Front Cover: A rare ┣   Midgley taken at the unveiling of a plaque in   ₋tion, commemorating the Institution of Civil Engineer ₋   ₋0 Award for Excellence. This was for the remodelling work done on the station tracks and the approaches – John and the author come under the title of 'Contractor'.

We can only say that it can be seen by crossing over the first span of the footbridge and down onto the platform. Platform numbers have a tendency to change from time to time but it is currently platform five, formally nine. The plaque is on the wall slightly to the left of the bridge.

In the back ground is Arthington Viaduct where the Leeds–Harrogate lines cross Wharfedale.

TOO BUSY TO DELEGATE –

More Railway Characters

TOO BUSY TO DELEGATE –

More Railway Characters

Mike Collins

ATHENA PRESS
LONDON

First Published 2007 by
ATHENA PRESS
Queen's House, 2 Holly Road
Twickenham TW1 4EG
United Kingdom

Printed for Athena Press

Dedicated to all those who appear within these pages, and to my wife Thelma, who has encouraged me enormously in my writing, and I dedicate it to the memory of John Midgley, a brilliant engineer and a first-rate colleague.

Unless otherwise indicated, all photographs are by the author.

About the Author

Mike Collins worked thirty-three years in the civil engineering department of British Railways and British Rail, avoiding Railtrack by being made redundant. This came about when Mike's speciality, new permanent way projects, sunk without trace, along with the spectacular dash into the doldrums marked by the privatisation of the railway industry.

Setting down on paper the hundreds of riotous antics – and the unintentionally hilarious remarks of characters – began in 1976, when the Leeds Civil Engineers Department's Annual Newsletter was born. This, without any malice, recorded most of the indiscretions, pratfalls, and humiliations of the staff over the year, soon expanding the basic threads of one-liners into full-blown, comically-padded narratives. From its start, the initial pamphlet of four pages expanded to a magazine of forty-two. There was one day, just before Christmas every year, when Mike was detested all round the offices, as the readers found personal references. Thankfully, this turned to universal applause as the far-worse escapades of others were studied.

This Newsletter formed the basis of Mike's first book *Railway Character Lines* in which stories of staff antics were told. In the current tome, themes are developed: how the railway industry taught you to eat, how it taught you gardening and the railway's attempts at educating its staff, with wide-ranging degrees of success.

There is also a long and affectionate look at one man whom Mike regarded as not only the greatest character and involuntary source of amusement to hand, but also the finest railway engineer he ever met.

Finally, there is an irreligious glossary of railway civil engineering terms, along with extracts taken directly from the *Annual Newsletter*.

The two books are *not* for sacred enthusiasts, who see the railways as glamorous. They are designed for those who relish memories, and who derive enjoyment from great characters.

Contents

Introduction and Catch up on Characters

Characters don't all need to be older than you to be characters. One of our young messengers appeared always plugged into his transistor radio by earphones. 'It's to keep me insane; if it wasn't for this I'd go mad in this place!'

We had a young trainee graduate maiden of great intelligence, but lacking the code to unlock it. The conversation was about homing messenger pigeons, sent out abroad by plane in order for them to return with information. 'Why fly them out?' she asked. 'Couldn't they fly there themselves?'

This is Book Two on railway characters... Didn't you? No! Well, put this one down right now and go buy it, you'll get a better introduction there than here. Briefly, that was based on the myriad of characters that I have met and enjoyed throughout my railway career, mainly in Huddersfield and Leeds, in the various offices of the Civil Engineer.

As a reminder, I'll list these in order, omitting the Chief Civil Engineer's potting shed at York where I spent my student days. (Here my weekly take-home doubled from my university grant to a mind-boggling £4 a week!) Following graduation with a 2:1 in Technology (Civ. Eng.) at Bradford University, I started with nine months in the glories of No. 23 Wellington Street, Leeds; a place I was to visit almost twice a week, after my initial spell, over the next fifteen years or so. Then Huddersfield Area Assistant Engineer's Office called. This was the famous block which Don Newell raised from the uninhabitable to an acceptable slum. It was, you may recall, roofed by an enormous water tank, and still is, for that matter. I spent ten happy and heavy years there. Having been tricked back into Leeds, following the temptation of a trail of scattered minor projects, I was back in No. 23 until the 1976 move to the characterless confines of Compton House, near the *Yorkshire Post* buildings. York Remodelling Project, and the amalgamation of Leeds and York Project Teams led me to share another shed in York with the magnificent John Midgley. During this time the newly combined District moved into the much more palatable surroundings of Aire Street railway offices at Leeds station. There I at first enjoyed, and finally survived to the end of my useful life. This last was in a year-long period as the railways slumped from being far-sighted and adventurous under BR to dull, dishevelled and dangerous in the first scandalous years of privatisation.

Swiftly digging myself out of that one, a return to the subject in hand. I find out now that I have had a fascination with characters and personalities all my life. Characters have to be people that stand out from the ordinary, obviously because of their characteristics. They range from devious and disastrous to gormless and gullible, and many were left over from the first volume. I discovered, while ruminating in that book, that structures can be characters as well, which I will develop a bit within. Looking at it from some directions, I suppose it is difficult to find any person totally lacking in character, though that in itself would make them a character of sorts. The ones in my collection are those that make you grin just thinking about them.

Jack Coggan, for instance, Drawing Office chief, with his nicotine-encrusted lungs and alcohol-moulded nose, was one such. Using his robustly frail health as a reason, he would arrive, secretly (publicly) chauffeured to a point behind No. 23, by Percy at nine. He would take a couple of hours' spiritual retreat at twelve, and leave the office at three-thirty to go back round the building, where Percy would again be waiting.

Back in No. 23 Wellington Street, with the lift, as usual, in a state of hibernation, Jack Coggan's arrival at nine was anticipated by Keith Thompson, one who harboured an intensely merciless line of humour at times. Keith would be standing just inside the door to the stairs and lift, coughing and spluttering, before bending over to vigorously rub the backs of his legs and going into a one-sided discussion on the family history of the Chief Clerk, who should have seen to breathing life back into the lift. Keith would no sooner straighten up, than the door would be punched open, shut itself, and receive another thump, and Jack himself would be decanted from the stairs breathlessly into the office. He would lean against the wall and pant like Lazarus on first sitting up in his coffin, looking for a unified sympathy. Keith's impersonation was too fresh in our minds, and overly accurate, so instead of deep concern, there would be a concerted coughing, clouding sniggering. Jack, then bending over and massaging his legs, was simply too much to take, and handkerchiefs were out and emergency evacuations made, leading to muffled laughter in the Print Room, round the back, out of sight.

Jack, when for once kept in by the Engineer over dinner, caught Chris Metcalfe coming in five minutes after two. 'Are you and me working the same hours, mister?' he growled sarcastically at Chris.

'No, Jack,' replied Chris, 'I'm on eight-thirty to five!' However, on those normal days, after his liquid lunch, Jack was everyone's best friend.

Chris was working on Jack's current pet project, a minor siding running into a new trading complex, which represented a few dinner invitations to Jack and 'my lovely Joan', and several bottled trophies at the end of the job. Jack slung his arm round Chris, seated at his drawing desk, leaning heavily and breathing out 5% ABV fumes, while trying to focus on the drawing. 'Whatsh the score then, shon?' he managed. Chris shook him off and rounded on him: '125 for four, dad, chasing 270.'

'The *job*, you daft sod, not the friggin' cricket!' Jack was a self-made character, but one lacking any sort of personality.

Personality is a rarer commodity. It carries with it a persuasiveness that can get other people to work to the wishes of the one that is blessed. It is character with a particularly endearing manner. To me, someone with personality is far more attractive than one lacking it. In this, appearances count for little. As a bonus they may be either pretty or presentable, depending on sex, but this is just a bonus. For myself, by way of going through descriptive prose, I hope that I can prove character by the written word. But I cannot show personality by the same means.

Mentioning Keith, above, brings to mind Joe Stanley, with whom he worked in his early days at No. 23. Although they were there officially as a work study unit, they would not have withstood scrutiny in that field themselves. Perhaps an hour of the day saw their work completed, studying work returns, after which, led firmly by Joe, they would get down to the serious task of entering every newspaper and magazine competition they could find. Resulting from this was a plethora of rewards, which they shared generously – with each other.

Keith Thompson once illustrated a characteristic of Jack Todd while doing one of the competitions. In those distant days, Jack was a jolly person with a very distinctive laugh. (Life became disgracefully tough for Jack before his retirement, years later, under whiz-embryonic leadership, but I can happily say that following that retirement, the Toddy of old has returned.) Jack's laugh came from a head thrown back, eyes full of tears and a steady 'Ho-ho-ho-ho' in stuttering hoots. He reminded you of a lorry reversing.

Anyway, the current competition was to put names to towns from given clues. 'I'm stuck with "Noddy's pride and joy",' said Joe. It turned out later that the answer was 'Redcar', but suddenly, out of nowhere, Keith suggested 'Okehampton'. I understood the meaning of 'pregnant pause' as Jack Todd, shut his eyes, bent back, and began 'Ho-ho-hoing', carrying on for a full half minute, leaving him wet-faced and panting. Laughter like Jack's was desperately infectious.

Going back to Joe Stanley, for a moment, he was almost a clone of Jack Coggan in appearance. The same pain when the lift felt itself too attracted to Three to leave it for other floors, the same slouching walk with a hunched back bearing the world's idiosyncrasies, but not, by a long chalk, the growling manner of disgust in the misfortunes imposed by life. Joe was an ever cheerful and unstressed person.

Left on his own, one day, Joe had a newspaper spread out on his desk while he scrutinised it in great detail. The Assistant Engineer, Steve Bell, appeared in the office, noticed Joe, and sidled up behind him. While the rest of the office appeared to be in heightened enthusiasm with work, bent severely over their drawing boards, Joe, unaware of the presence, continued studying the paper. A sixth sense came into operation, and Joe turned suddenly to look up at the hard face of his superior, and then back to the paper. Turning again to Steve, Joe said casually 'It's OK,

Mr Bell, it's yesterday's paper.' The absence of any logic defused Bell, and he turned away, confused.

Characters, like Joe, are usually people older and more experienced than yourself, but as you might have found in the earlier volume (now that you've gone out and bought a copy) they can be spotted developing from an embryonic daft grin. As regards 'older' there's one that breaks the rule for me. We have already had a tempting taste of John Midgley, who I regarded as a contemporary, being in fact my junior by one or two years. Here, with my contrived stumble into management, John figures largely; he demands a chapter all to himself. I compared others to Midge when it came to rating their character value, as he was the unintentional all-time star.

Repeating myself yet again, I must stress that John was the most competent and professional railway engineer I ever met in thirty-three years on the railway. That must be hammered home, because in these pages it is the character, and therefore the dafter side, that is faithfully recorded, not sufficiently the outstanding competence and ability. That's relatively boring.

Much the same applies to personality. Along with this goes the same competence I acknowledge above. In this department I will not name the cutest personality I had to work with, since she still has a job to go to, and a reputation to keep under control, but I think she makes herself known within. Oddly enough, Moira Midgley, John's gorgeous wife, fitted this role to an extent that meant controlling the most outstanding of characters; my young work nominee managed to take over from Moira at work and did much the same. Only because of her position in Midge's hierarchy was she treated with far less trepidation than Moira. The odd competitor runs in at a close second, yet even my number one at work comes runner-up to Thelma, my wife of over forty years. That isn't necessarily a surprise, as Thelma would not have got the job otherwise.

In this book I attempt vainly to leave behind my old Huddersfield Area mates, Bill Boyes, the hilarious imp, and the chainmen, Wilf and Percy, men of intelligence and integrity, though fans will be happy to know that they do crop up here and there in the inevitable flashbacks. What might seem a bit odd is that some characters who before I cloaked in a thin anonymity now appear in their true clothing and names. Before, there would have been far too many names to grasp, so I had to attribute some of the true incidents to an established character who had become familiar. The aka also went towards deflecting any legal action! In this volume both the actions described and names are true. The most striking change is Don Newell, my first long-term boss, in the Area office. Before I had him known as Elliot Milner, but he has since complained that he is not getting his share of the royalties, and that the truth can no longer damage his chances of appearing in the New Year's Honours List.

I still have a load of stories that for decency's sake I will not include. You could always search out the heroes of these tales and get the histories first hand. So, at this point, I can say to gentleman and welder extraordinary, Gordon Reed, that there will be no mention of calls of nature and overalls, or in the same field (well, not literally) Denis Durand's gang's idea of fun when one of their number was taken short. Ian Dickson can forget about getting a mention for calling on me, a fearless reporter for the official office glossy magazine at the time, to come down and take a photo of the 'Thing' in Trap Three on the Works Floor. In a different way, Bob Sissons and Roy Little can sleep easy, my computer cartridge having run dry as far as they are concerned.

What I *have* included are stories that wouldn't fit in before, events beyond the last collection in terms of time, and tales that until I started writing things down, I had simply forgotten about – the first chapter is an example of this. Hence there is the occasional throwback, when Bill, Wilf and Percy make guest reappearances.

By the halfway point, you will find me being dragged into a managerial position, rather than the subordinate one I cherished, and all those things we got up to behind Don's (for example) back, were now going on behind mine. The search for fun became a little bit more difficult, but it was still there, if in a slightly different way. It is now a matter of the noting down of things I found funny about my managerial colleagues at the time.

I even go into the characteristics of seasonal weather and its effect on the surveyor and railway in general. We examine what lies behind the statements 'typical March' and 'usual July weather'. Then, as an addendum, by special request of Sandy, who reads through all this to point out the dull bits, or the incomprehensible railway terms, there appears a glossary of such. (At this point I can claim no blame for any longueurs that remain – these must be down to Sandy.)

Unashamedly, I almost conclude the present tome with more or less universally acceptable, as opposed to parochial in-joking, extracts from the *Leeds Civil Engineer's Annual Newsletter*. Even throughout my major working commission, the remodelling of York station, I was still regarded as the office sponge for tales of others' misfortunes, despite becoming more and more the potential for such myself. It was out of this annual chore that the tales and characters within grew.

After this, and winding the thing up completely, I have inserted the un-technical glossary of railway terms, mainly in civil engineering. This will not help anyone wanting to look up a particular word or phrase, as it is not in alphabetical order; rather the order that the readers' questions might come in. You might like to drop into that section straight away. Don't worry about it spoiling the plot – there isn't one, and even if there was, I possess little more imagination than deciding that whatever it was that was done, it was the butler who did it.

Go forth, then, and hopefully enjoy, even if you haven't yet dabbled in Book One. Remember, the main object running through everything in life has to be to chuckle and have some fun; in between work breaks, of course.

The Office Trip

Once and only once did I try an office trip. Just the one time, for that experience was enough. Analysing this, I realise that I was on a day out almost without there being a single character among the joy-seekers in the party. Characters were met in abundance in the course of the day, and they stood out from the grey crowd I was with. This, I think, is why I never chanced another such trip.

We're back in my earliest days in British Railways' Chief Civil Engineer's Offices at York, and during my only summer there I signed up for this trip on the advice of my more senior colleagues, as it was apparently a good thing to be seen on. It took up one day out of my annual allocation of fifteen, and set me back 12/6d, but I was told that for my career I could do nothing better. Come the day, and I noticed that not one of my advisers had signed up, but the special two-coach train was filled with lower managers and the year's greens like me, along with a number of sad loners. As an extra enhancement, I noted that two of the York chainmen were included. This pair were conscripts, and they stood out like tomatoes in spring. I found out why they were there all in good time.

I knew these lads pretty well considering the few weeks that I'd been on the railway. My meeting up with them was as they booked out and returned items of surveying equipment. It became apparent that one of the ways to get rid of the office junior for a while was to appoint him custodian of the tackle for a couple of weeks. This involved going down to a room in the cellars, which smelt of leather and old brass, where all the theodolites, levels and tripod mounts were kept. My job was to book them in and out and to dry up any that had got wet in the course of the day's work. Emerging from the depths of the cellars every day at about four, I was welcomed back into the office with 'The troglodyte's back!' I had to look that up, but I was happy with it on doing so.

As a reminder, chainmen are the lads who hold the tapes and level staffs, with the surveyor virtually acting as their clerk. The York chainmen had a room next door to mine in the dungeons, and they seemed to welcome me into their midst. Perhaps this was because of the respect that must have oozed out of me, overawed at meeting these wisest of men, and being allowed to join in their conversations. For them, this social gathering allowed them to tap one who was steeped in higher education, a thing denied to them because of the system. In very little time I realised that the only difference between them and me, apart from age and language, was experience – but that was a vast chasm. They were deep and curious thinkers and allowed me to have an opinion on things, which they welcomed. For me this was the real world, with real men, and I matured faster in that environment than anywhere else in my working life. Subjects for conversation and discussion varied, but popular at the time was space travel.

'Says 'ere that they'll have a man on t'moon within t'next ten years,' said one, quoting from one of the day's broadsheets.

'Does it say 'ow many are likely to miss?'

'How dusta mean, *miss*?'

'Well, look at t'size of it, and how much of t'neet sky isn't moon. It's goin' t'ave to be one helluva good aim to cop for t'moon, like, 'cos ah've seen no sign on a steerin' wheel in these space rockets that they keep heavin' up inter t'sky. It'd be a reet easy thing t'miss, ah reckon.'

'Aye, and another thing, they allus shoot off in dayleet, wi no moon showin' to aim for. They must 'ave some way of 'oiking t'thing rahnd into t'reet road for hittin' t'moon.'

To me: 'D'they 'ave a rudder of sorts on 'em t'steer wi, like? Same as airyplanes?'

Educated juvenile: 'It'd be no good, because there's no air up there for the rudder to work in. Don't they have little booster rockets on the sides to move them into a different direction?'

'Years to come they'll 'ave set out a railroad between us and t'moon.'

''Ow can they? With t'earth spinnin' faster than t'moon goin' rahnd, it'd get all tangled oop or snagged on summat.'

And so it went on, every day for perhaps half an hour over one of the best pots of tea I've ever had on the railway, especially when measured up against some of the stuff Bill brought in to the Huddersfield office, during one of his experimental periods. Earl Grey – and it looked it – Oursam, Geedarling and such. This was a happy time for me after my first fortnight's boring experience of colouring up the compulsory map of the British Railways system. (And this was much bigger pre-Beeching!)

It appeared that in inviting the chainmen on the office trip, the men at the top had someone on hand to do the fetching and carrying as necessary. I was delighted to have them there as I had someone I felt I could mix with, so I became an honorary chainman for the day. I was later to discover that these York lads saw themselves as a little superior to the Wilfs and Percys out on the districts like Leeds. I could easily understand the language, which is unvaried in their area, whereas you can't go over a hill or across a valley without meeting up with a new dialect in the West Riding. Slaithwaite was a case in point, where people a mile apart pronounced their town differently, and words for common objects varied with every fence you climbed.

'So, where's this place we're going to – Rothbury, or something isn't it?'

George, one of the York chainmen: 'Ay, that's weer they're aimin' for, burrit's evens as to whether we get theer. It'll be a bit like aimin' for t'moon, like as 'ow we was sayin' t'other day.'

'Why? Is it a long way?'

'Nay, it's nobbut a stone's throw from t'main line, burrit'll be nowt but awkward. T'line's nivver used – well, nobbut t'odd train once a month. Thur's nowt of a passenger service, it's only theer fer silly buggers lahk us t'try and get through, wi nobbut a big owse t'look at when, nay, if tha meks it.'

'What might be the problem? Sheep on the line and the sort?'

'Oh, thur'l be sheep on t'line fershoor. T'Rothbury Branch is more like one gurt big ruddy field which 'appens to 'ave a railway meanderin' through it, nor owt else. Still thur's allus t'folk in't buff to seek aht. Aif way up thur's this nutter's colony weer they all walk rahnd bolluk-naked. Noodists, or summat. Ah woodn't walk through them thur woods wi mitrowsies rolled up, let alone wi owt danglin' in t'wind. Anyroad, thur happy, so who're we?'

'So what is there at Rothbury?'

'Buggerall, wi buggerall in front on it and buggerall at t'sides and back, and buggerall into t'distance, 'cept for t'big owse. Ah went up on a mystery coach trip once. It were a mystery why we'd bothered. We parked t'coach in t'village, and that's so small that theer were a bit of t'bus hangin' out of t'place at both ends. Ah c'n tekit or leave it, burrit's a free day aht ferrus.'

It was bouncing down with rain when the morning of the expedition dawned, which didn't enrich the prospects that George had mapped out. Fortunately, just before we set off the sun came out and stayed out for the rest of the day. All the same, picnicking on the mansion lawns (promised) looked a loser. We were lined up on the platform at York for a 9.32 start. By 9.33 all was well except for the absence of a train. It was then that for me the tone of the day was set.

'I say, you, young man – what's your name?'

'Mike Collins,' I admitted. It was always Mike at work, and was made Mike at home later on when the trouble started. I was always Michael Collins until the film of that name ran high on the headlines in the late 1980s. After several death threats over the phone in thick Irish accents, I demanded that in future it would be Mike, home and away, and we also went ex-directory. Happily, those daft enough to make such threats were also daft enough, it seemed, not to associate Mike with Michael.

'Well, Collier, show us what you're made of, and take Ashworth with you to the signal box and find out where our train is, there's a good lad.'

Harold Ashcroft was George's fellow chainman, and he happily trotted off with me. I had no idea where the signal box was at York – like our train, it too had taken up the cloak of concealment.

'We're not oftat Siggy Box,' said Harold, 'we'll ring t'bobby from that theer signal phone; come on, ah'll showthi.'

The first problem was with Rothbury. 'Weer the buggery's Rothbury?' said the signalman.

'We don't knaw,' said Harold. 'It's t'office mystery trip, civil engineers, tha naws.'

'Oh,' we got back. 'Now that'll bi t'three-car DMU [diesel

multiple unit] set what's up in t'yard waitin t'come aht. Burra still need to naw weer Rothbury is so ah can send thi aht of t'station in't reet direction, like. Ayoop, lads!' To his colleagues in the box, he called, 'Wiv fund aht weer that special's goin'. It is Rothbury, like what it said in t'train notices, burrit don't say weer it is – anyone dahn theer heard on Rothbury?'

'Well, theer's a Newcastle driver on t'platform wot's to go wi'it,' reported Harold.

'Reet, tharell do. We send it up north. Cansta see a short bloke in uniform arahnd, wi'is head on upside down?'

'Dusta mean Neville Althorp?'

'Oh, tha knaws him.'

'Same bowls team. He's here at side on mi'.'

Neville, as it turned out, was a man of economic build with a completely bald head and a bushy grey beard to compensate for it. Harold put him on the phone.

'Ah herd that, Binksy! Tha's a bloody nerve! Tha's not exac'ly a picture of golden locks. If they sprayed thy head red tha could stop trains wi'it. Wot's t'awant?'

'Ayoop, Nev! Nah that three car set up in thi yard; it's t'go inter number nine. And try and find Rothbury on t'station indicator roller on t'front onnit. Failin' that, just bung up "Special" or "Private" or summat.'

'OK, lads, tell thi mates we'll have it dahn in five minnits, orso,' promised Neville.

Such was the way that control situations were resolved. We were able to go back to our group, which was now visibly swollen by the numbers who knew that the train would be late, and had been in the refresh up to now. Management seemed quite satisfied that the train would be with us in 'five minutes orso', but were still a little miffed that they could see the thing in the yard, not fifty yards away.

The estimated time of arrival turned out to be 'orso', when it was eventually shunted onto Platform 9, and we all clambered aboard. There was a furious flurry of duffle coats making for the seats behind the driver. It was certainly going to be a mystery trip for them. They were obviously lacking any geographical sense, as the driver had only brought it out of the yard and into the platform. It was the other end that our Newcastle driver settled himself into.

George and Harold, who fully understood why they had been picked for this treat, struggled on board with a large boiler and two water carriers, which they set up in the guard's compartment. By the time Management had discussed with the train crew which lines they would be taking to Darlington, just to show that they knew the geography, we were well down in the pecking order as far as traffic was concerned. We had missed what is now known as our window with the confusion as to where Rothbury was. So it was a good thirty minutes before we set out behind a booked tanker train, to follow it up the Slow Lines to Darlington.

Instead of the usual forty minutes to Darlington, the tanker train took the full hour, so we had to follow suit. There was another slight hiatus there as once more the location of Rothbury was outside the signal box's realm of knowledge. All that their train workings told them was that we were a special from York to this place that could for all the world be fairyland. One of the porters on duty was from Morpeth, and knew Rothbury well enough to tell us that we needed to head for Morpeth after which we should ask again.

We now sped along merrily until we caught up with the tanker train again which was quite happy to lead us to Newcastle's South Yard. Again we experienced a delay, and Management were getting their feathers ruffled once more. The guard was getting it full face from them, so he nipped over to the stationmaster's office to ask if some movement could be made as 'the chief of all t'northern railways was on t'train, and was demandin' that we got off towards someweer or other'.

It showed the influence of such managerial skills that within five minutes we were on the move. Strangely, instead of turning left out of Newcastle, we went right, back across the Tyne. It was a scenic trip as we travelled through Gateshead and back over the Tyne again to manage to return to the platform we had left in Newcastle fifteen minutes earlier. The guard claimed that the manoeuvre had been justified, to allow an Edinburgh express to pass us.

Now just let me recap a little here. We had left York thirty minutes or so late at ten past ten; Darlington ten past eleven, leaving at twenty past and managing Newcastle by noon. We then had an unscheduled tour of Newcastle and Gateshead, plus waiting and complaining time; that filled us in until twelve thirty. It was then that we set off to the land of Oz which was Morpeth district. Things got so much easier now, except that for a few confused minutes, the signal box there thought that because of the late time, we were actually returning a little early from Rothbury. That sorted, we were on our way at a line best of 30 mph on the pretty route to Hexham. Twenty-five minutes later we arrived at a station that announced itself to be 'S ots p' on the ancient platform sign. Later enquiries showed an aging process had attacked the board and we had actually been to Scotsgap.

What struck us now, for the first time really, was that with the steady beat of 30-foot long rails, the two transistor radios on board, tuned to different channels, didn't gel. I suppose that they had been numbed to near silence by the roar on the fast sections of track with the train's motors going at full belt. Management stepped in somewhere early on and declared, well ahead of their time, that two coaches – theirs and the guard's – would be declared quiet coaches, or at least radio-free. This way the two transistors were confined to one space, each with their followers. All right as long as they agreed on programmes, but somewhere between the two there was a mad clash of pop radio, light classical and train beat. Instead of finding this uplifting, I was slipping into gloom.

If I haven't made this clear somewhere before now, I am one of nature's pessimists or, as I like to see it, a realist. I certainly don't believe that things will necessarily get better round the corner. As it happened, there weren't too many corners between Morpeth and Scotsgap, but my occasional view of the rails we were running on showed them to be a fair deal rusty in colour. Word had it that the occasional train of one wagon went up and down, but the line was devoid of any kind of passenger service. Here a sort of innocence was helpful, as in later years I was to see dead sidings where the build-up of rust exploded the odd rail-chair lug, leaving no support for the rails – many track abandonment trains had fallen foul of this sort of thing. However, when the visiting signalman at Scotsgap had to appeal to our two erstwhile trackmen, George and Harold, to bar the points over for the Rothbury Branch, and later bar them back, my hopes for what was left of the day were both dimming and inquisitively rising.

Dimming, because the state of the points suggested that our chances of attaining Rothbury, a dozen miles ahead, were heavily reduced. Inquisitive, wondering just what a romantic bit of railway, deep in the heart of Border country, could bite us with next.

'There's bound to be sheep on the line,' I remarked to the lad next to me, who had a railway atlas open and had been devouring it since Morpeth. Looking over his shoulder, I couldn't see any sheep marked on it, but rather worryingly I noticed that he had it open at Aber and Llanfairfechan. But things were about to develop according to the script. It took less than a mile before we spotted them.

Not just a couple of sheep and accompanying mature lambs, but a whole flock filling the shallow cutting. It wasn't so much the fact that we had come upon the expected sheep that was concerning, more that they also had a shepherd and two dogs in tow, and were following what must have been a regular route. We drew up alongside the man in brown boots and with baggy trousers tied round the ankles with string, topped off by a vest that looked as if it harboured as much life as the Serengeti. He looked up at our driver, back to his sheep, and then, obviously upset, back at the driver. Despite his very broad accent we could gather that he wanted to know what the buggery we were playing at bringing a train up here. Fruitless discussion ensued until he admitted that he was only taking them to a field about three hundred yards away. So we decided that the best we could do was to crawl up behind him. The dogs momentarily seemed to see this as invading their territory, pushing the sheep along, and viewed the driver as if demanding a sight of his Equity card, or whatever union sheepdogs belonged to.

George and Harold offered to get down and open the gate for him, but he made it quite clear that the only part of the fencing to the field that was still standing was the gate.

All the way from Morpeth we had noticed that the early morning's heavy rain had caused the lineside trees to lose their clear-cut shape of the loading gauge, as the occasional train had stripped them, and they were now leaning well over the track. This line so far had been fairly straight so, apart from the cracks and brushing as we ploughed through the trees, we could still see our way fairly well. Now, on the curving Rothbury line, things were a good deal more exciting with visibility cut by drooping trees and sharp bends to just a few yards. It was only as we paused yet again to allow the few still doubtful sheep to make their minds up that we noticed the signal a short distance in front of us. It was a yellow semaphore, one of those with a fishtail cut into the end of the arm, known as a 'distant' and giving warning of a stop signal ahead. The arm was bouncing up and down from 'caution' to 'all clear', as if the signalman was desperately trying to pull it up. Even so, the peculiar bouncing up and down didn't seem quite right. As we edged past the last of the sheep, ignoring the victory signs from the shepherd, we saw the hound.

It was fastened to a long rope which itself was attached to the signal cable. This appeared to be a clear case of cruelty, and the lady clerk among us looked up from her knitting for the first time since we had left York and started getting overheated about cruelty to animals, abandoning a poor sweet little dog like that. She was alone in seeing the bulky black and white hearthrug as being either poor, little or sweet, for at the sight of our train it started behaving somewhat wildly, in time with the signal arm. It was only as we got that bit closer that the picnic family came into view.

It was obviously their dog, and it was excitedly trying to take its share of the dinner on display. Cushions had been arranged on the rails, with the cloth laid out on the flat ash and sleepers in between. They claimed the middle of the track was the only piece of dry railway, 'due to the disgraceful way the trees were allowed to overhang'. It was now getting so late that a few of us were quite happy to call it a day, get out the packed sandwiches, and join them. Our guard was less charitable and started quoting from his rule book about trespass and the like, until the convinced family – mother, father and two kids of about six and eight – began seeing this as a hanging offence. Reluctantly, they gathered up their belongings and asked if we knew of anywhere else they could settle down. Almost as a body we invited them aboard, promising to drop them off again on the way back so that they could scramble down the embankment to their car. The dog was suddenly our friend, as it saw us as yet more providers of food. It was becoming a little too much our best buddy, so the father tied it up to a bit of chain. It was noticeable that the dog was twice as large within the confines of the guard's compartment as it had been down on the track. So off we tried to go, except the train appeared to like the current view overmuch, and had decided to stay put. All attempts to get started failed until George spotted the dog lead tied to the communication cord...

This was a bad spot to come to a halt, as early-fallen wet leaves decided to join the party. There were a few minutes of stop-start and spin before we actually moved off. It was the inclusion of the young family that at last got us all chatting, and it was a little disconcerting to find one lady on board whom nobody seemed to know, and who was asking what time the train would get to Rotherham. She took quite a bit of convincing that Rothbury was the nearest thing to Rotherham she would see that day, and that it was no use getting off as we would be the only chance of her getting back to York.

We were all very friendly by the time we reached the level crossing, and it was clear that the lady crossing keeper brought back to duty that day to look after the gates was delighted to see a train again. She lived in the signal house and was technically retired. There was a very pleasant little smallholding attached, and she was more than happy to allow some of our ladies to clamber down and bargain for some fresh vegetables.

For some reason I suddenly remembered about the nudist colony, reputedly on the lineside. This held a healthy curiosity for me, and a promise of a new experience. I tackled George who had first brought it up.

'Nay, ah've only heard said, like, 'cos ah've nivver bin upeer afore, except for t'coach trip, but we did get wind of it from some Newcastle lads when we had cause to go up theer. Might be nowt innit. What's up, anyroad? Hasn't it bin excitin' enough already forthee?'

'It's just that I think it would score a maximum hundred in my "I Spy Things from the Train". It would come under rare animals, I reckon.'

'What dusta reckon they get aht of it? Ah mean up 'ere it's nobbut ower nippy t'be swannin' arahn wiout thi clothes. Ah'm not agin rollin' mi trousies up fer a paddle, like, but even that's enuff in ahr climitt.'

'I've flipped through a leaflet about naturism that I found in the messenger's library. Apparently they only strip off when there's others that feel the same around them, and never if it's over-cold.'

'Weer d'they come from? Ah've nivver met one – well, not s'long as ah knaw. They don't exactly 'ave a uniform, d'they?'

'Apparently there's over sixteen thousand of them coming from all sorts of backgrounds. There's loads of clubs that they call sun clubs, so I suppose it's no good if it rains.'

'Bit dodgy for t'blokes, ah'd've thort. Tha knaws, like mekin' thur feelin's obvious.'

'It seems that this doesn't occur from what I saw.'

'Tha did a fair bit o'flippin' thro' this leaflet, didn't tha? Tha's not thinkin' of tekin' it up or owt?'

'At those prices! Their clubs cost an arm and a leg!'

'Nah that would look diff'rent!'

We drifted on another few hundred yards, rather looking at the state of the track than bothering about lineside entertainment. Then: 'Ayoop, sithee!'

The two horses and riders coming down towards us in the cess did not take us so much by surprise, as there was plenty of evidence that this was a regular route for them. What surprise there was lodged firmly with the couple and their mounts. These horses had little experience of trains on their normal day's ride, and showed it. Their acceptance of us was not helped by the driver having to sound his horn at the direction of the whistle board prior to an unmanned crossing ahead. We had to stop and reduce the engine sound before there was any chance of control-ling the beasts, and we needed to wait until they had comfortably passed us, as they moved steadily down the banking on a well-worn path. The driver amused himself by revving up over-enthusiastically before setting off again, as he had just woken up to the fact that it was our railway and not theirs. It certainly tested the amount of control the riders had over the horses, which the rear coach almost unanimously rated as two out of ten.

What had really aroused interest in the couple, who George reckoned were in there mid-sixties, was their riding gear. They were kitted out in smart bump caps and riding boots – and that was all. Faced with this apparition we were all rather embarrassed, instead of feeling lustily aroused. On the way back (have I spoilt things by admitting that we did actually get there?) I was nonchalantly scanning the bottom of the banking, along with a few dozen other casual stares. At the well-worn path where the horses had gone down was a gate, obviously constructed out of the existing fencing. The gate was labelled 'Dunnwi Clarts', a colloquial form of 'Finished wearing clothes'. George's 'nudist colony' was a retired couple living at the side of the line, and having certain preferences. His disappointment was obvious.

'That were nowt on a show! He looked as if his saddle were ower cold, and she looked like a set of Venetian blinds that could've done wi ironing.'

It was then that we had the most extraordinary experience of moving along at a steady 20 mph (compulsory limit) for about two miles, and even the sight of the four or five cows ahead didn't unduly worry us. A sounding of the horn sent a couple trotting off back into the field, but the others (three, as it turned out) were intent in two cases with the lush grass of the trackside, while the last was steadily chewing its cud and contemplating the meaning of life, laid out in between the rails. It was now ten to two, and we were due to make the return journey from Rothbury at half three.

They were a sort of cow I hadn't seen before. Not one of your black and white map-of-the-world sort, or the golden Channel Island kind. These were big and black all over, and a bit shaggy, looking as if they'd just washed their hair.

There aren't a lot of cows in the centres of Leeds or York, and we were communally ignorant as to how to persuade them to move beyond making a noise. This interested them slightly, but they were not encouraged by the addition of the two radios, still playing at odds and now wound up to full, to see such as being a reason for abandoning a particularly lush sod. Searching through our gathering we alighted on a girl who admitted being brought up on a farm.

'Come on, Gloria, show us how it's done. How do we get these three mobile barbecue kits moving?'

'I don't know,' said Gloria.

'But nay, lass, you must know how to handle a couple of cows, with all your experience on t'farm.'

'I was only six when we moved into town, so I never got sort of involved. Besides, even if I had, I still wouldn't know much of any help.'

'Just tell us what to do, you must have watched your dad.'

'He wouldn't have been much help either. He grew wheat and barley and tatties and sugar!'

So it was down to the ground once more, but at a much re-strained distance. Townies all but one, we were useless. More horn and the upright pair of cows turned in defiance. Braver souls broke off small branches to give themselves thinking time. These were brandished along with half-hearted shouting, with 'Cush, cush' being the most popular conversation piece. After a few minutes we were getting bravely close to actually touching them. It was the first whack across the buttocks that got things moving, and the two standing animals were persuaded at least off the line and into the bushes, so we only had the one left, casually aware and making notes of all the cowboy stuff that was going on behind it, but still remaining unmoved.

It was a picture of contentment and contempt. After all the foreplay had been gone through of shouting, clouting and shooing, we became as used to the animal as it had apparently become of us. We got to walking all round it, prodding it, actually slapping it with bare hands, all of which it seemed to regard as signs of endearment. One thing that was clearly established was that we had nothing to worry about approaching this particular cow.

There was no established game plan, which was a bit of a setback, and the cow amusedly glanced from one to the other of us. The guard produced a length of rope from his compartment, presumably there to serve some emergency problem. This inspired the idea of lassoing the beast, since this was a common sight on the Westerns of the day. The trouble was that this particular steer had neither watched one of these epics nor read the script. Purely for effect, the lad with the noose had to twirl it round his head before throwing it out over the cow. By these means he managed to lasso himself twice, and the trains buffers regularly. More by luck than accident, one throw captured the cow's horns and pulled tight. So we'd managed that; now what were we supposed to do?

We began to appreciate the size of the animal when three or four of us took hold of the rope and pulled. The cow pulled back with a shake of its head. Foothold was not too secure due to the combined effect of rotting sleepers and normally functioning cows. No actual descent into the slurry occurred, but our wholehearted enthusiasm for throwing ourselves into a deter-mined tug of war was a little below maximum.

An idea to fasten the free end to the train buffers met with objections from both the driver and the guard. They couldn't quote a specific reason and the Rule Book couldn't provide any guidance: 155 stated that finding cattle on the line the crew must report it at the next station. This boldly assumed that the said obstruction did not prevent them actually reaching the next station. Further unhelpful advice informed us that they should exhibit a red flag to any oncoming traffic and put detonators down. We all agreed that although this might be obeying the rules and passing the time, it was far from providing an answer.

Then the cow raised its head and mooed. It was not a particu-larly friendly moo, in fact it was downright aggressive, as we all agreed after we had scrambled back into the coach. But it was here that inspiration hit us. One volunteer – George said 'Harold' and Harold said 'George' – was all that was needed to nip out again and tie the rope to the track so that the cow could not move even if it felt like it. Then we could all circumnavigate it and walk the rest of the way. One sad and inevitable looking lad eventually said that he didn't mind, so he climbed back out again and gingerly approached the end of the rope. The cow had once more lost interest, so tying it down was the work of a moment.

For myself I'd had enough of the cow; I felt I was becoming

one of its family. I had my Hanimex round my neck with thirty-six shots to take as souvenirs. In getting over involved with events I had so far failed to take a single picture, so I satisfied myself by getting some of the lads to stand round the cow, putting one foot up on its very large back in the pose of big game hunters. So, after helping a number of the older fun-seekers down from the coach, quite a few of the others not willing to face the drop to the ground, I decided to march off with about half our company in tow, on to the station just half a mile away. We now had a scheduled hour to play with.

The spectacular house, known as Cragside, with its main claim to fame being that it was the first house to be lit by electricity, was what we had all come to see. It was, of course, shut, as it was every Monday, but the gardens were open. There was just time for a quick circuit of the exterior of the house, taking a couple more snaps, and I felt that it would be wise to return to the station, as there would be another ten-minute walk back to the train. I was quite surprised to see it now drawn up at the platforms, with the rest of the party getting off. I questioned the driver, who said that after we'd all stopped playing with it, he'd untied it and the blockage became bored with lack of attention, got up, and sauntered back into the field.

'Why man yee knaw, when it stud oop, we foond it wisna a coo at'll! Hae ye seen a phone box a'where cos I'm ganna ring Control t'see if wis can hang aboot 'ere till fower, les there'll hae been nae point in comin' bonny lad.' (That is the sound of a Tyneside train driver, collected with difficulty. The essential being that in contacting Control we might be allowed to stop on till four o'clock.) With which, he and the guard secured the train and wandered off into the village. I reckoned that it would be safe to saunter along too, as the train was going nowhere without them. We found an unexpectedly thriving little place, almost a town. Civilisation was there in the form of a cinema, which I doubt exists today. There was a phone box next to the post office, and so our return was worked out without resorting to messages passed down the line.

Four o'clock we were all loaded again. Organisers had also been on the phone to the restaurant back in Morpeth, putting our booking back an hour and a half.

The cows had obviously learnt the rules of the game by the time we came back. Sure enough, they were back on the line, but this time they allowed us a very slow passage among them. There was no sign of the bull who we'd made our best pal.

We dropped the young family off near their car. It had obviously been the first time the children had been near a train, let alone on one, so all that had happened while they were on the train with us must have made its mark on them, such that they would be thinking that this was how the railways always worked. I hope that they have had that illusion corrected by now.

After the early morning rain, the day had broken out sunny and very warm, quite warm enough for the track buckle ahead of us. Obviously this minor branch had suffered a lot from a lack of maintenance, and many of the fishplates had gone ungreased and had seized up. On the severe curves of the branch, the 'misalignment', as we were later taught to call buckles, was inevitable, and had probably occurred after the first passage of a train for months. So here was a fairly ordinary track problem presenting itself to the cream of the civil engineering department. As one, we 'new boys' reverted to being innocently inexperienced, and watched happily as the seniors got out to view the situation. Eventually, taking their reputations to danger point, they allowed the train over at extreme caution, possibly having hunger outweigh prudence.

For the rest of the journey it seemed as if we had been the first train up the branch following a blockage by snow. All our outward trouble spots were now clear and safe for our 20 mph trundle. There was a slight problem at Scotsgap as we tried to return to the Morpeth line, the signalman booked specially for our trip claiming that his shift was up, and that it was 'morethanmijobsworth' to let us through the junction, with the switches now set for the through line. Promises to clear matters with his superiors finally convinced him to release us, and we returned to the heady speed of thirty. Wet trees were but a memory after the day's sun, so the view was clear ahead.

We jumped ship at Morpeth for the hour's restaurant break, and almost as one ordered beefsteak, as if getting our own back on earlier difficulties. My impressions on setting off down the main line back to Newcastle and York was of immense and scary speed after the hours of crawling on the branches.

'What was t'trip like yesterday?' I was asked when I got in the following morning.

'Interesting,' I said. 'Definitely interesting!'

Courses – Attempted Education

Education on the railway served two purposes. It was there for whenever a minor change in procedure might need broadcasting, or a specialist piece of training was required, but it existed for most of its time to justify keeping schools and staff at places like Derby, Watford and Harrogate on full time. Around 95% of what it churned out was useless, unnecessary, inappropriate, purposeless and a complete waste of time. Career records kept by whatever the Staff Section was calling itself that week, had within them details of all courses attended, and any spaces without ticks were an abomination to these people. That is why, as a Drawing Office Permanent Way Technical Officer, having very little to do with bridges, I was sent on a course for Bridge Marking. This was rather like sending a probationary Roman Catholic priest onto a course on performing circumcisions.

Within four weeks of attending the course I'd forgotten completely how to mark bridges, and was never faced in future years by any such need. Had they arranged the course before I went up into Bradford Exchange Station roof for three months, walloping great chunks of paint and bird-manufactured topcoats off to get to what was left of the actual metal, then it would have been marginally useful, if only in pointing out that safety glasses might be a good idea. As it was, during the Bradford period, I had to rely on basic common sense and a grasp of the downright obvious.

Bridge marking was a pretty straightforward idea of finding out how strong a structure really was, and not how well it looked. It was a matter of stripping off the fancy veneers of make-up and posh clothes and seeing how good the body was in reality, though it never seemed quite as evocative as that. (Is this the secret behind beauty contest judges, or are my original thoughts on these inadequates correct?) Bridge marking only really involved a very few people, but to justify the cost of the course, every poor unfortunate in the District Civil Engineer's technical departments had to go. It was based in Harrogate and lasted a week. As far as Harrogate and the poor works inspector who covered that area were concerned, this was not particularly good news.

During the period that this course ran, the whole class would be marched out to a couple of bridges, all supplied with little hammers, and encouraged to wallop away and assess the basic dimensions of the bits that go to make the component parts. The fact that many students had gone before, and that many were to follow, meant that those particular bridges were left in pretty poor shape by the time all the chipping away had been completed and they were almost clouted into oblivion. This course would be run for about a year, which would mean the test bridges would have gone from being sound to badly weakened in all accessible places. As a whole, bridge marking was a scientific step up from declaring a bridge either in good nick or knackered, which was the case previously. Now they could declare to what extent of goodness the nick was, and how serious the knackerment. The course was interesting, and an insight into the workings of another section, but to me a completely wasted (but paid) week.

★

Statement: The length of a railway course varies inversely to the significance of it.

Getting the longer and usually most inappropriate ones out of the way first, I have consigned the Induction Course at Derby to a chapter dealing with food and the instructions for devouring it. That particular course, designed for completely green new entrants, was presented to me after well over two years of actually working on the railway. I'd somehow been missed off when I first started, or someone had ticked it by mistake in pencil, which had now worn away. Suddenly, a fairly well-informed draughtsman had to go off with a load of lads with no more than two weeks behind them. It became, as I explain elsewhere, a fortnight devoted to teaching me how to behave when eating socially. It did also serve to explain to too many of those present that there was more to the railway than just collecting numbers off the sides of engines.

I met a lot of this sort of lad during my time in the Area Office at Huddersfield, where, from their seat looking out of the windows, they had sight of distant steam and smoke approaching up the viaduct. This led to a dash to the door and a flopping mouth with dribble down one side. I was, and still am, a hoarder. In this capacity I had acquired the old drawing office's book of seven-figure logarithms when it was being thrown out. These were unknown things to my visiting gricers, and I would persuade them that this was a secret wartime list of loco numbers. Quite a few spent time reading through them – Bill would help by pointing out the one or two that he'd worked with. All these lads were destined for my own education system, including an introduction to the beauty of steam close-up course that was held in Bowling Tunnel, a hole that was rarely free of the stuff. A couple of hours in there, in complete darkness, with smoke and steam swirling around and negating any usefulness from our lamps soon put a lid on the romance of the noxious smog.

'Tha's got technical competition starting on Monday. Another poor sod comin' for thy speciality two month course on how t'get clarted up to t'eyebrows.' This was one of many of Bill's announcements of impending enthusiasm or apathy.

'Have you got his history, then?'

'No, but Don has; it were specially sealed up, but it fell open while ah were mashin' t'tea. It really come yesterday, but it's teken since then for t'Gloy to work, stickin' it upagin.'

'So?'

'Oh,' he replied, consulting a scrap of paper exhumed from a trouser pocket, 'Tha's got a reet bobby-dazzler this time. Name,' he consulted the paper carefully – 'Humbert Hildebrand Willoughby, which according to t'wife's book o'names means "bright giant, battle and sword". Ah thort that might interest thee!'

'Education?'

'It said 2:2 at Leeds University. Dusta reckon he'll be any cop?'

'I don't like it much so far. Anything else?'

'Only t'best bit. Tha's bahn t'be ower t'moon wi this. Hobbies…'

I groaned. Anyone willing to list their hobbies must be right keen about them, and therefore talkative to the point of boring.

'…Country sports – what's them?'

'Hunting and fishing, usually. Is that it?'

'No, theer's best t'come. Military 'istory, and, wait for it – *model railways!*'

Humbert, when he came, insisted on Humbert. Bill's attempt at 'Bert' was impatiently stamped on. He turned out no better nor worse than any other, and scoffed at our aging levelling equipment, and ate packed sandwiches from tinfoil. Any time that I did not fill for him was spent designing model railway layouts, as expected. His main mistake was in not rating Don Newell, our boss, asking at an early stage about Don's education. He was amazed that I had no idea of it, and that I didn't think it mattered. I provided him with my standard education, only accepting graduation by the permanently blackened nails, and fingerprints on his crustless white sandwiches. For the likes of Humbert, his first two years working for the railway were a continuous course broken into two-month sections. I was later delighted to see him working with a track gang in Leeds station platforms, picking up discarded wrappers and drinks cans.

★

I suppose that I should admit at this stage that I developed a great skill through courses of ways and means to avoid going on them. Delaying tactics could be employed so that I would be at an indispensable point in a particular job, and could not afford any time off, even for holidays. Pregnancy only helped if it was in the very late stages, and that I could swear it was my wife. I had also started collecting medical appointments, or I would arrange strategic meetings. By the time that the Staff Section had offered me alternative dates, I had blocked all possibilities so skilfully that I had to have the support of such as Don Newell, my boss at Huddersfield, for verification of my unavailability. There I was the only experienced technical officer in the office, and Don had a similar attitude to me about wasting time on irrelevancies. There was one occasion when I confounded the Staff people by agreeing to go on two courses, which I noticed had the same starting dates at two very different locations. On the Friday evening I rang both venues and told them that I had another course to attend the same week. As a result I went on neither.

My last straw was the work study course at Harrogate. Details of this have drifted off into my subconscious, and although the relevant documents are still stuck under the bed in the small bedroom, just half a dozen paces away from where I now sit, I simply can't be bothered to get them out just to bore you. I do remember clipboards and stopwatches being handed out, along with reams of forms and tables. This one lasted a fortnight, and was residential even though I was only half an hour from home. Meals and accommodation were in a minor Harrogate hotel, which, like the lecturers, did very well, thank you, from these lapses in significance that the railway saw as essential courses. The insistence on spending evenings and nights together was in the hope that we would compare notes on the subject of the day. What we actually collected by the weekend was a comprehensive list of decent pubs in Harrogate.

It is wrong to give the impression that this work study course was a complete waste of our time. We actually picked up on all the essentials of what we were there for by the end of the second day. This could easily have led to boredom had we let it, but one or two of us, over an evening pint, devised a plan for the rest of the fortnight. We would apply work study principles to the four lecturers employed to tell us how to carry out work study. This meant that over the ensuing days we asked some very pertinent questions, such as the difference between elements of waiting time, inactivity and taking rest; thinking time and investigation. We studied speed of approach and loss of precision and effectiveness due to too fast or too slow a delivery of speech, and presentation and legibility of board work. Throughout the lectures and exercises at least four stopwatches were trained on the instructors, picking up later on the actual coursework from others, in less than fifteen minutes after the evening meal.

Results of our studies on the working efficiency of work study instruction were both disappointing and highly revealing. One of the four being studied achieved a working efficiency of 30%, but only by patiently going over certain points several times before we all agreed that we'd got it. The others were rated around 15–18% efficient, due to the enormous length of time spent just walking up and down between the tables instead of preparing the later sessions. Added to this, only two at any one time were active, except when we went out to some workshop to study various belligerent examples of workmen. On these occasions all four came along. These hands-on visits were interesting from the point where some of us would chat to the working lads, swapping stories and such, later marking these chaps down as having been observed as performing at a zero efficiency while we were there.

Our obvious attention and perceptive questioning in studying the lecturers earned us very high ratings after the course, a thing we discovered when we returned to our various places of work, only to have invitations to join our respective work study teams on the divisions. After what we had seen at Harrogate, not one of us took the bait, even though the worm was large and fat. Until I blew the truth of our studies on the course, I was actually asked to stand in for holidaying work studiers, which I did just once. It was not engineering, but going through hundreds of submitted sheets of data of manpower achievements. I managed to award impossible bonus payments to all, including one gang led by Adolf Hitler, and including a dead pope and a ripper called Jack.

I totally dismissed the principles of work study while at Huddersfield after noticing the ganger at the station staying all day in the hut, while the rest of the gang worked. He spent his time filling in all sorts of exciting and exhilarating performances, and as a result earned himself and his lads bigger bonuses than he would have, had he actually joined in the work. Work study was a fashionable fad, because other businesses where it was more appropriate did it.

Useful courses often cropped up due to some incident that reached the national press involving an aspect of civil engineering. As a result everyone was sent down to Watford in waves of apathy. The substance of the instruction took a quarter of an hour to put over, yet we were all to travel down at intervals for one afternoon each, to sleep in beds almost warm from yesterday's complement, take welcoming tea, three meals and coffee, for three hours of morning class work, necessarily going over the obvious and what we had long before gathered by experience, just to offer us a slight change in procedure. Had the work study of the previous section been applied, then the lecturers would have done the travelling, dealing with us all in half a day at our home stations instead of two days each in an old Victorian workhouse.

Breaking off for a moment (and this is entirely your fault), I have become profoundly depressed. Feeling that it was miserly and uninformative of me to deprive you of detailed information, I have dug under the spare room bed for the old papers. Things that I have read among them include performance reviews and arguments over pay. Following the hefty York remodelling job, the amazing achievements of the people who made up our team and led to an outstanding success, I received reflected high ratings in my performance reviews. Arguing for something better than the average marking of three (out of five), I was told that this would be impossible as it would mean that someone else would have to be marked lower than average to maintain that same average. I gave up on reasonable discussion on personal grounds after that. Having now been reminded of the unfunny side of the railway, I will down fingers temporarily, leave this writing job on hold, and go down and see how England are doing against Australia, in so doing hopefully regaining my composure.

★

HASAWA was a new word to us, and we were all to go on courses to learn about it. (Health and Safety at Work Act, if you're unsure.) Here we were shown stunted movies of work staff doing the daftest things, just to underline points of unsafety. There was a lookout man standing in the fourfoot with his back to traffic, busy lighting his pipe, followed by a dramatic shot of an approaching train. A blindingly obvious full-size dressed dummy was cut in here, being flung up the embankment. This was followed by a poignant shot of the pipe lying between the rails. A gang of four men were seen sat on a trolley, which gradually gathered speed, resulting in four moaning bodies sprawled out on the track, and a derailed trolley with one wheel spinning against the sun. The film improved to the point of a bloke walking across four tracks, reading a copy of the railway free magazine. He finished up being printed on the front page of the next copy, surrounded by a black border.

Now sensible parts of this Health & Safety week I did get a chance to apply to work conditions on my return to Huddersfield. Don, who had also been called up on the course earlier, requested some risk assessments done of various worksites, along with preventive suggestions. I covered the PWay Stores, housed in a minimally converted second-class Gents. This was where the PWay and Works Supervisors, Drawing Office and Don had their famous single-stall lavatory, until Don had his delusions of grandeur, and built a dry, warm, covered one inside. This was why, as I spent the best part of a day in there, all sorts of rumours about my medical condition sprung up, due to the regular visits of various members of the supervisory staff in order to use the facilities, and finding me there looking thoughtful.

'What's tha game, Mike? Tha's spent all morning in 'ere. Aren't you up to scratch or summat, lad? Dusta see t'need of an 'andy bog all t'time?'

'I'm carrying out a risk assessment for Don.'

'Tha'll be well at risk if Harry comes in. He nobbut goes once a week, and it's a matter of sendin' up some white smoke when he does as a warnin', along wi shovin' a canary in afore thee to test t'air.'

'No, I've to see if things are stacked safe, and that no one's in any danger by coming in here. No hazardous substances getting damp or owt, and no dangerous sharpy things or matches within reach. Take these floor slabs with the great gaps between them; they're what's known as a recordable hazard. So I've to spot this, assess the level of risk and work out a remedy.'

'Tha means that a collidge eddication has put thee in t'position of lookin' at cracks in floors, and decidin' that some daft bugger might trip up?'

'There's more to it than that. I'm on the lookout for anything with a chance of falling over and such, like them bars stacked in that old urinal stall.'

'Thee'r all safe wedged in t'piss run gulley. So's t'shovels and forks – tha's worryin' abaht nowt!'

'What about noxious substances and gases?'

'Ah, that'll be Harry agin. Ah'll give thee that. No fun comin' in 'ere after Harry's been loggin'. Has ta got yon leet on this list, then?'

'No, the bulb's way out of harm's way, and the switch is dry; I don't see a problem with that.'

'Hasta ivver bin t'fust in 'ere of a mornin'?'

'Not that I know of.'

'Well, tha wain't knaw abaht t'leet, or rather t'switch. See this 'ere?'

This was a length of three-quarter dowelling with what looked like an old bicycle tyre wrapped round it. 'What's it for?'

'It's fer turnin' t'switch on wi. Touch that wi thi bare 'and to turn t'leet on an' theer's a flash an' a reet crack up thi' arm. Wi this stick, theer's justa flash! Nah, that's wot ah calls dangerous, and it isn't even on tha list!'

You see? Once more experience wins over learning! Mind, men such as this did get a chance of a bit of learning in my early days. There were after hours classes for volunteers in basic track design and components given by senior lads from the Drawing Offices. They were known as A and B courses. Having passed one, the men went on to the other. Although there was no overtime paid for them, there were rewards in extra days' holiday, and passes on their records did no harm to them when jobs came up.

In later years, fired by many minor mishaps somewhere or other on the railway system, new working arrangements were brought in, all needing courses and pass marks before you were allowed out on jobs that you'd been doing since joining up. Suddenly there were PICOW – Person In Charge Of Work, PICOP – Person In Charge Of Possession, and PTS – the most important one of Personal Track Safety. Without that you were not allowed to set foot on the railway lines, let alone walk along them. All these were sensible, reasonably short courses – an indication of how important they were – and required a pass certificate at the end. PTS actually came up for regular review, and those among us who baulked at tests and examinations of any kind, found themselves in all sorts of nervous trouble.

A Training Section later dedicated to the Leeds Division (at last having the lads travelling in and back in a day) to deal with these track safety issues seemed to develop a phobia about having me on their short, but sound, courses on home ground. They would look increasingly nervous as I wrote things down, when the rest of the class wasn't. Obviously I was collecting morsels for the *Annual Newsletter*. However, they did bring a little of it on themselves, and it was asking for trouble, what with the trainers being former colleagues:

KEITH BROWN: (on the Personal Track Safety Course) Right, you're walking along the track and you find a large oak tree fallen across the line, blocking the road; what do you do?

AWKWARD SOD IN CLASS: Is it only blocking one line, Keith?

KEITH: Yes.

ASIC: Pretty incredible fluke that, isn't it. Being large, and an oak tree at that?

KEITH: Well, never mind that now. How far do you have to walk back to protect the line?

ASIC: Which way, Keith?

KEITH: How d'yer mean? Towards traffic, of course.

ASIC: So you still maintain that this fallen oak tree is managing to block one line, without even affecting the other, because I just can't believe that, since oaks spread and bits would be bound to go on both lines.

KEITH: Well, the other line's a long way off... (*inspiration*). It's the site of an old station, closed down under Beeching, and the two lines diverge round a long demolished platform, so the other road's miles away.

ASIC: That's another fluke, then, and anyway it's
                   unlikely that an oak tree's sprung to large between
                   Beeching and now, because it'd be bound to be
                   stood where there'd been station buildings, or
                   something. I still don't think it's likely.

Long pause.

KEITH: Right, you're walking along the track and you find
                   this broken rail…

Personal Safety is fine discussed in the classroom, but trying to apply it out on the track, every moment, is impossible. Walking towards Hull, on a line strange to me, in pleasant warm sun, I noticed a very colourful butterfly settling on the rail in front of me. As I walked it flew on a few yards and settled again. This was repeated over and over again. I'm thinking, as I watch it, that there's no protection on the railway for poor little butterflies. Like this one, they would just get run over. The action of moving on constantly was something that fascinated me, and I mused on how anyone could put a fear of the railway into this small mind, and teach it to watch out. Suddenly I realised that as I had been walking and watching the butterfly, and worrying about its future, in the space of two minutes I had not looked up once. Every ten seconds is the recommended interval for checking for approaching trains. So much for the butterfly – I hadn't even looked out for myself!

The Drugs and Drink course was known among the lads as 'Mike's Biography'. By late in my career I was known to be taking a large amount of pills for my chronic chest condition, and ignoring the instruction of not mixing them with alcohol; in fact many a time I used the stuff to wash them down, since it has been found to be more effective as a painkiller than the tablets devoted to that job. (Never knock the old remedies.) What interested the office most was my dependence on steroids, and a great number of cartoons sprung up of me as Supertech, but for one who could hand it out fell the need to be able to take it back in return. I got them all later at Christmas with the *Newsletter*, anyway.

Perhaps the most annoying thing about courses was the frequent display of arrogance and superiority shown by the trainers. We had a morning in York at the Welding School, going through new methods of welding up the de-stressing gap. This was over a 10-foot length of track in one of the sheds. At one end was the gap and next to it the welder's trolley. Our instructor was a useless piece of work who had notably failed to shine in the Drawing Office. Before starting he pushed the trolley a couple of feet away from the work point, and asked us, with a smug look, to go about setting up the weld. This was easy – we'd all done it dozens of times, so we got stuck in.

'No!' he shouts. 'Wrong from the start!' With which he moved the trolley back the two feet up to the gap. 'First of all get the trolley up to the de-stressing point!'

He was met with an amount of verbal abuse that no donator of wisdom should ever be subject to. Bearing in mind that we would normally have shoved the trolley perhaps half a mile up to the gap before this, two feet was of no significance. Some of us then told him exactly what he could do with his course, warned him to give us all adequate pass marks, because we knew where he lived, and walked off back to the station.

Now I must at last move back onto the hallowed ground of character studies by reintroducing John Midgley, the best in my collection (he appeared in a supporting roll in Book One). As we became a unit through the amalgamation of the York and Leeds Projects Sections, prior to the big build up to the York re-modelling job, we became to be thought of as one, and as such shared courses with each other. This was not a wise move for the rest of the world. Many things that appeared funny to me and not necessarily to others didn't help. Then there was Midge's reaction to any progress beyond steam and his immediate experience, plus his apparent inability (or determination) not to cope with anything new, with special reference to computers; but on the plus side, typical railway, we were taught every last thing that there was to know about them on a course lasting just one day. We were to go to Doncaster for this one, which put John in an antagonistic frame of mind immediately. This is just a taster of John, I promise much more later.

'Why do twenty of us have to go to Doncaster when they could bring their frigging computer here? Who needs computers anyway? Just bloody typewriters, and we've got typists to do that. I've more to do than be a bloody typist – anyroad, typin's women's work!'

John and I, being middle-aged ('You might be, burram nobbut forty-five!') were openly labelled as dinosaurs by our whiz-kid immediate superior, so much so that when he left to climb back onto his comet, we presented him with a self-construct model diplodocus. As usual I felt genuine sorrow for the little lad, never seemingly getting any job satisfaction wherever he landed. It was he who arranged for John and me to attend the 'basics of computing' in a one day course.

Our instructor was a disaster when confronted by John. He was keen enough, but exuded superiority, in knowledge if not in rank. To make matters worse he was a clerk and male. 'What's any bloke doing takin' a course on typewriters? It's not natural.'

There were twenty of us in the room and ten computer keyboards and monitors ('bloody tellys and typewriters'). We were told to work in pairs. ('You're workin' wi me, sithee. Cummon, let's grab two seats.' No way was John going to display his fallibility to anyone but me.)

The immediate problem was that two chairs do not fit in front of one computer. John solved this by pushing mine aside and plonking himself squarely in front of the screen. ('Nowt's happenin'. Is it plugged in? Weer's t'switch?') I advised him to wait until we were told, but exploration was natural to John. In poking and pulling our machine about, he managed to disconnect the monitors and keyboards from the computers of both our neighbours on either side.

'Right, now first I want you to switch on your computer. You do this by pressing the button at the front of the box.' ('That's norra bloody switch! That's a tit! N'wunder ah couldn't find it.')

Our screen lit up with an agreeable picture of a field with a mountain behind it. From both sides of us was a chorus of 'Our's is doing nowt!' The instructor became very unreasonable, accusing them of playing with their PCs and disconnecting things. ('That's one oop t'us, then!')

'Now let's get acquainted with the components. The monitor is the screen in front of you, and that displays your work. The box with the switch on is your computer, and the keyboard is your working table.'

'Ayoop! Our's is all wrong! All t'letters are mixed up, thur's "a" here, "b" dahn here and it starts wi "q" and finishes wi "m". Someone's buggered our's oop!'

'You are looking at a perfectly normal qwerty keyboard, common to all keyboards and typewriters.'

'Whose med this and buggered up t'alphabet? Ah bet it's them Japs – they've no idea. Has ta seen theer writin'? No wonder they've med a bollux of settin' this oop. Ay, theirs ower here is t'same, and so's theirs. We're all buggered to start wi!'

Our leader was becoming a shade tetchy by now. 'The layout of the qwerty keyboard, which is what you have in front of you, is the common layout of all typewriters!'

'Rubbish! Ah learnt t'alphabet afore you were an accident in a mucky weekend.' Then he added, to me, 'He is talking bollux, in't he?' A genuine question, now lacking in certainty. There followed a talk, which might have been useful to me, had I not got a grumbling heap of discontent sat next to me. When the subject of the mouse was introduced it brought a crescendo of confusion from my right.

''As he ivver seen a mouse? This is nowt like one. Ay, have yer noticed that arrer thing movin' abaht on t'telly when ah shift this thing? Is it supposed to do that? How duz it doit?'

At this point the mouse came under great scrutiny, a sort that only Midge could perform. It was examined front and back, before turning it over.

'Ayoop, look here under it! Thur's summat like a ball thing stuck under this rahnd plate. Ah think that comes off, sithee, a slot for unscrewing it. Lend us a penny, it's abaht slot size. If ah just… oops! Didsta see weer it went? Ay, thee! Our mouse's ball's just dropped out!'

The class, and he who was addressed as 'Ay, thee', now set about searching for the bit that had dropped off our disintegrating mouse. This took care of ten minutes until one of our neighbour's blew his nose and the ball came out of his pocket along with his hankie. The cool teacher now looked rather agitated and excused himself for a moment. He returned four minutes later with cigarette smoke coming down his nostrils. Some sort of calm returned, as did John who had visited all the computers to find not one of them with a correct alphabet on them.

Then came the moment we had all been waiting for – putting something on the screen. This involved opening a document that took an embarrassing length of time at one table. ('Gerroff, ah can doit! What did he say tha'd to press? Try this… no. This, then. Bugger, t'screen's gone dead. Are we on t'wrong channel, or summat. Wodderyer mean, "turned it off"? That's t'on tit. Oh, is it "off" as well? Ah'll press it agin.')

In an attempt to restore some order the instructor turned away from the rest of the eager class, and put all his attention on us. Bearing in mind that I'd yet to touch the machine, I was a bit dischuffed at the way he spoke to us both. Eventually the screen performed correctly and our mate (now) led us into a programme.

We were then invited to touch in the letter 'a'. Everyone managed this successfully except Midge. Neither I, nor the trainer, were ready for Midge's approach to this simple task. Starting with his finger at shoulder level he circled around before zooming in to the rough location of the 'a' button. Son of a farmer's fingers were wide and thick, hence the resulting 'qwa'. For sheer excitement we were then allowed to have a dash at 'b'. Sure enough we got 'hgb', again John's finger entering the atmosphere from two feet above desk level. He seemed quite content to have put something on the screen. Capitals followed with greater confusion, having to use two fingers at once, after we had established which arrowed button was the correct one. The morning was passing and I had yet to put digit to key, but I was quite content to watch and note my colleague's efforts for a report on our return to base. My turn came suddenly and quite unexpectedly.

Our instructor had left us, presumably for another calming drag, with the task of writing out a short sentence on the lines of *Hello, I am working at a computer*! He set us to it for a while and went out 'to jump that tasty bit at t'door' being John's usual interpretation of someone sneaking out of a room. John was still in control of the keyboard, and started well with the 'H'. After that, things went downhill at a similar rate, in which cursing, damning and blasting featured ever more strongly. Eventually frustration with the keyboard, me, the rest of the class, technology in general and all the instructor's relatives, led to an almighty slam on the keys with a fisted hand.

One thing that hadn't been mentioned was that the keys were capable of being removed. This we now found out because within the limits of 5, r, d, c, and 8, i, k, m, there was nothing but a hole with the best part of a Scrabble set on the floor. From aggravation to frantic took a second. Here began another arc of the learning curve. You can't just replace the buttons anywhere and expect the right letter to come up. By now all the class were around our machine offering helpful advice and directions as to where the correct locations were, all dodging about backwards and forwards from their own keyboards for reference. On the instructor's return, John was just left with a reluctant 'j', which I hastily managed to divert him from hammering in with his fist.

'We should've put 'em in t'reet order while we were at it. Look, they come out quite easy if you just prise up t'edge. Dusta think he knaws?'

The afternoon session was more relaxed, as all afternoon sessions on courses are, despite students having to leave the room at regular intervals. Our only interest occurred when one of our own Leeds instructors called in. Seeing Midge and me sat at one of the machines, he sang out for all to hear, 'What have you put those two dozy buggers together for? Do you realise that all t'signals round Donny have turned to blue?'

'We couldn't've done that, could we?' said Midge to me, in one of his stage whispers.

Doncaster became a favourite place for one-day jaunts, and as Midge and I were working alone together on planning out the York remodelling, we tended to be sent off as a unit – the thinking being that we needed each other in the planning process back in the office. This was good for both of us, even though initially being rather chalk and cheese, since we were both equally uncomfortable sat once more at the schoolroom desk. With our lengthening time together, we had both come to realise that, rather than chalk and cheese, we were actually two different breeds of Dales cheese, since our individual differences were nothing compared to our combined attitude to the rest of the world. This realisation formed a great foundation for cooperation.

What we also found was that courses dealing with things that we saw as useful, like this computer basics, after the initial stumbling start, were always dealt with in a day. Subjects of no importance or interest to the pair of us tended to take a fortnight out of our lives. By mutual cooperation we were able to support each other in avoiding going. One of our keener colleagues, returning from a management bonding week, enthused about the mock battles, firing paint bullets at each other, and competitive projects in the evenings, like constructing things with kids' building blocks. Midge at first couldn't believe this, but on getting confirmation, rounded on our leader with a rich articulation, involving kindergarten, group painting and bloody great kids.

Another such one-day course, like the computer crash day, was to give us the vital information surrounding the approaching electrification. This was the driving force behind the York Project, and so involved us greatly. The course also had a bizarre and very unsettling ending for both John and me.

By some extraordinary and sad coincidence both John and I had fathers-in-law confined to wheelchairs, and for the same reason. Both men had lost their entire legs due to illness. We discovered this one day while out on the road, and had to stop at a café, utterly confounded by the coincidence, to swap details and discuss what the effects were on the both of us.

Farmer's boy Midgley thought nothing of carrying Moira's father with him clung to John's neck and facing him. In such a way John could transfer dad from armchair to wheelchair. This I had never contemplated, and knew that the sheer weight and indignity would outface me. Otherwise our lives with the handicapped ones ran along very similar lines. While remaining opposites in some minor ways, on important matters John and I grew closer by the day; in fact it was mainly our socialising that stood us apart at all, but that was in general the difference between York and Leeds Districts.

Electrification lessons rushed us through the basics of mast and cable design and the matters where the civil engineer came in, mainly clearing trees back two metres from the masts, and dealing with overhead wires under bridges. The Works lads also had to be aware of avoiding induced currents in handrails and the like, running alongside the overhead cables. There were lots of other minor time-consuming needs, but these were the most costly. Then, after a DIY dinner break – the best sort – we had a basic course on first aid, with particular reference to electric shocks. This is where John and I had an altogether different kind of shock because of the unreality of the situation.

There on the floor was a truncated dummy body with nothing below its waist. Laid out on the floor it appeared virtually sexless, but it deeply un-nerved us both.

'It's Moira's dad!' Midge blew out in a breathless whisper.

'Just what got me – Thelma's dad!'

'Ah don't thing ah can do wi this! Can we slope off?'

We were trapped in a converted coach that was part of a mobile training centre.

'I don't see how we can – there's only twelve of us, they'd notice; and we're supposed to get a pass mark out of it.'

'Well, ah'm off fust, and gettin' out sharp!'

We were faced with an electrocuted victim who had stopped breathing, and while John and I were muttering between us, the trainer was explaining that we would all have a go at the kiss of life, until we felt a pulse in the dummy's neck – if we did it correctly. When the time came, John leapt forward to be first, in order to enable his escape. He was brilliant at it! One puff down the tube into the dummy's mouth and John 'discovered' a pulse, jumped up with a 'That's him sorted! Ah'm off out!'

The instructor was having none of it. He claimed that the dummy could take up to half a minute to be resuscitated, and that John must have felt his own pulse. He insisted on John having a proper go. With a large sigh, John returned to this intimate position over his father-in-law. On the count of thirty, he was asked if he could now feel a pulse in the dummy's neck, activated only when the correct procedure was completed.

'Yup!' said John, feeling the appropriate vein on the dummy's neck. 'He's fair pantin' now and rarin' t'go! Yup, that's gorrim goin'!'

I followed, shut my eyes, shoved my cardboard tube between the model's rubber lips and blew away to a regular beat. I did not enjoy it any more than I found John had.

'Can you feel the pulse, now?' asked the instructor. I groped around the area with two fingers.

'Oh, ay, there it is!' I said, and joined John.

'Didst'a feel owt?' he said as we withdrew to the back of the crowd.'

'Not a bloody thing!'

'Neether did I, burra weren't goin' to say nowt!'

It was the proud boast of my old school that no pupil left without being able to swim. That was one net I slipped through. Fantastic at swimming under the water, I found it impossible to take a breath on the surface and carry on without choking. By this method I managed a width, and nearly drowned in the deep end going for a length. I was happily forgotten.

Similarly, the Civil Engineer's Department of the railway wanted everyone involved in weekend work to be able to drive. Again this was a challenge where I found the mesh size large enough to slip through. This was a wise and safe thing to do. Many a technical lad has worked a fourteen-hour Saturday night, and has had to drive himself home afterwards. While based in Huddersfield I made suitable arrangements with the local gangs and drivers, and never had to get myself home, unless suitable trains existed. Young Tony McGowan, a very likeable, if quiet, young lad, who was never very fit, and sadly died early, once worked an extended shift through the night and well into the next day, overrunning wildly. On his way home, desperate for sleep, he wrapped the office car round a tree in the late morning. Thankfully he suffered only shock and involved nobody else.

'Learning to drive' was not a greatly organised course. It was just occasional lessons in a Leeds goods yard at dinner times. Not that there was much realism involved, as the training vehicle was not a car, which is what the candidate would be presented with later, but an old goods mechanical horse. That's the three-wheeler cab so popular in model railways as background. Its relationship to a car was like that of paddling a coracle against sailing a yacht. Only the keenest looked forward to these 'free' driving lessons with any enthusiasm, and I had no ambition whatsoever to own or drive a car, and I still don't and can't. I could not understand my colleagues who looked forward to their holiday in Penzance, driving down overnight, when I simply caught a train, complete with family, all travelling free. So that was another course I successfully avoided!

★

Education sometimes comes up behind you and hits you like a sock full of wet sand, probably some time much later than during the actual learning process. This usually turns out to be brief but deeply affecting, and by far the most intensely fruitful absorption of experience and knowledge that you ever go through. I had two such learning sessions on two separate occasions early on in my railway career.

Student and graduate trainees were invited on experience trips, arranged as powerfully voluntary invitations. These did not necessarily need to be taken up, but mental note was made of any refusals – not going on personnel records, but usually filed away in managerial pigeonholes, parading as brains. Admittedly some were fairly trivial, like trips round wagon shops or chocolate factories (a principal industry in York in those days), but one or two stood out as significant adventures. Fortunately I found these far more inviting than the socialising ones. My two stick forever in my mind.

A night spent exploring the London underground system on foot appealed to me for the tunnelling aspect, an early instinctively exciting adventure in my mind. (The popular psychologist would put my liking for deep dark places down to being pushed under the dining-room table when the air raid sirens went off when I was only eighteen months old.) Down below the metropolis we were shown the usual signalling and safety features, up until the time when the electric current was turned off for maintenance. Then it was down onto the tracks, and an exploration of the tunnels. It was there, during a refreshment break that we met the maintenance gang who doubled as a suicide clearance team. Relaxed and cheerful, they described a 'clear-up' of a couple of nights previously in graphic detail, while at the same time paying due attention to their snap tins full of sand-wiches. I asked whether experiences like this affected them at all. In reply they admitted that it did effect their immediate life, in that after shovelling up the various pieces of human pizza (the corpses tended to be fried by the current as well as being filleted by the train), they were instructed to wash down with great care before settling down to their sandwiches.

This was enough of a shaker for me, but we were next led out to one of the major junctions to examine the switches and crossings, somewhat different to the standard BR ones above ground. At about five o'clock we were standing in groups in the complexity of all the trackwork when a horn sounded and we were told that the current was back on in one minute, and that we should now take care. We hunched up our coats and delicately stepped in and out of the live rails, trying hard to keep any part of our bodies, and anything attached to them, well clear of the current. It was very difficult to see in the directional lights of hand-lamps the difference between a dead rail and one carrying an almighty jolt, and we moved very deliberately and slowly until we reached the safety of a nearby station platform. Fifteen minutes later a familiar breeze came down the tunnel and the first train of the day emerged. From the tight, dark confines of the tunnel, to the men who spent their uncertain working lives down there, I felt nothing but admiration. I thought then that I would never again in my life experience such a location for claustro-phobia. A few weeks later, with all this fresh in my mind, I was to undergo a much greater challenge to my senses in that direction.

St John's Colliery, Normanton, was on our itinerary. We thought at first that this one was going to be a doddle. Fully kitted out, we descended an incredible distance downwards, I forget how far now, but it took a long time – that I can remember. We then walked along a tunnel, attractively lit up, all of us having individual dancing fairy lights on our helmets. Items of interest were pointed out, the tunnel being the comfortable size of the average two-track railway equivalent. Then the leader turned and said, 'Right!'

This was ominous. We had arrived at a point where the end of a conveyor belt appeared out of a small hole to one side. At this point we were invited to either return to the lift, or go along the coalface. He pointed out that this was only three feet high and would mean crawling. It was after we'd done it that he mentioned that the length of the face was a quarter of a mile.

We knelt down in turn and started what was to be an immensely long crawl. There were many scrapes of helmet against roof as we made our way along the side of the conveyor belt on our left. Pit props supported the roof on either side of us, leaving us about another three feet of passageway sideways. It could have become monotonous except for the occasional rumblings and rock collapses that we had been warned about in our briefing. Apparently, as the face advanced the tunnel was allowed to collapse way over to our right, and we were instructed just to stay still until it went quiet again. The fallen roof and rubble could be seen, appearing to be about thirty feet away. No movement was ever apparent, the collapses always occurring either ahead or behind us, yet the feeling was of apprehension with each crash and rumble. Speaking for myself, all I felt emotionally was excitement, a sort of intense throbbing excitement.

Crawling is all right in normal conditions – when you can stand up whenever you feel like it; but when the slightest move upwards hits the constraint of the tunnel roof, a feeling of entrapment comes over you. As yard followed yard I found my head sinking from the sight of the bum in front down to the floor immediately ahead. I was happier leaving a gap between me and my leader. Rather than taking in the experience, as I progressed, I found myself in a hypnotic trance based on the ground. The main objective was now the end of the tunnel rather than the sights to right and left.

Only in our wildest dreams could we have imagined a carpet where we were crawling; instead it was rough-hewn rock. Hands and knees were being penetrated by grit. Eventually they went numb and so overrode the pain. We had been told 'old trousers', and we now knew why, because as we emerged most of us were without knees. There was a heat down there, an uncomfortable filthy still heat and we were forever spitting out from dust-clogged throats. Again lights hung at regular intervals along the seam, with the face of coal gleaming black and appearing clean. About halfway, I had drifted into my autopilot condition, stopping as instructed when the roof collapsed to our side with a crack followed by an echoing dullness, and had accepted this as one of those endless dreams of horror. I don't know how long we were crawling. We passed the odd maintenance man engaged on the belt, and managed decreasingly cheerful, 'How dos?' It was gradually becoming a hell.

We were still silent as we reached the end and stood up, all affected by the incredibly harrowing experience. Things began to dawn on us, and even now after over forty years I can taste that air and hear the rumbling collapse of the roof. Laughter, more of a nervous reaction than fun, returned among us in the showers. Good as they were, they failed to clean everything and left us mementos for a week or more.

I will here write down what I have said many times since that experience, and right through the various mining strikes and violent disturbances where pitched battles have taken place between police and miners, both migrating to battlefields way away from their homes, and through the tented HQs of the wives. In response to the ill-informed letters and articles which appeared in papers like the *Telegraph* and *Mail* decrying the exorbitant pay claims of the workforce, I repeatedly said, 'Do not even think about commenting on a miner's pay until you have once crawled a quarter of a mile, with three feet of headroom, through their everyday working environment.'

Evermore I have been overwhelmingly grateful for that one experience.

★

'Right, lads!' It was young Lindsay, our boss of less than thirty to his 'lads', averaging fifty. 'Weekend of the 24th, 25th and 26th we're having a bonding session along with Maintenance, Works and Bridges. I want your names in by Wednesday, unless you have some very good reason that means you can't go this time.'

'Is that the laking about with paint guns, and canoeing and wall climbing?'

'That's it, with indoor mental challenges in the evenings, based at this motel complex near Wakefield.'

'Can't go!'

'Neither can I!'

'Nor me!'

'When d'you say, 25th and 26th?'

'Yes, that's three weeks off, and I must stress that anyone not complying will not be looked upon kindly. It's not compulsory, but it is very much against your best interests not to attend. Morris Smith is going. Nigel Trotter would be, but apparently there's a big job on Newcastle Area he wants to see. So three weeks time, and let's have your names in now.'

'No good to me, I've got a funeral on the Friday.'

'I get a bath that weekend. Can't be putting it off any longer.'

'I've an urgent appointment at a field in Headingley – Saturday and Sunday. It should be all over by Monday.'

'Oh, come on, lads! It's going to go against you! Be warned. And I've promised a full turnout from PWay!'

'Well you can go and unpromise it, then!'

'Mike – what about you?'

'Nope! Important job that weekend. I've got a bale of steel wool, and I'm knitting myself a coal bunker.'

'Right! I'll put your name down. Midge?'

'No way!'

'And I'm serious about the coal bunker. Put my name down by all means, but I'm not going. And neither's Midge. We're too busy right now.'

'You will go! This is character building!'

'Look, lad. You wouldn't know a character if it came up to you bollock-naked with a traffic cone on its head. Characters built this railway, not little pillocks jumping around shouting, "You're dead!" Him and me are included out!'

And so we stayed.

Combinations of luck, weaving and lying, along with declaring an indispensable attendance on work kept both John and myself clear of all these trainee managers' courses and bonding sessions. What experiences we must have missed, so essential to managing a railway section! Our abilities suffered so much from lacking the determination acquired by playing Cowboys and Indians with paintballs and guns. We were quite ignorant of how to make tricky decisions while dangling from a rope alongside the rock face of a local feature, especially when forward planning and the efficient use of resources suggested using the slope up the back that the family picnickers took to the top. Neither were we convinced that our day-to-day working routine would necessitate experience at canoeing through minor rapids, so we determinedly refused, forgot to reply, or ignored instructions to sign up for one of these immature kiddies' weekends.

At one or two points in my career, roles were reversed. I was called upon to lecture on the project team's latest adventure, usually at one of the monthly meetings of the Permanent Way Institution, but once to an international conference at the Leeds Hilton hotel. PWI talks were all right in my earlier days, but towards the end the Institution became discredited locally, and merely served as a place to be seen. (Things have improved latterly.) Meetings were from seven at night, so some effort had to be made to be there.

In those early days a mixture of track workers to managers attended, and talks were geared to such a mixture. After all, in the '60s and '70s the only difference between the extremes was the benefit of a full education. The man on the ground could be every bit as intelligent as his bosses, and would sniff out condescension immediately, and treat it with contempt. I gave several illustrated talks in my time, with the follow-ups of the 'paper' being published in the Institution's journal. These seemed to pose a problem when it came to annual prize awards. The astute reader of these jottings may judge how my talks were presented, a slightly light-hearted approach being favoured, and they raised comments among the judging hierarchy ranging from 'breath of fresh air' to 'outrageously trivialising'.

Sadly what should have been a great vehicle for gentle education and information degenerated in the West Yorkshire area into a bandwagon for the upper inner circle. Ridiculously inappropriate foreign trips were organised, rather than travelling to places of real railway interest within a couple of hours of home, and some members of the committee arranged these fun-filled packages around one or two local remote and tenuous railway connections; and what's more, they went on fact-finding missions lasting up to a fortnight in advance of the main excursion. The shrewd track lads, who could never afford these extravaganzas, saw their leaders for what they were and turned their backs on a potentially useful organisation.

Dave Holmes from the Drawing Office and Denis Durand from the supervisors, set up skill-testing days themselves that sorted out the genuine trackmen from the casuals. Many stories emerged from their classroom at Stanningley Shops, usually of a technical ineptitude. These mostly came from visiting supervisors who couldn't wait to tell horror tales of some of the lads in their gangs.

One such was a case of a lad on fog duty, placing explosive detonators on the track to indicate the clear or danger aspects of the old semaphore signals. After a few hours at his post his supervisor got in touch to see if he needed any more dets, only to be told that he had all his left still. Suspicious, the supervisor paid the lad a visit, only to find the detonators strapped to a guard rail at the side of the running line.

★

Finally, after all the above there has to be a highlight in the ways and methods in which British Rail attempted to train and teach a mostly hostile work force. This has to be the Metrification Course. A moment in our engineering life when the great and good tried to wrench us away from rods, poles and perches, gills, pecks and bushels and dehumanise us into the world of the milli, centi, deca, hecto and kilo.

With a message akin to the Sermon on the Mount, men and women of all stations and corners of the railway kingdom were called together in groups of about twelve at a time, which in itself had some significance. Were we called together as disciples, or in units that we could understand, as opposed to metric groups of ten or twenty? In the introductory blurb justifying the course, we were told that following the ancient Indian philosophers' discovery of the unit zero many thousands of years ago, the time had arrived, here, now, at this moment in AD 1970 for us to pick up on their idea and apply it to our work. There were a few who empathised with this statement, declaring that there was a distinct lack of zeros in use today, especially when it came to payslips. It was not an advisable initial approach to tell us that this course was all about nothing (or 0), as we already had experience of many courses where the fundamental basis of the tuition over the ensuing week was based on next to nothing. Not much more than nothing was ever said, nothing from the week took root and the results of our indoctrination in the weeks following was nothing.

Our twelve, an undisciplined dozen from the Leeds Drawing Office and Area, was a doomed mix for such an educational experience. Because of our positions – we were all technical officers of some years' standing – our Messiah was to be Peter White, the current PWay Assistant, a man with a reasonably relaxed view on life, known as 'Peter' to us all, ever with a modicum of respect.

Perhaps the main barrier towards us appearing to pick up on the metric system was the fact that most of us had had a university or college spell lasting three years during which the terms yard, gallon, mile or pint were never mentioned, and we worked exclusively in metric units throughout. Only after this did we return to the railway life where the basic unit of measurement was the chain. There was no way that we were going to admit our prior knowledge, as there appeared to be some mileage to be gained from this day of needless metric indoctrination. Still, the Training Section had to have a tick for every name on their books against the 'Attendance of Metrification Course', so we were forced to go back to potty training and learning to eat with a spoon. The day – it was only a day because of our presumed greater intelligence – was doomed from the outset, and Peter was wearily aware of the six hours in front of him (which he sensibly and appropriately reduced to five).

We were initially exhorted to dismiss thinking in terms of any comparisons between imperial and metric – we must not say that a metre is a yard and a bit, it is a metre, full stop. We had to stop thinking in terms of inches and feet, and speak only in millimetres. Not centimetres, you understand; the railway industry only recognised metres and millis. For mischief and winding up this was a perfect base. Peter, after his initial chat, unwisely asked for comments and discussion.

'It's going to make life more difficult in loads of ways. I mean, have you ever tried pacing owt out in yards, Peter? It's bloody difficult, unless you're abnormal like Holmsey there; and now you're asking us to do it in metres, which we're not supposed to know are about three inches longer. That's beyond anyone's stride – even yon stick insects.'

I added a personal note. 'I tell you, if they stop serving in pints I'm stuffed because I've had enough after two and if I've got to drink in litres, I'll be no bloody use next day, what with the tablets, and all. Everyone says "Are you coming for a couple?" '

Keith was good for an unhelpful point. 'And then there's cooking, Peter. I always like three eggs in an omelette and I reckon five, which is half of ten, which will be the basis, will be too many. We'll all be egg-bound. And anyway, t'milkman always brings 'em in boxes of six. Will he have to sell them in fives and tens? Ten's too many, and if you only have five and have a metric omelette, that's all your eggs gone in a week. And anyway, how do you design a box for just five eggs?'

We were getting carried away by now, and question was falling out on top of question. Mind, there's always one:

'Yes, and what's a "tablespoonful" in metric, and a "pinch"?'

That one caused a moment of silence, until someone muttered, 'They're the same as now, you daft sod!' Things were now entering the absurd.

'How about when you're measuring and planing wood and just want another thou off, what will it be a thousandth of? It can't be a thousandth of a millimetre, 'cos that's impossible, and it shouldn't be a thousandth of a metre, because that's a millimetre, and that's far too much, and it's not a thou but a millimetre anyway, and you wouldn't say you wanted a milli off, 'cos that's a deep chunk!'

'Yes, and then there's a drop of. You know what a drop of is in imperial, it's a drip; but what's it going to be in metric? Could be a thimbleful, and that might be far too much.'

'Look,' said an irritated Peter. 'This is getting silly. You'll still be using drops and thous as before; that'll stay the same.'

'No, Peter, we've got to start thinking in metric only.'

Dave now had another problem. 'That's not always possible for the first year or two. Take my bike, for instance. It's a 26-inch wheel. What are they going to be giving me now? And if I'm having to get a new wheel for my old bike it's either going to be too small, and I'll have to be pedalling harder, or it's going to be scraping t'mudguard.'

Peter was ready for once, 'They'll still supply the same size of wheel, it's just that they'll sell it in metric. Your 26-inch wheel will be sold as a 660-millimetre wheel.'

'Bloody hell, Peter, that was quick! Did you just know that?'

'No,' Peter confessed. 'I've got a conversion chart here.'

Chorus of, 'You're not supposed to convert, Peter! You've got to think in metric!'

Dave was not happy. '660! That sounds bloody big!'

'Not if you're thinking metric in the first place, Dave,' responded Peter. 'It's actually 0.660 metres, and that sounds smaller. The important thing is to get your decimal point in the right place. Supposing you ordered a 6,600-millimetre-size wheel, now you would be in trouble.'

'How big's that then, Peter?'

'Over 21½ feet! Now that won't fit!'

'You're still converting, Peter.'

'Mind you—' this came from Terry Ward, who I never saw as a wind-up merchant, joining in, 'I'm not so bothered about bringing in metric, but they've definitely got it wrong with temperatures.'

'Meaning?' said Peter, no doubt hoping for a bit of sensible debate creeping in. Terry was from Leeds Area Assistant's Office, and possibly not tainted by the crackpots of the Drawing Office.

'Well, Fahrenheit that they're doing away with; it's ideal for weather temperatures since the range in most countries is from zero to one hundred in Fahrenheit, whereas it's something like minus twenty to plus forty in Centigrade. Fahrenheit seems perfect for being a metric base for weather temperatures.'

'That's true,' Dave picking up on this new line of argument. 'You can't have a minus in measuring, can you? I mean taking it further, you wouldn't have a system where you could measure minus three metres, whatever that would look like, or a jug with minus two litres in it, would you?'

'I don't see your point, Dave,' hoping beyond hope that there wasn't a point.

'Well, talking temperatures, the scale below freezing goes to minus something, doesn't it? So you've got measurements of minus so much. That being the case you're bound to look at other metric things that could have minus readings. Say you'd a leak in your jug, would you then have minus a litre in it? And supposing you were digging a two-metre-deep hole and it turned out to be 2.2 metres deep. Would it be minus 200 millimetres too deep?'

I now could see this line of discussion drying up by getting too daft, so I decided to add a bit more coal to the fire. 'Seriously, though, Peter. Isn't this change in thinking over just the thin end of the wedge, like?'

'How do you mean, Mike?'

'Well, I mean the clock. What's to stop them deciding that there's going to be twenty hours in a day instead of twenty-four? And then a hundred minutes in an hour, and a hundred seconds in a minute. Seems to be the logical progression.'

'What about the week, then, Mike?'

'Oh there'd be ten days in a week in future.'

'That'd mean we'd only get one Sunday in ten, rather than one in seven! That's bad news, I mean apart from overtime being hit, you'd be getting less anyway on an hourly rate, and there'd never be enough Sundays to get a year's programme of relaying in.'

'That's a point. How come there're always just enough Sundays in a year now to fit a year's relaying work into? I mean, if there were twice as many Sunday's, would we have every other Sunday off or would the programme get bigger to fill them?'

'They'd be smaller jobs in that case, because you'd only be allowed ten men on instead of, say, sixteen. So if they took up Mike's idea where there were fewer Sundays, the jobs would be longer in length and you'd have twenty men instead of sixteen.'

'Half a mo, though…'

'That'll be a full new "mo" now, Dave? How many mo's are there in your new minute, Mike?'

'No, silly bugger, just listen! Mike's gone and shortened the Sunday to twenty hours from twenty-four, remember, so that might take care of the programme.'

'It's going to be costly, this metric, isn't it?' This was Keith joining in again – a reliable thinker and stirrer.

'There'll be some initial expense, yes,' admitted Peter.

'No, it'll carry on being more expensive. Just look at your mileposts, they'll all have to be changed to kilometres, and there'll be a lot more kilometre posts than mileposts, along with .5 and .25 and .75 posts.'

'Yes,' agreed Peter. 'As I say, there'll be some initial expense, but the government is subsidising a lot of that. It'll be the same as before afterwards.'

'No it won't,' persisted Keith. 'All those extra posts will need painting every ten years, and there's more of them than miles, so the expense goes on after the beginning. Do we get an annual grant for painting kilometre posts?'

This was taken up by the class. 'And, there're more numbers to paint; I mean you'd get up to one hundred sooner in metric kilometres and have to paint three numbers instead of two. You get to one hundred in metric while you're still only in the sixties in miles. And there's the 50-foot tablets in tunnels, what will they be changed to? Probably 10-metre tabs, so there'll be more than now, and they'll all need painting up every so often.'

'Changeover day's going to be a belter – they'll need a fair few sacks over the road signs, and they'll all have to come off at something like two in the morning, along with all the weighing machines changing.'

'I'll tell you one good thing about this metric measuring: it'll improve Holmsey's bowling!'

'How d'yer make that out?' asked an intrigued Dave. 'And what's wrong with it anyway?'

'You do bowl short, Dave, you know that; I mean batsman's only got to stand there and the ball's whizzing over his head all the time. With metric, the pitch'll be down to twenty metres, which is a bit shorter, so you'll be pitching them further up and taking his head off then.'

'Well,' said a relieved sounding Peter. 'I reckon that's dinner time. We'll be doing a few exercises after.'

'How many, Peter?'

'*Ten*!' he snorted, catching up fast. 'Back here for two – I mean 1400.'

'Have you owt on over dinner, Peter?'

'Not specially.'

'Fancy a pint then?'

'Why not,' said Peter.

Accidents

In a fairly light-hearted collection of railway anecdotes and memories, it might be thought that there should be no place for the serious topic of accidents, but I have no control over where my mind will flit next. The trouble is that one person's accident is often another's day made.

Imagine, for a moment, that you are privileged to be watching a master surveyor at work, on a high-profile job such as the realignment of part of the high speed East Coast Main Line. You watch as this paragon carefully picks up details on either side of the baseline and transfers them to his book. A bunker here, a drainage catchpit there, a telegraph post here, and the odd signal box that might show up, there. Accompany him back to base, watch the drawing emerge, followed by the perfect proposed new alignment, so beautifully designed that you are bound to wonder why in tens of years this better alignment has not been apparent before. But therein lies greatness.

In awe, you travel out to site to watch this genius have wooden pegs hammered into the ground from his plans, marking the new centre line of this epitome of perfection, leading gently away from the existing line of the tracks to this supreme excellence of new alignment. Wonder at the composure of this latter-day Stephenson as he sees his line of pegs heading straight through the south wall of Ferryhill No. 1 signal box, which has miraculously upped foundations and moved several hundred yards down the line… apparently. Re-examination of the survey book suggests that, although measurements from the base to the box were accurate, the actual recorded position along the line was a tad out. No great damage done, as the signal box is immediately apparent as being in the way of trains following this new line. But there is a visible dent in the pride of a top surveyor, brilliant engineer and eventual famous leader. (He, he, he, hee!)

Not as lucky is the York Headquarters PWay design lad who

produces a magnificently detailed drawing of a new crossover to be laid into the complex that is Leeds station layout. As an observer, I was suitably impressed in the confirmation that the correct insertion of check rails in such a layout are very functional, fixed as they are alongside the running rail in this situation, and essential. Their purpose is to hold wheels to the correct running rail at points where, in theory, the loco might seek an escape leading to derailment. This is borne out on the Monday morning when the first loco over the new installation settles comfortably onto the sleepers and stone formation, for the lack of a missed out check rail, blocking three lines through the station. Despite there being extenuating circumstances for the error, the young designer is for evermore known as 'Chekhov'.

★

'Never, on any account, admit any responsibility, for yourself or for your colleagues or your department. Deny everything!'

This was a lesson taught to a very green Mike during my first month at Huddersfield, after experiencing the unnerving sight of a large locomotive settled half on the sleepers and half on the rails. When your Hornby Dublo screams round the tiny track on the dining room table and encounters a sudden bend without slowing down, it leaps cheerfully into the air and onto the tablecloth. This is annoying, meaning you have to lean right over and try to reposition driving wheels and undisciplined bogies back on the track, turn over the carriages, and wipe up the mug of tea that you've dislodged in stretching. In real life, with full-size, very heavy locos and trucks, I tended to just look on in disbelief. It is a very troubling sight, a bit like having the unbuttered side of the toast staring up at you from the carpet. It's not how you are supposed to see it.

The instruction heading up there in *italics* was delivered to me by Permanent Way Inspector Dick (Mr) Simms, back in his office in Huddersfield, in a kind of 'When did you last see your father?' position. He sat with his back to the unnecessary blazing fire, facing me over his enormous old desk, as I looked at him with the apprehension of the apprentice standing before his master. This was all wrong. Simms had no right whatsoever to lecture me; that was the job of another. He should be asking me if I'd mind taking a few measurements of the track after the loco had been removed, and could I please let him see them before I showed them to Don Newell – my and his boss. Instead of which, in the presence of his assistants, he was giving me what turned out to be an inquisition – and a totally unjustified one at that. In place of the judge's wig was the permanent way inspector's official equivalent – a brown trilby.

Mr Simms, only allowed to be addressed as 'Dick' by Don, was near retirement and was deeply venerated and feared by his own. He was a fairly pleasant Welshman up to being crossed by those he saw as his inferiors or opponents; then he would become a bully. He was out riding the territory when a message came through of a derailment in the yard opposite our offices, and I trotted over, more out of curiosity than to get involved. However I found myself regarded as the Civil Engineer's representative, mixing as I was with the shunter, the yardmaster, the local Carriage and Wagon man and the signals. I studied the scene for a minute, and said that the problem seemed to be clearly a PWay fault, only to have Mr Simms bear down on us and take a completely opposite view. He argued for about ten minutes before demanding my presence in his office for what turned out to be the dressing-down.

In *Simms v Collins*:

PROSECUTION: You *never* accept responsibility!

DEFENCE: There was an 08 shunting locomotive standing on the badly rotting sleepers between the spread rails. Five chairs consecutively before the loco had their fixing keys missing, so that nothing could stop the rails dividing. A further seven or eight chairs had their restraining lugs broken, some by the derailment, but some with rusted faces indicating old fractures. There was nothing wrong with the loco – no wheels missing, no

> drunken driver, and no sign of it hitting the
> siding at 100 mph. No signalling was involved. A
> very clear case of bad track.'

It was just a game that had to be played out. Everyone knew whose fault a derailment was, or perhaps what coincidental factors could call more than one department to be at fault. For example, if an unevenly loaded 10-foot-wheelbase wagon with a broken spring were to encounter a poor section of track where over ten feet of it twisted at more than 1 in 200, then there would be faults on both sides.

SIMMS: *Never* accept responsibility!' (For the third time, in a guttural South Wales bass sing-song tone.)

COLLINS: The track was rubbish and had simply disintegrated.

SIMMS: The track was just as bad further back, so why hadn't it come off there?

COLLINS: Luck.

SIMMS: (Rising in tone) There's no *luck* about it! We've no idea what state that engine was in. It could have been going up and down after it hit the rail joint, (I had noticed that the fishplates had dropped off) if the springs are faulty. It could have been jumping if the fuel was down. The windows were dirty... well, the bottom of one was. There could have been a boulder on the track. (That might have shown up!) There's no end of things that might have made it jump the track!

COLLINS: And make the chair blocks disappear, and make the broken lugs rusty, and unscrew that fishplate, and—

SIMMS: I've heard enough from you, young man. I shall be reporting you to Mr Newell. Get out of here!

I got out. Don turned up an hour later, and together we went over to look at the broken track.

'Measure the gauge and cant every sleeper for twenty up to the point it came off, please, Mike. After dinner will do, but before that sly old devil can make repairs!'

I shuffled off happily. Don went straight through to Dick Simms and I had the satisfaction of listening through the connecting door to Don giving Simms his considered opinion of the state of the track. I did hear Mr Simms, at some point where Don stopped to draw breath, whine a bit about the young upstart saying that it was our fault in front of other departments.

'He was damn well right!' shouted Don, in one of his very rare vents of temper and frustration. 'I'm going to have him measure up and examine all those sidings over the next few days, and we'll have his report to discuss by the end of the week!'

I did the few measurements that Don had wanted, but he asked for no more. We were both quite happy to see old Simms and his deputy out there all next day, scrutinising every yard of track.

★

The City of Bradford is very similar in shape to a wok. It is a large pit with a handle running along north to Shipley. I suppose that is the writer's way of trying to gain sudden interest, coming out with a statement like that. I plead guilty.

When I was being educated in every facet of civil engineering, with the exception of railway work, at the Bradford Institute of Technology, lecture time was pretty intense. While I turned my back during my gap 'year' for fifteen months, doing some actual railway work at York, the Institute turned into a University, and became a new building, but none of the intensity changed. Lectures were back to back from nine to five, with the important exception of Wednesday, when lecturers were all struck dumb and thirsty at exactly 12.30, and we were left with the rest of the day to either study alone or reclaim some life. I usually went home to do coursework, but as the end of the four years approached and exams had been taken, we were in a kind of limbo, so one fine day I decided to put my wok theory to the test.

What gave me that image was the fact that all roads into

Bradford ran downhill into the centre, marked by the Town Hall. The exception to this was the valley, or handle, that ran from the city out to Shipley, along the line of a small beck. My theory was that from anywhere within a radius of two miles of the city centre it was downhill into town. To prove the hypothesis, or at least to put it to the test, I caught a bus out of town, avoiding the wok handle route and got off after ten minutes. I then set up my experimental equipment on the roadside.

Admittedly this was a fairly simple apparatus, and to the casual onlooker – and there was quite a collection of such during the course of the experiment – the tackle used very much resembled a worn tennis ball, because this is what it was. Restricting myself to the pavements, I dropped the ball to the ground and followed it. Experimental rules allowed that when the ball came to a step up after crossing a side road, it was permissible to pick up the ball and drop it again a yard further on. Much the same applied on the approach of a small dog whose parents had apparently had no leanings towards xenophobia. It was an amalgam of every known breed. The animal mistook scientific exploration for play, and made a dive for the apparatus. A swift boot to what I took to be its tail end reduced any interest it momentarily had in scientific exploration.

At the time I was living a life of experimentation up at the university, so strict guidelines were demanded, and any obstacles to scientific advance were there to be surmounted. Laboratory investigation of contour lines had convinced me that the ball would end up at the Town Hall steps, wherever I chose to drop it. An hour later, by which time I was thankful that then many shops still observed the half day closing tradition, so keeping the pedestrians at bay, the ball stopped rolling in a grating about a couple of hundred yards short of its target, which to my mind signified success.

I decided not to repeat the experiment from a different location, mainly due to embarrassment. You will have seen on news programmes a reporter talking and walking to camera surrounded by milling people. The camera pans out from close-up slowly as he talks, revealing him to be working alone except for the curious passers-by, who are wondering who this nutter could be walking with a fixed gaze upwards and talking away – apparently to himself, as the camera is out of sight. I bet they have to do loads of takes, as people come up and stare, or ask him if he's all right. Following a tennis ball down a city street is very much like this as far as audience reaction goes. The Bradford man in the street is very questioning of the oddity seen following a rolling ball down a hill in the centre of his city.

Having dealt with the above experimental details in depth, I've rather lost the thread as to what the point was... Yes, it's come back: Bradford is proven to be a large pit, coming in from most directions.

Now, this of course applies equally to the two railway lines running into what was, in those days, Bradford Exchange Station. However, there is a difference between a sloping road and a railway going downhill. On the road a gradient of 1 in 50 would be fairly insignificant, but on the railway trying to move several hundred tons up the same slope, or holding it back from running away, tests the system to the limit. In the old steam days, trains often needed the Bradford banking loco at the back, especially freight trains coming out of the yards on the Manchester route. This was all right for trains going uphill, but there was no method of assistance for braking trains travelling down into the city.

One day, towards the end of the steam era, an aging loco and tender set off backwards towards the city from Laisterdyke on the Leeds line. It soon became clear to the crew that the brakes were not working as well as they might, as the engine began to slowly but surely gather speed. After trying everything in their power, the driver and fireman decided the wisest move was to abandon ship, choosing a rare stretch of long grass to leap into. Sizing up the situation, the signalmen down the slope guided the runaway for a mile off the main line and into the remote wall-top siding at Adolphus Street Goods Yard, way up above the streets below. This tricky steering exercise ran out of options with the approach to the buffers, high up on the retaining wall, the loco doing something like a steady 30 mph ploughed through them and the wall, landing with its tender upright and in the road, and with the loco resting at an angle between the wall top and the tender. The road was fortunately empty. On its final journey in life, the locomotive at last made headlines in the local press. It was offered, as it lay, to local scrap dealers. The first of these turned up with a horse and cart, half loaded with old washers and radiators. He looked at the towering loco, and back at his two-wheeler cart, and announced that he'd have to go and get his mate who had bigger, but similar, business transport.

Such runaways as this can be controlled, to a large extent, though their eventual fate is in no doubt. The alert signalman and shunter on the ground can divert it into an area where it is reasonably safe from causing serious injury. One of my most tragic experiences was the brake failure of a diesel multiple unit travelling down the hill from Halifax into Bradford Exchange. It was a late afternoon train, and carried among many others our local PWay Inspector, Aubrey Mortimer, on his way home from his office at Halifax. With the driver struggling with the brakes, Aubrey shepherded all the passengers into the rear coach, and returned to try and help in the front cab. The train hit the buffers, cleared of people, killing both Aubrey and the driver. I was accustomed to the sudden death of older colleagues, always a sad time, but Aubrey was in his thirties, and a very promising supervisor. Bradford's press declared both him and his mate heroes – an understatement.

★

Don had a bump in the car one evening on his way back home in Leeds. He rang me, working late on some important drawings in the Huddersfield office, asking me to let his wife, Irene, know that he'd be a bit late. Now what words do you use to tell a wife that her husband has been in a car accident, over the phone, without the wire melting with her response?

'Hello, Irene,' I would announce in a sing-song, happy voice. 'Don's been in a bit of an accident.' 'Nothing to worry about' would be drowned out by a scream at the other end. *No…*

'Oh, hello, Irene, Mike here…'

'What's happened? Is Donald all right?' in the crescendo of a panicking cry. *No…*

'Hi, Irene, how are you? It's Mike here. Don's rung to say

he'll be a bit late home.' *Better.* 'He's having to make his own way home because the car's a bit poorly.' *Go on, keep it up, doing fine.*

'What's wrong with it, Mike?'

'Oh, nothing to worry about, just a few scratches.' *Ruined it.*

'Has Donald been in a crash? Where is he? What's happened?'

I found no way to get it right, and failed magnificently.

There's a stretch of the A62, Leeds–Huddersfield road where, should you get a total stoppage of traffic, you could park four cars alongside each other across the road with comfort. The time was before the M62 appeared, so this piece of road was always very busy. Don in a hurry could easily overtake, even with another car coming the other way. If, by sheer coincidence, another Don, or a Don clone were driving a car in the opposite direction to Don, he, like Don, might think that there was room enough for four cars, which standing still, we've seen there was; but these four cars were doing forty and sixty in one direction and sixty and forty in the other. The two sixties do not now fit. Scrape, crash, tinkle, tinkle. Drivers come to a halt a hundred yards apart, both having to climb over into the passenger seat because the drivers' doors won't open.

'There was enough room for four cars, m'lud.'

'Prove it!'

Fired up, and needing clearing, Don desperately wanted to know the width of the road at the collision point. Ideally this could be fitted in on our way home one night. It was a simple job, in theory, of using a steel tape across the road and reading the measurement. In practice, thirty feet of steel tape, in a gentle breeze, takes some unwinding and laying flat without snagging it on a passing car. It was to be my job to take the dumb (ring) end of the tape across the road, unwinding it as I went. Have I made it absolutely clear that this was a busy road with cars passing one way or the other constantly? After ten minutes of, 'Now! No, hold it! Now! No, no, no!' we gave up.

But we didn't totally. Don has not ever been known to give up. What had been of mild interest – was the road wide enough for four cars travelling at speed, a question which I felt Don had proved in the first place to be in the negative – now became a point of honour. When I sarcastically suggested using a theodolite, Don jumped at the idea. Instrument duly borrowed from the Leeds store one morning, we parked up and measured out forty feet along one pavement, set up the theodolite and panned through an angle of 90 ° to the other side of the road. All three points were marked by nails driven into the tarmac and chalked up on the walls, one side on an electrical wholesaler's car park, the others on the boundary to the Jewish cemetery. Returning that evening we planted the theodolite on what became the near side of the road, by the electrical showroom, and measured the angle between the two nails in front of the cemetery wall. We now had a triangle that I plotted out next day. Four cars, assumed to be identical Ford Anglias (the car in question) were placed on the plan showing eighteen inches between all the four cars. Triumph for Don, in his eyes, and dubiousness in mine, and in those of the officer in charge. Case declared fifty-fifty.

Not an accident, but an incident which might have developed. I was running up to near Marsden in Don's car with Jack Senior, PWay Inspector, driving. We were going down a typical twisting lane running roughly alongside the railway, when I noticed that we were slowing down a bit.

'Do you know owt much about cars?' said Jack.

'Next to nothing,' I told him. We ran on, the experienced passenger (me) noticing that Jack was not changing gear at all, despite the ups and downs of the lane.

'Just wondered,' he said. 'So I don't suppose you'll be much help.'

'Doing what?' I asked.

'In telling me what to do with this,' said Jack, and he turned towards me, waving the gear lever in his hand.

★

It would have been mid-morning, coming up to noon, high noon in fact, when news filtered through to us in Huddersfield that there had been a derailment of a passenger train near Mytholm-royd on the Calder Valley line. A freight train derailment is a nuisance; it damages the railway and probably spills whatever it has been carrying all over the tracks, or what's left of them. It would often be a train of short wheel-based wagons, the sort that find every fault in the track, but in the end it is only a freight train, and not a people carrier.

As soon as we found out that it was a three-car diesel multiple unit, with passengers aboard, it made a big difference. Our concern was immediately for their welfare. Before dashing out to site, phone calls were needed to ascertain how serious it was, and if the emergency services had been called. The train was reported upright, involving minor injuries. So it was some short time before high noon when we set off on the 45-minute trip to site.

It would have been about the same late morning when the Carriage and Wagon department set off from Leeds, so we were to be in confrontation at about the same time, just before high noon.

Our information was that the track damage started between Mytholmroyd and Hebden Bridge, meaning that if there was a track fault, that is where it would be. Nearest access was Hebden Bridge station, which is where we started our walk. C & W, with different concerns, made straight for the derailed train to assess the damage to it and whether it could be moveable in a conventional manner once re-railed. They carried out a quick assessment before retracing the path of the train back towards Hebden Bridge. Had we known it, they were far more perturbed than we were, having discovered that their train was minus one gearbox, a rather large thing to move. They needed to search the route, obviously for the odd gearbox that might be lying about, but also for smaller clues.

Don and I, working from the other end, were looking out for the derailment point. By chance one of us noticed a severed bolt in the middle of the track, the break shining brand new. We dropped back a little and found a few more. Marking the discovery locations up in the web of the rail in yellow wax crayon, we carried on.

We spotted the orange safety vests of the C & W representatives about half a mile away, walking towards us. It was now almost high noon.

They were stopping at intervals to pick something up, we continued towards them looking for signs of track fault or damage. It was now exactly high noon on the dot as we arrived at welcoming distance to each other. Almost to perfection we found the point where part of the train had jumped the rails. The shooting began.

'Looks like a straightforward derailment to me,' stated the senior carriage man, looking Elliot directly in the eye.

'Track's perfect. Long welded rail, no joints,' responded Elliot. 'You found anything missing off the unit?'

'It's suffered by running three parts of a mile on the sleepers. You'd expect that.' A shot echoed down the valley, just missing its target.

'Missing any bolts?' Elliot with a direct hit to the shoulder. 'Like these?'

'Could have come off anything.' The wounded carriage man was faltering slightly, his gun beginning to hang limply.

'Bit of a coincidence, and the breaks have all happened within a couple of hours. Rain last night – they'd be rusted today. I think we'll get them to Forensic.' (Derby Research.)

As the stand-off continued, the two juniors, me and he who I came to know of as Frank, were casually looking for evidence at the track side. I was hopefully searching for more sheared bolts. He was not letting me know that he was looking for a massive gearbox. We saw it together, part way down the be-shrubbed small embankment.

'Bugger!' said Frank.

'What is it?' said I.

'*Harry*!' '*Don*!' we called in unison.

'Bugger!' said Harry,

'That's interesting,' said Don.

When they make the film version of this book, then that will be the point where the tension music stops and we go straight into the typical Western big tune...

'I'll need those bolts,' tried Harry.

'They're safe enough with me,' said Don. 'We've marked up where we found them.' At this point the two swapped phone numbers and some cordiality returned. We left Harry and Frank giving the gearbox the last rites, and walked on towards the train.

Damage was mainly to the timber sleepers after the initial

jumping-off point, where a number of baseplates would need replacing. We later found that the gearbox had dropped from somewhere near the middle of the train, bringing off the last trailing bogie – a good derailment from our point of view, with sleepers heavily scored, but for a while acceptable. Had they been concrete ones they might well have shattered, needing immediate replacement.

The train had travelled some 1,300 yards, at around 50 mph, the driver feeling a sudden sluggishness as it parted company with its gearbox. Trained for such an event, he applied the brakes gradually and then pulled up. The breakdown crane had already arrived on site, and the last coach was re-railed within an hour and passed fit to travel at 10 mph back to the depot.

Our Halifax gang were soon at the derailment point, be-moaning the fact that the train had come off during the day, and not within any conceivable overtime scenario. Only two men benefited, being sent straight home to come back and caution trains through the night.

Final big tune reprise and credits rolled.

★

Mytholmroyd was also the site of a memorable meeting with the legendary 'Old Man Geeson'. He was far from being old, say late fifties, but he walked with a heavy limp and leaned on a walking stick, which ages anyone automatically by ten years. Nevertheless, he was remarkably agile, and moved around and under the loco with some ease. He had a reputation for solving derailment problems with speed and at minimum expense. His name was applied as an indication that we were in the presence of a great. Interestingly, to me, was the arrival of his son, Ted, to spend a period of training under me in the Huddersfield office. Ted never played on the great parent's name, but his air of slight superiority let you know that he was who he was by birth. Ted, on very rare occasions, displayed a genius at improvisation, if perhaps not perfect judgement, which must have been inherited.

A shunting error had left a very large steam loco part derailed at the entrance to the sidings, and I was only there as a casual observer. In this position I was able to watch in awe the methods of O M Geeson in getting the derailed bogie back on track without the need for cranes. He had the surrounds and run-on of the bogie jacked up on timbers, and eventually swung it bit by bit back onto the rails, all the time having the loco inch forward under its own steam. It was a performance of great skill, derived from many years of experience, and a willingness to break every rule of safety in the book. The man was a genius, but would be totally thwarted if he could have applied his approaches today.

★

Sundays were popular and frequent days for derailments, mostly on worksites. Popular from the point of view of the gangs who were performing boring work like de-stressing. They provided the possibility of a much longer Sunday, and the attendant financial bonus. Frequent because it is not that many years ago that Sunday track relaying work had uncertain levels of risk attached to it.

Shipley, daylight, installation of the first ever crossover and turnout using concrete bearers instead of timbers, high profile, honey pot for senior engineers.

We were laying in an innovation that was to follow us ever-more afterwards. Concrete sleepers for plain track had been with us some considerable time. Their advantage over timber was that their lifespan was much greater, and they provided more weight and stability to the track. (I would imagine that Greenpeace will approve of them, too, as against timber.) Point and crossing work demanded precise accuracy in setting up and positioning. With the introduction of the heavier and stiffer concrete bearers the accuracy had to be even more so. Our main concern was the new league in weight terms. Despite many calculations as to the cranes' capacities, the supervisors still pushed things just that little bit further, and we had the common Sunday sight of a crane tipping up slightly so that the rear wheels rose above the rails. As long as there was no movement sideways, the wheels settled back where they belonged when the load was released. This morning there *was* a little movement sideways, and the crane missed the rails and sat back on the sleepers, at this point fortunately still timber.

It was just before this juncture that the first raft of brass drew up, and obviously they were attracted to the crane work. This was where our luck was in, as they turned out to be the Divisional Civil Engineer, Geoff Holmes, and his PWay Assistant, David Kealey. These were a new breed of senior staff. They knew all their staff by name, and out of office hours were known as Geoff and David. They were also seasoned engineers who had learned that jobs don't go any better by dancing up and down and shouting a lot. As the crane released its lift and settled down neatly off the track, Geoff Holmes marked himself up as a boss of great sensibility by turning to his colleague and saying, 'I think, David, we ought perhaps to go down to the other end of the job for a while.' With which they trotted off, leaving the supervisors and men to set aside rules and regulations, and turn to experience and common sense, re-railing the crane before the engineers' return.

When a derailment or other accident occurred on the railway, all Area Drawing Office work stopped and we had to concentrate on getting out detailed plans in time for the inevitable enquiry that would be held within a week. In all my time on the Area I never fell for a fatality, but did do injury drawings. One such was in Standedge Tunnel, when a lookout man was floored by a slow-moving shunting loco within an engineers' track possession. I was in the office that day, with Wilf and Percy, the chainmen, who were waiting to go out on a job with the lad who was the junior at the time. Such jobs with lesser experienced surveyors, the chainmen either put up with or disliked due to the lack of leadership and ideas. It was gently raining, and there seemed little point in them going out at all. Don was visiting one of his out-based supervisors, and Bill had completed the morning's filing and such. An early tea was the order. I was trying to do a bit of calculation work, but was totally hampered by the deep discussion in the background, inevitable when these three got together.

'Didn't say nowt abaht any rain today on t'telly last neet.'

'Ah reckon all t'accuracy went when they left off using straightforward charts.'

'You can nivver tell wot they're forecasting nowadays wi them theer fancy magnetic clouds and suns they've got. Thur allus slippin' dahn t'map. Tha starts off wi heavy rain in Aberdeen or some such, so heavy that afore tha can look rahnd it's slipped dahn ower Yorkshire.'

'Ay, burrit don't mean that if t'clouds do wander dahn t'chart ower us that it's bound t'actually rain here, tha knaws; norrifit's just t'magnetics that's failed and they've slipped dahn from Scotland. Same wi t'sun, though that don't seem t'be as heavy, 'cos it don't drop as fast as t'clouds.'

'Can't see why they bother wi magnets ower Scotland. It's allus rainin' theer. They could nail t'bloody clouds up there and still bi reet nine times aht of ten.'

'By t'end of t'forecast all t'weather's sloped off dahn t'London. Couldn't be a better place forrit.'

'Just as well they only give 'em two minutes for doin' t'forecast, otherwise all t'weather'd be dahn on t'floor, and they'd be treadin' watter.'

'Has tha noticed that when they start theer's nivver no weather in Ireland, except in t'north?'

'That's becoss it's still Britain theer. Wot wi it bein' t'British Broadcasting thingy wot's worked it all aht, they can't go givin' t'south free weather, can they?'

'Dun't matter any road, 'cos after a minnit it's all slumped dahn inter t'south.'

'They're settin' a lass on t'do t'weather next week, accordin' to t'paper. That won't seem reet – it's a man's job, is doin' t'weather.'

'It were bund t'happen after they let 'em loose readin' t'news. Ah can't be doin' wi'em. Slightest bitta bad news and they're face slips and t'voice goes all miserable and wobbly. Think what they'd be like doin' t'weather. Drop of rain and they'd be cryin'. Gi'em a good thunderstorm and they'd break dahn altogether, or be hidin' behind t'board out of t'road of t'lightnin'. They should be all like that theer Alvar Liddel character, or whatever his name is. Tha's no idea wot's comin' up by his voice. Cheerful or miserable, he allus talks in a reet dead soundin' way even if he's sayin, "The fifth and final test match has concluded with a win for Hengland by an hinnings hand two 'undred runs, which means that they retain the Hashes." Then his voice goes dahn another notch wi, "Haustralia were hall hout for forty-nine runs, and Geoffrey Boycott made an hunbeaten two hundred and fifty and then it started pissin' down becorse t'clouds had slipped dahn t'map ower t'Hoval…" '

Throughout this I was struggling with some tricky figures, but getting tangled up in basic meteorology. The phone rang; it was Don.

'There's been an accident in Standedge; one of the lads has been knocked down by the loco. It'll mean an enquiry; get out there and start measuring up. Have you still got the chainmen? Good! I'll meet you up there.'

This was not a job for the lad, although I'd never done an accident survey before where someone had been hurt. I mentioned this to Wilf who said not to bother as him and Percy had done one or two in their time and knew the drill.

What had been happening was that the Works Department had had the double track tunnel blocked while they worked getting materials run in, to carry on repairing the lining. They had the use of a shunting loco with four wagons and a guard's van. While they had the tunnel blocked, the PWay lads were doing some track repairs too (which wasn't going down too well as that was clearly Sunday work!) The short Works train was on one line and the PWay 'Whickham' powered trolley was on the other to take the lads in and out. Apart from anything else, the Whickham was a noisy brute, and had apparently taken away the attention of Ernie Hardcastle, the Works lookout, and he had missed the train moving quietly towards him on his line. He was standing at the tunnel side and just got knocked over into the wall. Not too much damage, but a lot of shock, so they got the ambulance there sharp and moved him out of the tunnel in the guard's van. I was to do a survey of an accident without a body or a train.

The Whickham had been sent out to Marsden to raise the alarm, and it waited there for the chainmen and me.

Now, surveying in Standedge Tunnel has one downside – its length – over three miles. If you are carrying tackle it gets even longer. Thank goodness, therefore, for the Whickham, in our early days, when there were four lines through Standedge. Up to a point – yes. However, the machine was no more than a motorised platelayer's trolley. There were seats (planks) fore and aft with a padded bucket seat for the driver, and more back to backs along the sides. Separating these was the engine, which was largely open to the elements. The important feature, or lack of, was the springing – there was none. In those far-off days of the sixties, the track throughout the tunnel was jointed, so for the mile approach from Marsden, and anything up to three miles following, there were two heavy bumps every sixty feet. Added to this, the track gauge was the standard four feet eight and a half inches. That of the trolley was apparently the same, less the half inch, so it would be lurching from side to side all the time as well as hitting rail ends.

George, the driver, did have the padded seat, and this was generously sprung, by means of a single large coil, central to the padding. As a result, anyone at George's side or behind him would receive liberal amounts of George swinging into them as he bounced and swayed with every wild movement of the trolley. Top speed was something like 15 mph, which felt nearer to a 115 in the dark. George used to tell of having a full day ferrying men and materials in and out, and getting home for his tea, still swaying and bouncing. Knife and fork were near useless as he kept missing his plate.

With just a tin sheet covering the motor, the racket was thunderous, and nullified George's ability to carry on a conversation throughout. We who had experience of this, and the fact that we could not hear a word George said would bellow out on occasions non-committal things like 'Aaagh' or 'Ummmm', which neither agreed or disagreed with George. Hence when a stranger, like the Engineer, were to get a lift in with George, then George would say afterwards that the Boss was a 'stuck-up bugger who hadn't a civil word to say'.

Our journey in was of 2½ miles, starting at Marsden station. Hanging on was a feat. Not only did you have to find a non-operational part of the trolley to grab on to, but you also had to hug the level box, legs and staff. With all the bouncing and surging, you soon became convinced that you were gradually slipping off the seat, and clung on even harder. There was a thoroughly uncomfortable effect on your spine, it alternately bayoneting the seat of your trousers or going through your cap. This was the vertical challenge to put up with, painful gripping of anything fixed was the other. Hands that had done such an excursion were hardly fit to handle the delicacies of the theodolite at the end of the trip.

George pulled up slowly as he sought the tablet numbers on the wall of the tunnel, pointing his Tilley hand lamp hopefully in the right direction. That, of course, was another encumbrance in the tunnel, in that every man had to have his own paraffin lamp. The brake was applied – a long wooden pole levered down to a block grinding against one wheel. This in itself caused a violent searching of the trolley to the rail nearest to the braking wheel, if done too quickly.

'This 'ere's it,' he announced. 'T'body, ah mean Ernie, were just lying ower theer or theerabahts.' He pointed to a section of darkness. 'T'shunter come dahn 'ere from yonder and tapped Ernie ower theer. Tha'll see t'marks on t'wall.'

We measured up the tunnel width, the track spacing and the clearance to the walls, and the point where Ernie had involuntarily scrubbed the wall to a near-new perfection. George showed me as near as he could how and where Ernie was lying, and we measured that to the nearest tablet on the wall. The loco apparently ran on another ten yards or so after thumping Ernie, so I made notes of that as well.

'Right!' I said 'I reckon that winds it up. Can you think of anything else we haven't picked up?'

I felt something in the air, I couldn't be sure in the darkness, but I felt that Wilf had nudged Percy.

'Nay! We've scarce begun!' said Wilf, 'There's all t'evidence still to get.'

'Like?'

'Look here on t'wall. Dusta see scuff marks in t'sooit? That'll be where he tumbled ower and tried to grab summat wiis fingers. Tha needs a picture of that in thi book.'

'Was Ernie cut, George?' asked Percy.

'He'd got a nasty graze on his nut wot were bleedin' a lot,' said George.

'Bring thi lamps ower 'ere,' ordered Percy. 'Cansta see owt?'

'Nowt bar t'back of thi 'ead!' said Wilf.

'No, look 'ere. See that? It's blood!'

'Oo ay,' agreed Wilf. 'Get that measured oop, startin' 'ere… and finishin' oop… 'ere, sithee. That's what? Eighteen and an aif inches.'

Percy was on a roll now. 'Look 'ere,' he said, touching the wall with his finger and examining the result. 'That's scalp, that is… Look there's hair onnit!'

'And here's his flags. How dusta think they got reet ower 'ere? He musta bounced a bit. And that looks like fresh stone on t'floor. He's scuffed it as he went down.'

All this was faithfully being measured up and put in the survey book. Wilf's lamp was now roving up and round the wall.

'Thur's more scratch marks up theer!' pointing at the roof. 'And is this his hanky?'

He waved a bit of cloth that had more than likely been dropped by one of the navvies building the tunnel seventy-odd years back. I was getting a bit fed up with them.

'That's been dropped years ago, it's just an old rag. Ernie wouldn't have been using that as a hanky.'

'He weren't ower fussy, weren't Ernie,' George added.

DCI Wilf was now on his hands and knees. 'Nah then, wot have we 'ere, then? This, unless I'm very much mistaken, is a bit of fingernail. Get on to t' meat shop weer they've teken him and ask if he's missin' a fingernail!'

That did it. I'd no intention of complicating things by ringing the hospital. I'd had enough. 'Right, that's it!' I said. 'You're not having me for a silly bugger!' I knew fairly early on that they were playing on this being my first casualty survey, and were jointly winding me up.

'Don't you want any more details, then? Just tryin' t'help…' Injured voice now.

I replied as I always did in such circumstances, in fact it apparently became my catchphrase. 'Percy… theeee bollux!'

Tunnel survey books are not the easiest things to interpret back in the office, what with bringing back a fair proportion of the tunnel with them. Also, I didn't have time to get hold of another casualty drawing to compare with, so I was working in the dark, so to speak. Despite my exasperation with the chainmen, I was gullibly uncertain as to just how much of their information should be drawn up. So, with the exception of the handkerchief and fingernail, I put it all down.

At the enquiry, Don was congratulated on a magnificently over-informative drawing, and was asked if it could be a little simplified in a final version, leaving off residual bits of the victim.

★

For much of its life the civil engineer's railway was under the curse of the 10-foot-wheelbase wagon and its dislike of twisted railways. Twist is present in all tracks; in fact it is designed in through curve transitions where the cant (or superelevation of one rail over another) goes through any changes. If there is a fault – say a dipped joint – within a section of twist, then that twist may be increased to an unacceptable amount. Much of this problem has disappeared with the introduction of non-jointed track, along with many of the short wagons having fallen apart and been dumped.

Imagine a bit of twisted track and a stiff wagon going through it and you will see one wheel rising up and possibly over the rail, hence the chance of a derailment. Wagons badly loaded so that the weight was in one corner were more susceptible to twists in track; and where do you get badly loaded wagons? In my experience, in cold wet tunnels on a Saturday night with diggers taking up an old mucky track formation. (Why they had to be cold and wet, I do not know – perhaps it's those nights that stick in the memory.) Filled wagons were taken off to the railway tip, where, during the week, another digger would plunge its bucket into the wagon of spoil and occasionally and unwittingly take with it part of the floor of the wagon. This truck would then be made up into a train for the next weekend. Now the wagon would be part filled, with much of the spent ballast falling through the hole and onto the track. At night, or in a tunnel, or both, this might go unnoticed, so that when the train was moved along, the faulty wagon would ride up over its own spillage and derail. This was a nuisance, and should call for the breakdown crew to re-rail it. That took a lot of time, and was often of no use as the adjacent track had been lifted out, so the rescue team would have to use their initiative. Initiative can be a double-edged sword!

However, before the breakdown was considered, similar initiative would be abundant within. Dubious use of the digger to lift the wagon and jacks to push it sideways, accompanied by a lot of shouting and much swearing, generally did the job. There was one occasion when shouting and swearing alone re-railed a wagon, but I can't give details as I have a pension to consider. Such derailments would not be reported, as it might lead to disciplinary action. Visiting engineers would be escorted past any such incident, while having the condition of the tunnel roof pointed out to them. This was a fairly common occurrence, and was regarded as one of the accepted snags, like rain and snow, of weekend work. It was a very different matter, however, when a short-wheelbase wagon was derailed in traffic, when a short period towards the end of the life of such wagons and the strengthening of health and safety coincided. Here the railways' romance with piles of paper and masses of detail was in the ascendancy.

Longwood Goods was my first encounter under new re-cording instructions. A wagon in the middle of the train left the track at around 30 mph, causing extensive damage and encouraging many other trucks to come off in sympathy. With rails and sleepers extensively torn apart, my orders were to take levels of both rails, at every sleeper, for one hundred yards up to the accident and twenty yards after; also cross-levels, extremely detailed curvature measurements and the names and addresses of everyone living within a mile radius. I made the last one up, but the other two were almost as easy. Imagine there are the remains of a railway intricately entangled with what was a goods train, with the wagons' blood and guts everywhere. And all the measurements (impossible) and drawings with tabulated readings (time-consuming) required to be neatly presented within two days.

These things were drawn up by headquarters staff with no grasp of reality, as were the instructions about the panel selected from a variety of departments put together to investigate such accidents. The only time I ever had to sit on one of these Old Bailey enquiries, making up one of three, all smoking with the light behind us, concerned a multiple unit which drew into a bay platform at Huddersfield, hit a patch of oil on the track and slithered into the buffers at an estimated 4 mph, causing a few passengers to sit down again. We had to grill the driver, guard, stationmaster, signalman, PWay supervisor and ganger, and the café proprietor who heard the bump. Enough questions had to be asked to make the resulting report look thick and thorough, and to justify the two days of enquiry and the bank of typists taking turns at shorthand and typing up as the inquisition rolled on. Defending from the civil engineer's corner, I was reduced to asking what time the driver had got out of bed that morning, whether he considered that he'd had a good night's sleep, and what he'd had for breakfast. These were among the more relevant questions asked. It had nothing to do with the driver, who acted exactly as he did six times a day, five days a week. What had appeared on this occasion was a patch of oil. We did not discover where that had come from, but we had filled in lots of paper.

Finally, on the subject of accidents, apart from ones involving injuries, there's my personal saddest ever. With Don away at the Leeds office and guaranteed an early tea, I got my work sorted out so that I could catch the early express home at 16.32. This was an exciting train, the only one of the day to go via the soon to close Spen Valley line, a route of vicious curves and gradients, built very late on in the railway age, and therefore encountering many established obstacles, like towns. Failing this, I had only the slow 17.10, late into Leeds, and late for tea.

Coat on and bag packed, I made for the office door, when the phone rang. It was Don to see if there were any messages. From the background radio I could tell that he was already at home and no doubt taking sherry and cocktails. By no stretch of the imagination could he have been checking up to see if I was still at Huddersfield! As I put the phone down I heard the sound of a departing horn outside as the express drew out of the station, and resigned myself to another late trip home arriving at quarter past six. Three minutes later the phone rang again. It was Hilary on the switchboard

'I've got to ring round everybody to tell you that a train's come off just outside the Leeds end of the station!'

I went to the door, and sure enough my 16.32 was stuck half in the platform and with the front end out among the approach's point and crossing work. The loco was at a funny angle. Not only did my personal express immediately disappear, but the following stopper couldn't get through either. I was marooned in Huddersfield. Then the sun came out as I realised that I had now to ring Don, just sitting down to his usual lobsters and caviar, and get him over here, with the car, as soon as possible, without delay.

Sporting Diversions

There were four defining moments in the history of the Leeds District or Divisional Civil Engineer's distinguished sporting existence. The first was the introduction of the ice hockey table. This, apart from the odd game of cards, brought the spare time activity life indoors and extended the sporting season to all year round. Second was the discovery of an abandoned table tennis board in the Goods Offices, coincidental with the move of much of the Drawing Office out of No. 23 Wellington Street into the Railway Offices in Aire Street, attached to the Queen's Hotel.

Later in 1976, the moving lock, stock and barrel out of No. 23 and Aire Street into 'Cramptup' House was hardly significant, except that it brought all the sections back together again. There we were a contented, docile and superbly average crowd of sporting talent, using the otherwise uninhabitable underground area in the basement for our collection of indoor sports. Happy there, with competitive league tables of eight different activities, we bumbled along through summer and winter indoor leagues, with no predictable overall runaway champion, when into our midst came Graham Whiteley, a new clerk, with 'athletic sportsman' written all over him. This was our third moment of truth.

Graham was over six feet tall, with snarling good looks, flaring nostrils on a superior, upturned face, and from what conjecture insisted, rippling muscles. This had to be the superb sports character who would upset our mediocre equilibrium. Our fears were immediately justified when this elegant, lithe figure mooched in alone on his first dinner time and picked up the darts, before flighting a series of doubles on our dartboard. Here in our midst we now had a true natural athlete.

Our final shock to the system came when Leeds and York Divisions were merged, and based at Leeds, much to the chagrin of the Yorkies. On their first day with us, a block of them moved into the Cramptup sports centre and took over the table tennis. Among them was Arthur Barnard. Arthur played the game as we'd never seen it before and, like his companions, proved fierce in the area of competitiveness. Up to then we'd had the late youth club skills of John Marshall, and the deceptive Methodist League guile of Bob Newell.

At first it seemed that Arthur played without a ball, as you faced him over the table, until suddenly there it was flashing past your ear. It wasn't long before the supremacy of the York lads could be explained. Life on the old York District was fast and furious until Friday dinner time, when it was the custom for the Drawing Office to be out as a block in one of the many city pubs. Games vied with pints, as they did in the evenings as well, since most of the York folk lived within York, whereas the Leeds crowd came from all over the West Riding, and hardly ever saw each other after hours. York worked and played together; Leeds just worked together.

Starting with the ice hockey: this was a metal stadium, a sort of tin tray with 2-inch-high sides. It was about three feet by eighteen inches, with finger operated rods through the sides, much as in the larger game of table football. On the five rods per side were fixed 2-inch-tall players with hockey sticks. Rods were less than a quarter of an inch thick, and were housed such that the rows of players could be moved to cover the full width of the arena. By twiddling the rods, the hockey sticks came into play, utilising some far too intricate gearing beneath the table. This was much too delicate for the enthusiasm that the games inspired, and frequent derailments occurred. Dropped cranked gear wheels are a far more serious injury than the odd spot of cramp, and the St John Ambulance maintenance team were called on quite a few occasions with their magic pliers. The puck was scaled up much larger than it should have been, compared to the players. This enlargement was necessary just to make it visible. (Unlike the full-size game where on TV you can hardly catch sight of it.) About twelve of us formed individual teams. (I was Porridge Wednesday, as that was visiting day at the local Armley Prison.) With the ice hockey being a novelty it attracted the crowds, probably as much as twelve in number. You might scoff, but imagine a dozen hyped-up hockey louts, high on Co-op tea, surrounding an arena 3 x 1½ feet in size. There was standing, high drawing office stool seating and table-top stands.

So came about the Leeds Civil Engineers' Sports Club. In the weeks that followed, skips and attics were raided and various other games emerged. A snooker table, little bigger than the ice hockey, with miniscule balls and two-foot cues appeared. Darts came along in the form of a Yorkshire board where there are no trebles. Dominoes, and the less popular draughts, were easily sought out, as was a cribbage board. This was ignored as it was thought to be too posh (complicated) a game. (Chess was introduced once, but was found to be incredibly boring, and not given to cheering crowds of spectators.) Blackboard and chalk (the Stationery Clerk was one of us) allowed me to introduce the game of 'crut', which I had played at school. This was at first sneered at, but soon became addictive. (No information of this game will be found in any indoor sports compendium, but it was so mentally testing that a later boss's wife, Valerie Smith, introduced it into her maths lessons at school.)

Regardless of all the other attractions, the ice hockey held the attention, and for critical matches, like top of the table fixtures, there would be a maximum crowd round the board, commenting loudly throughout. This caused the first altercation we had with the fashion company on the floor below. Porridge Wednesday forever languished in the lower half of the league, me never managing to coordinate lateral movement with spinning the stick.

To compensate, I virtually ruled the snooker table. So much so that a demonstration match was arranged for me to play Terry Ward from the Leeds Area Office. Terry was for a time a world amateur billiards champion, travelling to exotic places like India for the championships on special leave. On the day of the match, the ice hockey was abandoned, and the crowd concentrated on the snooker. Conduct was suitably adjusted to quiet concentration, with the odd gasp now and again. Although Terry's skills were apparent, they were by no means overwhelming. It turned out that he was a mediocre player away from home, and severely reduced by the bonsai table he found himself on and not playing his natural game of billiards. The anti-crown green dip in the centre of the playing area was another aspect that he had never come across anywhere else in the world. He only just scraped through to win by a very narrow margin.

Here, then, were two grown men, with 2-foot cues of dowelling rod, pushing marble-sized balls around a green baize table, hardly 4 feet by 2½, and into pockets, where they fell straight through to the floor below. Although we were playing legitimately, in our lunch hour, there was a feeling of great embarrassment when one of the senior engineers happened to poke his nose in one day.

About this same time I was playing men like Fred Davies and John Spencer (then world champion) at Pontin's, due to winning the week's snooker challenge. There I played on a central table in a room of nine, with 400 men and women surrounding me. (I must record a near win against John after he got annoyed with me for snookering him. But for just one good break of 104 by him, I might have clinched it.) Nerves on those occasions at Pontin's were nothing compared to the tension on the toy table in No. 23, playing against another world champion.

As the lease approached its end on these offices, more space was created as desks moved over to Aire Street. This was when the table tennis board was discovered and set up in very dangerous circumstances.

Two old and abandoned clerical desks were arranged more or less centrally in the free area. These were stable and solid, and excellent bases for the table. They were at slightly different levels, so unlike the professional game, you could elect to play uphill or down. Unfortunately the board top area was slightly smaller than the desks, leaving bits of them sticking out from under it, and some nasty collisions occurred with the exposed sharp corners, at the very sensitive male level of loose change, etc. However, a greater hazard was the lino. This was obviously cut to the shape of the original layout of drawing desks, and displayed raised edges around the player's feet. We tried nailing it down round the perimeters; we tried gluing it; we tried turning the ragged cut underneath itself; whatever, there remained a treacherous proud and damaged edge. This proved to be a tripping hazard, evidenced on the occasions of rushes in to the table to get to a ball dropping short, with half-somersault results and crunching encounters of nose to table.

It was no safer when leaping sideways. An indiscreet positioning of the toe would send the player crashing across the floor, hopefully landing on a soft spectator, but now and again sailing into an anything but smooth wall, arrayed, as it was, with coat pegs.

Rivalling the lino for danger were the electricity junction boxes. Again, these were placed on the floor convenient for the old desks. That is as far as their convenience went. Raised, round boxes with conduit running in and out of them managed to make them the highlight of risk. A competent player could place balls in such a way that his opponent had to brave not only the worst of the lino, but with great precision direct him towards the junction boxes. With all this to contend with, even changing ends was an adventure.

After circumnavigating all these hazards, the expert player was then constrained when playing high, looping shots by the low-slung lattice of the ceiling, such that with luck on his side the ball would find a way through, but more often than not it would strike the ironwork and fall back onto the player's own side of the table. However, enthusiasm reigned and some of us even went so far as to buy our own bats. Better this than using the two bare plywood paddles which had been found with the table. Reluctantly, we also coughed up for a net. This proved far better than the two stacks of calculation books and a surveyor's pole.

How things changed when the move to Cramptup House came about. The basement was below ground level and subject to occasional flooding. This was not only worrying from the point that water was getting into the building, but also from the fact that it had a distinct tidal flow. This started in what had become the games room, and reached so far up the central corridor, depending on the severity of the rain. To trained surveyors like us, this meant that the whole building had to be sloping. With this in mind, the technical staff had one over on the clerks in that we chose to play games from the shallow end, especially the table tennis.

Despite the flooding, which in fairness was restricted to a couple of times a year, the floor was covered in wall-to-wall blue carpet. The walls themselves were plastered and smooth, and the floor was free of any protrusions. (Momentarily returning to the central point of these chronicles, this room, like the rest of Cramptup House, had a character rating of absolute zero.) A single large clerical table, lost in the move, now formed the base for the table tennis board. Now the protruding corners disappeared, and at last true skills could be evaluated, rather than having the more timid players watching their footsteps all the time.

Two distractions in the table tennis direction were the welcome additions of Stephanie Thompson, head of the typing pool, and Denise Collins during one of her fuller phases. (Denise would over several months go from slim and shapely to rather substantial and then back again, all the time retaining a compelling attractiveness.) Steph had played in the old No. 23 office, where as a fit young mini-skirted lass in pumps she provided not only skill but quite some crowd-pleasing entertainment. Her expertise at table tennis betrayed her Girl-Guide-leader private life. As for Denise, who saw herself as a distant niece of mine, she insisted on partnering me in mixed doubles, what with being family. This caused my only serious injury in the inside sports arena, when, leaping for an impressive smash, Denise came down fully on my foot. Explaining my limp on arriving home proved tricky.

Denise was, unsurprisingly, a pub darts team captain, and was the only one who could give Graham a run for his money. That is until the York contingent arrived, who due to misspent Friday afternoons seemed to be superior in most of our indoor sports. Our initial games at the table tennis matched the Leeds careful ping-pong approach with minimal movement, for historic memory reasons of undisciplined floor coverings, against the overenthusiastic athleticism of the newcomers.

Two serious snooker tables arrived, discarded from pubs on the feeble excuse that the slates were cracked. One was actually broken, and the unnerving sight of snooker balls leaping up in the air added a new aspect to the game. This crack was at a slight angle to the line of the table and led to one of the middle pockets. Any ball propelled gently across this fault line inevitably found itself in the pocket. Most spectacular was the occasional opening shot which would hit the crack at a particular point, rise up in the air, and land squarely on top of the triangle of reds. A very unusual split of the balls ensued, with often two or three reds being pocketed. This board was most definitely a 'home' venue – occasional visiting workmen had no chance on it.

On the second table the term 'pocket' referred to four corner holes and two middle ones. This meant chasing a potted ball as it dropped through to the floor and shot down the corridor. Denise's mum did a bit of crochet work and sorted that problem. Its individuality was the fact that all the cushions had virtually perished such that there was a breakdown in Newton's law concerning a ball striking the cushion and being repelled with an equal force. (It is a little known fact that it was Newton who invented snooker, after watching a red apple fall from a tree and roll down a nearby rabbit hole.) This table's cushions merely welcomed the ball with open arms and engulfed it in the soft rubber.

From the same pub source came a first-rate bar billiards table and equipment. This stuck out among our cobbled sporting artefacts, in that there was absolutely nothing wrong with it, except that it came without a set of rules. More expense, and one of those slim 'Sport Rules' books, this one on pub games, was purchased. There were the bar billiard rules, and reading on led to some basic changes in our rules for bar skittles and dominoes. Thereby another skill was laid open for the billiard sharps among us, mainly me.

The bar skittles came on loan from a Methodist youth club, and never found their way back. Here a suspended heavy ball had to be swung round the supporting rod to strike the nine pins on its return from earth orbit, this being the tactic applied by most. On its journey it became another missile of danger, to match the York-driven table tennis ball, and its re-entry would either miss all the skittles and provide the launch pad occupants with a nasty shock, or scatter all nine pins in nine different directions. Our new book of rules allowed for one circuit only of the spine, not having it going round and round until it had wrapped itself up.

Prior to the York invasion we had set up a sports fund (which bought the rule book). Because of the inspiration provided by an unbelievable expanse of carpet, we invested in the set of carpet bowls. Being new, and perfect, with an excellent playing surface, the bowls executed enormous sweeps on the floor, so vast that obstacles were often circumnavigated and tables run under. As it happened Dave Thornton and I emerged as equal champions – at last something else that I could perform at. The only snag with bowls was the chances of interference. Table tennis balls, especially after York arrived, could be despatched to any part of the room and down the corridor. Being light, they had little effect on the bowls other than causing the players to fire extravagant shots when surprised by a ping pong ball on the back of the neck. Other things were far more disruptive, like the skittles missile escaping gravity and becoming detached, so that it flew across the room and into the bowls. Failing that, a successful strike might find the bowling green suddenly awash with skittles. Also, before the snooker boards had definite pockets, balls would drop through, ricochet off the moulded table legs and shoot out in any direction.

As to the darts, it is best that a veil be drawn over the hazards that game inspired. Health and safety at work it was not! It wasn't so much the chance of crossing the line of flight, rather the violent bounce-back when a dart hit one of the generous wires. And it always came towards you point first!

So, we now had a full complement of eight activities on the go, shove-ha'penny joining the ranks through a drunken theft, which I suppose introduced the dominoes as well. (Here was a slight throwback to character. These boxed and perfect dominoes lacked all the blatant characteristics of our Huddersfield home-hewn ones.) From this fully equipped gym came the winter and summer challenge cups. (More carefree expense.)

There was, in theory, still room. That is, until the table foot-ball and stand were spotted in *Exchange and Mart*. By universal agreement we had to have it, and we swooped on it. With its arrival, everything else became rather peripheral. But how the old comradeship disintegrated! Put mature adult males alongside a table football game and nature was reversed, somewhat like getting behind the wheel of a car. We had the disquieting sight of Bob Newell, a respected senior member of the Drawing Office, stripped down to a string vest, to be later sat back at his desk, gently steaming. Roger Bean, Chief Clerk, remote and disdainful, suddenly turned into a whirling dervish. It was Roger who managed to bend two of the bars, and no end of attempts ever got them back in shape. It also attracted a wild and mobile audience. I only saw this ferocity again during office cricket matches. Sadly, there is no record as to the fate of the ice hockey, this being totally ignored in the face of the new table football and the other Olympic-style disciplines.

Feeling ourselves to be getting in a rut, we bravely took our skills to away matches. My church in Armley, St Bartholomew's, two miles up the road, was a very far-sighted organisation. As well as the normal hall, at the back was the fully licensed social club. The Railway took with them as many of their games as they could and augmented them with the club's pool table and floor tiddlywinks. This raised the question as to whether the railway was playing at home or away. Taking our own pitches into someone else's territory must be both, so which side is awarded double points in the event of a draw? These things are important on the international circuit.

At these events we managed to have a fair representation from the ladies of the office, no doubt attracted more by the chance of drinks than sport. We even devised a team strip, designed more with the resulting appearance of the girls in mind rather than through any camaraderie.

This led to outings for pitch and putt, and tenpin. Golf was viewed by two different camps; those who thought that they could play a bit, and those who knew they couldn't. The skilled mob went off to do their own things on serious courses, but found themselves levelled when it came to pitch and putt. We non-players prodded, poked, clouted and swung through fresh air, getting round the course and taking much of it with us. After teeing off, we often were left wondering whether we could count the distance travelled by the tee rather than that of the ball. The 'players' were still determined to show off their prowess, and struck some mighty shots on what was by their standards a miniscule course. As a result of displaying their powers they would constantly overshoot time and again.

When it came to the putting part of the activity, the experts were once more equalised by the optimists. All the 'greens' were indistinguishable from the course in general, less a tree or two, and with the addition of impossible sandpits designed on the lines of World War I trenches. The golfers would eye up the shot, look for slopes and whatever else they have to go down to kiss the grass for. Meanwhile we hopefuls would continue using whichever club came to hand, clouting through the rough of the green with as much precision as before. As a result the experts made painfully slow progress towards the hole, while we would cheerfully hit out for the flag, thoroughly surround it and trust in the law of averages.

Scoring was something which occupied the great and good for minutes after each hole, reliving the last ten minutes in detail, while the rest of us were putting down 'about ten or eleven' every time.

One excursion took us to a sort of pretentious country club place with a croquet lawn. We soon found ourselves hampered by the hoop things and dispensed with them, reducing the sport to a mix of hockey and golf. We were escorted from the premises. This was not such a tragedy as an exploratory expedition discovered that the après-ski pint cost an amazing ten bob a throw, far in excess of our norm.

There was a sedentary management group who played an oriental game called My John, or something, with elaborate-looking dominoes while the rest of us knocked lumps out of the basement and each other. This alternated with poker, and welcoming leers of invitation to join them led us to one conclusion: whatever management played at was too expensive.

Before leaving indoor activities, brief mention should be made of the invented indoor sport of slalom, as in skiing. These were still the heady days when drinking in the dinner hour was a perfectly acceptable thing to do, and we had two particularly devoted participants in Brian Mosedale and Martin Squires. Brian was our Drawing Office PWay chief, and was a great enthusiast of real ale, this being the early years of the campaign for such. What's more, Brian could handle it, and three good pints held no fear for him. Equally enthusiastic, but a little less accomplished, was Martin. This was clearly displayed by his many close contacts with doorways or some extraordinary amounts of leeway he introduced as he made his journey back to base. For Martin we constructed the slalom.

This consisted of carefully placed chairs, waste bins and useful bits of surveying equipment. There always would be a straight way through, which Brian found, with no effort or deviation. Martin could not, and would take extravagantly wide avoidance tactics round the obstacles, causing collisions and ricochets off the fixed desks and filing cabinets. He also took on an inward compensating gait into each object, as if on the Isle of Man TT track. The object of the game was to try and produce wilder and wilder arrangements, causing Martin to take more astonishing avoidance routes. These were measured up and drawn out, all the time trying to increase the travelling distance while keeping the start and finish constant.

Outdoors, football made a brief entry into our sports agenda, but we found it aggressive and dirty. However, at least we gave it a go. Warmth, reasonable comfort and minimal sweat, along with an adjacent public bar, were our usual conditions for exercising ourselves. This meant that if we were to get any fresh air down us, there was really only one way to go.

For as long as I can remember, No. 23 had a cricket bag. It didn't have a uniform content, and at any one time might have three full sets of pads and six extra left legs. There were two bats, a varying number of balls in a wide variety of conditions, full wickets and two protective boxes. This was the only item of equipment for which a personal ownership was encouraged.

We played on a variety of pitches around West Leeds and Pudsey, from club fields, with cut and rolled strips, and controlled outfields, to what became our regular ground in Armley. This was council 'maintained', inasmuch as they cut the grass on a monthly rota basis and the playing strip received probably a couple of passes extra. Two-inch grass managed to hide a strip of treachery, where history had held onto the years of bowlers' footmarks, such that as well as providing excitement for the batsman, they presented an ankle-spraining opportunity for contemporary bowlers.

Local kids, especially enthusiastic Asians, used the pitch regularly, so keeping it distinguishable from the rest of the field, and forming something that took on the quality of an average footpath. I fear that we never challenged a team drawn from these youths, since quite frankly they scared us. Thirty-yard run-ups, even with a tennis ball, can be lethal; give them a corky and we'd have needed the St John ambulance on standby.

We once, by accident and default, managed to get through to the later rounds of an interdepartmental competition. This found us, with pay, travelling to Shildon, up north, to play a Durham team. The ground was of minor county standard, and we had never set foot on the like before. It was certainly superior to either of our snooker tables back home for predictability. Balls sped to the boundary as our lads, wary of bending too low due to the vagaries of our normal outfield, letting slip dozens of runs. When we came in to bat, facing some two hundred and fifty, mainly acquired by what turned out to be two Durham county lads, we found ourselves tied down on a perfect pitch. Never having experienced perfect before, we were hopelessly outplayed.

If our home strip could present a challenge to the batsman with indiscriminate changes of direction of the ball in the last microseconds of flight, and to the bowler in remaining upright after each delivery, then the outfield around the boundary forbad all but the criminally carefree the bending down to ambush a travelling ground shot. A hard struck ball would approach much like a flat stone across a pond, landing and leaping at random. I still bear the marks of a scar on the bridge of my nose, caused by my final foolhardy act of bravery in this position. Better the well-placed leg and foot, or as Neville Edwards always did, slinging his body across the suspected line of travel, he being rather hazy at sighting the ball, and relying on guidance by encouraging calls from his teammates.

Nev spent the best part of his cricketing career on the boundary, chatting with the opposing team. This became, twice a summer, a group drawn from the church Social Club. As good Christian lads they took Nev to their hearts and were sporting enough to drop him a hint as to when the ball had been hit roughly in his direction. There charity stopped and gamesmanship took over, as they did their best to countermand the directions being shouted at Neville from his colleagues.

Naturally, Neville wore glasses, and equally certain, during his moments of weightlessness while in flight, they would detach themselves from him. For safety reasons, so that he did not step on them while searching, Nev took on the pose of a statue, frightened to put a foot out. At such points the game had to be stopped while his mates came over to look for the glasses in the long grass. This would always take some time simply because a member of the opposition had them in his pocket. By means like this the team fielding would find time passing and light fading As a result their innings would be in twilight. Combining this with the corrugated pitch made batting second desperately dangerous.

There was another reason for the batting side, along with wives, girlfriends and any injured in battle, to be sat or reclined in a row behind Neville. This was to ensure that the game did not finish prematurely with the loss of the ball. The pitch was set in a field which was a general sort of community sports area belonging to the Parks Department, whereas behind the line of spectators was the municipal golf course. It isn't enough to say that there was simply a golf course there, since the boundary between the cricket field and the golfers was also the rather dramatic start of the valley of the River Aire. In less than ten yards, the ground changed from approximately level to decidedly downhill. Golf was played from one side to the other, with three greens on the way down the hill, all at right angles to the slope.

You may have seen on television the ancient practice of cheese rolling, where a round cheese is set off down a very steep hill with thirty or so of the local brain donors proving their virility by chasing it. They start off running, then leaping, followed by tumbling, somersaulting and rolling, waking up with concussion in one of the waiting ambulances at the bottom. The golf course, together with the unlucky boundary fielder, was very much like that – up to a point or points. Those points being several bunkers on the way down set as small horizontal oases against the slope, a stretch of smooth, slippery grass used by kids for dry sledging, and real sledging in winter, assorted surprised and dismayed golfers, and two frisky German shepherds who would take it amiss to find men tumbling down the hill. The out-of-control fielder would leave the golf course to plunge through thorny shrubs, thick grass and broken iron railings to finish up in the Leeds and Liverpool Canal. Neither ball nor pursuer ever got any further in life than the Leeds and Liverpool Canal.

The line of opposition players more often than not was an effective barrier along this crucial section of boundary, except in the case of a six. With luck the ball would encounter a bunker, a dog or a golfer before completing the otherwise inevitable journey into the canal. Of these only one of the three would give up the prize without argument or discussion.

Our opposite boundary was a traditional line at the foot of a 3-foot drop in the field. It had been thus for many years, and stubbornly remained so when the park authorities took over a section here to plant a nursery of young trees. Thus Neville's opposite number, in later years, stood at the foot of a small embankment amidst a year-by-year thickening copse of trees, with much consequently impaired movement.

Infielders had their own problems, one being a concrete practice pitch, advisably used by tennis balls rather than corkies. This ran parallel to the grass wicket and about six yards away. It wasn't so much a tripping hazard, more of a surprise when diving sideways saving a run. The prudent fielder would gradually move away from the strip as the attention of captain and bowler was distracted. This concrete had led to a large amount of grazing and bruising over the years, and amazingly only one broken finger.

Our pitch ran east and west, so making the sun a peril for batsman and deep mid on and off alike. The experienced batsman, with his back to the evening sun, soon worked out a safe trajectory into the deep, forming on its way a minor eclipse from the fielder's point of view. The option of fielding down there always caused a fight to escape it, and the sad loser donned a cap or poker eyeshade and dark glasses, through which battered ball and ground appeared much the same. Then, not to be forgotten, was the tree.

It was an enormous beech, with some historical connections in Armley, being mentioned in chronicles way back in time; something like a king hiding in its branches, or the last red squirrel in Yorkshire being spotted in it. Whatever, it was famous to a few. (This is not as unlikely as it may seem. It is a historical fact that the remains of two ancient hippopotamuses were once dug up, down in the valley, only two hundred yards from the pitch. This has got nothing to do with anything we are talking about at the moment – it's just something I know, and felt it only fair to share!) There had been a proposal to fell the tree once, as it stood halfway between wicket and boundary, but this found so much disfavour with the local historical and green brigade that it remained. (In those days they weren't called 'Greens', were they? But they were the same interfering dedicated protestors as today, ready to join any bandwagon going.) Nevertheless, today the tree has gone – condemned as rotten. But in its day it was a hazard and an immovable object within the cricket field, so it had to be catered for in the rules.

If a ball hit it without bouncing, it was declared a four. If it was struck so high into the tree, and failed to come down, it was called a six, and the match a draw, since it was usually the only ball we had. On the rare occasion that a ball lodged in the branches and began to find its way down, it could be caught and be out so long as the catch was one-handed. There remained just one further possibility – that a member of the opposition climbed the tree far enough to reclaim the ball. This was a case of six and out. One other tradition was observed. The person living closest to the tree (me) was instructed to visit the site during high winds in case the ball was dislodged. If in the unlikely event that I was there when it fell, and caught it with the stated one hand, and with a witness, the drawn game was belatedly awarded to the fielding side. As if it mattered.

There were other reasons agreed for abandoning play, besides a be-treed ball. Heavy rain was, of course, one, though the heaviness was hotly debated (while sheltering under the tree), depending on the state of the game. Should the street lights come on along the adjacent Stanningley Road, then bad light was declared. Debilitating injury to players was another ruling. Should any mishaps to one side at any time number two more than the other team, after assessing the likelihood of the return of the injured one within ten minutes, then a draw was decided. From time immemorial, on this field there had existed an ancient ruling for a local farmer of dairy cattle to retain grazing rights on the condition that he used it at least once a year. We did play the next day once, but apart from slipping hazards being greatly multiplied, there was a universal reluctance to recover the ball on certain occasions, there being no washing facilities nearby. Apart from this, any soiled player found himself barred from the club afterwards. This was sensible, as the Social Club's heating was stuck to 'on', or 'tropical', all year round, as nobody understood the workings of the control clock.

(I should have made it clear that following matches between Railway Civil Engineers and St Bartholomew's Social Club, we always repaired to the bar after the match. These games confused me so much. I was supposed to be captaining the club team, but was so used to playing for the Railway that I would forget my position and run onto the field while supposedly waiting to bat, and save a certain boundary. I was never called upon to umpire.)

So, coming round to me, I have yet to relate what my part was in the game. I always seemed to bat at number eight, not because I could be relied on to produce some hefty late innings swipes for a quick twenty or so, but rather because there always seemed to be three people in the team who were even worse at batting than me. When it came to fielding, I always adopted a position around cover point or midwicket. These were spots where amateur sloggers rarely managed to direct the ball, yet they looked to a hapless captain to be usefully filled gaps. I didn't possess a strong arm, and needed a runner if I was ever employed on the boundary, so a halfway position was ideal. From my point of view it gave a valuable second in time to decide where the ball was going, and whether or not it was going there fast enough to warrant avoiding rather than intercepting it. So why was I there at all? The secret weapon, that's why. On good days I had a disproportionate amount of success bowling.

My position was as a right-arm, slow, round the wicket, leg-spinner. Although that lot is a mouthful, or a lineful in the present circumstances, it hardly described my delivery. From leaving my hand with a whirring sound, the ball climbed high reaching a peak about halfway down the pitch. Its descent was amazingly slow, considering the fairly constant effect of gravity, and the batsman would be taking practice strokes as he waited. Should he be momentarily in the wrong position for making a real shot, the ball would bounce and turn violently. Given a badly scarred bit of ground, I've seen the ball almost turn at right angles. With experience, and when I was playing for the Railway, Bert Glover, the stumper, would be poised in entirely the wrong place. This further upset the batsman, yet he was ready for the ball passing the left stump when it looked destined to be a wide to the right. Bowled out occasionally, stumped unexpectedly (successfully ricocheting off Bert two yards away from the wickets), caught in the slips often, but most satisfactorily trodden on wicket now and again. In any over I was good for a wide over the stumps, a ball stopping dead, two balls being accidentally hit, and two wickets.

One or two of us took to some light practice in the vast and vacant third floor of Cramptup House. The room, with occasional pillars, was the full length of the offices, and comfortably wide. My only problem was the statutory minimum height of the ceiling. This was constructed in aluminium angle supports with polystyrene infill panels, and a few lighting strips. Invariably my bowling ran the ball along this ceiling, leaving a red scar on the tiles. These, being square, were then systematically distributed around the room, which must at some time later have confused the new tenants. By this you will realise to your amazement that we were using a relatively new proper cricket ball in a low room with windows down both sides, but bowling into a blank wall. We were careful to respond to the gentle bowling with forward taps to avoid any damage. All this dinner time activity ceased suddenly when I edged a ball off the shoulder of the bat and straight onto the casing of the fire alarm. One inch to the left and the building would have been evacuated.

Our matches were of twenty overs each side, two per player

except the wicketkeeper, and with the temporary retirement of anyone on reaching twenty-five runs. Scores of around a hundred per team were common. Apart from the odd galumphing journey down to the canal, one event stands out in my mind – the occasion when a nine was scored.

The ball was a friendly full toss and had been hit for a quick two down to Dave Holmes on the boundary. Dave was good in that position as he had a strong arm that could be both useful and costly when he was bowling. Should a batsman ever decide to give Dave his rope, and leave the crease to stand as a square leg observer, in his two allotted overs of long nomadic run ups and wild deliveries, Dave would probably have hit the stumps at least once. The rest of his spell would have balls going in all sorts of directions, both high and low, either hitting the ground a couple of yards in front of him or soaring gracefully to a first bounce way beyond the wickets. He always employed an agile longstop.

So when Dave bent down to collect this particular ball, only to have it hit a wayward sod and rise steeply into his face, he became angry, and took it out on the offending sphere by throwing it back far over the still crouching stumper and down to the opposite boundary, where it sought out Neville. He was quite surprised to find a ball which, by way of noting the batsman's stance, had been struck to the far side of the field, suddenly turning up in his territory, alerted as was the norm by cries from his team mates of, 'Yours, Nev!'

With his usual gymnastic approach to fielding, Nev stopped the ball by way of a looping dive, initially using his chest, with the ball rising to the underside of his chin and causing him to painfully bite the tip of his tongue. Time spent recovering and picking the ball out of the folds of his pullover, where it had lodged, led to three overthrows being run. Nev's lofty return to a bewildered Bert came to him out of a twinkling background of sun sparkling from among the leaves of the famous tree. Somewhat diverted for reasons explained later, Bert caught it on his shoulder, so sending it flying onwards towards an incoming Dave, who was in the process of seeking out some temporary repairs. Bravely, in all his discomfort, he noticed that the pitch was congested at one end by both batsmen, so he could sense a run-out somewhere. Still smarting, and a little blinded by blood trickling down from his head wound, Dave returned a blistering ground shot to a now totally disorientated Bert, only to see it shoot off back towards Neville. Sadly, Nev was searching for his fallen glasses, disturbed during his recent brief flight and landing, thus allowing the ball to run gently over the boundary for a further four.

While all this was going on, the batsmen first ran a quick two as the ball hopped down to an incoming Dave. By this time it was apparent that one of the two was considerably fitter than the other. This situation was obvious after the previous ball had been hit into the copse, short of the boundary, and four runs had actually been run. This left one of the batsmen gasping, and in no position to take on the exertions demanded by this next delivery. As the ball journeyed from Dave to Neville for the first time, one batsman ran another four while the ailing other managed to stumble through three. This found them both at the same end, the stumper's, arguing as to which of them should attempt the journey back to the bowler's end. Bert was now clearly distracted by this impromptu gathering and failed to have any productive contact with the passing return ball from Nev. Had he stopped it, he would have remained in confusion for a short time, not knowing where next to send it. With the shoulder ricochet he was saved from having to make any decision, and the time taken for the ball to arrive back in Dave's care allowed the batsmen to sort themselves out; and by now the fitter one, returning to the bowling crease, had managed the equivalent of seven runs, with his mate achieving a desperate five.

Puzzled disbelief had hit the crowd, who as a man were cheering on they didn't quite know what. Dave's second misguided missile launch was heading straight for the invalided batsman, who in carrying out avoidance tactics, stumbled a short distance down the pitch with a muffled whimper. He noticed in the process that his team mate was once more bearing down on him, screaming for another possible two, taking the other's leap for safety as a willingness to go that extra mile. The exhausted warrior staggered, gasping, through the remainder of the 'run'. The sanctuary with which the bowling crease provided him led to relief and an inevitable collapse to the ground, with the blue sky seeming to beckon him to his rest. By now he was reunited with his enthusiastic colleague, who had completed the suggested two, so leading to the pair of them once more being at the same end of the pitch as each other – but with only one of them upright and still interested. Considerable debate and argument between the vertical batsman and the two umpires, who had come together to compare opinions as to what score had actually been clocked up, was assisted by the ball obligingly bypassing the groping figure of Neville, and just managing to make the boundary into the now helpless group of spectators. The unfortunate one of the two high-scoring heroes had to be helped to Neville's boundary to recover, while his pal was hopefully trying to convince the umpires that they had in truth scored the equivalent of eleven.

There was an amount of varied confusion among the rest of the field. Those close in tried to back up Bert, but with him managing to divert the ball with his shoulder, they were all leaping in the wrong direction. Similarly, Dave's scorching second attempt, which caused the now exhausted batsman to leap down the pitch, revealed Bert, who was standing slightly behind him. Either Bert fearlessly managed to kill some of the speed by getting the back of a leg in the way, or Bert failed to avoid being struck a glancing blow on the shin, possibly because he had his back to the throw. Whichever, the ball was again slightly rerouted out of reach of the otherwise efficient back-up lads on the farther side of the stumps. Others not included in the area of the main action ran around in enthusiastic circles, shouting all sorts of conflicting advice. Jack Pinder, down at long leg, squatted on the ground to watch with mild interest, while relighting his pipe.

In all this the scorer, one of our supporting elder statesmen, was faring badly. He had recorded the two, rubbed it out and added three, and then scratched that out to make way for his decided seven. Checking by semaphore with the umpires, he had to erase the score yet again to change it for the ultimate of nine, by which time a hole had appeared in the scorebook. As it happened, he was also the team's first aid representative, and now had to turn his attention to the padded pulmonary disaster laid out at his side, gasping and inhaling passing flies by the dozen, leading to a coughing fit. The by now challenged first aider was being gallantly assisted by the opposing team's amateur medic, and they both stood looking down at the glazed eyes of the panting mass, remarking on the amazing colours his face was taking on, like a world-weary chameleon. Demanding more textbook attention was Dave Holmes with a bleeding forehead caused by his first encounter of two with the ball. Neville, feeling his impressively Jimmy Hill chin, was swilling water around a loosened tooth and bleeding tongue, and belatedly Bert had managed to hobble to the boundary, stopping to rub alternately a bruised shin and a grazed shoulder.

As a result of all this confusion the nine agreed runs were never recorded in the book, which meant that there had been an awful amount of energy expended, much blood and bruising and one near coronary, all for nothing.

As custom demanded, both teams made for our church Social Club, some on foot, with the injured being distributed among the three cars available. A momentary shock came when Roger Bean, a man always capable of staying on his own when drinking, ordered two pints of lager; but such had been the excitement that one pint went down without touching the sides, with the other following in a more relaxed manner. An interesting discovery that evening was that a perfect cure for suspected thrombosis and pulmonary collapse was a pint of Guinness.

Having left the scores in an unsatisfactory state, the result was decided on the pool table.

★

A sports chapter cannot be complete without a brief mention of an out-on-site dinner time activity at certain locations. There were four tracks of fairly swift traffic up and down the Colne Valley, with quite often a running culvert near at hand. Experimental surveying of drains at Huddersfield recently led us naturally to the idea of 'Pooh sticks'.

There was a large element of danger in dropping a twig at the upper mouth of the culvert, negotiating the crossing of four tracks between trains, and reaching the lower end, only to find our team twigs way there before us. The game was considerably slowed down when one of us suggested swapping to 'Pooh bricks'. We still await a result of our first and only attempt at this.

Food and Drink with Extras

Work at Huddersfield was not only an education and an experience in railway civil engineering terms, but it also became a lesson in life itself. We had within the office men who had picked up habits in eating which were novelties to me, though care had to be taken when being offered anything by Bill Boyes. Though naturally naïve, and initially fairly gullible, I soon had this well and truly knocked into the shape of eternal suspicion. Bill generally left me alone, and practised his art of monkey business on the occasional youngsters that joined us briefly. Dave Thornton was long term, and in my consideration a great success. In overcoming his naivety, though, he made very little progress, and Bill never tired.

Young Dave drifted into our world at Huddersfield at some stage when I had become pretty well settled, and was forever dubious about company being foisted onto me. I had little hope for Dave as regarded progress in the railway system. He was initially a sad little lad, having done time as a sort of office gopher in York Headquarters. However, after a year with him around, I began to realise that a cracking little practical engineer was emerging from unpromising academic beginnings. Perhaps it was his curiosity that worked well for him.

'What's that, Bill?'

'Plum cider!'

Bill had a deep maroon concentrate of a cleaning fluid in a pop bottle that he was 'borrowing' to try on the kitchen floor at home. He'd just spent a messy ten minutes decanting it from a 5-gallon drum in the stores. The experiment intended for the kitchen floor had now been inadvertently extended to include brown shoes and trouser legs. We were trying it out for cleaning up tools and trackside machinery, and Bill was as usual stretching its possibilities a bit further. He had not intended that to be as far as young Dave's innocent gullibility might extend, though. Bill sometimes found himself on an unstoppable train of mischief, not knowing how to get off. He was still working on Dave, and hadn't quite fully assessed the lad's bounteous innocence.

'Can I try some, please.'

'Er… ah suppose so…' He looked toward me with a rare glance for guidance. I was not inclined to make life easy for one who used me for his fun when there was a shortage of Daves.

'I'll go get my cup,' said Dave, and shot off in the direction of the Drawing Office.

'He's not serious, is he? This is bloody cleaner, what if he drinks it?'

'That's up to you, Bill.'

'Ay, but…' Dave reappeared and tried to relieve Bill of the bottle. Bill resisted, but still couldn't bring himself to pull out.

'Ayoop, hold thi 'ossies. Tha just wants a drop to try… *No!*' – This was uttered as Dave put it to his lips.

Bill does have limits, after all, I thought.

'Tha's supposed to dilute it wi a load of watter…'

Dave was still not deterred, or even suspicious, when the resulting solution frothed way over the top of the cup, and eagerly took his first and last sip. After dropping his cup, Dave raced for the sink and drank an amazing quantity of water, holding his head sideways under the flow. He eventually emerged and fell into a deep sulk.

Bill, just for a moment, looked full of remorse, and picked up the remains of Dave's cup. However, all penitence evaporated when he took a mop to the spilt liquid.

'Ayoop, sithee! This stuff's brilliant on lino an' all!'

Dave had many unnerving encounters with Bill, and between them I suppose quite some working time was lost. But thinking back, and knowing how the lad later developed, I reckon that these confrontations went a long way to giving him his confidence in life. Sometimes Bill appeared downright hostile, as on the afternoon when he decided that Dave's fashionable shoulder-length hair needed bringing into line. Armed with the long office scissors, he chased Dave to ground behind the drawing table which ran the length of the office. It was offset from the wall by a space about an inch wider than Dave's greatest dimension. There

Dave stayed until Bill went home at four, insisting that I pass him the calculations he was working on, and a hand lamp.

On other occasions Bill would be overwhelmingly helpful, should the young one have any small problem – but only in the hope that his assistance could turn it into a bigger problem. Again, Dave's devotion to fashion demanded that he wore his trousers upside down, that is, with massive flares around his ankles and horrendously tight accommodation for his bum. A twisting bend during a session of wet day corridor cricket led to a belt-to-bollock split in Dave's fashionables, and his disappearance into Don's toilet with an attack of schoolboy modesty. Bill's sympathy was immediately displayed by his filling up the stapling gun, and passing it through the door crack. Considering that the material had never allowed for any spare, it was asking a lot for sufficient overlap to even allow stapling; but Dave did it, and got back into them, thanking Bill pathetically.

He couldn't see the effect from the back, which Bill told him was perfect. There was a dash-dot effect of bright red underpants alternating with straining staple, from top to bottom.

'D'you think I'll be OK going home in them, Bill?'

'Best road test 'em a bit first, lad. Try sitting down.'

Dave took a position on his stool that was as near to sitting down as a plank might manage.

'Ay, tha's OK theer. Tha'll be all right on t'train, at least.'

'I think I might just stand. This isn't really comfy.'

'See if tha can bend ower a bit… oh dear, tha can't!' A mixture of tearing material and the pinging of escaping staples fired Dave back into the lavatory.

'It's OK, lad. Cansta sew at all?'

Dave claimed he could, or at least he was willing to learn.

'Ah've got a needle here, ah'll just go get thi some thread.'

Bill trotted off to the PWay office, and returned moments later with a wad of cotton waste and a broad grin. He explained to Dave's nose, which was all that was visible, that he might have to tie a couple of pieces together, but it should do the job nicely. This was stuff supplied to wipe down oil spills on generators and such, and I knew for a fact that there could be no piece longer than a couple of inches.

Dave was a full hour and a half loading and reloading the needle, trying to sew in the BR duster which Bill had thoughtfully supplied to line the inside of his trousers. He emerged just as Bill had to leave for home, and so shelve any further helpfulness. Our once fashionable youth now had trousers that were certainly more roomy than before. Sadly, the blue and red chequered duster was visible as a vertical plug that widened from the top to a maximum of about an inch before bringing the two edges of trouser back together again. It clashed violently with the light fawn of the main material. I had to break it to Dave that the results of ninety minutes' labour were far from convincing.

He went home wearing a borrowed greatcoat. If he'd not wanted to stand out, he failed badly. Now that the rain had stopped, the steamy heat of midsummer had returned, and there were very few other passengers on the packed train that evening wrapped up in winter greatcoats.

★

'Never eat anything until you've seen it eaten by someone else' became my self-preservation motto.

George joined our office team from the gangs after a long illness that ruled out ever going back to manual work. He took on the role of room warmer, arriving first in the morning and either lighting or reviving the fires, or flinging the windows open in summer. George was incredibly long, a truly 2 ¼ yards man, who before his illness had been a little too well built, but had now slimmed down to around thirteen stone. He was a man of very pleasant countenance, a little ravaged by past pains, but amazingly handsome, given a smart pair of overalls. These were one of two such, washed regularly and pressed by Mrs George. Above all was his amenable attitude to everything. This in part was brought about by a touching gratitude for being given a job to do, and not being pensioned off through ill health. It was George who extended my gastronomic horizons to new depths. In this he was ably assisted by Bill, someone who was determined that I should experience some of the more revolting-looking traditional diets of the lads.

Prior to Bill's arrival, as a newcomer to life at Huddersfield, I was a Hagenbach's habitual. This was a fair-sized and popular café just below the station, and as such harboured a good representation of railway white-collars. It wasn't really for Don, who had higher dietary demands and preferences. When in the office at noon, which was rare, he favoured an establishment that viewed the label of 'café' with a certain disdain, and chose to represent itself as a restaurant. As far as I could see and taste, the trough was a little more decorative, and the menu stated that something called *pommes* was served, which looked suspiciously like what Hagenbach's dished up as potato; but apart from that and the price, I could hardly separate the two places. Hagenbach's for dinner represented poor economics, as a meal had to be paid for and no expenses were claimable, since it was at our home station. Don's 'Princess' restaurant was economically disastrous. However, I always took up Don's suggestion that I joined him, as this was yet another fruitful chance to cook up some new schemes that the Area definitely needed. It was swings and roundabouts; whenever I was out in the Area with Don I could claim his expense rate, although I still had a meal to pay for.

Hagenbach's were good value for their 2/10d fixed menu of four choices with pudding, though their liver and bacon usually won the day for me. I noted and tried stewed steak there, and found it to be identical to the Princess's steak and ale, which made a bigger hole in my pocket to the tune of another shilling. Final endorsement came from my father, in his last days as a railway goods clerk, when he occasionally came over to Huddersfield, with his remark that Hagenbach's was as good as what mother served up at home. I never tried him at the Princess; he was a shade more careful with his dinner money than even I was, despite the fact that he would be entitled to his expenses. Those occasions confirmed in me that he now regarded me as a fully fledged individual, and no longer anything to do with him, in that he always allowed me to pay for myself.

Expenses were daft. They were generous, and my scale allowed me to dine in Don's style of luxury if I so wished, but they became to be regarded as far too much a significant part of my wage. They were awarded as soon as I left a geographical magic circle that in theory made it uneconomical for me to return to base for a meal, and go back to site afterwards. They were daft in that for when I was once, for three months, seconded to Leeds District Office into the Works Section, who claimed they were overstretched as regarded staff, I was able to go home for dinner and claim full expenses for doing so, as I was away from Huddersfield. (That short experience proved to me, and to Don, that they didn't know what hard-pressed was in the Works Drawing Office. Three months were spent mooning over a single drawing designing cladding for a train depot, when at Huddersfield I'd be tied up with at least four different jobs at a time.)

I soon learned that Don's attitude towards paying expenses was somewhat relaxed. He argued that if the chainmen and I shot off early to do a job, and returned to base before dinner time, I could claim them. The alternative was for us to dawdle starting out, make the job span dinner and wander back in later when there was little time left to do anything useful. This also got the dominoes, or cricket bat, out for half an hour of genuine relaxation. (I've just now dug out the famous hand-made dominoes in order to take a picture of them for possible use in my first book, and they really are a disgrace, both from a workmanship view, and also a confidentiality aspect – all the backs looking individually distinct.)

Mention there of the bat. This again was home produced, here from a programme item peg. These pegs were made using most of a tree, being 1½ inches thick with a 6-inch face. Just the weight of the thing meant that you had to be lifting it off the floor way before the bowler started his run-up, and the following shot had to be decided on well in advance of seeing what was to be delivered. We played on the shingle area outside the office, with boundaries represented by the massive retaining wall above Fitzwilliam Street and the nearest station platform. With four of us involved (Percy, Wilf, Dave and me) fielding positions were dictated by the lay of the land. One would patrol the wall edge, while the other took up a not-too-silly mid-off, in the middle of the yard's sidings. This latter position was somewhat static as movements in any direction were hazardous in view of the rails and sleepers. Clearing either boundary, onto the main lines, or down to the street below, were calibrated as six and out. Obviously a soft tennis ball was used, and, should it go into the street, was regarded as lost, since a search among disgruntled shoppers, as well as a 400-yard trip round the George Hotel, meant that recovery would take up the rest of the dinner time. There was just one possibility of scoring a six and remaining in, that being getting one into the 4-foot deep tank of water that made up the office roof. Should balls become scarce, then a fishing trip up the iron ladder would be undertaken, the prevailing wind being very generous in that it shepherded the floating balls to the ladder end of the tank. Generally, though, balls were easy to come by at the foot of cuttings, even real leather corkies at Gledholt on Mondays after the weekend's club cricket.

We thought our cricket days were over when Don (who very rarely saw these matches, since if he was in the office, his car would be parked at midwicket, making play impossible) decided that Huddersfield needed a concrete vehicle washing area right where our pitch was. I was given the job of designing the destruction of our game in the form of the new apron. However, I put an intriguing pencil to paper, fixing the drain itself near the bowling end and banking the concrete in all directions very gradually for water to be directed into the drain. We now had a greatly changed pitch as a result. I will admit now that a novel cricket pitch was the basis for my designs; a secondary consideration was that it should be suitable for washing road vehicles on.

Instead of uncertain ash and shingle, we had solid ribbed concrete, meaning that the ball could rise or dip with excellence, but above all other features in effectiveness were the sloping sides to the pitch. All cricket pitches should be like that – inverted crown cricket. Balls cut in from impossible angles, and what with keeping low or rising to shave eyebrows, we had all the hallmarks of professional bowling without any of the skills being needed. The pitch is still there for any cricketing authority, or fan of vehicle washing areas, to examine.

Bill, taking his dodgy heart condition into consideration, adopted a stationary square leg position, most often in a folding canvas chair. He took no part in the bowling or batting, but was extraordinarily active in the commentary and advice department. His health situation took enough potentially dangerous knocks when he started laughing, just once tipping his chair over.

I suppose that it was the financial situation at home (wife no longer working, young son, and later two, to be looked after) that put the brake on the Hagenbach's extravaganzas, and certainly kicked the Princess into touch. Coincidentally it was at the same time that Bill, with George's willing help, decided that my gastronomic history needed some advanced adjustment. Between them they gained my confidence by introducing me to black pudding. The thought that I had spent thirty years on this planet without experiencing this most luxurious of foodstuffs was to become a source of great sadness to me, and horror to Bill. One day a week we fried some up when we were sure of possession of the small cooker in the corridor outside Don's end, along with his absence. It turned out to be the food of the gods, and I became addicted. Bill, finding his culinary coaching to be going much better than it should have, for it was the initial intention to have me eat what the lads had, and be disgusted by it, began a campaign of trying to curb my enthusiasm by reciting the ingredients of the pudding, but this affected me not. It was time to try another tack.

"Course, t'finest stuff that tha can chuck dahn thi neck is tripe. White or brahn tripe, it doesn't matter, but it's t'stuff they'd feed thee every day in hospital if they could get enough on it.'

Now, making a window-shopping trip round the market butchers made it certain that a conversion to this unlikely looking delicacy was remote. So Bill set it before me as a challenge, not on a plate, but in a shallow bowl, explaining, 'Cos tha needs a load o'vinegar onnit afore tha dips in!'

I discovered early on that the white variety was served best as a bowl of vinegar, with pieces of tripe floating in it. The stuff by itself I found as attractive as a wet pullover, and without the lake of vinegar, inedible. But for appearances' sake I was obliged to put on a hungry grin before launching into it. It was Percy who stopped me in my tracks one dinner time.

'How come' – (a usual start to an in-depth enquiry) – 'how come that if that theer is the lining of a beast's stummick, how come tha can digest it? And if tha can, how come tha don't digest thi own stummick?'

Bill hadn't faced this one before. 'All beast meat's eatable. Theer's no big difference between a cow, and a sheep, or an 'oss, or rabbit, it's all meat. We're not, we're different.'

'Ah don't see as how we can be any more different from a cow as a cow is from a rabbit, we're all med on t'same stuff, so ah don't see as how our stummicks don't cotton on when they've snapped up all t'tripe wot tha's shoved dahn, and start eatin' themselves.'

''Appen it's t'vinegar what does it. Sort of warns that what's got vinegar on is to be et up.'

'Howsabaht them theer cannibals, then? They eat folk, probably wiout any vinegar, an' all! And vultures don't leave nowt, so our guts must be edible, so how come we don't eat usselves? And anyroad, once t'vinegar's got down theer, tha own stummick's sloppin' wi t'stuff and all.'

I never liked to see Bill down and nearly out, so I put in a suggestion.

'Could it be that live tissue cannot be eaten, whereas dead can?'

'Theer,' added Bill, 'that's eddication for thee, and he only studied surveyin' and figures!'

'Weer's tissues come into it, then?' Percy was watching his argument falter, and decided to fade out gracefully.

'We'll try brahn tripe ferra change next week. Ah'll admit it looks a shade better.'

Brown tripe was better by far, not needing drowning in vinegar, but it was with a flourish that Bill and George played their trump card. The saddest thing is that I cannot remember what the stuff was called locally; 'elver' or 'elder' or something. Anyway it turned out to be the cow's udder, and it was absolutely delicious.

[Hot news! I have discussed this with two aged members down at the church Social Club and have been told without hesitation that the udder meat is called chicklings, so elver and elder weren't far off!]

After more ventures into belly pork and other delicacies, the lads found themselves exhausted of new ideas, and we settled down to quarter pounds of cheese and pickle, and other safe eatables. That was until Dave came on the scene, and the whole process began again. Very soon Dave took to going out for his own choice of sandwiches, suspicious of anything else put before him, and refusing it outright.

Six months into Dave's time with us, and his initial naivety and greenness was beginning to fray slightly at the edges. He had the first signs of cockiness showing. Jack Senior, the PWay Inspector at Huddersfield, noticed it, and Bill Boyes noticed it, and they both made sure that I noticed it too. From this position the crossword scheme was instituted.

Crosswords were all the rage at dinner time, so long as you could keep them away from Harry Hanson, one of Jack's assistants, whose unique way with them I have explained before. Briefly, as a reminder, Harry would concentrate on the *Daily Mirror* Easy Clues puzzle, the *Sun* having yet to appear, otherwise this would have been his chosen level. Harry was not put out by the strictures of black squares and the rigid grid. If he thought that he was right, and the space was insufficient, he would add a square or two onto the grid. If his word was too short, he'd install a full stop. If this was still not adequate, he'd fill in another square black. So when I introduced the Sunday magazine 'Ximenes' crossword to the company, he totally lost interest. No black squares, just thick lines at the ends of words, and clues that made no sense at all. Jack and Bill once got a single word right, and rejoiced as if they were in a position to claim the prize. Answers always appeared the following Sunday. It was this that gave me the idea.

I explained to Jack and Bill that once I had got a new magazine I would give them last week's crossword and just a few words as a starter from the current Sunday's answers. By this time Dave had been showing an ineffective interest in the pair's regular cross-word, and was as mystified as Harry with the new hybrid. Jack and Bill knew that they had an old copy, but Dave didn't, until I took him to one side and told him, saying that I had the answers in the latest Sunday's copy. I suggested to him that it would really make the two of them sit up and take notice if he popped in now and again with one of the impossible answers. I later explained to Bill what I'd arranged with Dave, and prompted him, with Jack, to show great amazement whenever Dave came up with the odd answer. It was one of those lovely situations where I could just sit back, with one of them thinking that he was going to show the other two something, not knowing that the other two knew perfectly well why he was performing so effectively. I could relax and watch, just curbing Dave a little when he was tending to get a bit too clever by solving two clues instead of one.

This went on for a few Mondays, with Jack and Bill showing increasingly mock amazement at Dave, and with the lad getting cockier by the week. Eventually we thought that he had become as conceited as we could allow (he was boasting to Wilf and Percy when they visited, which only increased his perkiness as they two were in on the deception as well, and expressed amazement equal to the others, Jack and Bill). The following Sunday, Jack bought a copy of the paper, so that by the time Dave arrived he and Bill had copied in all the answers in the space in the previous issue in an impressive thirty minutes. It was now Dave's turn for amazement, along with some disgust that his incredible ability with the answers could not now be demonstrated.

When we eventually told him what had been happening the last week or so he slowly grasped what a prat he'd made of himself, and descended into one of his sulks which lasted a full week. He had been gently dealt with.

★

We've gone pretty thoroughly into our adventures with food, although special occasions have not been mentioned. Any excuse, such as a retirement or someone we liked leaving Huddersfield, called for a sending-off dinner, always at Dunford Bridge. This was miles away, up in the Pennines, but Don had once been taken there by a contractor, and the pub became the only place to eat, if he had anything to do with it. It invariably meant a large slice of grilled gammon, and quite a few drinks to slake the salt. The return journey was always an interesting experience for me, aided by three pints of Guinness. As a passenger, I remember the vague superficial interest I had regarding the cars coming towards us, merely wondering if we'd miss them.

Christmas dos rotated round the Area and were predictably the same. They were a fairly lukewarm mix of Don, Area Drawing Office, and supervisors, and had a little bit of the wariness of the Engineer's Saloon, where opposite ends of the social spectrum were thrown together. However, it only took a couple of pre-trough drinks for Don to become Don as opposed to Mr Newell. We had a moderate amount to sup, far from the league of another District that will not be named for legal reasons (no, I've already let that cat out of the bag; it was York), where Friday afternoon was a licensed period of drinking, and nobody appeared in the office until about four, to pick up their weekend gear.

The Saloon restricting drinking from the allowed couple of bottles of Double Diamond down to a bottle of shandy, introduced by a teetotal Chief, marked the beginning of the end for drinking. In my later days no alcohol whatsoever was allowed for all staff, working from drivers and guards, to the entire industry for fairness' sake. Celebrations meant that staff had to book a half day off, or risk instant dismissal. The 1950 Rule Book, 240 items long, mentions drinking only once, and then as an aside:

> Rule 3 (v) Employees MUST NOT consume intoxication liquor while on duty.

This appeared under the forbiddance of wasting or squandering office equipment. (Which was interpreted to mean that as soon as you had collected enough pencils, rubbers and paper clips for personal use, you were to apply the rule thereafter.)

★

'*Tea!*' was about the limit of Don's drinking needs. '*Tea!*' was demanded from the new recruit, whoever he be, whiz-kid or of graduate status didn't count. He would be given leeway on his first day, and thereafter be made to understand that Don entering with an empty cup meant '*Tea!*' *Now.* Not one minute past ten or one minute past three, but ten and three precisely. What's more the little rocket had to make mine as well. I have had my tea made by some eventually very senior managers, to my personal delight. And, it was apparent that many of them had never made a cup of tea in their lives at home.

'*What's this?*' was often heard at about five past ten on their second morning. It was Don again, with a very un-humorous and sinister smile on his face. The instant chef would then usually look at me with a questioning stare, or, sometimes mistakenly, in defiance. Defiance was soon quelled by Don, who would remind the defiant one who it was that would be making out a report on him in two month's time. To the apologetic one, I would explain Don's preference in the tea line, and to the offensive I would direct them to Bill in order to get his version of advice.

'Nah what tha's done, lad, is mek it nobbut ower weeak. Don likes a bitta body in his tea. Nah what tha should do is mek it abaht quarter to ten, wi two bags in his mug and two in't teapot. Let it stand for quarter of an hour, stirrin'it up nah anagen, an then put three dollops o'sugar in. If t'spuin stands up innit then tha's gorrit abaht reet. And milk, use t'cream offat t'top – that's the way he likes it.'

In actual fact, Don preferred a hot cup of average strength and one sugar. Bill's recipe to the reluctant learner produced a tepid tea that only moved when you bent the spoon forcing it to rotate. With any luck the sugar wouldn't dissolve totally, but the milk would form an oily top on the surface. Don liked to dunk a digestive in it, but would find that the tea rejected it until it was forced below the surface when the mix would produce an instant mush. Result: '*What the heck is this?*'

It was never a good strategy to enrage Don, so I would undo Bill's damage and direct the now quivering bundle into making a Don-perfect mug. Never coffee so far as I can remember, except after a good dinner.

Tea is a dangerously deceitful drink to make. If anyone offers a cup it is best to first accept it without milk and assess the strength of it. Some cups you get have difficulty negotiating the climb out of the spout, while others cannot escape due to a gridlock in the escape hatch of combined bags. This applied in later years when I was attending top project meetings in York. The tea lady, now reduced from a team of six to one only had time to bring in the pot, the milk and the cups, along with tiny packets of sugar. The chairman would then have to sign for this before she bustled off to create a welcome diversion in another eternal meeting. But this is leaping far too soon into the era of meetings at York, a most tedious occurrence.

★

Going back to my nine months in the Leeds District Office before indulging in my happiest period at Huddersfield, I experienced my first Leeds Christmas. It could hardly be like the event at York in my student era, when all departments were called over to the Regional Headquarters Kremlin across the road, and arranged themselves all the way up one of the two open staircases, where carols were sung. We couldn't have attempted this on the 15-watt staircase at No. 23, Wellington Street. There would be a need for a coordinator travelling up and down in the lift to announce the next carol, should it be likely that anyone bothered to attend.

I found that the festive season started with an anticipated message from the Goods Claims Department in the sidings at the far end of the Wellington Street. There was to be the annual sale of 'lost' items – consignments where the labels had come off, or the paperwork had gone astray. It was to be held throughout the week at around dinner times. I could tell from the air of excitement that this was one event you did not miss.

I was more or less swept along in the crowd down the street at spot on noon, finishing up in a large goods warehouse, with all the orphaned stock around the walls on tables or stacked on the floor. At another end there was an auction of lost property. My humble haul amounted to a half-dozen crate of hock at a ridiculous price. I had never experienced hock, or wine of any kind really, so I had no idea what I was buying. It dawned on me later that I had acquired a very good vintage for next to nothing. Wine, in the Claims Office, was simply marked 'wine', with the same price for anything coming under that title. There was a distinct shortage of connoisseurs in that department. To top off my haul, I ventured to take a part in my very first auction, coming away with a handsome camera tripod with only the holding screw missing. I had it knocked out at thirty bob – worth, at a guess, around £50.

The years at Huddersfield were barren as regards this venture. Notice of it came through too late, and Don would take a dim view of a trip to Leeds just to make a shout for some cheap wine. Although not in the same teetotal league as the famous Stanley Mole, who poured many bottles of contractors' Bells down the sink at Christmas, Don was not an enthusiast in the alcohol department. I did once manufacture a visit to Leeds a year or two later, halfway through the sale week, but the best had gone and I was left with a choice of one hundred or so umbrellas.

★

I am far from being happy at formal troughs, indeed I have managed to go through life without ever donning a suit with bow tie. Dinners are, in my mind, to be eaten – and eaten while still warm. There is no place at my mealtimes for incidental and trivial prattle. This was the sort of thing you got on the Engineers' Inspection Saloon in two distinct clumps: eager young hopefuls listening to every word of wisdom dropping along with morsels of food from the dignitary mouths, and then me and the supervisors, chomping away with hardly a word except between courses.

Not that I'm happy with courses, either. If my entire dinner doesn't fit flat on one plate, then there's too much. I think I'm at one of my lowest moments when faced with a tablecloth and an array of consumption weaponry. This being the case, I was not a willing candidate for railway residential courses. Very few of these can be fun, and only just a bit informative. They betray the notion that there are three and two half days in a learning week, and that the lecturers have coincidentally just that amount of knowledge to impart. Many, I found, could have been concluded in a day, given inmates of average intelligence. This is why my first course at the Derby Training School caught me at my nadir. It was called an Induction Course, intended for brand new recruits to the railway, in all fields. I wasn't hunted down for this event until I had been in railway employment for 2½ years. For this reason the whole fortnight, with the weekend home and returning on Sunday afternoon, was a total waste of time, as I had already met up with most of the exciting things that they had to show us. I went all the way to Derby to be brought by coach and shown a new marshalling yard at Healey Mills. Not only was this a chair screw's throw from home, but I'd already assisted in a bit of the setting out. I tried to melt into the crowd, but could not avoid Jack Todd and Alan Barker recognising me, and greeting me in a way that some of my more potentially illustrious companions found most strange.

But it was the dismal formality and schoolroom approach to presenting us with a dollop of grub to sling down our throats that really got me depressed. I had been forced to travel down by Pullman on the Sunday afternoon, in order for assembly early on the Monday morning. It was a hot weekend with much to be done, but here I was stuck on a boiling train that had ground to a halt ten minutes out of Leeds, just beyond Ardsley Tunnel. There being no public address system in those days, my fellow passengers were becoming sullen and grumpy, while I was just hoping that all lines to Derby were blocked, and that we'd have to shuffle back home. Then the gang of lads, many of whom I recognised, came sauntering along the low retaining wall top, past our coach. It was the supervisor, Denis Durand, who spotted me. All windows were wide open.

'Ayoop, Mike! You're a bit out of your league on this thing, aren't you? All these others'll be posh folk. Just keep your mouth shut, and they probably won't notice. Bet you haven't got a ticket, either. Weer are you off to, then?'

I could hardly ignore him, apart from the fact that the whole coach was by now roused and watching me. I stood up with the table blocking my movement and craned to reach the sliding top window.

'Oh, hello, Dennis. Derby. A course.'

'They're not going to bother to try and educate you after all that you've done, are they? Do these folk know abaht your problem, then?'

Terry Ward and friend at World Billiards Championship – an old photo! Photo: British Rail.

At Denby Dale. An explosion of growth in the track, after a sewage spreader got stuck on top.

Badger sett near Keighley, with rejected bones from adjacent graveyard.

Seasonal arrangement in Huddersfield Station by the relayers, made up from stones and track components.

H.A.S.A.W.A. "DISCIPLE"

BRADFORD AND HALIFAX PATROLLMAN

*Cynical track patrolman's representation
of all he is supposed to carry with him.*

An example of track managing a zero in work study assessment.

Jack Pinder, works supervisor and cricket star.

Graham Whitely, the epitome of sporting excellence,
and fan of Father Christmas.

Drill holes in rock cutting, near Halifax Station.

Bob Newell during an enthusiastic treasure hunt.

Old photo of the weedkiller train, steam hauled. Photo: British Rail.

York chainmen, invaluable on the York Remodelling Project. John Hodgson, John Barker and leader, Bob Ashton.

I had done nothing and I had no 'problem', other than Dennis, but I could see that he was more than a bit amused by his train-bound audience.

'What's up, Dennis?'

'Classified information. I can't go worrying these good friends of yours. Gi'us a biscuit!'

Complementary biscuits had been handed out on leaving Leeds. I threw a couple out, only to have half the coach and the attendant contributing more for all the lads.

'Now, what're we stuck here for, Dennis?'

'Buckled rail, about a hundred yards up front. It's bloody hot out here, tha knows, not like in thy air-conditioned posh coach.' There was no air conditioning, and he knew it.

'Is it a bad one?'

'Nobbut half an inch or so, but it's short on shoulder ballast.'

It was now required of me to address my fellow interrupted travellers to pass on and translate the information. I explained that the intense heat in the steeply banked cutting had caused the track to buckle out of line, and that we needed some cooling and remedial work before we could safely go on. I returned to Dennis for more information.

'You're not waiting for a stone train, surely. We'll be here hours!'

'Ten minutes, most, Mike. All t'lads were just down t'road and had finished their shifts and were getting tanked up a bit before going home when they gave us the shout to come here. I've lined them up along the buckle, and they're just about ready.'

'What for?' I asked, as I was supposed to.

Dennis looked up and down the coach, making sure that he'd got maximum attention. 'They're waiting while they're all set, and then they're going to do some synchronised pissing on t'rail to cool it dahn.'

If he'd wanted reaction, he got it.

And so, some fifty minutes late, we arrived in Derby. Organised taxis were meeting all major trains and lifting us out to the school. This turned out to be a solid brick building of typical railway architecture, forbidding and enormous. My heart sank. It lifted a little when I found that we all had rooms to ourselves, and went up another notch when faced with my kind of meal – a buffet. It being Sunday evening, no teaching staff there, a meal of easiest preparation and available to arrivals at all times; but this was my last taste of informality.

No, I tell a lie, breakfast was necessarily informal, served between 7.30 and 7.45, and you could see immediately those who had popped out to the fleshpots of Derby the previous evening, and others who seemed to have no previous experience of breakfasts whatever. Parts of it were quite foreign to me, who always sat down to cereal and the top of the bottle, along with grilled bacon misshapes and toast with chunky marmalade. On offer here were exotic things, like special sausages, mushrooms, and baked beans together with the standard eggs and bacon. Also there were kippers, or rather complex fine skeletons with traces of fish among them. I think that there was also black pudding, but these were the days before my *cordon bleu* education in Huddersfield, so I ignored it, as I did with anything that I didn't recognise. I should have made use of the wide choice, as from there onwards choice was not on the cards.

From 8.45 we had Induction Introduction, during which it was made abundantly clear to us that the industry we had joined was the Railway, in case we had any doubts. An exciting timetable for the fortnight was set out before us, consisting of things that I had mostly experienced already at the hands of the lads. We were going to look at a bridge somewhere miles away, as if Derby had none; we were going to visit a station, and again Derby itself failed to make the ratings. A signal box filled half a day, not a tall old hand-lever job, but a bungalow of bells and flashing lights, just like York where I had been the week before. On one day when the organisers had planned that we should have rain, we sat in a classroom studying parts of the Rule Book – mainly those bits which tell you that it is an offence to get yourself knocked over by a train.

We went to Birmingham to look at some railway track (again, Derby apparently having nothing suitable); and what's more we went by coach, as we did for the unforgettable experience of going up to Healey Mills marshalling yard. Then there was another coach ride to look at a tunnel. Not walk through one mind, as I had hoped, but to just look at one end, then travel a mile to look at the other. Towards the closing section of the fortnight we were put on 'intensive', and visited a stone arch overbridge, a canal underbridge and a viaduct – all in the one enthralling day!

This was the itinerary as laid out on that first morning. There was time for questions, during which the keen children in suits made their faces known by asking the screamingly obvious. Apparently exhausted at ten we broke for coffee and biscuits and integration, where the two lecturers circulated among us in perfect co-ordination to me circulating round the opposite side of the room. The coffee was unrecognisable, being poured from a large Thermos jug thing, rather than being instant and mixed in a mug. By 10.45 the teachers were in need of a rest, so we were put into groups of six or seven for the purpose of discussion. We were supposed to discuss 'The Railway and its Place in Society'. Every group was exactly alike, and reminiscent of classes at high school. Every one had among it a suit and glasses with an air of deep seriousness and no sense of humour, a loudmouth whose questioning hand had earlier been up and down like a piston... and, of course, a fat kid.

It was only a matter of minutes before the rest of my group found out that I'd been on the railway some considerable time already, and I was for ever after regarded as being there as a plant, to report back about my two-week colleagues. I think that if we'd had a playtime, some of them might have had a go at me. Others used me to help answer questions. One sinister thing that emerged fairly early on was the fact that a number of those present had opted for a job on the railway purely to get close up to their passion for steam engines. From just a short experience, to be consolidated later at Huddersfield, I knew that such characters were little more than of questionable usage in railway space.

We did have a playtime after all. It was called 'Recreation and Intercourse' and lasted between twelve and half past when the dinner gong went. No, sorry, this wasn't dinner, it was something called 'lunch', another new word on my learning curve. Apparently we were to have dinner at teatime, or even a bit later. This was when I faced my first lunch of main course and pudding.

Meat and three veg, followed by what I was informed was dessert, it certainly looking nothing like pudding at all. It was in this way that every day of the fortnight was mapped out, except for the all-day trips, when we went to some posh café. By now I was set up for the day in the eating department. Lunch had been substantial and there was need only for a nibble later on before bed, and then to look forward to breakfast, the next day. It was then that they really pulled the rug out from under me by subjecting me to half past six dinner.

A change of clothes was expected, for which, I'm glad to say, I was not the only one to be caught out. Two shirts and an extra pair of trousers, and that was all most of us had brought. After coming up against this event called 'dinner' for the first week there were some changes for the next, after a weekend at home. One or two even brought black suits and bow ties for the evening meal for the second week. By now I was in total rebellion, and came down for 'dinner' in an open-neck shirt. However, before I could enter the room the border guards at the door picked me out, ominously called me 'Sir' and suggested that I'd forgotten something.

We were allocated serviettes in rings out of numbered pigeon-holes, into which we had to return them later for cleaning and analysing (presumably). This was so reminiscent of my very first day at nursery school when I was presented with a special peg for my coat, marked with the picture of a little sailor boy. Others had all sorts of objects and animals, but I was haunted by the image of that damned sailor boy. It appeared everywhere I went in the class, on my chair and on the register and on the 'good child' chart every week. Now it was a numbered serviette ring.

There was a seating plan that was changed daily in order for us all to mix, and also to meet a different member of the staff each evening. However, the main function of the roster was to ensure that every one of us took a turn at the 'Top Table'.

This was where the Principal sat, in a noticeably grander chair. I dreaded my turn, that was programmed for the middle of the second week. When it came around, my guardian angel had been very busy. It turned out to be the day of one of our coach trips and dense traffic had delayed our return to a point where we were offloaded and sent straight into dinner, all looking as scruffy as the next. My manner of dress, therefore, could not be scrutinised with any degree of criticism, and I felt remarkably comfortable.

Moving around among my fellows I soon worked out that I was Mr Average: not all pretentiousness like the penguin-clad brigade, and neither completely out of my depth as regarded table manners. Concerning the table armaments, I knew enough to start on the outskirts and work my way inwards. Not like one of my early neighbours, who managed to power his way through the various courses, finishing up with just a soup spoon for the cheese, butter and biscuits. Undaunted, he used the handle. Another, possibly from a frugal background, managed just the opposite by discreetly wiping his cutlery clean, on the tablecloth after each usage, so arriving at the chequered flag with a full armoury still at his disposal.

One thing the majority of us had obviously never encountered was the absence of a mug for our after dinner coffee. Not only that, but the stuff was dribbled out into thimbles with minute handles and doll's house saucers. We had to utilise the butter that accompanied the biscuits in order to discreetly extricate one poor lad's finger from this tiny appendage. This, and many more similar minor catastrophes happening to others, helped me to gain more optimism and confidence for the big table later.

Wine was served at the Top Table, as opposed to water among the common herd. While it being of assistance in calming nerves, it proved yet another etiquette hurdle to overcome. I hadn't honestly come across wine before, as far as I can remember, until that consignment of 'lost' hock came my way through the Claims Department, and even then only one bottle had been shared round a family table up to this introduction to the stuff at Derby. I had no idea, for example, that it was stronger than beer, or that it came in a choice of two colours. I wondered idly how much this sort of thing was part of the 'Induction' process of the course.

I can remember that one of the bottles doing the rounds was called claret, though what the other was I couldn't remember an hour later – it was something foreign like 'Sauvignon' or 'Appellation Control'. What I was wise enough to take note of was the amount that the Principal accepted, and so followed suit. I also noticed that when one bottle was finished another danger-ously took its place. As the stuff came to affect me, I suddenly realised that I was talking a lot, so I put a stopper on it... not like one pair at the table. Requests for buckets instead of the 'poxy egg cups' didn't go down well, and sat as I was at the right hand of the boss, I noticed him consulting a small table plan in front of him at any slight indiscretion. It must have been something like taking a driving test and wincing at every note made by the instructor. The denouement came when one of the two invited the other to try the rosé wine, pouring equal parts from the red and white. With hardly a move or a significant signal, one of the albino gorillas that were standing in as waiters tapped the two on their shoulders and advised them to vacate the room.

Menus were printed and placed on all the tables, which seemed a bit pointless as there was no choice as to what was available. Fortunately, vegetarianism had not been invented in the 1960s, so there was no trouble in that quarter, but the menus, apart from being superfluous, gave no real indication to most of us as to what was to be dished up. Posh eating apparently had to be done in French, and beyond *pommes de terre* I was stuck. 45% in GCE French, achieved at the third attempt, was of no great assistance in solving the evening's offerings.

Another shock to my system was the amount of waste, particularly among those who had turned up looking like magpies with bow ties on. They always left some of their dinner on their plate before folding knife and fork into the 'finished' mode. These lads were immediately marked down as useless in my book, as the vegetables were self-service out of great pot buckets. What good were they going to be in economic planning if they couldn't work out how much to put on their plates before they started? I was a war baby, and often sat day after day facing the same plate of semolina pudding until I eventually ate it. Waste was simply unheard of during rationing.

Fish had always taken one of three distinct forms for me: a choice between a flimsy gold-red shimmering object dodging round in a large tank of water with illumination from above and a stream of bubbles rising from a tube at the bottom; a hot lump of white flesh with yellow batter all round it, followed by newspaper; or the third option, where it obviously grew in small tins, abbatoired as soon as it filled the tin, sealed and labelled 'sild' or 'sardine'. There was, for me, nothing else, until Derby. It was a trout, appearing very much like option No. 1, but lying still with a large accusing eye staring up at me, and it was intended that I was to view it as either option No. 2 or 3. We glared at each other for minutes. In this I was not alone. The insensitive suits from down south were already picking their ways through the fish while engaging the thing's eye in a sort of conversation of admiration; we in the tank or batter brigade had no idea how to cope. Fortunately on our table that night we had a son of the earth among us whose father was a chicken farmer. He too was a little nonplussed at having his dinner hypnotising him, but it seemed that he'd decapitated as many chickens as he'd had chicken dinners. We watched as he picked up his fish, twisted its head round and used his biggest knife to chop it off. He then chucked the head under the table. Without a word, one by one, we passed down our aquarium tragedies for them to undergo his gourmet guillotining, receiving back mauled, but palatable, results without accusing eyes.

Duck and orange came as another shock, mainly because I never associated the two together. Ducks came from a large pond in Golden Acre Park back at home, while oranges came from goodness knew where, but it certainly wasn't Golden Acre Park. So what culinary prat had at some time put them together on the same plate? Tuna salad was viewed with disgust, salad being a very rare seasonal thing with many of us in those times, and not dissimilar to grazing. Which leads to the embarrassing moment when we were served cold consommé instead of soup, and found it had grass cuttings floating on it. We discussed it round the table, wondering whether we should inform anyone that our table had been served cold soup, but we were still a timid party and pretended that it was all right after all.

So here we were, being inducted into the railway industry, but mainly discovering how to cope with vast amounts of food: free-range breakfasts, dignified coffee and biscuits, piled up 'lunches', tea and small cakes, and just when you wanted no more at all, a vast four-courser, lying like lead way into the night. There was a bar to help it down so long as you were a fan of lukewarm bottles of fizzy beer, and for entertainment we had a snooker table. This we could hardly bend over after dinner, so we usually dispersed to tackle our 'projects' that were dished out during the day. (I'd ruined my chances of a game since some of the lads learnt of my meetings with Fred Davis and John Spencer in my past, at Pontin's, and was therefore not one to challenge for money.)

On the final morning, we all had to give a five-minute presentation on a subject of our choice. There was a distinctly predictable run of topics. I still have my notes on this. From the potential high launchers there was yet more crawling; 'On the Right Lines', 'Railways after the Millennium', 'My Career Choice', and such. From a significantly dismissible minority 'Black Fives', 'The Flying Scotsman' and 'Steam to Diesel'. Most subjects were honest and not meant for collecting Brownie points: 'Greek Philosophers', 'Famous Bridges', 'Fell walking'. Then there was the totally unsuspected; 'My Life as a Jehovah's Witness', 'When my Father became my Mother', and 'My Hopes of starting a Luxury Coach Company'. Mine was absolutely predictable – 'Railway Characters I Have Met'.

Summing up, the whole fortnight was dominated by food, with slight railway orientated distractions in between.

In the length of my career many courses surfaced for my attention, none as pompous as the Derby School Induction, but equally challenging on the intensive stoking and lack of exercise between meals. For evermore they were to be things for me to avoid. I was convinced that they existed for their own sake, to keep some chattering articles in work, dispensing theory, with the distinct impression that they would be of little use in practice.

So what, given many years of practical service to the railways, and as little as possible communal chomping, would be my ideal day, gastronomically speaking?

Assume breakfast, as previously described, at home. A mug of tea on arrival at Huddersfield, a drive out to site with chainmen, interrupted by a stop for toasted currant teacake and a strong coffee at a transport along the way. Job completed, make for Golcar around a quarter past twelve, when the hot meat pies would be coming out of the oven at the butcher's. Race back to the office, and pour scalding molten pork jelly down my throat without spilling too much. Later, a communal tea and chocolate biscuit, around three, and the journey home for a six o'clock steak and kidney stew with dumplings and veg. Finally, a bottle of strong beer in the evening, with a whiskey topper. Do you want all that repeated in French?

Gardens and the Like

Peter Sykes, sometime driver for the Huddersfield Permanent Way Supervisor, doubled as a smallholder in Marsden near the end of Standedge Tunnel. He had six cows – all with two legs shorter than the others for grazing on the hillsides – and was a little serious with a humorous straight-faced streak. Brought up in the Marsden gang, responsible for the tunnel lines, he was a keen countryman.

'Hasta a minute, Mike? Ah could do wi a word.'

'Sure, Peter.'

'It's really advice, tha knaws, if you don't mind.'

'OK, but I reckon if it's about work, you could probably tell me more than I can tell you.'

'No, it's a personal, staff thing, like. Ah'm wondering whether ah'll be allowed days off wi pay and wi out it coming outa mi holidays. Ah've been asked to join the Peak Parking Plan – the Pleak Pan Boarding – the Peak Plark Banning Poard – the Peakpar Boarding Plan…'

'Would it be easier to get a transfer to the National Trust, Peter?'

This came out of the blue. I knew Peter as a dour man with many undeveloped talents, but it would be true to say that he was hardly a man of words, suitable for joining the Peak Parks Planning Board; yet they had come seeking him, and not the other way round. On the surface I was surrounded at Huddersfield by uncomplicated characters, with mostly private lives. A lad I remember, similar to Peter with a thriving smallholding came in one day frightened out of his mind because the Inland Revenue had contacted him about money he made from the farming sideline. He had genuinely thought that they had some way of taking it all out of his railway pay, and was shocked to get a bill stretching back five years. The Railway, one of the best firms to work for as British Rail or Railways, helped the lad out by negotiating with the tax people and arranging for him to have the extra taken gently out of his pay over a number of months. This was a time when you had a Staff Section, which looked after the staff in every way, as opposed to the idiotically named Human Resources Section, which as implied in the name, see each man and woman as little different to a shovel or ballast fork. I use the odd barmpot in my stories of characters, but most of them are brain surgeon material compared to the thesaurus thieves who dream up the most inappropriate new titles for jobs we used to understand by name.

Peter got his day release to attend meetings, along with the congratulations of the Engineer, in that truly enlightened age.

Hillsides, fields, extensive gardens and small plots of vegetables all impounded on the railway for most of its length, and many of our dealings with outside parties concerned their property, large and small, in many ways. We might be seeking permission to run a drain through some manorial field to a suitable outlet, in return draining an annoying swampy area in the lower field. At the other end of the scale, I might be taking a train to Hebden Bridge where a neighbour of the railway has reported a landslide from us onto their garden. When I got there and raised the old lady who had rung us, and convinced her that I was not a bent gasman after her savings, she took me down the edge of her garden, which had a small retaining wall supporting an embankment and the railway. She pointed out a sizeable sod that had been dug loose, probably by foxes, and had tumbled onto her path during the previous week's heavy rain. It would have been possible to dismiss her as a daft old bat, more or less telling her so, but after an hour getting there it paid to explain to her what I thought had happened, and that our patrolman would keep an eye on that particular spot on a weekly basis. For this I earned a cup of hot water with milk and a threat of tea in it, along with one of those horrible 'Nice' biscuits. Resulting from this was a commendation from the District Engineer regarding a highly complimentary letter he had received from the lady, and a snort from Don, who knew full well that I'd hardly done anything.

When it came to negotiations at the 'Big House', for a drain through their field, these were, of course, conducted by Don himself, with me wandering up and down the site or waiting in the car. Discussions took about an hour and three quarters, way into dinner time, and when Don emerged he announced that he didn't feel the need for a café dinner, while brushing biscuit crumbs off of his shirt front. All I got out of it was an instruction to design the drain and to arrange it so that it would take away the annoying permanent pond near the railway. The field was used to house a riding school's horses, which I assumed were friendly, but taking no chances, I set up the level and legs on the track, and sent Percy over the fence with the measuring staff. It turned out that Percy had an affinity with the brutes, such that one or two of them followed him about for the peppermints he had in his pocket. This was all very well except that I couldn't read off the staff with the level's telescope, as it was permanently trained up a horse's bum, fully obscuring the target.

When it came for the 'Number Two Drainage Gang' to actually dig the drain and lay pipes, things did not go smoothly. They were led by a diminutive Irishman who did not share his nation's empathy with such animals as horses. Whenever one came over to have a word, he would lead his gang back over the fence onto the railway in a single bound, so the digging was done in fits and starts. As a result, when they reported the drain completed we were somewhat disappointed in that it had had no apparent effect on the pond. Don sent me out to check, again with Percy, and we found that the drain ran uphill towards the outfall, and at the end, the pipes were only a spade deep. This was one of probably five occasions in my career when I heard Don at his critical worst or best, depending on whether you were up-voice, or down with regard to his face. He explained in his terms that whatever water did in Killarney, in Yorkshire it did not run uphill. The drain was re-excavated, and by negotiation the horses were fenced off nearer the house, and the pond duly disappeared.

In later years, I was editing an official colour glossy magazine for the District Engineer, who, after several title changes with every reorganisation that came our way, was now called the Leeds Area Civil Engineer; hence the rather wimpish title of the magazine – *Lacenews*. Returning to my dealings with animals, one item I had to report on was the badgers.

We had to keep a close eye on badger setts, more so if they were burrowing into an embankment and under the railway. Continuous passage of trains can collapse these, with disastrous results, so we usually arranged for the resiting of such badger undes reses. Those in cutting sides presented little danger, but were still kept under surveillance. As a reporter, I was told about the one at Utley, just beyond Keighley, because there were peculiar things happening there.

Here the badgers had set up home near the top of the cutting slope, and some interesting debris was emerging with their regular clean-outs. Bones – and lots of them, large and small – were piling up and tumbling down the bank. More intriguing was the presence of some brass handles. There was heavy shrubbery along the boundary wall, so investigations could not go further than the sett entrances. However, the local lads were more than just a bit intrigued, and they cut a way through one less dense bush to get to the wall. Looking over, they found they were on the edge of a cemetery. The badgers had dug under the roots and wall, and were obviously a little put out when they came upon the remains of coffins and skeletons. Their spring cleaning involved raking them out as the debris fell into their back room lounges.

Rabbits, of course, were around in multitudes in the days before myxomatosis. Again, regular removal was essential in embankments, but we had the option of gassing, as they were not protected like badgers. Our usual view of a rabbit on the railway was a head only, lying in the track. With patrolling every two days, the bodies were collected as a useful meal, along with fallen pheasants. I was regularly offered the odd rabbit, but always refused as I could not face the reaction I would get at home that evening, placing a disassembled rabbit on the kitchen table.

Embankments and cuttings were the source of perhaps the only disagreement I had with Don. He would have trees cut down, blaming their weight for causing slippage in the banks, whereas I always argued that the roots held the soil together. We were both right to some extent, but I was overruled when the great debate started about leaves on the line. I can't remember steam power having a problem in coping with a brutal fresh sycamore leaf on the rail and virtually blocking the line, but the much lighter diesel units could be quite overcome with the beauty of the thing... so much so that they felt obliged to come to a halt, and take a look around. The engineer's answer was to cut down all offending trees overhanging or close to the lines. I met this again when overhead electrification came upon us, late on in my time, where one of the civil engineer's tasks was to cut down anything within a couple of metres of the masts. This edict amused me, because no sooner had a strict programme of lumberjacking been put in hand and executed, than the trees behind lost all support on the railway side and flopped over, almost embracing the masts come the first drop of rain.

★

All that above has turned into an almost serious lecture on civil engineering – I've no idea how it came in. So a return to the pottier aspects of railway life is called for.

Bill came into the drawing office with a letter passed on by Don. Such were often sources of doom for me. It meant something that Don didn't consider important and felt that he hadn't time to deal with. Yet all the while I was spending the time on it that he was saving, he would grumble, that is until a progress report by head office was called for from him.

The 'Beauty and Decorative Environmental Gardening Group' wanted to plant daffodils along the lineside and in cuttings. Why me! I was trained in civil engineering, and during four years of theory and practical learning I had never been introduced to a single daffodil bulb. Had I done so, then I would no doubt have been called upon to find what pressure would crush it, what tension would stretch and snap it, or by dissecting it determine its mineral make-up.

Bill handed over the letter, and an accompanying booklet detailing the purpose and aspirations of BADEGG, while humming 'Tiptoe through the Tulips'. He'd seen it before Don, of course, while sorting through the day's correspondence.

'Reet up thy street, Mike. To hell wi railway lines and bridges and suchlike, today's t'fust day of t'rest of thy life. Don reckons someone's got t'meet up wi these loonies and see they cause no damage or hurt themselves. All ta has t'do is walk through wi 'em and pick out t'best spots. Tha knaws, them places weer tha's often said to thissen, "Oo, if only there were some daffs along eer." '

'How come you seem to know so much about me getting involved in this, then, when it's the first I've seen of it? You been talking to Newell about it?'

'Well he were musin' ower it a bit and tryin' to work out whether it were PWay or Works wot should deal wi it, and ah may've mentioned that, seein' as how you were both, tha'd be best suited for it.'

'Sometimes, William, you can be a right prat, when you put your mind to it!'

'Nay, it's a gift,' he said.

I was called to a meeting in Leeds with the other three Area lads like me, and we all agreed that this was going to be a right waste of our time. It was chaired by Steve Bell, the Engineer, himself, so we could see how much importance had been thrust on him. There were three BADEGG people there, all looking more civil service than gardeners. It was a government-inspired plan and took one of the Suits three quarters of an hour to explain it to us. The other two said very little, and I was somewhat shocked when one of them was referred to as Miss Something-or-other. I had been convinced that the short haircut and severe suit was a bloke. I found out later that my mates were equally convinced. We all had uncomfortable fears that she would be the person to deal with us locally. One thing made perfectly clear was that Steve had as much interest in it all as Don, and that he was being leaned on from above. He required weekly reports and diagrams of progress, this looking like a right balls-aching job.

Don had obviously been got at during the next Monday morning meeting, along with his fellow Area Assistants, as he came back with more instructions, and an agreed date for a local meeting with one of the Suits from the Ministry. On the day, Don underlined the importance that Steve Bell had stressed, by sending out for biscuits, and borrowing some cups and saucers from the refreshment room.

Ten o'clock on the dot, a large black saloon drove into the yard and parked pointedly alongside Elliot's smaller Ford Anglia.

From the driving seat out stepped another Suit, thankfully not Miss Believe-It-Or-Not. He went to the back seat for a slim briefcase. Meanwhile, from the passenger side, the door was flung wide open, and nothing happened for a bit. After a moment or two the car was suddenly afflicted with violent spasms and eventually a confused assortment of arms, legs and other unidentifiable appendages, emerged, withdrew, and came out again in a different arrangement. Whatever it was seemed to be desperately trying to escape from the gravitational pull of the car. In time it managed to assemble itself into a single unit, and tumbled out looking like an accident at a small jumble sale. The earlier arms, and legs appeared to be attached to the main bulk at most unlikely points until it stood up. It shook itself, pulled a few loose bits of pullover, jacket and overcoat together and arranged itself into some vaguely human form. This, we were to discover, was Ernest, to become Ernie. Part of his problem in making a slightly more difficult appearance than at his birth was a large well-used duffel bag, with its cords slung round his shoulder and neck, and in some mysterious way, his left leg. If ever I'd been asked to describe a picture of a rustic daffodil planter, Ernie would have fitted the bill to perfection.

Don obviously didn't know what world he was in. The Suit introduced itself and shook hands all round; then he announced Ernest, who searched manfully for a spare hand and attempted to do the same. Ernie was described by the suited one as their 'operative', and he seemed to have a modicum of distant respect for the cordial bundle. They came into Don's office, Ernie snagging himself and his duffle bag on the door handle, and we sat round the desk to discuss what was required of us. Ernie didn't say much in the company of the stiff suit, but when he did it was in a softly rounded Lancashire accent. He was to make up for his silence later.

It all came down to Ernie arriving daily at Huddersfield with his essentials, and being run out to whatever site was next on the agenda. He required one lookout man, at Don's insistence, just to ensure that he didn't wander where he shouldn't. This did not seem likely, as his mission was to find his way along the boundary fences and adorn the upper reaches of the embankments with his monochrome daffodils. With Bill in the next office, out of earshot, I suggested to Don that my presence was not strictly necessary for all of the time, and that Bill could run him in the PWay van to a suitable access point and take the van on to the next to meet him and pick him up. Don thought that this was a good idea, and all I needed to do was to pop out to site once a week and make a note of what had been achieved.

'Bloody Newell!' said Bill, after our visitors had gone, agreeing to make a start the following Monday. 'D'you knaw what he's decided? Only that I've got to keep that mobile ragbag company all friggin' week for four weeks. Ah've haif a mind to knock sick!'

'You'll be OK,' I assured him, hoping that he got no inkling as to whose suggestion it had been. 'Drop him and the lookout at a bridge, and nip on to the next to reel him in again later. Plenty of room to stretch out with the paper, job's made for you!'

'But he's a nutter! He's just come inter t'PWay office and he starts goin' on abaht bloody daffs and wandrin' lonely like a bloody cloud and such. He's crackers, and ah'm stuck wi'im for t'best part on four friggin' weeks!'

'Pity I can't drive, Bill, or I'd do it.'

'Dusta fancy some quick lessons, eh?'

Bill, of course, turned up as usual on the first Monday, armed with a stack of magazines, a book and a transistor wireless. The weekend had obviously presented one or two silver linings.

The 10.15 from Wakefield, apparently the hub of the daffodil planters' universe, duly ejected Ernie onto the platform, from where he made his way round to our offices.

'Bloody 'ell, Mike, he's brought two mates wi 'im!'

At a distance this seemed to be true, but as he got nearer his 'mates' turned out to be two large and very full sacks. His duffel bag was slung round his neck, and had a length of wooden handle sticking out of it. This was his working tackle – a long-handled trowel. The sacks were filled with daffodil bulbs. I was immediately quite taken by Ernie. He answered my need for yet another character to add to my collection.

He dumped his sacks next to the van and gladly accepted the offer of a mug of tea. He sat awkwardly on a drawing office stool using only one cheek and juggled the hot mug with his duffel bag, which now had the added danger of the trowel sticking out of it. All the time I met Ernie he was never separated from the bag, even when I came across him and Bill having a sandwich between planting sessions. All this was done through a mild September, but Ernie kept topcoat, jacket and pullover on throughout. He added to this during light rain with a monumental plastic mac.

I engineered two days away from Huddersfield, one of them at a meeting in York, and I was late in on the Thursday, so it wasn't until well into the afternoon that I encountered Bill again. He was very chatty. Bill was known to utter the odd adjective now and again, but today I got a year's supply in just two minutes.

'Bloody 'ell, Mike, ah'm goin' home bloody knackered at neet, and ah'm hardly doin' owt. It's him – bloody walking daffodil 'cyclopaedia. Oh! And theer not daffs wot he's plantin'; them theer's really narsissusisis, but ah'm allowed to call 'em daffs; and dusta knaw how many bloody different kinds of daffs theer are? Ah'll tell thee how many theer are, theer's ninety-bloody-two! And dusta knaw how many different shapes on daffs theer are? Well ah'll bloody well tell thi. Twelve! And…'

'He's interesting then, Bill. Good to talk to an expert.'

'*TALK* to 'im? Tha gets no bloody chance t'talk to 'im; tha's theer t'listen, and tha's bahn to bloody listen too, now, 'cos ah'm bahn t'tell thee all the different types wot there are…'

'I've just…'

'No, tha hasn't. Tha's bahn t'bloody listen, cos ah've had to. Thur's trumpets, they're this wide and t'same length, and thur's big and small cupped, and thur's double and trianure… triandles… trandurals… thingummy's, and thur's cycla-whatjacallums, and thur's, oh aye, jonquils – they niff a bit, and, and… Well, thur's twelve or so, and thur all different, and he tells thee wot differences are in bloody detail.'

'By crikey, I didn't know…'

'Ah've not done, yet… remember thur's ninety two different names, all in Latin, or summat, and thur all different whites, yellurs, oranges, bits of pink. They've big trumpets, that stick aht a bit in t'middle, long uns, wide uns, short stubby ones, high uns, miniatures (that's little uns), and they've all got names, all ninety-friggin'-two…'

He can't be going to, I thought, not all frigging ninety-two.

'…and dusta knaw, thur's one called Rip Van Winkle? Didn't surprise me, cos ah dropped off a few times while yon Ernie were goin' on. Seein' as how I reckon tha's got summat t'do wi droppin' mi in this, ah've told him that tha's particular interested in narsissusisis, so he's goin' t'run through t'other ninety-one for thi.'

'I'm going to be out,' I said.

'Aye, ah knaws, tha's out t'morrow, cos it's wi us, cos thas checkin' wot's bin done for thi chart! Ah hopes it rains so tha can sit in t'van while he tells thee ninety-two stories. Oh, ah, and a tip for thi, when he asks what t'biggest daff is, it's four foot high.'

'Is he really as bad as that, Bill?'

'Tha'll see! One thing ah didn't understand – well, thur were lots – but one thing was why they have s'many different names, cos he were on abaht that if tha fancied it tha could go puttin' a bit of dye in t'watter when tha cuts 'em and mekin' them any colour tha likes wimout worryin' abaht givin' 'em a new name, like – ah think ah'll try that next spring.'

Bill was now calming down, but over the next hour he'd keep sticking his head round the door with yet another fascinating thing that he'd picked up about daffodils.

True to reported form, as Ernie walked me through his week's work he regaled me with much of the sort of information that Bill had found so un-riveting. I didn't dare slide off early, or Bill would have really had something to say, so I stayed through dinner, and discovered a few more named varieties and their distinguishing qualities. At a suitable moment I made my excuses, and walked off to the nearest station, Bill happy in the knowledge that it was over two miles away.

So Ernie more or less took over our working lives for about three weeks or so. In some ways we were both a bit sorry to see him go, me because I saw him as a new kind of character, and Bill because the supply of daffodils that accidentally spilled out of Ernie's second sack and into Bill's suddenly produced shopping bag was about to dry up. On the whole, though, we were both mightily relieved that the flow of information was to cease. Bill was altogether quite cheerful on Ernie's last day, telling Don what a great mine of daffodil gen the man was. He brought Ernie back early for him to have a few words with Don. And to pick up a letter that had been forwarded to him through us. After several attempts, still fighting back the duffel bag and associated trowel, Ernie managed to open it.

"Ow, this is interestin',' he said. Bill and I looked at each other, doubting that it would be. 'Way went throw a sim'lar program arahnd Preston last yore, and thor's bin a greet pooblic reacshun this Spring, so tho're goin' to have me troying aht snowdrops on yoor Area next yore. Now if yow thought narcissi wor interestin' yor'll be fascinoited wi snowdrops. They're galanthus t'bi rait; yor won't believe it, but thur's…'

'*Bugger*!' muttered Bill, under his breath.

Ernie was fully accommodated in his planned distribution of daffodils, except through the triangle of Heaton Lodge Junction. We had to slightly dull his enthusiasm here as it was the site of a long-burning underground fire. We had two of these during my time on the Area, with another one at Mytholmroyd threatening to burn itself under the railway. Both sites were areas of old sidings and were made up of partly combustible ashes. How the Mytholmroyd one started we never found out, but it was eventually brought under control by pumping into the red-hot orifices a very weak concrete mix to seal up the air intake. The fire at Heaton Lodge started by the lads burning some old sleepers.

The smell from these fires was something indescribable. Hot, acrid fumes caught the back of your throat and caused a choking cough. Smoke, like steam, oozed out of the ground as if volcanic, and when the surface was disturbed, allowing air in, flames would shoot out for a while, fading back into a red crackling glow. The Heaton Lodge fire was treated just like one in a forest by digging a deep trench along a hopeful firebreak line, well away from the main fire, and back-filling it with sand.

Because it was there, the local gang took to baking potatoes on the surface. This was purely out of interest, and both experienced judgement and experiment were needed to rescue them when done. Needless to say it was akin to walking across burning coals, and a stink of melting rubber was added to the general hellish atmosphere. The potatoes had to be placed and rescued with ballast forks. These needed removing as the handles tended to catch fire. Even then welders' gloves were required in case a slip occurred and a steadying hand touched the hot surface. But, as the gang were keen to tell us, there's nothing like a naturally baked potato as opposed to one done in the cabin stove.

Fortunately, this was before the barbecue was invented, otherwise all manner of foodstuffs would have been surrendered to the smouldering ashes; though they reported success with bacon and sausage, but technical failures with eggs. They really concentrated on the spuds, because, as the gang said, there was nothing that could compare to the potatoes baked in a bank fire, and they were very proud of their natural cooker. The chainmen and I were welcomed in the same way as any other visitors in that we were treated by having a potato each placed on the banking when we arrived. The job in hand was done, as apparently were the potatoes. These were carefully lifted from the simmering sulphurous inferno, and we eagerly settled back in the cabin with a dollop of margarine each to bring out the full flavour.

They tasted absolutely abominable, but still the gang lads ate them determinedly.

It was lads like these, and retired lengthmen living next to the railway, who used to take over any wide cesses and turn them into small allotments. Vegetables were the most popular choice in these places, as they were fairly well protected by being cut off from the general public by the railway. If the gardener was seen to be on the plot, some slow-moving goods trains might pull up and make offers for produce. If he was not there, then the first 'pick your own' scheme was inaugurated. We were once working above Batley, where a pleasant little plot had been set up near the cabin, when a light engine pulled up and the fireman jumped down and started to help himself. Our lookout was infuriated, and dashed up to the now departing engine, banging his flags on the side, and issuing the dire threat of 'coming oop theer and pissin' on thi coil'.

Incidentally, the locomotive footplate, as opposed to a bank fire, was where you really could get the perfect baked potato, on a shovel placed in or near to the firebox. Tales of cooking bacon and eggs on a shovel are also perfectly true – I've had some on a cold winter's morning when we had old locos stood in steam on the job. They were fantastic, if a little difficult to handle.

There was many a gang who would have a small plot attached to their cabin, which was tended during the dinner break, or at other times such as weed-killing days, when they felt justified in including their small allotment, so long as they thought that they could do it undetected. The length ganger's calendar had one regular day strictly set aside for weeding, and others dedicated to the many varied activities listed among the gang's duties. Here was where a noticeable difference appeared between teams. To some the calendar was sacred, and had to be adhered to precisely; others would use it merely as a guide, and were conditions unsuitable, they would go on to some other activity that was possible. Hence one gang might be sat in the cabin on weeding day if the ground was frozen hard, while others would bring forward their plate-oiling, a regular job in early spring. This was unscrewing fishplates, oiling the surface behind, and refitting them, so allowing expansion and contraction of the rails come the hot sunny days.

Weeding has long been a thing of the past with the arrival of the weed-killing train. This is a string of tankers full of some atrocious solution that has a devastating effect on anything green. On the end of it is a kind of observation coach, fitted with spray nozzles through 180 °. It was not a bad thing to be on, but you needed to be aware of its presence in the area if ever you were working on the track as it passed by. The spray could have interesting effects on clothing, and it tasted foul, should there be a bit of a wind blowing.

This specialised train is excellent for clearing track weeds that clog the ballast, but it is indiscriminate between railway weeds and neighbouring gardens. This is particularly true for the banks of flowers around Slaithwaite, which used to tumble down from the houses and spill over onto the track. Come the weedkiller train, and a neat demarcation line would appear a day or two later. Don once had to call on an irate gardener at Stanningley whose garden was separated from the railway by a small retaining wall holding the railway three feet above the masses of proudly grown blooms. Normally the crew are warned where to cease spraying, but communications fell down, and the chemicals, aided by a slight southerly breeze, killed half the garden along a very neat line. Don's problem was not only placating the householder, but having to explain the strength of the killer, and its persistence. Negotiations led to some recompense for the loss, plus a gang digging out the polluted soil and replacing it with new enhanced topsoil. The following year we were sent a photo of the phoenix-like garden, more splendid than ever.

Rather an opposite effect occurred just beyond Denby Dale, on the Penistone line. A timber farm bridge crosses over the railway joining two of the farmer's fields. One season at muck-spreading time, old Giles was doing one side, and found that he had enough to make it worthwhile starting on the other. He was using one of those heaped wagons, with manure hanging over the sides, and a rapidly turning sling throwing it well away from himself and the tractor. While crossing over the railway, Giles made two mistakes. The first was in not turning the whirligig off, so spreading enriched muck all over the track formation; and his second slip-up was in stopping on the bridge to find out how much he had wasted, so enhancing his initial distribution onto the tracks. Ideally, in this tale, we should invent a train passing through this unique shower, but I cannot tell a lie – nothing came for a while, by which time Giles had passed clear.

If you read the first book in this pairing, you might recall Percy's bag of treated sewage having to be discharged from the step of a tram, so producing a richly verdant grass verge for many years to come. Much the same happened at Denby Dale. I believe to this day that there is a band of accidental garden under that bridge, easing off away from it on both sides. A half-hearted attempt by the track gang to clear the fertiliser failed for various reasons, not least being the abundant aroma.

Another very unexpected bit of gardening was once done in the wide space between the platforms at Huddersfield station, where a gang of relayers had been working. These bodies of men turn up prior to a track renewal to prepare for it, execute it at the weekend, and repair it during the following weeks. They have no particular affinity with any section of line, so it was all the more surprising when we found that they had artistically laid out a Christmas tree in various colours of ballast and track components in the midst of the station. Naturally, while passengers commented favourably and occasionally excitedly about it, and the local *Huddersfield Examiner* came to record it, there were movements among the stiff collars in head office to initiate disciplinary proceedings. Had time been wasted? Misuse of railway equipment... dangerous activity. Was a lookout man posted? They could get daft at times, and this the spirit of goodwill to all. A nudge towards a pal in the press was enough for this to be quashed.

Some stations are noted for their displays of flowers, both official and locally inspired. I have mentioned the efficient gardening force who had nurseries at Poppleton near York, producing displays for functions, and instant gardens to hide unfortunate things like toilet signs from the sight of royalty. They would also produce decorations such as hanging baskets and Christmas gardens, but many stations had proud staff who produced their own floral results, like at Selby, where old barrows and trolleys were decked in seasonal blooms.

Bill took a particular interest in the pictures of the Selby floral adornments that appeared in *Railnews*, the staff magazine. So much so that he cut them out and stuck them above his desk. It was some time before I smelt danger.

The first real threat appeared as a holed bucket filled with soil, and his last year's discarded Christmas tree. Until all the needles fell off, it just looked like a discarded Christmas tree, but brushing past the thing caused dead twigs to snap off and eventually it could no longer be distinguished as a discarded Christmas tree, rather as just a stick. It had suffered by both a lack of tender loving care, and from the fact that Christmas to March is a long time for it to survive on a garden dump. It was replaced by a few wallflower seeds, which were scuffed into the soil.

Bill made a horticultural breakthrough here in discovering that cold tea and the accompanying leaves thrown out from the pot was not a recommendable substitute for clean water. However, he claimed that the dandelion that appeared had to be a triumph. Other planters turned up as the local gang rescued them from the public tip known generally as the railway. Broken chimney pots, empty oil drums, kettles and a 1950s Silver Cloud perambulator all proved possibilities to the would-be Percy Thrower that was Bill. I gave what support I could, but we were sadly inadequate to the task of potted plant growing.

It was the pram, for some reason, that spoke to Bill. In its time it was a gem in child mobility, and sociable too, in that the enclosed child and its source of power faced each other, unlike today's pushchairs where the forward-facing child is there just to test the speed of the traffic. This pram had various knobs attached to the sides for supporting hoods or netting, or for fastening down waterproof covers. 'Borrowed' (a term Bill tended to use persistently, and which meant more correctly acquired, begged for or stolen) sink plug chaining was fastened to four of the projections. At the side of the offices there were two projecting pieces of metal, roughly in hook form. Such things were common in old railway buildings. Industrial archaeologists would search for their various origins with keen interest; to me they were of no consequence or allure, nor was the whole idea of a suspended pram forming a hanging garden. I managed to take no part in the project, despite Bill's sales talk, and as it was Jack Senior's office wall, I suggested Harry Hanson as an assistant, with Harry being well up in local gardening circles. Due to the generosity of the chain donator, the pram was suspended by about six feet, and settled at just over Harry's head height. Soil, with our sad experience of damp moorland peat, was collected from a dry disused embankment. The pram was filled by heaving up shovelfulls of soil, with about 40% not returning to earth. Two pieces of tumbling ivy were hopefully slung up last, followed by a couple of optimistic shovels to cover them.

There it stayed, unnoticed by Don, always landing by car, well past the wall end, and ignored by me. I mean, it wouldn't have been so bad if they'd bothered to take the handle and wheels off. As soon as the design team realised that they could not easily water it, their interest also fell away.

As a side issue at this point, have you any idea of the weight of

155

a pram filled with soil, and, over the space of a year, rainwater? The pram appeared to be perfectly sealed below, and didn't leak until after a thunderstorm, when water spilled over the top, showing that it was now most definitely full. Of scientific interest is the strength of four lengths of sink plug chain, as against the unknown support value of two ancient metal hooks attached to an old building wall. The sink plugs chains have it. First one hook and seconds later the other left their housings of years, causing the hanging basket to momentarily swing startlingly across Jack's window before landing with a great thump on the ground. To me it was now a little more convincing since the wheels had broken off on landing.

Bill, as stubborn as ever, emptied it, and fixed it with string onto Jack's outside window sill. It didn't look for one minute like a window box, only an old broken pram tied up on a window sill. Jack and Don, returning from a day out, definitely saw it as an old broken pram tied up on a window sill. It was duly taken down, but not before I was unjustly held in some part to blame. Bill was annoyingly about thirty years ahead of his time. Nowadays it would still be an old broken pram tied up on a window sill to some, but a prize-winning art exhibit to others.

Horticulture had long lingered in our spare time discussions as a small ambition. We had dabbled with it in the past with the monumental structure on Jack Senior's window sill (on the inside), but the effect of permanent late evening illumination in the office, brought about by the Forth-Bridge-like arrangement and the abundant foliage, produced an edict from Jack that he would prefer it if we regarded his window sill as set aside in future, inside and out.

Bill launched the discussion. 'Nothin' extravagant, tha knaws, just a small plot t'brighten things up a bit out theer.'

'What sort of things do you fancy, Bill?'

'Oh, ah don't know, them theer wot come up once when tha plants 'em. Whatjamacallums? 'Ardy hannals or summat.'

'We're not asking Harry again. I wasn't over sure about his muck formula – pure sheepshit with that there peat at t'bottom. No we'll bring some soil in with a few bags – *just* a few at a go.' I was remembering the last time we transported a fair chunk of Yorkshire by car in goodness knows how many bags. Don had got a new Anglia since then, and I wasn't going to let Bill's ambitions drop me in it again.

'Nay, just ord'nary muck this time, from t'bank side.'

'We'll have a chat with Wilf when he's next over – he's got a grand garden at home.'

'Harry's OK wi plants, ah reckon.'

'We'll still ask Wilf!'

In the meantime Bill was coming to work armed with gardening magazines, seed catalogues, books with glowing pictures of masses of varied flowers, rockeries, and even guides to some stately homes. They had balustraded balconies with trailing plants falling from them and covered in a kaleidoscope of blooms, rockeries bedded out with thousands of miniature flowers, shrubs of varying sizes and neat tight ones cut in the form of swans and the sort. One mansion even had an immense staircase in stone with water tumbling down it, leading to a lake with a huge fountain in the middle.

'I was thinking,' I told him, 'more on the lines of a box made of sleepers about three high, up against the outside wall.'

'Ay – but tha needs some ideas afore tha goes rushin' in. Ah mean, ah knaws we can't quite match up wi this fountain, but we could have a small one, like.'

'Where do we get a steady run of water?'

'Bloody hell, Mike! We're sat under abaht ten thousand gallons reet now!'

This was true, the office roof water tank being of generous dimensions; but I couldn't see how we could get a regular trickle out of it. However, I didn't want to upset his enthusiasm too much.

'What syza bed is tha thinkin' of, then?' said Wilf on his next visit with Percy. His mate was fairly useless in the debate, as Percy's garden was given over entirely to rhubarb, with a privet surround. Wilf's was a planned annual garden of masses of colour and varying height.

'Bill's thinking along the lines of a country estate rather than a plot. I have in mind coming out from the wall half a sleeper with two lengthways.' This would be about four foot by eighteen outside measurement, effectively three by sixteen of soil, hardly matching Bill's ambitions to foliate most of Huddersfield.

'Reet,' said Wilf. 'Ah can let thee have enough plants acos ah allus gets too many to use myself, so tha gets whatever ah've got goin' spare, OK?'

'Fine and very generous,' I told him, 'No tunnel work for six weeks for you!'

'Tunnels are OK, it's rain tha can keep mi out of! So ah'll tell thee what ah've got going. For t'back, up agin t'wall, annual dahlias and African marigolds, boot eighteen inch high. In front some French marigolds and ageratum, them's purpley, wi yellow and gold for t'marigolds, both sort, all colours for t'dahlias. Then along t'front we'll 'ave mixed lobelia, light and dark blue. Tha can get it to tumble and spread ower t'sleepers if tha likes. That should fill it up fine.'

'Sounds great to me.'

'No red-hot pokers, and sunflowers, and fewsher bushes, and flowering cherries trees, then?' commented Bill.

'Look, tha plot is this' one long pace, bi this,' said Wilf, measuring five easy paces. 'Tha's bahn t'need a bloody field for them such!'

'Jus' thought, that's all,' said Bill, after which he fell into a slight sulk.

'Mebbee a coupla sunflowers, if tha can get hold of 'em,' Wilf generously allowed.

Bill brightened up a bit. 'And watter, wi've got t'ave some watter runnin' someweer.'

'That's up t'thee; ah'm strictly flowers.'

For no specific reason, building work was delayed until Don went on a fortnight's leave. We were sure that he would have approved, but at times he ran short on imagination, and could easily mistake a garden construction site as an undisciplined heap.

Sleepers were duly sought out, arriving second to a load of old floorboards due to some error in Bill's off-the-record requisitioning. These were put aside in deference to Bill's philosophy 'that they'll come in for something'. They were eventually used to even up the timbers that were otherwise on a slope, running away from the wall. Why these had to be level was a mystery, but the floorboards were run in from the front in layers of one at the back and four at the front with their ends sticking out three feet beyond the sleeper line. I have realised in later years that we invented decking.

Considering the water, Bill had already suggested a siphon system from the tank on the roof.

'We'll need a pipe,' I hopefully suggested, for gaining time. As usual Bill did not stick fast, and within the day thirty feet of hose had appeared. I have to admit that up to then I was fairly happy about the project, but the water aspect left me cold.

I was now working to Bill's instructions and had given up thinking for myself. Carrying one end of an increasingly heavy rubber hose up a vertical iron ladder is a major feat; fixing it at the top while balancing on two very old planks is just short of plain daft. I submerged about six feet of it in the water, slightly above the century of sediment, and firmly attached it in a gap between the boards using a few huge staples – I was trying to make sure that I would not be called upon to perform a second trip. The hose ran well down the side of the ladder and was easily fastened to it by office string. At the lower end it slotted in between the sleepers and into the middle of the plot where it was threaded through a rail chair bolt hole, leaving about three feet rising centrally from the soil. As a control tap Bill had rescued a rail clamp used to hold temporary fishplates together. These are not like carpenter's clamps, except visually. In practice they are great lumps of iron, designed to hold fishplates temporarily to rail ends under normal traffic. Bill's was fixed to the ladder, using three pairs of hands, in such a position that when it was screwed closed it would squeeze the hose and in theory cut off the water.

This was all very fine, but the final phase of the siphon plan was now due – sucking water down it from the tank. Apparently I volunteered. I didn't actually hear myself volunteer, or have any memory of broaching the subject, but Bill was determined that I had volunteered.

It took a full dinner time to get the right mouthpiece fitted. Despite Bill's assurances as to the hose's history, I was not prepared to put mouth directly to pipe. Finally we got water, a procedure that always demands getting wet to some extent. With my thumb over the pipe end, Bill wound up the clamp screw until it was tight against the ladder. He cut the pipe just above the fixing chair and bound a watering can rose to it. A slight relaxing of the clamp proved that the siphon was working, and at the same time reassured us both once again that water is wet.

Next day the carrier bag of embryonic plants, which looked more like rejects than the results of over-sowing by Wilf, was brought to site and the pathetic limp seedlings planted. Initial watering was done with a kettle, mainly because I had one of my premonitions of doom. After a hectic week, Bill was ready to declare his fountain open. This was done in the presence of all the office, fortunately with Don's exception, though he had failed to see any harm in the project in principle, but without access to Bill's brain and the plans. Wilf and Percy had taken up a position that seemed to imply respect for others, but I could tell it was a reflection of their faith in anything Bill had conceived. Bill performed a dramatic little 'ten, nine, eight' etc. and began to unscrew the clamp.

We agreed later that the clamp should have been better secured, at least enough for it not to fall off altogether. We also agreed that the watering rose was not a good idea as it distributed water in a widespread and violent manner, rather than to merely allow a single spout. It was also brought home to us forcibly, that a 25-foot head of water was far too strong a force to cope with. Wisdom after the event picked out the need for the clamp to be some distance from the exploding rose, rather than well within its fallout area. All this we felt could have been better handled, including the publicity angle. This should have taken into account a platform fairly well filled with waiting passengers who were entertained by the spectacle of half a dozen grown men getting soaked by an impressively powerful fountain. They should have savoured this and retreated, because when the rose finally blew off, the now free-flowing swirling deluge reached new distances.

Panic does make people run round in circles, which in the prevailing situation merely ensured a continued creditable soaking for all. Every solution shouted around seemed to me impracticable, so I took matters into my own hands, shot up the ladder, and pulled the pipe out of the water until the siphon failed.

There were no recriminations, only a sense of sadness as the last of the seedlings floated off among the sidings and car park. Bill's vision of a miniature Chatsworth drifted off along with the plants, but the strangest thing was that he did not appear to be deflated at all – just the opposite. When Bill found something hilarious he would collapse in a fit of laughter and coughing. This he was now doing.

Seasons and Reasons

I've rattled on about buildings as having character, and I'll get round to character in other structures, like tunnels, viaducts and bridges soon. Here I'm looking, as an ex-surveyor, at how the seasons have character, especially where you have an Area with at least half the railway in unpredictable valleys. They go chelping away about tomorrow's weather on TV, after the news. (Sorry – that slipped out. For 'chelping' read 'chattering on aimlessly.) They tell you what the weather's been on the journey from home to the studio, and assume that the Shetlanders are really pleased or sorry for them. You get a very substantial idea of what they expect for the next day or two in and around London and its human reservoir, the south-east, while the entire expanse of Scotland is treated as one equivalent lump. Weather information is often provided as a direct proportion to the number of bodies under it on average, which I suppose is fair enough. Of course, it has to be accepted that they cannot mention all the many small locations that have their own peculiar rules, but the Vale of York is an exception. There, thick fog descends with the slightest provocation, and always gets a mention in the forecast, because it's a certainty. We at Leeds theorise that it is a result of all the hot air coming out of York Headquarters meeting the cool reality that is Leeds District.

Thinking of other local situations, the Colne Valley in particular laughs at the promised 'light breeze and occasional showers', since it has up its sleeve sudden bursts of gale force and menacing black clouds bubbling down from the Pennines and rolling along the valley, each primed with a torrential downpour. On the other hand, 'mild and sunny' for the broader area can mean belting heat reflecting off the valley sides and almost frying you as at the focal point of a radio dish. So on our Area at Huddersfield, the character of the weather tended to be a massive exaggeration of that of Yorkshire in general. Nowhere else on the Civil Engineer's

Leeds District was there such variety as on Huddersfield's patch.

With that in mind, this part might appear to end up as a set of excuses, but in reality *reasons* as to why I, or the other pedestrians of the railway tracks, did not always work as efficiently as we might. In fact it justifies much of our extra-curricular activities, as it could be argued that working out on the railway is beset by so many problems, you can hardly get anything done. To be fair to my customer, I must stress that what follows is not good light reading matter if you are subject to bouts of depression. It may be a bit dull, and you'll miss nothing much affecting the rest of the book, so you might find this a good moment to pop out and make a cup of tea. If you want a plentiful amount of talking, you have my permission to skip this chapter. However, there are no discounts in price if you do.

INSIDE AND OUT. BASES FOR COMPARISON:

Inside (Offices)

Winter: Closed doors and windows, rooms variously heated, slightly stuffy, pleasantly warm at around 70 °F.

Spring: Heating still on, windows opened at appropriate times, pot of daffs on windowsill. Locally in Huddersfield, once, and only once, tomatoes as well.

Summer: Air conditioning makes office a welcome retreat from outdoors, if you have it. I've heard of air conditioning, but have never experienced it in a railway office, unless you count doors and windows propped open and Jack Senior's fan in operation. No. 23 Wellington Street, Leeds, had virtual air conditioning due to the state of the glazed roof. This changed with the seasons, in winter being known as 'that frigging draught'.

Autumn: Occasionally heated with windows slightly open. On one particular unspecified day it suddenly defaults to 'Winter', above, except that the negotiated heating was brought into action on an agreed date, not temperature.

On the other hand, the railway surveyor outside:

Winter: Cold and damp, stiff and numb, in the worst of it.

163

Brass monkeys are nervously counting up to two, and polar bears are beginning to wonder if they really are polar bears because they feel so cold. Here on the railway we have the labourer, with a duet of conditions, shovelling and digging away, and forming a sweat, (confined within his coat) between himself and the outside world. Gloves protect the more delicate extremities, until the mid-period point where he has to dispense with them and unzip his flies for necessary relief up against the bridge abutment, or if conditions are suitable, challenged to writing his name in the snow. (Our old friend G B S Thorpe-Gardiner, the well-born relic from No. 23 Wellington Street, was extremely handicapped in this challenge.)

Now consider the surveyor. At best with fingerless gloves, he's operating dry sub-zero stiffened metal screws on his instruments and their supports. The early signs of frostbite are producing fine cuts and sores in the fingertips. He is trying manfully to pierce the frozen ground with the tripod legs and securing their adjustment screws. These have to be tight, and tight is what he has extreme difficulty doing just now. By the time he comes to the fine adjustments on the instrument itself, fingertips have transmuted from pink, through white and blue to near black. Steamy breath obscures the spirit level, the bubble now elongated with the contracted liquid. Involuntary tears ooze out and freeze on chapped cheeks. Needles of fine ice are stabbing his face and piecing his ears. A miserably cold damp breeze surrounds and eventually drenches the theodolite, his book and his back. He has to try and fight against this to see through the telescope and also to stand back far enough so that the tightly pulled down cap neb doesn't touch the instrument. The information then has to be transferred into his surveying book using what is an assumed pencil, so, because he can no longer feel it with his anaesthetised fingers. Should he be lucky enough to have some feeling in them, he will still not be controlling the pencil at all well while shivering. Notes in the book are also enhanced by the dripping stalactite-style glacier of unexpected dewdrops from the end of a numbed nose. Back in the office, he reads occasional clear figures, but has to indulge in some intelligent guesswork in the frequent smudged places.

Given a damp freezing day and a mile of levelling to do, only the chainmen get any exercise to speak of, and that's merely walking to the next survey point. Shivering approaches to the mounted instrument make occasional stuttering contact, disrupting the fine settings. These conditions will have to be suffered for at least two hours, before relief can be sought. Coming back in for dinner, you cannot handle the sandwiches for the lack of feeling in your fingers. Golcar's scalding hot pies with their molten juices are out of the question, as liquor would scorch an unfeeling throat. You can't easily chew with the pain in stiffened jaws, and the numbness allows you to burn your hands on the hot mug, and not notice it until later. Then follows the lingering stinging pain of finger recovery as feeling slowly returns to them. Coats are steaming gently on the backs of chairs, while trousers retain the characteristics picked up during two hours of exposure, with the hope that lack of sensitivity has not mistaken weather dampness for anything else. Everything slowly changes condition from soaking and bitterly cold to soaking and chilled.

Most miserable of all is the freezing fog, where the levelling staff disappears beyond fifty yards, involving more setting up and handling hostile knurled adjustment screws. Nobody wants to be there, and all want to be back in the office as soon as possible, so the slightest movement of the surveyor's hand is taken by the chainman as a sign that the reading has been noted, thus allowing him to march off to the next point, while you shout in vain to frowned upon balaclava'd ears.

Steel tapes are, without exception, several degrees colder to the touch than the surrounding air temperature, and the only benefit is that when you cut yourself on the fine edge of the rule, you don't feel it. In fact you know very little about it until you have wiped blood all over the survey book.

Sleepers, especially wooden ones, become lethal to the confident step as the air damp freezes in a very fine layer of ice. Carrying a level and legs over the shoulder makes you more vulnerable to slipping, as your centre of gravity is moved upwards. Torville and Dean you are not, neither are you humming Ravel's 'Bolero'. Walking in the cess at the side has its own problems in winter, as everything, including the meandering and treacherous bramble twines, has turned ashen-black and has become indistinguishable from the surrounding hostility of winter death.

The misery of the above is still capable of enhancement when all that accumulated weather has you enclosed in the black ice of a Saturday night. There you may have officially little part to play other than a bit of measuring out, or providing technical advice and observation. You fall easily for the temptation of an un-accustomed shovel or pick, with the threat of personal damage which that, and your cold uncoordinated limbs makes possible. Or sometimes, if you're lucky, a pneumatic hammer becomes available to augment the natural shivers. This, rather than wandering through the dark, damp, icy, stinging potential frostbite of simply watching. In reality the surveyor is at the peak of the choice pyramid. He has the acceptable option of spending much of the time in the cabin. Under him, the supervisor controls decisions as to when warming breaks can be taken, or if the weather is too severe for reasonable work – and at a weekend that severity has to be life-threatening. Lying at the base of the pyramid are the lads, with no control over their condition, and obeying the whims of those in charge. Very few technical staff have the nerve to take cover while the lads suffer, so the plight comes out as universal.

The pneumatic hammer was a one-off experience for me, breaking up the edge of a sharply curving disused platform at St Dunstan's, near Bradford Exchange, in order to improve track alignment. I had grabbed a chance with it while the lads had a tea scalding break. That was an interesting night, as around two o'clock the place was swarming with police – British Transport ones, thankfully. Two youths had decided to sleep rough in a string of carriages that had been run into St Dunstan's sidings from Exchange station after forming the last London train. Their search for leftover morsels had led them to face the dead body of a man in one compartment. After leaping out of the carriage, their unavoidable screaming had one of our lads, working only a couple of hundred yards away, investigating. The youths pointed to the coach and ran. Work stopped for a minute or so while we all had a look, before calling the BT police. Had we alerted the civil police, we knew that our job would have been stopped, as cordons were put up all round the site. However, scrupulous searching discovered a disorientated chap who had been sleeping off the half of the buffet car that he had consumed, and who should have left the train at Wakefield. He had slept through all the door slamming both there and at Bradford, along with our chattering hammers, to be aroused by a copper. This lad was somewhat startled when the corpse sat up and asked where he was, and traditionally of a policeman, what time it was.

In case you were getting comfortable while that story was in progress, let's go back to the character of winter weather. In its simple straightforward cold form, it had few problems for the trains. On jointed track you notice the usual clickety-click of the rail joints has become thumpety-thump, with the expansion gaps widening. It's only nowadays when you get the additional treat of snow that things might become iffy for the locos. (The surveyor wisely takes advice and stays inside at this time, as most of what he wants to survey, and the fixed reference points, are covered over… or that's his excuse.) But the mighty diesel engines have their unusual problems – made highly popular in the press – with 'the wrong kind of snow'. How the papers enjoyed that, along with the steam anoraks! Yet the explanation is simple if they could be bothered to listen, which the press can't because it's not news.

As I understand it, not being a mechanical engineer, fine, dry powder snow enters the grills in the loco body and in greater amounts gums up the works in a way that large damp flakes cannot. Yet while cars are sliding all over the road, the railway is expected to be unaffected. Heavy continuous snow can build up in point work, with the gas heaters valiantly fighting back and melting it in the immediate area, only for it to slide to the side and turn to ice. Before the advent of the heaters, all groundwork stopped for the PWay engineers as men were distributed all over the Area on snow duty, their job being to keep the points from clogging up. This used to be a dangerous occupation, and often a losing battle, with men working in conditions that they were normally advised to avoid, and with approaching traffic being virtually invisible and their sounds dulled in the snow. In the past, more attention was given to the protecting signal if it was visible, hopefully a semaphore, which can be read from behind. Modern signalling is useless in that it displays a 'cry wolf' green aspect all the time, unless a train has just passed.

Snow, and the surveyor stays put. It doesn't matter whether it's the crippling fine powder stuff, the Christmas card brand – all big, pretty and fluffy – or just sleet. All snow is dangerous for visibility, so work is restricted to the warm office, the gas heater and the kettle. Oh, and the drawing board, of course!

Frost, when particularly severe and combined with its associated stillness, could even beat the point heaters. These were initially propane gas fired, and during a stiff breeze were capable of being blown out and not reacting to the ignition sparks. I once experienced a situation where this had happened, and the gas lay heavily on the ground, in a widespread invisible blanket, not reaching nose level. Suddenly a spark worked, and there was an enormous *woosh* as cool flames shot across the whole area, fortunately causing no personal damage.

Frost also amuses itself by making levelling certain track tricky. It can freeze any damp under the sleepers and lift the track a considerable amount. You can get an inkling of this when stamping the tripod legs into the ground, and finding them resistant, until they break through a crusty frozen surface layer. It's very much like plunging a knife into an overdone rhubarb crumble.

Hard packed snow can be as supportive to the new railway as stone ballast. If it is tamped into new track during a frost, then come the thaw and the track levels are all over the place as the packed snow melts. I have discovered that wooden survey pegs, set to the final planned track level, rise up out of the ballast with the onset of a keen frost, thus becoming not only wrong but dangerously so. Weather, or its creator, certainly has a developed sense of humour, always poked towards the railway surveyor.

Safety boots, being as they were made up of steel soles and toecaps, during frost were like having your feet strapped into a couple of small refrigerators. After an hour out in them, toes were following fingers into rigor mortis. On the positive side, the edge of the toecap could no longer be felt chaffing the tops of numbed toes; back to the negative, and your socks wouldn't later come off, as they were welded to your toes by congealed blood along the line of the toecap edge.

We were discouraged from keeping our heads warm in hoods because of the safety aspect of being blinkered and not seeing or hearing, except forwards, so the all-weather cap was the only acceptable alternative. For ten years while out on Huddersfield Area, and doing my share of winter surveying and cold tunnel work, I took to growing a very effective full beard late on every summer, shaving it off at a carefully calculated moment in May. This practice ceased sharply one autumn when the first white hairs appeared. I was fully aware as to what my seasonal appearance would be by the time Christmas came round. Up to then it had been an excellent natural substitute for a scarf.

One secretly added luxury, used by many stationary technical lads, faced with the promise of suffering exposure, was a pair of their wife's tights. These, however, had their drawbacks when the night's four o'clock leak was needed. The lads had to retreat into the shrubbery and virtually get undressed, which knocked out all the advantage gained in the first place. There was one lad who admitted to wearing tights, but never had any undue trouble when it came to getting relief. We discussed how this was among us, and some amazing variations on the possible were suggested. However he did it, we were sure that he would have been deeply embarrassed were he to be hospitalised during the shift.

Spring: A season of treachery. The sun rises high in the sky, but is only partly effective behind the dark billowing clouds. If by chance it is dry, then the surveyor has no great excuses to stay inside. Now, though, the level or theodolite is being buffeted by gale force winds. Perhaps it's not moving visibly itself, but looking through the telescope shows that the small shifts in the wind are magnified to impossible limits on the target. Finding yourself in a cutting, and the wind has two choices – either to blow across the top of you at right angles to the line of the track, or deviate slightly to become a funnelled blast, bouncing off the bankings at the side. On top of an embankment or viaduct, whichever way the wind blows you've completely had it.

Wind is another real hearing danger. It's like having a couple of seashells strapped to your ears. If you have some reliance on the sound of the approaching train, the wind can, in the wrong direction, negate the horn or whistle. Sensible decisions have to be made as to the level of danger, and maybe when out on site, demand a return to base. Meanwhile, base itself looks out of its window at the fluffy clouds hurrying past, with intervals of warm sunshine, so that the failure to do the job of the day is looked on with some disdain. This is where you need the backup of your older chainmen who knew your boss when he was in your position some fifteen years earlier, and can talk to him with some authority and determination.

Stringing is the method of measuring the curvature of a piece of railway. This involves stretching a nylon line between two points on a rail, a chain apart, and then measuring the offset from the cord to the rail at the halfway point. Overlapping measurements are taken at every half-chain point. Blustery wind blows the string all over your measuring ruler, and a dangerous mean value is often guessed at. A steady directional wind is little better, in that readings are constantly higher or lower than they should be.

I don't know whether I'm still answerable for jobs I did thirty-five years ago, but there is a certain curve, about half a mile long, which carried a 50 mph speed limit. It was a raggedy curve, changing radii throughout, and Don Newell felt that it could be improved. Off I went with Wilf and Percy, and we strung the curve, noticing a regular breeze blowing across the site. What I didn't realise was that the versine readings of offsets were all about 3/10" too low, and the subsequent working out produced a curve fit for sixty, the line limit. Realignment to my scheme followed, and we proudly removed the ancient speed limit.

Train drivers enjoy such things, as it means one less instruction to remember, and they immediately took up the sixty, with their customary 10% addition. We noticed a certain amount of wheel and rail screaming as trains went round the new curve, but it didn't worry us unduly. A check two or three years later, locally, at a point where a new footbridge was to be installed, showed that the curve was still broadly fit for the original fifty restriction only. It is much easier to remove a speed penalty than it is to install one, and a lot of paperwork and explanation is required. Discussing it with Wilf and Percy, after we had discovered the error, led Wilf to the usual conclusion that 'It's near enough for t'Railway' – and sleeping dogs were left undisturbed.

For a period around the sixties, the March winds sulked. Progress was taking away the lineside telegraph poles and the invitingly vulnerable wires began to be replaced by troughed cables. There was nothing to blow down. Apart from that, when the odd phone wire was demolished, it didn't do anything too dramatic, like stopping the trains running, so it was just a bit of fun really. Then morale among the winds picked up significantly when, up our way, the nineties introduced a much more effective toy, in the overhead electric conductor wires. Tougher, and more of a challenge, the wind's greater efforts could now cause considerable real disruption.

In order to amuse itself in the gap years and beyond, there was always the challenge to the wind of bringing down an embankment tree. Growing in such a location obviously gave more stability up the hill than down, so that would be the chosen way to tumble – right across the tracks. In the 'olden days', signal wires running along the cesses might give warning of an obstruction as the signalman found he could not pull off his signals, and would sense danger. Now, nothing but a driver's alertness can spot a tree across the track ahead of him.

April showers could be great fun. They were most effective when you had reached the limit of the length being surveyed, and were about a mile from the car or cabin (should one be open). On deciding that this was not just a shower, but serious rain, you made up your mind to dedicate the next twenty minutes' soaking, to hiking back, with the leafless trees offering no protection from the deluge. It is then that you discovered that it was a shower after all, and the car or cabin was bathing in warm sun...

There is another act of weather deceit that I have experienced with April. Out on a rail stressing job in daylight, and expecting spring temperatures, there was no stretching gear on site. Rails were put up on rollers, and when they are at an acceptable temperature a chunk of overlapping rail was cut out for the two ends to be welded up, knowing that the condition of the rails is

171

stress-free because of the natural temperature. It was then that April sprang into action, a sharp shower cooling them down by at least 15 ° Fahrenheit. This meant that the small welding gap that you had made is suddenly an 8" chasm. Job stops, and overruns had to be reported to the Duty Engineer at home, sitting in a deckchair in his garden, bathed in sun, watching cheerful fluffy clouds bouncing along his horizon, and full of sympathy for your plight.

On occasions, spring could be benign, producing the odd day of gentle warmth, without the discomfort and surveying problems of summer. The survey would be a mile long, and was characterised by the small piles of clothing left under bridges as the work progressed. On the return journey to the car, the obligatory tie and pessimistic pullover were collected; another few hundred yards, the inevitable jacket, and finally the precautionary coat were reclaimed. This has been one of the few days in the year that are kind, comfortable and amenable to surveying. Such a day should be stuffed and mounted for future use.

Summer: Three months of happy surveying out among the hills of our two valleys, the Calder and the Colne. After sufficient experience, this young surveyor wears his sun-shielding cap and just rolls his shirtsleeves up, keeping his back protected from the deceptive heat of the sun. Embankments are a blaze of colour, and chainmen are generally in a benevolent and cooperative frame of mind. Leaving aside the times when the sun overdoes things and causes tracks to buckle, there can be nothing to hinder the surveyor, with good visibility, a gentle breeze and pleasant warmth. For once the tackle is friendly, and handles comfortably, as it has taken up the surrounding temperature; the pencil is apparent and the survey book dry. Perfect – or is it?

The theodolite and telescopic level are useless. Heat is shimmering off the cooking track, causing all but the closest target to dance wildly. Level readings off the graduated staff at fifty yards away, jump over a couple of inches, and it is impossible to guess a mean value. Trying to detect the nail set in the wooden peg, the theodolite is impotent, and cannot fix on the peg, let alone the nail stuck in its top marking the survey point. There is a constant feeling of leaking, as little rivulets run down the inside of your shirt. Damp starts around the bottom of your necessary cap, and drips onto the survey book, once more damaging its credibility. Your legs are damp, and you hope you know why. To cap it all, you have the draughtsman from York Headquarters with you who designed the scheme, and he's busily trying to work out, in a supercilious manner, how much longer the 100-foot steel tape is now, compared to when he did his survey at a much cooler temperature. The chainmen don't help. Any heated discussion between the surveyors and they are stretched out on the banking, with their caps over their eyes.

Did I mention the bankings being a blaze of colour? On the down side in steam days, track sides were also just ablaze, brought about by dropped ashes or sparks from passing locos onto tinder-dry grasses. Suddenly, as far as the surveyor is concerned, he's back in the days of fogs from a season long forgotten. The telescope fares as well at piercing through dense smoke as it does during the November panoramic disappearances. You may have picked 'gardening day' for your survey, in which case the gangs are deliberately lighting 'controlled' fires – that is, ones where the fire brigade are considered a close backup to fire brooms.

Then there's the hay fever. Running eyes blur the vision, and sneezing takes over from the winter dewdrop. This combines with the sweat droplets in merging the recorded readings. An explosion while handling the instrument, and it's knocked out of true. Certainly, in summer, you can feel to use your handkerchief, but its constant appearance acts as an unintended signal to the chainmen, meaning more running back and forth in order to bring them back under control.

There is a constant demand for drinks. Bottled water has just been invented for the gullible, but certainly not for the clear-thinking survey team, still less for the older chainmen, who cannot conceive of people actually paying money for what comes free out of the tap. Instead, large bottles of flavoured water were purchased (by the surveyor, 'who could afford it on his Sundays').

However, summer came with a physically nasty side to it. There was a tendency to produce violent downpours during thunderstorms. Locally, cutting sides were vulnerable, with mud flows down the sides of slopes and full-blown circular slips in embankments, especially when there was some inbuilt potential catalyst. Along the route of the River Colne, double lines had been cut into the valley slopes. When these were quadrupled, then a false embankment was tipped from the existing double lines, creating a frontier roughly down the centre of the formation where firm excavated ground abutted looser built-up material. Circular slips might give some warning, starting with a visible crack between the tracks, probably some time after the storms; whereas cutting slope surface slides would be sudden and immediately dangerous.

There is an enormous circular slip at Golcar, on the Huddersfield to Manchester line, where the made formation of the old Fast Lines is slipping very, very slowly down to the river. This can be seen today as a huge bulge at the bottom with a loss of level at the top, and a 5-foot drop in the adjacent footpath and railings running alongside the railway (originally). For the non-railway person, the slip is to be seen face on from the A62 at Linthwaite, looking across the valley. Take your camera in case it finally goes after forty years, with you watching it!

Summer trees are now full and heavy with leaves, so the merry seasonal storms would add to the burden. Hence, on branch lines, the wet trees would overhang the track. There would be a disconcerting scrunching noise all the way down the train as it passed through tree-lined cuttings.

Unlike the spring winds, the summer sun was always direct in its disruption. It closed the expansion gaps covered by slotted fishplates and caused buckles at these joints. Misalignments, which are PC track buckles, and discreetly referred to as such, were much more common in my earlier days when mostly 60-foot panels of track predominated. Track ballast was either ash or light power station slag, which slowly disintegrated under traffic. Continuous welded rail, ironically without expansion gaps, is much stronger, as the rails are artificially tensioned to be stress-free at normal summer temperatures, and the track has now become more of a structure.

The Engineer had a seasonal planning problem about now, especially in the close-knit communities of the West Riding. Calculating his Sunday manpower was a nightmare, since one fortnight in the summer would be Huddersfield holidays, another Halifax, and yet another Dewsbury. These were when all the mills in one locality closed down together, and the tradition hung on after many had closed down permanently. This parochial shutdown resulted in great chunks of his workforce locally being away for two weeks. Fortunately, no two overlapped, so he could reliably work out where planning manpower must be avoided. For once, religion played a part in the availability of manpower on Sunday. Hallowed to the extent that having a holiday at Christmas is, was the weekend of the rugby league cup final. All season, games were played pretty well within travelling distance of each side; then suddenly, the most popular game of the year was held 'dahnsath', necessitating a weekend stopover. This marked another dead Sunday for planning work.

Autumn: Perhaps the surveying team's happiest season. It still held a gentle summer warmth, without causing too much shimmering heat to rise from the tracks. Storms were now rare, and so were slips and landslides. Rails scarcely reached an overstressed state and everything was fine. Sadly not. The infamous leaves now fluttered down onto the rails, decomposed, and mixed with light rain to produce what is apparently the most effective lubricant known to man. In these conditions the lighter diesels are sorely troubled. I cannot recall leaves upsetting the heavy steam locos – they only faltered under large loads and steep gradients when combined with signal stops. Just one wheelspin could gouge out a deep curve in the rail head. Rails had to be changed as the fault became a thumping point for subsequent traffic, severely testing the strength of the metal. Small lightly loaded diesel unit wheels can spin wildly and produce a small indentation in the rail. This has then to be watched as a possible cracking point. Such trains are reminiscent of the roadrunner cartoons, where a figure would be shown with whirling legs, before suddenly getting a purchase on the road, and shooting off screen.

The term 'autumn' means that planning a week ahead, for booking chainmen, is awash with problems and possibilities. October has on occasions burst out in surprising 'Indian summers', for only a week later there to be night frosts and freezing drizzle. It is a fraught time for the surveyor, still hanging on to the summer-style clothing, and finding himself grossly underdressed for a spell of open air work, standing still levelling.

We are now drifting into the peace of late October and November. Traditionally, fogs should be the blight. In the enlightenment of cleaner air, these are rarely troublesome nowadays. Combine this with the much more effective signalling, and there is little, if any, disruption to traffic. Not so up to the late twentieth century. No work would be done, partly because of the danger of not being able to see, but also because every man would be out on fog duty. A little sentry box and coal brazier was set up under vital signals, each with a man in it along with a sack of detonators. He had to be constantly on watch, looking up at the signal arm, and laying his detonators in accordance with its position. With this being twenty feet up in the air, it would be further obscured by the drifting smoke from the fire. In practice he would have tied a small rag to the signal wire, and sitting reasonably comfortably, would only react when the rag moved. Some fogmen of advanced thinking and innovative ideas made scientific advances on watching the wire move, by balancing a tin can between a stone and the wire, so being able to give the newspaper full attention until the can was heard to bounce off. There's many a telecommunications engineer that could learn from this.

Surveying was out of the question, but there was still a need to go out and mark up the weekend's work, assuming that the fog would not last that long. In these conditions I found the work nerve-wracking. Even with an alert lookout man, it took a second or two to get clear of the tracks, and a 60 mph train only appearing when fifty yards away could be most disconcerting.

December brought us full cycle, and the reader must wonder whether we got any work done at all the previous year. That reader who has absorbed Book No. 1, with all its little sidelines, will now be certain that we never ever got any real work done. Don Newell, here reading about those days when he was not around the office, and by now retired into his comfortable seventies, must be wondering at the effectiveness of his powers of supervision in those days long ago. Fear not, Don! 'Play hard and work hard' was our motto! At Huddersfield, we always had the option of escape into tunnels. It is a little ironic that to the general public, the thought of finding life easier in the supposedly hostile environment of a tunnel must engender doubt, but the actual case was that on a safety and relative comfort basis, you were better off than out on the open tracks. Not that it's always that simple in the tunnel. All levels and theodolites had cross hairs marked on the lens that showed up admirably out in daylight. In a tunnel, at some distance, locating the marks against the thin light of the measuring staff and its surrounding blackness was nigh impossible. It was like trying to see the whiskers on a black cat down a coal mine at one hundred yards! Yet the tunnel is still the better place to be in general. The trouble was that if you weren't on Huddersfield Area, you'd very few tunnels to escape into.

Which of course reminds me of the special seasonal treats mostly peculiar to our Area. Summer tunnels and winter ones can be very different animals. There used to be mixed feelings about tunnel work on hot sunny days. Whereas you could escape from the heat and the dancing theodolite, you could feel a bit cheated that you were not enjoying that sunshine.

Winter tunnels were generally frigid holes, although at times of sudden temperature loss outside, the tunnel could retain a little warmth. This would be visually enhanced when a steamer slid by as you stood clear in a refuge in the tunnel wall. Initially, red smoke from the funnel would be followed by a split-second belt of heat from the footplate, contributing to a psychological warmth. This would be immediately dashed by the subsequent draught caused by the train, as it pulled in the rest of the world's shivering cold.

Wet tunnels were so all the year round, and the dripping water was either cold or colder. Also, water is wetter in winter than it is in summer. Damp seemed to come in lengthy patches, where underground streams might have been attracted in through the roof. On timber sleepers there was an ever-present opportunity to go arse over tit without any warning, as the dropping water combined with the soot of ages to produce yet another perfect lubricant.

Tunnel shafts were either impotent at producing updraughts

or over-brilliant. This meant a local enhancement of the general ambience before and after the vent. In near-surface tunnels, where the shafts almost naturally lit up the railway, there was a temptation to set up camp there when surveying. Many a time a deceitful little device called a ring dam would come into play. This was a channel built around the base of the shaft, supposedly to catch water. It managed this fairly well, only to discharge it at some point of blockage, in waves onto the track and disillusioned surveyors. Moving a moment away from the natural conditions, there was an added risk at the bottom of near-surface shafts, as the Great General Public imagined signs on the exposed upper portion marked 'General Litter Dump'.

A cold winter tunnel often had an unrelenting biting draught throughout its length, when the wind was in the right (or wrong) direction. Outside you would get gusts and calm. Inside it was reliably constantly cold, with the occasional damp area multiplying the effect. Pleasant enough in summer, tunnels could become real ice holes in winter.

At the ends of many tunnels would be the accompanying viaduct or high embankment. I was to find out for myself later, after leaving the railways behind, that wind speeds increased dramatically with exposed height above ground level. In the wild depths of the 2000/1 winter, I had the opportunity, which turned into a job, of climbing our 180-foot high church spire, by way of scaffolding, in order to photograph restoration works in progress. While there was a slight breeze on the ground, only fifty feet up this could become a howling gale, producing a questionable situation as to whether it was safe for the men to work. Viaducts have the same effect.

I am told that the Ribblehead Viaduct is such because an embankment in that spot would encourage winds so strong up the valley that they could blow a train over. A viaduct is an embankment with holes in it. Unlike the tunnel, it doesn't matter which way the wind is blowing, it's giving the surveyor and mounted instruments far too much wallop for accurate working. And another thing: why are winds so much colder a few feet from the ground? Everything conspires to make surveying life impossible. Hence, the inevitable conclusion about the working ability of the railway surveyor is that at all the time he is at the mercy of the season, leading to a reason.

So that proves it, m'lud; in general, working on the railway is next to impossible.

Trials

We'd had field trials on the Area before, usually because we had the necessary facilities. Take Standedge single tunnels, when they wanted to have pressure tests in connection with the proposed Channel Tunnel. That we could understand. But considering that the Area Engineer's Office at Huddersfield contained the most cosmopolitan collection of reactionaries, traditionalists, crackpots and mischief-seekers, it remains a mystery why we were constantly being selected to carry out tests and trials on innovative ideas. This in areas where our situation was not particularly peculiar compared to other candidates.

How about the glue, for example. The very word conjures up potential for tomfoolery. On the track, the running chainage, and the cross-level cants, were usually marked by small cast iron plates nailed to the sleepers. As concrete began to take over, we were asked to try out this newfangled epoxy resin glue stuff, as yet unavailable to the public, for sticking the iron castings to the concrete. Chainages had often been left to the ganger to paint up on the trackside, and you'll still see old numbering on fence posts, retaining walls, trees and under platforms. These were marked out between quarter-mile posts, which had been carefully located; but it often happened that if at a particular point there was a total absence of a post or tree to paint a number on, then the marker would walk on until he did find something, so mucking up the integrity completely. (In a moment of devilment, acting under strict instructions before a programme inspection, one ganger could find no suitable point to mark up on, and ended up painting a large 26 on a cow, one of those marble cake sorts, while distracting its attention with a bunch of grass.)

Eddie O'Brien, setting off from the 39 milepost at Mirfield, managed to confuse himself with a conviction that the 66-foot chain was 26 sleepers long. It very nearly was in the days of ancient certainty when 60-foot lengths had 24 sleepers to each panel. But Eddie was working on continuously welded track where sleepers could be 26, 28 or even 30 to a length, and so he introduced for the first and last time long welded expanding chainage. He took advantage of a continuous low retaining wall, and adorned it with figures eighteen inches high, in brilliant white. Marking up a particularly bold 75, he realised that the 40 milepost, at 80 chains, was only just in sight, and he must have been marking short chainages all the way so far. To compensate, he determinedly increased his paces to 30, 36, 45 and a maximum of 52 to make it fit. Gangs relied on these numbers for entering on their bonus sheets, and Eddie's gang soon discovered that they could earn a lot more nearer Mirfield than they could a mile away, near the 40 milepost.

Bill Boyes, as office man, storekeeper, correspondence clerk and uninhibited disruptive monkey, took delivery of the glue, and eagerly checked what he'd signed for by opening the packages before either Don or I arrived. There were two boxes, marked A and B, each with a quantity of plastic sachets, with instructions to mix one of the golden syrup in A with a similar pack of the disgustingly suggestive off-white creamy stuff in B, stir together, and use within five minutes. It was like dropping Smarties in a nursery school playground and expecting none to go missing. Also included in the experimental pack were a quantity of plastic cups and spatulas for mixing.

Before I could get out to have a crack at using the stuff in various conditions (exposed track, oil-soaked station areas and tunnels, etc.), half of it had gone missing. On the very first morning Harry Hanson's high stool, tucked under his desk, became permanently attached to the floor, my tea mug, unusually filled up by Bill from a teapot, divorced itself from its handle as I tried to lift it off the lino-topped drawing desk and Tommy Avison's dinner-time apple was defying Isaac Newton's convictions by stubbornly refusing to come down from the ceiling. Don's lavatory seat lid remained up forever, and the front row of items in Jack's stock cupboard left the shelf and swung out, firmly fixed to the doors,

Tommy took a table and chair to get himself near enough to cut slices off the exposed areas of apple, and Bill reunited handle and mug using, as he put it, 'This brilliant glue wot we've just bin sent!' The mug now had a permanent ring of linoleum extension, giving it extra outside depth, and the desktop had a corresponding circle missing, a situation repeated four times in the case of Harry's stool. Bill 'repaired' a pair of his shoes by fixing a layer of brown lino to the sole. He now found that he could see over walls where he couldn't before, and also proceeded to trip up every time he encountered the outside step. From the introduction of the glue, the kettle had to be filled through the spout, and the cup and saucer Don saved for special visitors had become a unit 'in case one bit gets lost'. Although I was sure that Bill's investigative interest had by now been satiated, I hid what was left of the new glue in Don's car.

My first proper try out was with Wilf and Percy, but only out of necessity. The two of them combined were no more than twice as trustworthy at taking it seriously as Bill had been back in the office. I'd picked a length of concrete track where we could back the car up to a gateway in the fence, and use the boot as a mixing base. It all started off sensibly, but as tradition demanded, got silly. The further away we had to take the mixture, the faster we had to move with it before it set, until we found ourselves managing only one marker per mix, one step from total failure. If we carried the packets and mixing plant out to site by way of a jacket pocket we found that a peculiar permanent sticky residue from the resin seeped among all the fluff and valuables therein, haunting us for weeks after.

'Bugger this for a game of soldiers,' said Percy eventually. 'Why don't we just empty ten of this treacle inter one cup, and ten of the come juice inter another, an' mix 'em as we need 'em?'

'We need to keep the amounts exactly right for mixing.'

'Easy! Birra this an' a birra that! Mix 'em up straight on t'back of t'thingummy, and Bob's yer uncle, t'job's a guddun. Come on.'

It seemed OK as an idea, but it wasn't long before the 'birras' became 'lotsofs', and we were getting the two gunges everywhere. Things came to a head, literally, when Wilf found he couldn't get his cap off without a selective haircut, and Percy had a problem blowing his nose. The three of us had covered half a mile, but when it came to tackling further sites, I decided I'd cope on my own. Results were certainly impressive, but the idea of trusting full-scale onslaughts to the gangs, and the latent inventive genius within – well demonstrated by Bill – was felt to be not on. This was brought home to me when we handed some out to Bill Hargreaves, our PWay Supervisor at Dewsbury, who apparently mixed ten of A with ten of B in his tea mug, using his pipe as the stirrer, and successfully fixed twenty iron plates before ending up with a unique piece of art nouveau. This spent the rest of his working life on his window sill, entitled 'A Pipin' Mug Of Tea'.

Another innovation we were to test-fly at Huddersfield was the first electronic calculator. It was the size of a transistor radio, and cost an astronomical £68 in the late '60s. We persuaded the higher levels that it would save time and money, which is the language that speaks volumes to them. We wanted it to help out on one of my most boring jobs – the quarterly assessment of the masses of data churned out by the track-recording vehicle. These came in groups of figures for each quarter mile, along with the graphical traces, and I had to make some overall sense of the data. I'd bought one of those bygones to help, a mechanical tin calculator with a series of slots and sliding cogged inlays for hundreds tens and units, and so on; the sort of thing that turned up in *Innovations* magazine, and minor adverts in newspapers: 'Miracle calculator; does away with fingers and thumbs'. It was a laborious and unreliable piece of tackle, which destroyed pencils by the dozen (they were the only thing which fitted the slides to move the toothed bits up and down, once you'd lost the original metal probe).

The calculator, on the other hand, which had to be plugged into the mains, via a transformer, was immensely popular.

'Bloody hell, Mike, this is reet handy! Sithee, Wilf, toooo… plus threeee… eeequals… five! It's brilliant!'

'It may come as a surprise to thee, Percy Kellet, burra got theer abaht ten seconds afore thee!'

'OK, try three… nine… four… seven… two… eight… plus six… five… nowt… nine… nine… sithee… four five nine eight two seven. There, ah berra bet thi that time!'

''Ow dusta knaw it's reet, then?'

183

'Look, ah'll show it thee on paper; what were it ah said? Three seven two... no, 'ang on...'

'Ah could've done it bi now, though! It's useless!'

Wilf's dismissal did nothing to stem the flow of visitors who'd heard of our new machine, and came in a steady stream to confirm that five and six added up to eleven, and similar mathematical certainties. Some even went into the heady world of multiplying seven and nine, progressing thereafter, as Percy had, to exotic six-figure numbers. They'd then gaze at the split-second answers, without a clue as to whether they were right or not, or what they were going to do with them now they'd got them. Bill tumbled to tapping 71077345 into it, and turning the display upside down. It was beyond me, but this seemed to add to the amazement of the various worshippers at the numeral shrine.

Once we'd tested and proved it, the calculator was passed round the four Area Offices on a rota basis, and occasionally booked by the Central Drawing Office in Leeds for especially long calculations. It all seems a long way away from the promotional playing card calculator I've got in my pocket as I write, given free (though, admittedly, most of the numbers have now rubbed off their pads).

★

BR's Research organisation at Derby wanted four different types of rail grease testing. This is the stuff that is plastered onto the baseplates supporting the moving switch rails in point and crossing work, to ease movement. Traditional grease eventually failed after heavy rain, or became relatively ineffective in frost. On heavy freight routes it was often contaminated with droppings from the wagons, such as coal dust or fine sand, producing a paste rather than a lubricant. Huddersfield Station area P & C work, perched as it was atop a viaduct, combined heavy freight and a full range of weather to perfection.

I painted up the point end sleepers as to which grease was to be used where, picking four sets of switches per sample. The station gang was clearly instructed on what to use and where to use it. Their ganger dutifully negotiated extra bonus time for the buggeration of having to lug four different grease buckets around, so everyone was happy. Plenty of the four greases were supplied, more than enough for the amateur mechanics among us to fully satisfy their instincts to take home their percentage of railway property before the railway used it all, so everything was set fair for a winter of scientific analysis.

Don was required to examine the test beds once a fortnight, and assess the condition of grease under all of the point rails. So on fine, dry, sunny, mild days, at approximately two weekly intervals, he would potter out and take a look, no doubt all the time aware of his name going forward for inclusion in a high-powered report, in the process collecting one or two Sunday School attendance stars to stick on his career record. (On wet, windy cold days it turned out to be my turn to go out and do the assessments.) My main involvement – and here it suddenly becomes interesting – was the simple job of manning the small weather station which came with the tests, on a daily basis, come rain, sun, wind, snow or frost, including weekends on a rewarded 'voluntary' basis. Derby wanted a comprehensive record of all that their various greases had had to survive.

The apparatus consisted of a rain collector, a maximum-minimum thermometer, a rather basic sunshine recorder and an unconvincing little wind gauge. The rain monitor was a copper cylinder, about twelve inches long, surmounted by a funnel leading into a measuring glass tube, familiar from chemistry lessons. Temperatures on the thermometer were taken at five feet above ground level, so it had to be attached to a stout wooden post. Maximum and minimum readings could be read off as each tube of the apparatus had a small metal spring in it, which rode the mercury, or was left behind as it retreated. Everything could be reset using a small, supplied magnet, which I confiscated immediately to keep it safe from… well, bluntly, from Bill.

Sunshine was recorded on a piece of graduated paper wrapped round a clockwork rotating cylinder, under a bird table affair. Indeed, it was often adorned with breadcrumbs and bacon rind when I came to take readings.

The whole miniature scientific weather station might just as well have had a large notice board planted within it, bearing the invitation, 'Please muck about with me!'

I had doubts from the first mention of the idea, only because of the mischievous morons I had to work among, led by the evil little master himself. This was all justified on the second day when I noted that after a few hours of light drizzle and a weak north-westerly breeze, the apparatus informed me that we'd had twelve inches of rain, with temperatures soaring into the low nineties. What's more, the water in the rain gauge was still tepid when I tipped it out, obviously introduced from the office kettle. On the third day, following a 12-hour downpour, only 1/10" was discovered; this was itself remarkable, seeing as the night-time temperature had apparently dropped to minus fifteen at one point. Then an overnight flurry of snow, leaving the ground barely covered, had managed to concentrate its efforts into the rain gauge to the extent of suggesting 6-feet-deep drifts. One day was particularly notable, what with the sunshine record paper catching fire during a day-long dismal fog.

These recorded extremes of weather continued through the first two weeks of the experiment and coincided with the appearance of a watering can, a small magnet and a large magnifying glass behind Bill's desk. How he manufactured storm force winds escaped me until I overheard him giggling to Jack about the wife's hairdryer, but by then I hardly cared. I'd discovered early on that precipitation on Huddersfield consisted of a very large variety of liquids, some of them slightly corrosive or disgustingly smelly, and I soon learnt to handle the measuring container with gloves. It was the purloined parking sign set at the side one morning that concerned me, with its invitation to 'P here'.

I think that the last straw came for me when Bill casually dropped a match into the cylinder of last night's rain, causing an effect somewhat similar to an oil well going up. With Don's reluctant approval, I moved the weather station some twenty miles, into my own back garden, and the winter settled down to one of monotonous normality. Bill tried to help, now, by suggesting that to obtain a truly scientific situation, by taking home the four greases and treating four of our back garden steps with each one.

'After all, tha's teken t'measuring tackle home, so tha needs t'grease summat in t'same hole for proper testing. Just daub up each step and see which one tha tumbles dahn t'most!'

All the results, amounting to a daily record of measured readings over 4½ months, together with Don's observations on the ground, were carefully written up, and in late March, my leader went over to discuss the various greases with the gang. He was quite put out when they at first appeared ignorant as to what he was talking about. But he went limp when the ganger lit up in recognition.

'Oh, them theer tins of jollop they gev us a month or two back, tha means. Oh ay, we tried 'em like tha sed, but they was all bloody rubbish, so we went back to t'old stuff what we allus used, after a coupla weeks!'

Results were still sent in to Derby; all the weather records, and Don's observations – his minute distinctions now appearing remarkably inventive since we'd discovered that all the greases were one. Control observations on other points openly using the old grease were put down as marginally better, and the ganger's considered blanket assessment of 'bloody rubbish' was carefully translated variously as 'ineffective', 'poor', 'disappointing' and 'unsatisfactory'. None of the four new lubricants found its way into service. Is this the way of scientific tests involving the public, then? So what price *Which*? and the Consumer's Association? Perhaps they don't have impish prats and reactionary spoilers on their books.

★

Everything you take for granted nowadays was a novelty at some time or other – like the epoxy resin glue – and like polystyrene foam. I can't remember when foam entered our lives, but once it became readily available, the construction industry leapt at it. It was handy as formwork for concrete laying, particularly where a hollow or hole was needed. Take electrification masts, for instance. To set them in a base of concrete, simply use the foam block where the mast will eventually stand, surround it with concrete, and dissolve the foam – forming an instant slot for the steelwork.

Jumping a little bit on to the York remodelling, one day while we were all assembled in the site office, previously the Selby

Diversion HQ, polystyrene raised its head. The works supervisors next door were using some to enable concrete to be poured into large and convoluted shapes. Polystyrene blocks were the answer, cut to the unfriendly shape of the ends of the bridge parapet girders. The idea was to use the blocks as a kind of formwork to lay the girders up to, and when everything was in place, to dissolve the polystyrene and pour concrete into the void remaining. There suddenly came from the Works Office uncontrolled and hearty laughter. In time one of them came through, followed by their wagon driver. The supervisor was still in hysterics.

'What's up?' we asked between peals of laughter. The job and the use and purpose of the polystyrene was explained.

'You ever worked wi these foam blocks, Mike?'

'Only once, but that was for keeping muck out of drain manholes while we were digging in Morley Tunnel. They were only crude, not precise like those you have in bridgework.'

'We've just got some back that're really precise, for Bridge 104, what we're workin' on at the moment. Irving were given t'list for ordering by Leeds, so he had no measurin' up to worry over. Bloody big things, though. Biggest were two an' 'alf metres by one. Sent t'lorry down this mornin' to Derby where they cut 'em to order. We thought that it might mean two trips, they were so big, and I were worried over keepin' 'em held down – could jus' see 'em flying off of t'back, cos there's nowt to liftin' a metre cube, y'know. Light as a feather. Any road, he's just got back. Just as ah feared, there were nowt in't back, only this on t'passenger seat...'

The driver felt inside his jacket and pulled out a small poly-thene bag. It was full of minute perfectly shaped pieces of foam, cut into cubes and variations of cubes.

'It's Irving! He's hardly bottomed feet an' inches, let alone metres. Only ordered everything as centimetres instead of metres! Bloody gurt lurry all t'way to Derby and back, for this! Harry here were wettin' hisself when he brought these in!'

We first came across foam in an experiment we'd to set up, trapping oil in a bay platform drain at Huddersfield. I'd drawn up a catchpit at the end of the drain having two separate chambers, with a way for the water to run from one to the other through a hole at the bottom of the divider. The idea was that oil and water would run into the first, with the oil coming to the top, and the water running through into the second half and away. This was done to separate the oil, and to soak it up with this specially impregnated foam that we were trying out. It was loaded into string bags and dangled in the mixture, and regularly changed. As with all such things, regular meant three times on a weekly basis, then again after a couple of weeks, then a month later, and after that whenever someone thought on. But the foam, when it was delivered in large three by two cardboard boxes, was a novelty – the first we'd ever come across. It therefore had to be useful in many ways yet to be discovered.

The first box, by tradition, was devoted to personal use and experiment. After we'd ripped open the lid, Bill piled in and stuffed three carrier bags with the foam. It smelt a mite peculiar, and left some sort of colour on your hands. Later they itched a bit, but all these new materials did.

'Ah'm none too sure abaht this foam stuff,' said Bill, a day or two later. 'Tried it on our drive to soak up t'oil stain. Can't see as owt's happened, 'cept for next door dahn gettin' a load of foam blown among his roses. Telled him it were a mulch, and would blend in given time. Seemed happy 'nuff. Burrit's doin' nowt for t'oil on t'floor!'

'Maybe it'll be OK for getting any fresh up as it drops.'

'Mebbe, but how does ah get it to stay put? First puff of wind and it's away! 'Sides, ah've tried it on fresh oil. Dipped it inter some sardine oil ar lass spilt on t'table. It were still gainer to go and get t'dish clout t'wipe it up. Ah'm not ower struck on t'stuff! Oh aye, and ah tried rubbin' it inter our young 'un's greasy hair, cos he uses a barrer load've soap when he's washin'; jus' thought it might sam a bit up, like, so's he didn't need to soap it as much. Didn't seem t'mek much impression, though! Tried some in t'cat's box, but it nivver took to it. Done nowt but chase its bum round since, daft article!'

'Have you tried it on your hands, instead of Swarfega? That should work, as far as I can see.'

'Is theer much left in t'box?'

'No, we're near down to t'bottom. I reckon I ought to fill up this string bag thing first and try it for what we got it for. Help us get the last up before we have to open another box.'

Bill obligingly plunged into the box, head and shoulders, scraping around, while I stuffed the string bag with whatever he could get out.

'Ay, theer's a note at t'bottom 'ere. We must've opened t'wrang end! Happen it'll tell us just what this stuff will do! Here.'

'It says, "Warning! Do not allow the chemically impregnated foam to come into contact with skin. Keep out of eyes. Do not breathe in. Keep away from plants and animals".'

Bill pulled himself out of the box. 'Ah think ah'll just go wash mi hands.'

'You've got some in your hair as well, Bill,' I said.

★

We will now have a short period for reflection.

I have described how we on Huddersfield Area were chosen to test-fly so many new products that today are taken for granted. Epoxy resin glue and repair pastes are massed on the shelves of the DIY shops, yet we played with the first batch ever released, sticking everything to anything, occasionally usefully. Computer technology introduced the pocket calculator, and the first model (only describable as 'pocket' so long as you were a kangaroo) was purchased at enormous cost, to be tried out in the Huddersfield Drawing Office, and later passed around the District.

As to the point grease, it's perhaps best to draw a veil over that. We tested it, or thought we had, and declared it to be in chocolate fireguard territory. Then there was the foam in its various forms, tried in many ways until the really practical usage emerged. And let's not forget the Channel Tunnel trials, held in Standedge single line tunnel, which proved beyond any doubt that it would never be possible to take trains through because of air resistance, should it ever be constructed.

There's just one more thing that we were presented with, which today is as common as muck: reflective strips. Postmen, road workers, bike pedals, unsuccessful burglars, they all have them now, worked into their fabric. We had them first.

Lamps in tunnels varied in effectiveness. Despite the remarks of my re-emerging colleagues, I was not of the age where I had to walk tunnels with a candle stuck to my cap neb. I came to darkness in the age of the old paraffin Tilley lamps, with their sensitive components. They used to light up a large area of tunnel wall to a very comforting extent. When they died for lack of pumping, or blew out, or the silken gauze mantle covering to the flame disintegrated, comfort turned to panic. A fireside glow transformed instantly into complete and lonely darkness, followed by disorientation. With the battery lamp, at least fair warning was given of failure, but this had a sort of laser-like beam in comparison. However, both lamps were next to useless at picking out tunnel refuges built into the walls, where two men could easily stand clear – or in haste, three. These were the days when the woofter was an animal yet to be discovered by the ordinary man-in-a-tunnel, and momentary close contact with others was not a cause for alarm. On the approach of a train, you had to walk along the tunnel, shining your lamp at the wall, until a sudden indentation materialised, and in you stepped.

Now here was one case where it was acceptable that Huddersfield Area should road test luminous material, with us having more than our fair share of tunnels. L-shaped plates of aluminium were fixed to the far edge of the refuges, in the direction of walking, prior to the delivery of the sticky-backed reflective plastic. This came in rolls, like table top and shelf coverings, and was made up of millions of minute glass crystals entrapped in the surface. It was most unspectacular when looked at in normal light, appearing as a rather dull cream colour. I will ever recall the day I walked with the sub-inspector, tearing off the backing paper from pre-cut sheets, and sticking them to the wall plates. At the end of the run we turned round, shone our torches down the tunnel, and every refuge suddenly sprang to life, inviting us in to their individual safety. What's more, they only required a damp cloth once a year or so, with the traffic now being diesel.

OK, so we've got a success on our hands, but it, like every other innovative substance or material, had to pass through the alternative experimentation of Bill Boyes. First to the office in the morning, and first to open the packaging, Bill had not sat idly doing some useful work. By the time Don and I arrived, the dark passageway between offices had been delicately picked out in reflective tape. Bill was jumping around in childlike glee, and as we entered he turned out the light. He used a handlamp to pick out every little detail of the corridor, adorned as they were in reflective tape. It looked like two dozen black cats down a coal mine.

The sink taps stood out like chapel hat pegs. Doorknobs were immediately identifiable. So were the kettle, the gas ring, the row of coat hooks and the toilet flush handle. For some reason the light bulbs required to be identifiable in Bill's mind, though he'd forgotten why when questioned. Keyholes were surrounded as were light switches. Turning the electric light on and all these features appeared a dull creamy colour, as the tape lost its effectiveness.

'How many rolls have they sent us, Bill?' enquired Don, looking at the best part of one plastered around his corridor.

'Twel... er... ten, altogether, Don, but they're pretty long rolls.'

A week or two later, Bill and I were out in the car, not far from his home, so a tea break was most surely written in. I discovered where one of the rolls, at least, had disappeared to. Bill had a fairly narrow driveway down to the garage, probably ten yards long. From the gateposts onwards were creamy daubs of the reflective plastic, culminating in a splendid show on the garage doors themselves. Garden gnomes had abandoned their traditional red bonnets for a dull cream, and a slightly overhanging bush had reflective strands hanging from the lower branches. The decorations were completed by a central run of raised bricks, all with the now ubiquitous tape on them. Bill said that it had been the wonder of the neighbourhood. Apparently, I eventually discovered, it was not all good.

We were at a time of light evenings, and Bill was not one to go out after his tea, until one night they, Bill and Florence, had to visit a sick relative. It was dark when they returned home, and Bill had more or less forgotten his luminous decorations, as it was a week or two since he'd put them up. Turning sharply into the driveway, Bill slammed his brakes on hard and grappled violently for reverse. The whole world had suddenly, and fiercely lit up, with what appeared to be a jumbo jet coming in towards them to land. Ghoulish little men lined the drive and the trees were decked in screaming waving lights. Seat belts were in their infancy, and Florence shot forward into the windscreen, while Bill's dodgy heart was debating whether to fail again. Recovering his composure, but not his eyesight, Bill switched off the headlights and coasted in until he gently bumped into the garage doors.

Bill got used to the effect as the nights drew in, and labelled the experiment on the whole a success. Even more positive was the now luminous collar on the cat, as it was never again mislaid at night when it was due to come in, though the sight of a broken halo drifting among the garden flowers was reportedly a little unnerving.

As a further aside, the reflective plastic was something I felt would be useful at home, and for the first time, I borrowed a piece of scientific advance from the Railway. I laid strips of it on my father-in-law's wheelchair, covering all surfaces facing forward or back. Approaching cars veered madly when he was picked out in their headlights. John (Thelma's dad) later became a collector of railway innovations, the most useful being some non-slip grit and glue, meant for platform ramps, to make safe a couple of sleepers (OK, hands up to them as well) which ran up the two steps to his back door.

We ordered several more boxes of the plastic rolls, as Derby Research appeared to have miscalculated how much we would need to cover the Area's tunnel refuges. Perhaps they had not brought a garage, a cat and a wheelchair into their estimates.

★

This, and much of what has gone before, must persuade you that Bill and I were deeply interested in the science of things, and always willing to go along with experiments, either thrust upon us, or of our own making. Long after Bill had departed this life, to try the patience of the saints, I got involved in a scientific test, described in the most pretentious way, and carried out with a crudity that was beyond belief.

I'd begun to specialise in curve realignment designs and calculations, mainly on the trans-Pennine route, and most particularly on the stretch that ran through the Huddersfield Area. This took in about twenty-four miles between Diggle and Morley, near Leeds. By now I'd been surgically separated from the Area, and had supervised schemes beyond my roots, through York and on to Scarborough, a total well beyond the 100-mile mark. So when the Chief Civil Engineer's Track Design Unit decided on a field test on the route, running at speeds above the comfortable design ones, I was naturally included.

This sort of idea is what the bumble-headed berks, who flashed briefly before my eyes as graduates at Huddersfield, would dream up. They hoped to make names for themselves (they did in fact manage that, but not as they would have wished), by querying the rules and guidelines set down for a century. In an age of galloping hysteria along health and safety lines, these inept inexperienced ones were allowed to flout good tried and tested rules, that had been checked both in theory and in practice. Sadly, they had been put in positions of superiority over wise and dependable lads whom I would consult on any PWay matters, men in the Chief's York Drawing Office who threw away more experience and knowledge when they cut their toenails than these upstarts would assimilate in their entire railway careers.

The Engineer's diesel multiple unit inspection saloon was used, filled with test equipment, drums of graph paper and vibrating pens, along with a representative of every remote department you could think of, that was even slightly interested. Above all, there was an element present from the above rocket-driven twerps who were to delight and make my day – a mixed group from Headquarters, spearheaded by the Cocky Young Graduate, seconded from Derby Research. Now this CYG takes the opportunity of a delay at Scarborough, waiting for a 'window in the timetable', as he put it, to variously bore some and expound to others on the topics of grandmothers, eggs and sucking. He was soon interrupted by the Operating Manager, who told him that when it came to testing comfortable riding on curves, he relied on the coffee-cup test, where the said equipment, filled to within half an inch of the brim, was watched as the train took the curves. Any spillage equated to bad riding.

This, to me, was a fair comment. Designs were made on the basis of passenger comfort, when it came to putting the correct superelevation, or cant, on the track. It was well into uncomfortable riding before the questions of damage to the track or, beyond that, danger of derailment came into play. Ideally, the coffee should not rise in the cup on a correctly designed curve with the train doing the designated speed, so coffee cup science was good enough for me. But no, not for our CYG.

'Well, you must understand the dynamics and laws of circular motion as applied to the movements within the liquid material filling the receptacle.' (Coffee slopping round a cup!) 'As the train enters the full radius of the curve, the superelevation should be such that the centripetal forces drawing the liquid towards the centre of the circle, caused by the acceleration emanating from the constant change of direction, should equal the centrifugal force which is evidenced by the liquid rising above its at-rest position.'

'What's he chuntering on about? There's no changes of direction – we're heading for York all the time!'

'Ah, no, that's just it.' This accompanied by the sort of smirk reserved for the idiot child failing to grasp the very basic lessons of life.

It was here that I felt CYG lost forever, the sympathy of his audience, who took to talking among themselves.

'If I can just have your attention for a moment longer…'

'Not if he's just going to talk bollocks!'

'Coffee cup test – count on me!'

'Precious young pillock!'

'Have you seen owt of George Greenfield, lately?' And so on.

But credit where it's due, we'd not just got an ordinary pillock here, but a rhinoceros among pillocks as regarded skin specification! He went on and on about his test gear, circular motion, radial forces on circling objects, mass m, velocity v and radius r, compound, reverse and simple curves, cant and deficiency, and then transitions. Had he but listened to himself here, we might not have had a problem later. 'E certainly equalled a mighty square crackpot, as Albert Einstein so clearly stated.

We had managed the curves on the way out at around 10–15% above recommendation, and apart from a bit of screeching, and a slightly damp saucer, we had experienced only mild discomfort. So much so that the adventurous amoebas demanded something more exciting on the return journey.

Running at 60 mph, we were approaching a 40 mph speed limit on a fairly tight curve across a bridge of longitudinal timbers, with no flexibility in alignment. I'd tried all sorts of schemes here, but only a new bridge (which was a possibility) could lift the restriction. It wasn't so much the radius of the curve, but the fact that there was virtually no transition from the straight into the curve. No motorist will quite understand the likely effect of this, because the gradual turning of the steering wheel automatically makes the transition on the road. This has to be built into the railway track, and wherever we have a restraint on this, a restriction to the maximum speed generally follows. You could create the same situation with your model railway (haven't you? I'm surprised and gratified!) Here you have straights into instant curves, and experiments with excessive speeds might produce the same effect as we were on the point of experiencing.

We were about twenty minutes out of Scarborough, and had travelled with ease round the curves so far at around 80–85 mph Taking what should have been a 60 curve at 70, we were nearing the bridge and what I regarded as the compulsory and irrefutable 40, due to its design. Our operating friend had set up his coffee cup trial, now wisely using a plastic beaker and water. He had already discovered a flaw in this method in that bumpy jointed track caused considerable splashing, but since Malton we had been running on continuous welded rails, and he was fascinated watching the water gently climb the side of the beaker. Sadly, as it happens, so were most of our other companions, if they weren't actually copying the experiment for themselves. CYG was trying desperately to interest them in his dancing pens scribbling on the rotating drum of paper, but the cups of water held the attention.

'Curve radius twenty-five chains approaching!' he sang out.

'Speed limit forty, we'll try it at sixty.' Part of his calculated risk should have been the driver's percentage. Many of this species had an unwritten rule of 'Plus 10%', and we were approaching the speed restriction sign at what I felt was a cavalier speed.

I had locked myself to various projections on the coach wall and finally called over to our cocky spaniel. 'What about there being no transitions at all?'

'What do you mea—?'

Which was the moment when we hit the change point.

We met the straight onto the bridge with extreme violence. Pens on the recording drum left the paper and became stuck in this position. The coffee-cup test was suspended as no account is taken of the beaker (in this case) actually following the liquid. At last some panic was aroused. Operators shouted at the driver on the intercom for him to slow down, with only sixty feet to go before we hit the even more severe curve off the other end of the bridge. With the brakes jammed on we probably lost a couple of mph. Then we hit the sudden curve.

Good news – the saloon stayed on the tracks! Bad news – any other eventuality you can think of...

I'd already moved to the outer side of the curve, and had taken my surreptitious grip on a row of coat pegs, so I was well placed to watch the more relaxed bodies of my fellow travellers taking an unplanned spontaneous trip around the interior of the saloon. CYG's centrifugals propelled the whole of humanity with scientific correctness towards the outside of the curve, some reaching the walls of the saloon, others finding fixed tables, and fallen chairs painfully interrupting the full sideways thrust.

Briefcases on the luggage rack shot across the coach, almost landing level on the opposite rack. Everything not screwed down leapt to life to become serious missiles. Bodies were flung outwards, not all reaching the comfort of the side of the coach, as fixtures intervened at all sorts and degrees of positional damage. Coffee cups that were previously transported to one side of the carriage as we went onto the bridge were now returning, mostly in dangerously sharpened kit form. Miraculously no bones were broken: coats, hats, jackets, rolls of plans and assorted soft things broke the impact of many of the items of hardware unexpectedly journeying into space, but with pens and pencils along with paperweights suddenly taking flight, and bodies being flung into various recesses of the coach, numerous sharp incisions occurred, and many widely located bruises began to form.

Of particular interest, to me, at least, was a lower set of dentures and accompanying pipe flashing past in front of my face, and I later learnt with delight that the CYG had swallowed a lit cigarette, evidenced by a clutching of the throat and some violent coughing. Happily, as a result, he was to speak no more. Perhaps the greatest indignity was that the secure cabinet, mounted centrally on the floor of the coach, containing the cylinder and stuck recording pens fell over. Our driver was not unscathed, finishing up half in and half out of his open window, leaving him having no contact with the controls, and leading us to go through the most violent emergency stop 200 yards further on from the bridge.

The two outward forces, created at each end of the bridge, were instantly replaced by one of forward momentum caused by the emergency braking. Forwards was a direction with far more potential, the usable space within the length of the coach being much greater than the restrictions across it, although those completing the full journey to the front were well outnumbered by the majority meeting up with the much greater density of tables and chairs. Finally, gravity took over as other forces became spent, causing everything to find its way to the carriage floor, in direct relation to former flight altitude levels. Thus unfixed chairs hit the deck first, breaking the falls of much of the human element, followed by every minor object still mobile. Most of what I suffered was indentation marks in my hands, mirroring the coat pegs to which I'd been anchored.

In these situations it is usual to describe or film everything in slow motion. There was nothing slow about the motion of the briefcase catching one in the small of the back, or the brolly coming handle first from above. It all happened in strict tempo, and in beautiful unison – side two-three-four, reverse side two-three-four, front two-three-four, down two-three-four. If it could have been translated into slow motion, then from where I stood, in the loving union of a fairly stable relationship with a row of coat pegs, the whole scene would have made the most effective ballet.

Due to my private knowledge of the transitions, or lack of them, I was one of the only people left in a relatively normal position, though I bore the imprints of my anchorage for a while afterwards. My down-to-earth Headquarters colleagues had had similar reservations to me about spontaneous airborne ballet. It was a scene of instantaneous camaraderie that lay before me. Blokes who had up to then found but two words to say to each other were entangled in a range of wild embraces that would have justified an addendum to the Kama Sutra. The subsequent disentanglements and separations did occur in slow motion, and in considerable and obvious embarrassment. Not only that, but each individual was then concentrated upon a personal examination as to any real damage, before, as a polite afterthought, enquiring as to the condition of their nearest companion. There was then the matter of reuniting themselves with everything about their persons that was not integral, such as pens, pencils, glasses, and in one case, teeth.

What had started off as the more straightforward of the experiments, the 'coffee-cup test', had definitely met its Waterloo. Not only was the equipment lost from sight, but the water had shot in all directions, ruining the integrity of any readings which might have been taken. It had not done the recording pen traces many favours, either. Momentarily attractive, the combining of them with the coffee test was causing the dissolution of all the coloured lines. Everything taken together led to the virtual abandonment of further experimentation. Added to all this were extensions of the cup test into teapots, coffee jugs and 5-gallon water carriers. CYG had totally lost first his nerve, followed by his ability to speak, and several component parts of his machinery. There were plenty of unblemished coffee cups left for the rest of the journey, but the body of opinion among the observers was that to return to their bosses following important trials and own to having spent most of the time watching water jiggle about in a beaker was not going to be over-impressive.

When we reached my home ground, we'd gone through a change of drivers at Leeds; and a fresh attitude, together with a lack of any unfortunate experiences earlier, allowed for me to sit with the replacement. I was able then to authorise more modest speed limit infringements, allowing me to get something positive out of the trip. Sadly, it seemed that it was now just the two of us. I tried to raise some interest in taking the curves at a slightly more exciting speed, but there was a unanimous lack of any real enthusiasm. It had been a good half-hour after the incident before they'd all finished rummaging through the first aid box, only managing to underline the superficiality of their various punctures and bruises.

The body repair cabinet was completely out of any hurt pride ointment.

★

Approaching the end of this catalogue devoted to pioneering, let it be known that life at the frontier of science and technology is not necessarily all glory and satisfaction. They laughed at… well, any revolutionary innovator you can think of, and I shared the pain of Stephenson, of Trevithick and of Brunel. My experiences, trying and testing one of the most embarrassing pieces of tackle ever conceived – the 'twistector' – beat any of the ridicule the other more famous lads had to put up with.

This is all about derailments. Regular diversions in the sixties and early seventies, more often than not were in part caused by clapped out goods wagons with short 10-foot wheelbases (the distances between axles). If you combined unequal loading, deficient springs, and a twist in the track you could spark off a derailment. At speeds of forty miles per hour, in a long train, a wagon jumping the track could cause no more than a slight jolt as far as the driver was concerned, and it might only be the guard who spotted it. Suddenly his brake van came to fulfil a purpose, and he would wind down his handbrake wheel, which took time to register with even the most attentive driver. Having no communication between the front and back of a train, a derailed wagon could run for a mile or so, before something significant like points and crossings brought it off completely, along with many others. So, just one fault could leave a trail of disruptive and expensive carnage.

Short lesson: for the PWay side, some means of easily detecting excessive twists in the track was essential. At the time it was a matter of spotting something by eye that didn't look quite right, and measuring the cross levels at every sleeper before and beyond the problem. As a sideline, I might mention that our PWay inspectors used to align curves using a system known as 'bi t'rack o' t'ee'. Even when translated to 'By the rack of the eye' it hardly explains the system of placing stones on the rail and sending the gang with bars to certain points along the line to slue the track over slightly, left or right. For cross-levels they thankfully used their 5-foot track gauges with spirit levels and adjustable foot at one end.

A 'twist' existed when the two axles of a wagon encountered two different cross levels relative to each other. This was inevitable in transitions between curves, as cants were reduced from the superelevation of the outer rail over the inner down to zero on a straight, but design rules kept these within acceptable limits. However, an enhancing fault in the track could take these beyond limits into the danger area. Track recording trolleys detected such things reasonably well, so far as the dynamic loading of the vehicle simulated a partly full wagon, but the boffins wanted something that the local engineer could use at any time; and so was born the twistector.

That all sounded a bit technical, and I think that I understood it, and hope you did too. All it means is that twists in the track are naughty things, and it was our fine body of scientific geniuses at Derby Research who designed and built the answer. They must have struggled through sleepless nights to both come up with a name like 'twistector' for a machine that detects twists, and for a way in which the humble technical officer at the bottom of the fool chain can be made to come out looking a complete prat.

We set it up outside the office at Huddersfield, on the bay siding.

'They must've seen thee cumin! "Ay oop," they sez, " 'ere comes a likely pillock fer owt we don't want to be seen doin' usselves." Tha should've put a cross in the "not bein' made a right prawn of" box when tha joined.'

Bill was his usual self. On this occasion he was hardly interested in the delivery, (a) because there was nothing in it he could use; and (b) it was painted yellow, and any old relayer knew that anything painted yellow on the railway meant 'heavy'.

'You don't feel tempted to give me a hand, or anything?'

'Nay, ah've bought a ringside ticket; ah'm here t'watch. Ah'm noan takin' part, burra bet that bit goes ower yonder!' He was determined that my struggles would be worth watching, and nipped off into the office, returning a minute later with two chairs and Jack Senior.

In appearance the thing was a large 'H', the two end pieces being the axles and the crosspiece the 10-foot-long central spine. This spine was bolted flat on to the back axle so that if the axle twisted, then so did the spine. At the other end it was welded to a rocker beam, which lay above the front axle. The rocker moved in the same way as the fixed rear axle, so the difference between its attitude and the front axle lying under it showed the amount of twist over the ten feet of the apparatus. Screw detectors between the beam and the front axle could be set to make a circuit if this twist exceeded a certain amount, when buzzers and lights would come into action. Overall, the effect was of two cross-level measurements being taken ten feet apart. By pushing the contraption along using a trolley arm attachment to the back axle, this measurement was being made continuously.

When called to attention by the buzzers and flashing lights, I had to mark the sleepers, and my boots and lower trouser legs, with spray paint. Legs and boots were not compulsory, or in any way helpful, but the decoration of them was an unavoidable bonus in the slightest of breezes. Everything was made out of tubular steel rather than solid rods so that the boffins could give it the 'one-man operation' tag. Later, lifting it off the track in the middle of the spine meant that five feet away was a swinging trolley arm, positioned perfectly to veer round and deliver a tidy smack in the small of your back, followed by your head. Bill was unimpressed by the 'one-man operation' tag.

'Ah'm glad t'one man's thee and not me. Ah c'n see thee liftin' it, but thur's a powerful lot of moving parts to mek it noan so friendly when tha's tryin' to side it away. Go on, gi'it a try!'

I wasn't inclined to do anything of the sort, and took to adjusting the two contact screws at either end of the rocking arm. This was too much for a dedicated faffer like Bill, and he just had to come and get involved. His wide experience, as a former relayer, with metal things painted yellow paid off, and he sussed out the fiddling bits in good time, lubricated by two teas. When inducing a twist into the frame, the contacts on the rocker beam could be adjusted so that buzzers buzzed and lights lit, indicating that the calibrated value of twist had been found on the track. Bill was by now totally engrossed, and involved. It wasn't soon before he wanted to conduct test runs up and down the sidings. This he did until the batteries went flat – not surprising, since the sidings were hardly up to main line standard.

Behind this tendency for heavy, folding, manhandlable track things to be painted yellow lay a deep suspicion in any hardened trackman. It very consciously gave a message to the 'one man' that it would be 'bleedin' heavy'. The overall effect of this monstrosity was that of an iron bedstead, pushed or pulled by a loose handle, with intermittent flashing lights and buzzers, and we were supposed to be happy shoving this thing along in broad daylight, within sight of people who knew us.

However, a hundredweight of uncoordinated metal tubing was hardly a substitute for a 12-ton wagon when trying to detect dynamic twists under load. Nevertheless, it was accepted with diametrically opposite degrees of enthusiasm from Don and myself. To one it represented two cross-levels taking constant measurements ten feet apart, comparing the two and giving an audible and visual warning whenever anything beyond the preset value was detected. To the other, it was an outsize lump of dysfunctional scrapyard components that buzzed and lit up a lamp at will, and realistically took at least three people to set it up, or to remove it on the approach of a train. Bill's practical trials in the sidings moved all but one of those trying it out towards my pessimistic outlook. Don Newell stood out like a beacon of positive attitude and confidence, seeing only the tremendous advantages of having such technological wizardry at his fingertips, or rather, at the fingertips of the poor twallop having to push it along. He also stood out as the one who would never have to touch or adjust the thing, and also as one who'd been told from higher up that he must make it work, or give very good reasons as to why it didn't.

I was more than happy to help provide those reasons, but Don was convinced that we were now ready to try the damn thing in anger.

For some inconceivable reason, he had decided that we would test the rail-mounted Meccano No. 5 Kit through Stanningley and its tunnel. This was where I learnt the complexities of getting the thing clear of traffic in a confined space. I had great apprehension about any part of this unpredictable bedstead swinging out foul of the track.

So it was a slightly bewildered signalman at Stanningley station who watched our team of six engineers placing the twistector on a siding outside his box.

'Tell thee what; t'patrolman fund a red and purple mattress on t'line yesterdi…, 'appen it's yours to go wi this thing?'

We thanked him politely, because his willing cooperation was vital, but said no.

'Can't say ah blame thee not admittin' it. Bloody vile it looked; ah wouldn't own to it bein' mine, eether!'

Every lift-off meant that the twistector had to be re-calibrated before further use. This, like the initial setting up, involved easy finger-tightening screws in summer, and rusted, immovable, freezing and painful twisting in winter. All screwing was by wing nuts, possibly the friendliest means possible. To the casual observer it meant one hot and bothered lad, with decorated bottoms to his trousers and boots, leaping about adjusting screws at all corners of his immediate universe, while five others stood watching. These included the two lookout men, whose attention should have been elsewhere; PWay Inspector Dennis Durand – a large figure in a ground-hugging black mac, who was thinking that thought that he had seen the ultimate in barmy technology, up to today; Don Newell, in a smart hat with a small feather, a car coat and gloves, and carrying a notebook; Bill Boyes, who was to drive the car round to a suitable meeting point; and Sub-inspector Donald Coates, immediately responsible for the detected twists, leaping around like an electrified Tigger, kneeling down, looking up and down the rail, changing rails and doing the same, all the time explaining in excited detail the cause of each splodge of paint.

Bill had stayed with us on the pretence of helping me set it up. There'd be no assistance from Don, who was only there to make notes and persuade the powers as to what an excellent idea they'd had. Dennis, unusually, lacked any appetite for what he could only see as a dangerous disaster looking for a place to happen, but his morose outlook was more than compensated by the leaping loon that was Coatesy. We'd lookout men posted fore and aft to warn of approaching trains, with Coatesy dancing back and forth to relay their signals, or lay down on the track to stop the train, or run and fetch his ball, or even to keep the sun shining – in fact to do anything else he was asked to. Dennis and I, acting together, were to be the 'one man' needed to operate the trolley, while Don followed, observing, and gradually feeling his enthusiasm drain away drop by drop. A Sunday had been chosen, when traffic would be low, which was rather against Don's idea of real-life situation testing, added to the expense on manpower. He had to be persuaded as to the wisdom of this, and we only succeeded by demonstrating the faff that went to re-calibrating the thing once it had been lifted clear. A weekday 20-minute service, as against the spasmodic average of half hourly on Sundays, did the trick.

I calibrated it on the siding, Bill justifying his existence by standing at one end and reminding me what I hadn't done yet. There was much furious chuntering between us, made no easier by Mr Coates wanting to be helpful, and stoked by Bill's philosophy that arguing at time and three-quarters was much more financially beneficial than saying nothing. Don tried to urge us along, but was hampered by not fully understanding what I was doing, and therefore being ignorant as to whether I was doing it well or not. Bill helped a lot in this; minutes mean hours, and hours mean prizes!

Bearing in mind that the inspiration behind the twistector was to detect possible locations for derailments, it was to the credit of the designers that after travelling twenty yards along the siding, it encountered its first insulated fishplated joint, rode up on top of it, and jumped completely off the track. Bill said he'd told me so, Dennis looked towards heaven, and Donald Coates did his re-railing dance all around the contraption, while Don made the first of his notes.

Within one hundred yards, we encountered a piece of switch and crossing work. I made to lift the machine off, but both Dennis and Don objected, since such locations are notoriously prone to twist problems. Resigned, I pushed on, and as I expected, the thing once more managed to gain its freedom. Less than a tenth of a mile, and two derailments. Don was already turning the page in his notebook. We decided to carry Derby's entry for the Turner Art Prize a couple of hundred yards, clear of all S & C and signalmen, and to set it up where there were fewer invitations for it to jump off the track. Once we were set up on the main line, Bill pushed off on his second assignment of the day, taking the car and three Sunday newspapers round to Duckett's crossing, a mile further on, to wait for us.

Leaving Stanningley Viaduct, and carrying on towards the tunnel, we encountered our first real curve. Pushing became tougher as the curve became tighter, and I noticed that for some time its little flanged wheels were no longer going round, and the whole thing was just sliding, and not even touching the head of the rail. Don enquired whether it could be adjusted. I said, 'Yes,' and kicked it for the first time that day. Dennis made his first real contribution by suggesting more weight to keep it down on the track, and sent his deputy leaping and bounding away to locate two scrap sleepers that they somehow balanced on the frame. What had been a difficult job, pushing this iron dinosaur round the curve, now became arduous to the extreme. On we went, very occasionally getting the hint of a buzz or a flicker of the light bulb, until a continuous squeal from the buzzer made us all jump. This was the signal for me to stop and spray yellow paint on the offending sleepers, and I noted with a little satisfaction that the slight breeze was directing any surplus across to Don's trousers. Heaving away from the standing start, we then entered Stanningley Tunnel, and a section of welcome straight track. Additionally, we encountered our first train.

Fortunately, it was not on our line, but safety decreed that the twistector be removed, and placed clear against the tunnel wall, which was all right so long as it was not expected that someone would have to hold it there at the same time. A chaotic panic dissolved as the train sped past, but Don decided that some routine should be established before we were faced with a train on the same line as us. This involved me pressing myself into a wall refuge, and gripping the thing tightly. A long held theory of mine was once more reinforced, that any plant or equipment taken into a tunnel grows to twice the size it normally was out in the fresh air, and any tunnel reduces to half the size it appears at its mouth when you get inside.

As it turned out, we seemed to have hit a lucky spell of no traffic on our line, and we left the far end of the tunnel without having had to put the practiced crash avoidance plan of action into effect. Rounding the bend, out of the cutting and onto the famous voyeur's garden bottoms, we could hear the warning bell at Duckett's level crossing sounding away. Taking this as ample indication that our first train was nearby, the hateful heap of daffodil scrap was lifted aside, and we waited. Nothing happened, and I remarked on the fact that the bell had stopped ringing. Taking this as a false alarm, the lump was heaved back on, and re-calibrated. This done we set off again, only to notice that the bell was once more belting away. While Dennis and I were looking with some alarm at each other, both having the same horrifying thought, Don was busy making further notes regarding the nuisance of passing traffic, and the work that was required each time they had to remove the device from the track.

In the distance, we noticed Bill get out of the car and get on the phone back to the signal box. Donald Coates was leaping back and forth, which made a minimal contribution to the situation, so Dennis figuratively threw a ball for him, sending him off to the crossing to see if all was well. For it was the two of us who had realised that the bell rang when the twistector was on the track, and stopped when it wasn't, meaning to us both that the track circuits were being triggered by our little trolley, and that as far as the rest of the railway system was concerned, we were a train – and a train in the way of others!

This was confirmed visually as Donald reached Bill, relieving him of the phone, only to be seen to immediately jump back, staring at the receiver, which was obviously shooting some agony at him. His return in thirty seconds over the 200 yards distance confirmed this. He had been told that there was a train stood at

Stanningley, another one two miles back and a third in Leeds station, blocking an essential platform, all because the signalling system could not differentiate between a train and our overblown yellow baby walker! We carried the twistector up to the crossing, dismantled it, helped with amazing eagerness by the formerly steady-away Bill. It was packed away in the bus that Dennis had thoughtfully arranged to meet us, 'just in case', before the first of the queue of trains passed us.

Bill put the situation to Don, and added an aside to me. 'Bloody bell ringin'! Tryin' to get me head down fer a bit, and on and on it goes! Thought it best to have a word when ah saw thee all comin' round t'bend.'

'Well,' said Don, 'I suppose I'd better go face the music. There's bound to be bother over this. I'll go down to the box and ring Control.'

'Ah wouldn't bother, if ah were thee, Don. Ah think ah might've sorted it, like.' Bill looked both smug and a shade apprehensive.

'But I've got to own to us tripping the circuits and causing all the delays.'

'No, as ah say, ah think ah've sorted it.'

'How?'

'Well, when ah got on't phone, ah told signal bobby that ah'd fund four big daft kids wi a load of scrap metal on't line. Ah told him that they'd buggered off as ah took after 'em, and ah were abaht to clear the heap of junk when tha lot really did turn up with it. They think it's just vandalism, and ah don't see as 'ow we needs t'say any different!'

We got away with it, up to a point. There was an internal enquiry. All enquiries end in recommendations. Recommendations are taken as instructions, which always become restrictions. So stringent were these that the twistector died, to be revived only to check through renewals, still under engineer's possessions. It was later fitted with insulated wheels, but all the fun had gone out of it. Supervisors returned to taking cross-levels every four sleepers in suspect areas. The machine rested in the Cramptup House cellar, useful only in providing somewhere to hang the dartboard.

★

Any good chapter in an uncoordinated book like this should finish on a dramatic or fulfilling note. There should either be a shock revelation, or the culmination of a finely judged crescendo. So it is here. Not, in this case a saddening body blow, but a tale of pioneering triumph, of world-shattering importance and the changing of lives forever – at least, railway area civil engineer's drawing office assistant's lives.

It is said that there is a book inside everyone. Likewise, I believe that there is at least one brilliant idea lurking there as well. The book falters for the lack of a pad of paper or a sharp pencil, or perhaps an implement designed to sharpen that pencil. There are no excuses for the failure to bring to the surface, and the publicising of the short, sharp mental act of genius, unless you are so unlucky as to be marooned on a desert island when inspiration strikes. I used to regard the object of my particular moment of revelation as a thing of beauty when at last I held it in my hand, not only in appearance, but also because, besides having had the initial idea, I'd the incredibly dexterity to manufacture it. However, looking at it now, nearly forty years on, it seems to have lost some of its aura. It is a pocket theodolite.

Many live wires and cables cross above the railway and it is essential that their heights are known. So when I was in the process of producing line diagrams, which had notes of such impedimenta on them, I needed to be able to give a fairly accurate idea as to this height above rail level. Should a crane jib come close to a bare electricity carrier, the first thing you noticed was the operator's hair going into Mohican mode. If it is midwinter, you are surprised when he leans out of his cab and asks whether it's him, or is it getting warmer all of a sudden. Touch the cable, and all sorts of interesting effects can be achieved, even to a chargrilled crane operator.

This pocket theodolite was made from three shaped Dexion corner brackets and a hacksaw blade. I then had to write the instructions in Taiwanese-English for the international market:

'Move to feet in ninety from wires from underneath. Take eye in head and lie along theodolite. Hold high in hand. Mind standing and pursue along at wire. Hit wire and fix. Do with finger to blade. Reading off with eye, first moving down. To high put on six feet. This high of wires.'

To anyone not familiar with this clear leaflet/instructions, similar to all that accompany any imported goods, I can provide a local translation:

To operate the pocket theodolite you measured out ninety feet away from under the crossing wires. Being alone, this was done by counting sleepers, generally thirty-six in old wood or thirty-nine in concrete. You then turned and faced the lowest point of the overhead wires. The theodolite was then pointed up at that point, lining the top edge with the object, and allowing the saw blade to swing against a printed scale. Clamp it with a finger and read off the measurement. Add six feet for operator's height and there you have it!

Now if this is not inspirational genius, I don't know what is. Having honed it and perfected it, and completed field trials, health and safety evaluations and risk assessments, and also having satisfied environmentally friendly requirements, I prepared myself to present it to my immediate boss, for him to no doubt place it with care on the car seat beside him, and race it off to head office, the patent office and finally to prepare a paper on it for the Institution of Civil Engineers for their amazed appraisal. The ingenuity of the pocket theodolite fell at the first fence, when Don started laughing at it. Such short-sightedness, and furthermore, no Nobel Prize for Inspired Technology! But it worked!

Things (such as Tunnels, Viaducts and Bridges)

I've had a lot to say about buildings having, or not having, character. This is easy to see, feel and smell. Our place at Huddersfield, for instance, a block of four rooms under a water tank, was oozing with character. What's more it was virtually nailed on to the main station frontage – one of the finest in the country. Leeds Wellington Street (No. 23), an office slum in my time, but a glorious 'home'. No doubt they've put all the character in a big skip by now, seeing as it has been 'refurbished', and it's interesting to note that in the thirty years since we were tipped out, and the place done up, nobody seems to have leapt at the new interior. It remains empty.

My railway world is small, but I think that I can speak for all areas of British Railways as consisting of the living remains of a surgeon, Dr Beeching. Amputated limbs remain on the OS maps, and many are amazingly undergoing resurrection surveys, along with the stations, the fruits on the branches. Real enthusiasts, rather than those who just talk about it, are giving many lines in industrial hospices the return of life, and in exactly the same form it used to have (or as near as modern Health and Safety will allow). So when I dwell on the West Riding, my personal patch, similar fields can be seen up and down the country. If you have difficulty with the notion of life after death, look at some of these reviving branches, and particularly at some of the relics administering this kiss of life.

York Chief Civil Engineers were housed in the old station buildings while I was there. What remains of the organisation has been shunted into a concrete and glass job, with low ceilings and dead carpet. Again, there used to be character in the old place. Just silly little things like a sudden two steps in the middle of a long lino-covered corridor, suggesting an original building cock-up, the Staff Section atop a long flight of winding wooden stairs,

211

going a long way to having old retired staff who are visiting suddenly being removed from the books. And what about the Chief himself being closeted behind an office front of framed opaque stained glass, with a door into his secretary's office bearing his name in gold Arial Condensed? Within was a private toilet, the whole appearing as a mix between a headmaster's room and a funeral director's display window.

Then you go on to look at stations other than York, most now re-vamped into a universal drabness. But try Hebden Bridge, where the character has hardly suffered, and has just been scrubbed up a bit; compare this to others on the same line, like Halifax, where there used to be refreshment and waiting rooms for all three classes, containing benches or chairs or upholstered settees – a sort of transport apartheid. Also, there was the Victorian correctness of ladies only rooms. Now all this unused accommodation has been ripped out, though I would think that if that had been proposed today, they would all have been preserved and converted into offices for architects and solicitors. Platforms remain, now needlessly tortuous with two remaining lines and lots of empty space.

Bradford had some magnificent stations; enormous cast iron spanned edifices. Now all we have are jumped-up bus shelters. Take Leeds station, the busiest outside London. Now, here I might see some element of modern character being built into the new, certainly after it's been knocked about a bit; but the old stations did have to go, if only for safety's sake. Usually platforms were roped off during storms as obscure panes of glass crashed down, or in the case of Bradford Exchange, sheets of tarred cladding first floating, then taking up a harpooning mode.

So, following on from that, it has lately occurred to me, that as well as offices and station buildings, so railway tunnels, viaducts and bridges also have individual characters. The offices have it from two directions – looking at the exterior and putting up with the inside. Taking the insides, these could be heavily camouflaged like our Wellington Street horror was, where the fourth floor was transformed by a fashion house into a palace of wonder, while the railway offices sandwiching it were cleanish, but indescribably ugly and unkempt. The comparison of an Ascot lady with a bag lady. Yet outside there was no distinction between the fourth and any of the other four floors.

Bridges have, in the main, not often been replaced, and the original character remains, be it the shape, the adornments, or the lack of foresight in the matter of worldly progress. Engineers mostly in the Brunel mould were artists as well as structural designers, and his bridges, to me, surpass most other railway spans. His broad masonry flat arches defy gravity (the Maidenhead beauty springs to mind). Character, usually pleasing to the eye, was built into all his work. The Stephensons went more for practicality, but this did not preclude character, rather, this was enhanced, as in the North Wales box girders. In general, however, bridges take a back seat compared to sweeping viaducts.

Yet the passing traveller suddenly plunged into a few minutes of darkness might find it difficult to see how tunnels can have character, or more particularly, differing characters. Faced with one in particular, your reluctant chainman, who could only look forward to booking four shillings' dirt money on his timesheet, would classify it as one selected from 'a mucky 'oil, an empty 'oil, a smelly 'oil, a slippery 'oil, a wet 'oil', or, most oddly, 'a dark 'oil'.

All tunnels contained a percentage of these descriptions, yet to the chap facing the prospect of spending the next few hours inside it, on a surveying visit, one thing would stand out from the others. To spend twelve hours on a Saturday/ Sunday night inside one, digging out formations and renewing tracks, then these differences in character tend to merge into a homogenous few hundred yards, full of diggers and diesel locos, all disgorging fumes to cripple you later in life.

Here I have to be very parochial, for I can give only examples from the multitude of West Riding holes; others are foreigners that I have only ridden through. (I would have loved a walk through the magnificent Severn Tunnel and Brunel's Box Tunnel.) It shook me only a year ago when I heard tell of Ipswich Tunnel. How does that work, for goodness sake? Could a land so flat warrant the possession of a tunnel? Anyway, for a Leeds District Engineer's lad, only those of Yorkshire could invoke any interest, in honesty because I have not travelled far in life.

ME:	Standedge next week!
CHAINMEN:	Oh, bloody 'ell! All that hiking…

Or

ME:	Morley Tunnel next week!
CHAINMEN:	Reet, what time?

Or

ME:	Bramhope next week!
CHAINMEN:	Both me 'an 'im 'ave funerals next week.
ME:	What day?
CHAINMEN:	What day was thee thinkin' of?
ME:	Tuesday.
CHAINMEN:	Ay, that's reet!
ME:	Well maybe next month, then.
CHAINMEN:	Fancy that! We've got funerals comin' up next month as well!

Morley Tunnel is a princess among tunnels. (All tunnels are female, but it's best not to follow that line of discussion too far.) It is both clean and gentle. Despite having sharp curves at both ends, it always seemed to have a safe feeling about it, even if it meant walking out on the wrong line. Trains run on the left, so walking on the tracks should be confined to the right, facing oncoming traffic. However, Morley was relied on in diesel days as one in which you could see a train two miles away, so 'bang roading', or walking on the left as you approached the dangerous curve at the end, was pretty safe. And there was the telltale draught on the back of the neck indicating an approaching train from behind. A scarf or turned up coat collar put paid to that, but there was always the train driver, spotting the smallest light within, and out would come his inbuilt cultural tendency, as he attempted 'On Ilkley Moor Baht' at' on the two notes made available to him.

Once, all of a sudden, Morley became a 'smelly' tunnel, at

least towards the Batley end. It was a stale oily smell that was quite unpleasant after a while. We didn't connect the two things, but about the same time that the smell turned up, a farmer a mile down the track complained about oil in the beck where his cattle occasionally drank. The complaint went on to the machinery of local authority, where it was no doubt passed from 'Water' to 'Environment' to 'Illegal Tipping' to 'Grumpy Farmers' back to 'Environment' to finally, in true homing complaint style, returning to collect dust in 'Water'.

The 'Water Department' would be expert in their field, and would be aware that water tended to run downhill (not a theory grasped by one of our District drainage teams, by the way). Following the farmer's stream uphill for about a mile, 'Water' came upon an input from a railway trackside drain. This must have been a moment of sheer delight for them. The matter no doubt then passed up the chain of 'Water', ending up at the monthly policy meeting, who passed it back down to its starting point, with the instruction to contact 'The Railway'. Their letter would then take on a journey that even 'Water' and the others could not match, from Batley Stationmaster, via many policy tributaries, and ending up at York, with the Chief Civil Engineer. Its journey from there was simple. Down to the Leeds District Engineer Clerical Sections, to 'Outside Parties', where it would be by now a yellowing note, into the capable hands of Bob Newell, master of indoor games and sweating. In an instant it was sent to Huddersfield Area Assistant and Bob's cousin, Don Newell, who marked it 'Investigate urgently' and put it in my box. (When I say it was marked 'Investigate urgently' I should add that there were very few people who could have told you that. Don had a distinctive way with the pen – very neat, but to the untrained eye appearing as the laid-back heartbeat record from an ECG.) So the letter has now travelled a considerable distance, only to end up in my tray, about ten miles from where it set off.

In passing, some momentary whiz-kid, working a spell at the Leeds Office, announced that he had experienced the problem of oil in the drainage, and recommended that we cut some blocks of polystyrene to fit the catchpits to soak up the oil. A month later an angry note from the same irate farmer was making its way round the complaints labyrinth, about lumps of polystyrene fouling his beck now, as well as the oil.

Wilf and Percy loved those days when I would tell them that we needed no surveying tackle, just a bar and a torch each. Then the words 'tracing a smell' entered the conversation, and interest dropped off like a stone. They both had painful memories of 'tracing the smell' from Don's lavatory and being swamped by the ensuing flood.

'What sortuv smell?' asked Wilf, suspiciously.

'Oh! Nowt like what you're thinking, this is an old oily smell, like a tin of sardines that have gone off.'

'What's it look like?' put in Percy.

'It's a dark black oil.'

'So we're lookin' for a dark black oil in a dark black tunnil, are we? It strikes me that we don't stand much ova chance, on the whole.'

'There's the smell, too,' I explained, not wanting to dwell too much on that attribute of the oil with this suspicious pair.

'Well, while we've no great objection to liftin' t'catchpit lids, it's *tha* nose wot's goin' dahn it!'

'Suits me,' I told him, knowing full well that the smell would hit us all whenever it showed up.

We knew that the oil appeared somewhere in the tunnel, but had never found out where. Anyway, a morning spent inside the dry cool of Morley Tunnel was appealing, as we had had nothing but overbearing sun for more than a week. Walking further and further in, and we found no hint of a smell from the drain catchpits. We rested in an air shaft.

This was another beauty of Morley – the shafts are wider than the tunnel, very airy and mostly dry. They had to be wide, as Joe Mallon had found when you're trying to circumnavigate an elephant. There were also odd crates and boxes to sit on, courtesy of the residents of Morley, naturally mistaking the tunnel shaft, which comes up behind the Town Hall, as a monumental dustbin. We were now at the middle of the tunnel, a mile in from both ends, and still no smell. This was also the apex of the tunnel and its drain, so that any smelly water coming out at Batley could not have come from any further on.

'It was before this where we last smelt it,' I said, 'let's have a walk down to the beck and see if it's still coming out there.'

Three-quarters of an hour later, after strolling out of the tunnel and hitting the wall of heat, we were cooling our feet off down where the farmer had first spotted the oil. There was none now.

'I never realised,' said Wilf, 'when I was in the gangs ten years ago, and thinking this chainman's job wot I'd put in for would be so arduous and mentally draining, that I might have to spend a whole morning wandering into a cool tunnel and out agen, followed by a paddle. Fancy – I've been trained up to a finely tuned instrument of technical expertise to be able t'do this!'

And so the smell had sorted itself. Two days later the weather broke, and we had several days of steady rain.

'Yon pong's back in Morley,' announced Don's confidential secretary, Bill Boyes. 'We've just gotta note from t'farmer. Tha three mustave med a good job of tracin' it!'

'That smell's back in Morley, and the oil's in the farmer's stream again,' said Don two minutes later. 'I thought you said you couldn't find it. I can see I'll have to sort it out by myself. Come on!' Which was Don's way of doing it by himself.

Sure enough, at the Batley Tunnel end the water was as filthy as before. Bill had come with us, and Don told him, 'Take the car round to Morley, and we'll walk through.' And so we set off for another two-mile hike through the hole.

As I mentioned, the drainage in Morley Tunnel slopes both ways from the centre on gentle gradients. As we walked in the smell got stronger and stronger, until it was like a white noise smell as you got used to it. At about half a mile from Morley we realised that it had gone, and we were no nearer finding the source.

'That was a wasted journey,' said Don as we emerged at Morley station to find Bill hard at work with a newspaper on one of the station seats. 'Found nothing, Bill!'

'Ah, well,' said Bill, 'ah think tha'd best come wi me a sort of roundabout way back.'

Bill drove, taking us away from the main road back to Batley, down a side lane, in sight of one of the tunnel shafts. Suddenly he stopped to allow a tanker lorry through a gate into a field. 'Come ower 'ere,' said Bill.

We got out and roughly followed the lorry along a muddy track. All at once we were at the edge of an old quarry, and there was our lorry pumping its load of dirty oil waste into it.

It took just a little working out to see that the level of the oil, floating on the flooded quarry lake, rose and fell with the weather. We had just ended a long dry spell where the water level had fallen, and the recent rains had brought it up to a much higher point. The matter was sent back to 'Water' and 'Environment', who eventually discovered that there were vents in the quarry sides at a level above the normal reservoir, and as the quarry flooded, so the oil went through the vents into the tunnel below, only being our – the Railway's – problem in passing. When they had got their act together, 'Water' and 'Environment' proved to be an effective team, and less than a year later we had no more problems from the drains.

★

My first real Saturday night track relaying was in Morley Tunnel, a great place to start, except that every future tunnel digging job was downhill in excitement from that point. Traxcavators, side-tipping diggers, were the weapons used – at least two of them, or in this case three. Two of the contract lads were the immortal Zen and Leatherbarrow, so good that it took a great deal of energy to keep up with them. We had to be on their tails all the time checking depth of dig and correct cross-fall, and to top it all we had to stand on all the drainage catchpits to ensure that the energetic trio kept clear of digging them in.

One odd thing that happened one night was a hell of a racket coming from one of the empty spoil wagons. Lights were played in the general direction of the noise and two faces appeared over the wagon side. Even in the surrounding darkness we could see that both frontals were somewhat damaged. The two were George Davey and Bill Hellewell, gangers from adjacent lengths, and both capable of taking on acting supervisory roles at times. We knew that they came from opposing political wings in the

Working Men's Club that they both belonged to. George was snooker and mild, while Bill, taller, was darts and bitter.

'What's goin' on wi thee two?' Both were very much out of breath.

'Ah fell ower,' answered George. Torches moved across to the other damaged beauty.

'An' ah fell ower 'im,' added Bill.

We left the two friends to themselves, with a vigorous muttering coming from the depths of the wagon.

★

Morley Tunnel has another great point in its favour; it is wide and high, making way for any amendments to alignment and level. It is also a romantic sort of tunnel, having an inviting appearance at Morley Low Station, certainly attractive to circus animals, once enticing an elephant in, and it ran out into the passion fields of the Up side embankment near Batley. It represents two miles of wrap-around comfort and near dryness. Of a similar length is Morley's antithesis, Bramhope Tunnel.

Bramhope, on the Leeds to Harrogate line, is the very opposite of the tranquil Morley; angry and threatening, with no tunnel end light in front or behind. It twists and turns as it makes its way through the hill separating the Aire and Wharfe valleys. For its full length it is sloping downwards from Horsforth to Arthington, having a large central drain, or more correctly a culvert. This is just as well, because it is distinctly wet and it's a 'dark 'oil'. This is partly due to the small apologetic air shafts, but also because there is no sight of either end until you are almost upon them. It also has a bad reputation.

This came about when it was first lit up by continuous electric lighting. As I have pointed out elsewhere, putting such lighting in tunnels creates things never before seen, such as bulges, and there was a beauty of one in Bramhope. These bulges will have probably been present for many years, possibly since birth, but the lighting displayed them as never before. Dark tunnels meant blissful ignorance; illuminated tunnels, with suddenly discovered bulges, engender dismay and expensive correction. (In Bramhope's case this amounted to drilling rock bolts through it, to stop it bulging any more.)

Bramhope is also pretentious. Approaching it from Leeds, you go into a sinister walled cutting to be sucked into the wet gloom beyond. At the posh end (Harrogate-facing, of course) the tunnel mouth is extravagantly ornate with a castellated frontage, to reflect on the gentility of the lands you are leaving. A scale model of this appears in nearby Otley graveyard, to commemorate the many men killed in the tunnel's construction. They died mainly because of the sudden outbursts of water from the rock faces. That water is still a major factor of walking through Bramhope. Incidentally, water coming through tunnel walls is not necessarily as much of a structural problem as water not coming out. At least you know that it is not building up behind the lining.

Like many West Yorkshire tunnels, this one bursts out of the hillside, with a fanfare from the extravagant portal, and immediately needs a viaduct to carry the tracks forward. As ugly as Bramhope is, when it is not wearing its disguise of a beckoning tunnel end, so the following Arthington Viaduct is of great beauty and nobility. This sweeps over the River Wharfe and is a glorious sight from miles around. Were it out in the wilds of the moors it would attract sightseers and photographers. As it is, if you are ever presented with a picture of the Wharfe Valley, you can bet that Arthington Viaduct features on it. It has retained a lot of original splendour, as it is far from the industrial smoke of the time of its construction. Arthington station used to lie between it and the venomous tunnel, but now the train leaps happily out of the hole on a sweeping curve and onto the viaduct, which strides majestically over the valley. The squalor of Bramhope is instantly dismissed. All this assumes that you are travelling to Harrogate; nobody but commuters used to admit to travelling from Harrogate to Leeds, that is until Harvey Nichols opened up a corner shop there.

Comparing tunnels like Morley and Bramhope is all right, except they're miles apart and under different hills. We had many 'twins', where tunnels are matched together. Obvious ones are the twin bores of Huddersfield and Gledholt Tunnels, running from one into another. Huddersfield North and South Tunnels are a disgrace to the name of tunnel, their shafts standing higher above ground than below. Once Huddersfield's Town Council were digging a trench in the town and came right through the tunnel roof. A very embarrassed town surveyor came knocking at our door, asking if we would either take levels on the South Tunnel roof, or accompany him while he did it. We chose the latter, as lifting a staff up to a very sooty tunnel arch is something you should not deprive any young above-ground surveyor from experiencing once in his life. Sure enough, the summer-clad young lad and assistant attended for half an hour in a cool dirty tunnel, and became much wiser men as they worked their way out.

Huddersfield Tunnels have their accompanying viaduct with the station standing in between. Here was a viaduct bursting with character, in that it had all but disappeared into the busy landscape. But for the one noble span over Fitzwilliam Street, the rest have all the appearance of a Turkish bazaar. Almost every one is filled with a workshop or store of some kind. We ourselves occupied two of them with the painter's store and the blacksmith's shop. Here was a place that Bill and I visited on many occasions for domestic repairs to metalwork, notably kettles and such. Bill had a gate made there, although the blacksmith didn't cotton on too quickly. Bill would take a couple of rods that he wanted welding together 'just theer'. Eventually two sections would reappear to be fixed together, until finally he appeared with two halves of a now obvious gate for them to be welded together. It just seemed to amuse him, doing it that way. He wouldn't have dreamed of asking for a gate to be made, using BR manpower and materials!

From a distance the viaduct looks like a high wall. Walking across it in the cess, avoiding the five running lines, and you worked your way along the inside of this wall. At almost every arch the stovepipe of a chimney stack would peep over the wall, coming from whatever establishment occupied that arch. There was a multitude of different smells coming with the wafts of smoke, the blacksmith's being the most distinctive.

It might have occurred to us that it would be amusing to place a piece of slate over the exposed flue. It did and we did! We gained a sadistic pleasure from timing the blocking to the appearance of the irate arch's resident from a smoke-filled shop.

★

Tunnels can come in families, all with some similarities. (Yes, I know that they're all dark with two ends and wet, but there's more to it than that.) Yorkshire's best offering of tunnels, in terms of frequency and number, is the journey from Leeds via Bradford to Manchester, plunging into the Calder Valley.

Leeds to Bradford Exchange manages to include three tunnels, in official terms. Armley Tunnel is just an awkwardly-shaped bridge. Hammerton Street, plunging into the plughole that is Bradford itself, was only notable in that the traveller could spend some time stuck in it waiting for the signalman to raise interest. To the passenger, Stanningley Tunnel was but a short absence of scenery, but to me it was one with problems. This is a special, and I'll look at it closer a bit further on.

From climbing out of Bradford to arriving in the countryside of Mytholmroyd, there's nearly as much darkness as daylight, or so it seems. I've described the steam-and-smoke-filled Bowling hole between the station and Low Moor engine sheds, having spent many a contemplative hour or so waiting for some slight clearance of the fog. Two locos coming out of Bradford up the steep incline (one a banker behind the train, pushing), and light engines among the normal traffic travelling in from the other direction. All those from Bradford climbing into the tunnel were belching out vast quantities of 'I'll see you next Sunday when it's cleared' type of smoky steam, while the light engines coming the other way from the shed dispensed more pure freshly made smoke from their new fires. This tunnel's character transformed almost overnight with the changeover to diesel multiple units. It now appeared to have two ends, and straight, with a bluish haze replacing the smoke and steam. After one or two of those had come through, stinging the back of my throat, I could almost feel nostalgic for the steamy confusion of old.

Emerging from Bowling at the country end in the old days, you were tempted for a moment to see yourself out in that countryside, until the mass of sidings, sheds and scattered smoke of Low Moor loco shed hit you, in the short mile before New Furnace Tunnel. In the present company, this is a tunnel in miniature, more of a long bridge, but still qualifying for the title. It passes under a hiccup in the landscape, and prepares you for the now speeding plunge into Wyke Tunnel. Now here's a place of mystery. Away from the smoke and clear, it is a bore always showing the two ends, without any suggestion that there were hidden secrets within. Sure enough, as soon as electric lighting was hung along its sides for a track relaying job, there were the bulges; none of great excitement, but all demanding that you try to estimate whether they were there yesterday. Added to this, disturbing mounds of sandy deposit were piled up in some of the escape refuges in the walls, many of them bare rock. Was the tunnel disintegrating? Amounts of the eroding lining were sent to Derby Research, who put all their resources together for an urgent and immediate declaration. This came six months later, by which time exhumed piles had been replaced by more new material. A long and tedious analysis recommended further observation, a conclusion we had already come to.

Wyke Tunnel was always a bit moody, suffering sudden changes in profile, something you only discovered on the tunnel inspection truck. This was especially apparent when we had fixed our novel measuring rods to the ends, and hasty withdrawal was necessary as the wall and roof, almost instantaneously, came in towards you. We had no indication as to whether this represented bad setting out during construction, or movement since. At moments of discovery like this, the first thing that occurs to you is the disruption that would be caused if there were any movement here. Only Don and I and the gang were aware of it, and seeing no recent traces, we decided to 'keep it under annual observation'. There are some things best not made public to the headquarter offices, as they would only lose sleep and worry.

Again, we have a case of a viaduct almost straight after a tunnel, except that here we are travelling into the Pennine range, and the landscape rises and plunges with no river valley as a reason – it just does. Somehow, Lightcliffe Viaduct, with no obvious character, is of little visual beauty. This is a structure that could do with one of those TV makeover things, and get itself a bit of publicity. It desperately needs a manager, as it does not seem able to look after itself. Perhaps it's because it stands out from the landscape as a black smear of industrial pollution, or maybe it is looking over to a disused sister on the old Hipperholme to Brighouse (Baliff Bridge) line. This viaduct is spectacular in that one of the arches is in the process of failing, and is rising at its crown. Watching and waiting for its inevitable collapse is an unrewarding occupation. Travelling to photograph it for this book proved equally pointless, as the powers had panicked and had it demolished.

Lightcliffe Tunnel is another short but tricky little number that takes you by surprise when you think you're going to get a bit of daylight for a while. It's tricky because, although both ends are visible, the curve through it hides many secret places. This very soon leads to a tunnel with stern character, reflecting its Victorian origins in the way its companions should, but don't. This is Hipperholme Tunnel – a favourite, at a quarter of a mile long, and dead straight, for walking through with the aid of a stick against the rail. It almost apologises, in a very diplomatic way, for even being there and interrupting the view. This is a pleasant, regular hole with few surprises. It is a severe but comforting tunnel, almost guiding you like a pair of hands as you walk through without a lamp.

Ahead now is the enormous hill separating you from Halifax. There seems to be no escape as Beacon Hill rises high above you, until you spot the discreet entrance to the tunnel at the end of a long plunging curve. The sight of this small hole set in a vast hillside convinces you that you won't fit, and certainly two trains could not pass within, but it's all kidology! Now you're in for a mucky journey on foot. I've never seen anyone go through Beacon Hill without them coming out attached to bits of the temporary tunnel lining of age-old soot. It was in there that we took a short-term local student to observe the track relaying process. Dave Thornton was assisting me on that job, and we sort of forgot about our charge, diverted by the problem of a wagon becoming derailed. This was a fairly common unreported thing, unless we could see no way of getting it back on the line. It was the usual cause, a wagon with a hole in the floor, unseen from the side. Muck got tipped in, with part of it spilling out over the line. With the next train movement the wagon rose up and over the spoil, and landed on the sleepers.

Re-railing a wagon used to involve a lot of shouting, especially if, as on this occasion, Donald Coates was the supervisor in charge. Enthusiasm oozed from this man, and with enough conducting to see you through the longest symphony, accompanied by the mixed voices of Donald encouraging the men, and the men replying in a chorus based on Donald's parentage, the wagon was slowly raised on jacks, which were then kicked out of place, dropping the wagon back on the rails. When Donald was made chief relaying inspector, his loyal band of colleagues presented him with a relaying manual. It had writing on just one page – Note 1 – 'metal side up'; Note 2 – 'eight hours? Call it ten'. Dave and I were about to set off home when we remembered our lost student. He emerged on one of the locos, blending in with the tunnel superbly.

Yet again, this tunnel, with an ornate entrance at the Halifax end in keeping with the Victorian town, leaps straight out of the severe hillside onto a curved viaduct. This is almost hidden from the streets by all the buildings alongside and under it. There is an overabundance of compulsorily cobbled 'Hovis' streets threading in and out of its arches. It is the most striking location of many on that line, and you have to wonder at the sanity of the original surveyors. They must have had immense optimism and courage to see any possibility of building a railway there. It would only be the inducement of hitting Halifax, and the barmy army of financial supporters, that made them work out a solution.

Leaving the town, and the smell of toffee, behind, the line runs through a steep rock-faced cutting. Here the track walker benefits again over the passenger in observing this vertically edged cutting of note. I can only think of two other such elongated gaps to accommodate the railway that could remotely have character of some sort (that would be the steep chalk hill on the Leeds to York and Selby lines, a character just by their incongruous position marking the dramatic edge of the York Plane). Halifax's cutting is distinguished by having the hand-bored blasting holes clearly visible for all its length and height. Bridges and tunnels can be easily dismissed, but the sight of these clean half-holes, all no doubt driven by hand drills, somehow brings home more forcibly the effort that went in to constructing this almost impossible route.

Keeping to the main line, we are led into a sharply curving and literally deadly tunnel, variously called Bankhouse or Copley. This is number two on my nasty holes list, now achieving the top spot with the singling of Esholt, which we'll come across shortly. It is a wickedly devious tunnel, with awful promise in its shape and darkness, despite it being quite short. It is a 'popular' location for telephonic friends of the Samaritans.

Bankhouse is twinned with Salter Hebble Tunnel, actually two single tunnels on the branch line that runs down to the left of the mains, forming a triangle with the Calder Valley at the base. These two tiny bores were only distinguished by the need to walk through them quickly, as there used to be little warning of traffic and not much room to get out of the way. This line was abandoned some years ago, and I was given the job of doing an assessment of it for reopening when the Bradford to Brighouse and Huddersfield service was reinstated. Nature is vicious and quick at reclaiming old railways, and it was a machete-type walk to get up to the tunnel mouths.

Back on the mains, Bankhouse is also, really, the last tunnel in the Halifax line family, and again sweeps you almost immediately onto a grand viaduct pointing down over the river. Here we have a viaduct with a real purpose in life, other than merely spanning a dip. Although the railway is doing its best to escape from the dizzy heights of Halifax, it relies on Copley Viaduct to perform the majestic plunge down to the river level. Here's one with character hidden behind industrial grime, although the environmentalists have probably got there by now to clean it up. It is a thing of shy beauty, visibly sloping down to the valley floor and hidden from most roads. It can be only really appreciated from the river bank. It needs a fan club!

Everything that goes through Copley and its tunnel also goes through Sowerby Bridge Tunnel a mile and a half away. This tunnel is around half a mile long and straight enough for there to be the small stack of strong sticks at each end for the man without his torch. It is also haunted. It has to be, running as it does beneath a cemetery for much of its length. Anyway, the man with a stick and no lamp says it is, and that's good enough for me. It is also hardly finished, being sparsely lined, for the most part cut directly out of the rock. In reality, this is some hell of a tough ghost that can come down through all that solid rock, but local lore says that he's there. (Yes, it's definitely a 'he'.)

Those who have found my determination at seeking out character in tunnels must hold their hands up at Sowerby Bridge. How much more character do you want than a haunting? I've not seen it, but I've had it described. He walks a foot off the ground and looks like a Victorian navvy. He carries a pickaxe over one shoulder, and for some inexplicable reason, a lamp in the other. What a ghost needs with a lamp is beyond me. I suppose that even the pick is unnecessary, when the wraith can walk through solid rock, but I'm hardly a fit person to question his reasoning. If you buy your informant sufficient pints, the ghost also makes a noise. One more, and a whisky chaser, and you can find out the actual words he says. It is reported to be, 'Where's the Sunday job this week?'

Now that we are out in the open Pennine valley it is a bit surprising that tunnels seem to peter out until you come to the famous Summit Tunnel, geographically matched alongside Standedge, since its job is to see you through the peaks of the spine of England. It was here that the disastrous fire from an oil tanker train closed the tunnel for many months, with spectacular firework scenes of flames erupting out of the tunnel shafts. But it was off our engineering area, and therefore none of our business, thank goodness!

Returning to the theme of twinned tunnels, the ones I was thinking of are those like Springs and Esholt tunnels, from Leeds and Bradford respectively to Ilkley. They are about half a mile apart as the crow flies, running under the same hill. A more un-identical pair of twins never existed.

Springs is like a gateway to the Moors from Leeds, with the tracks climbing up from the Leeds to Skipton line. It is short, on a gentle curve, and reasonably safe and dry. If you get dripped on in there, then you're simply standing in the wrong place. Esholt (Bradford to Ilkley), on the other hand, is a nasty, vicious and spiteful little hole on a sharp curve. It has improved its image since the tracks through it were singled, but before that it was so tight that you were obliged to walk on wet, slippery sleepers, on jointed track – which gave little warning of an approaching train. In places you got unavoidably soaked. Though only a few hundred yards long, Esholt has always been my least favourite tunnel. Again, this should not really be said, but it is a typical suicide fatality site, with drivers getting no warning of anyone in the tunnel.

Digressing slightly, now that I've been reminded, into the relationship that was unwritten but oft said in the days of old, between the British Transport Police and the Civil force. There are no instructions in the Rule Book as to a practical procedure on finding a body on the line, but the silent approach to be adopted was made very clear on Huddersfield Area – blessed, as it was, with a large number of tunnels. Following my first experience of a fatality on the track, I asked what the procedure should be. I was told, muttered behind a hand, that I should get hold of the Transport Police, not the Civil. The sole reason for this was that it was one of the interests of the Railway force to get traffic moving again as soon as possible.

Railway Police would take measurements, and possibly photos, and arrange for the body to be moved to the side of the tracks and covered, allowing traffic to resume. Any follower of TV death scenes will know the elaborate work needed before a body is moved at all. Photos, measurements, statements from everyone on the train, summoning of superior officers, SOCO, forensics, and maybe even the press. A far cry from the 'take a look and shift it' way of the Transport Police.

All the above would be strenuously denied if asked directly, but that's how it was in practice. Again as a further diversion, seeing as the Rule Book has come up, the 1950 version lays out the procedure should anyone be injured on the railway. The ganger of that length, which was usually about three or four miles long, would have to send a man in each direction to the adjacent gangs, who in turn sent a man on to the next until a station or signal box be reached, so that assistance could be obtained. Meanwhile, the poor victim presumably either recovers or becomes the sort of problem above.

This diversion from the theme suggests that tunnels and suicides are linked. That's how it is, and in all my years of walking alone through tunnels it was ever at the back of my mind that I might come across an example. There were two close calls: one where a driver reported a body, and I was the first there to discover a heap of old clothing; and another occasion when I must have disturbed a planned suicide, as from the timing of the report I could see that I must have been there only minutes before the deed.

I don't know how I might have reacted if I had found a body, though I did encounter a heap of old clothing in our church doorway at night once. It had given me a bit of a shock when I first stepped on it, so I gave it a retaliatory kick, at which the pile got to its feet and stumbled away, grumbling about trying to get a bit of peace.

★

Bridges throughout the system all carry a number, usually rising along with the mileposts. One of the students who came among us at Huddersfield was a desperate engine number collector. Locally, he had collected every number going, and was having to spend money travelling to other regions for new numbers. We solemnly suggested to him that he should widen his horizons to collecting bridge numbers. With him being somewhat green, he gave it a go one weekend.

Generally speaking, railway underbridges are lacking in character. For bridges carrying railways over roads this is probably explained by the fact that the load is directed over a guaranteed alignment, and the design tends to reflect this, often being easily designed straightforward iron girders. From the road they appear as plain iron parapets, the real work being done by the half-concealed cross girders underneath. In crude terms, the engineers of old would go into the Bridges 'R' Us department of Ikea and take away a flat-pack rail bridge of spans, short, medium and long. The only differences on offer would be the depth of the main girders and the thickness of their top and bottom flanges.

Viaducts deflect from this iron girder rule, having a continuous string of stone or brick arches. However, Paddock Viaduct, in Huddersfield, carrying the Penistone Branch, all lattice girders for some reason, is an exception, and obeys the bridge rule to a large extent. (It is local folklore that any would-be Yorkshire cricketer was put to the test by having to throw a ball right over Paddock Viaduct. What happened to it then is not mentioned; presumably some hapless Paddockian copped for it on the other side in one way or another.)

Were a new viaduct to be ordered today, there would no doubt be an outcry about it spoiling the landscape; whereas existing viaducts, like Arthington over the Wharfe, are regarded as a proud and beautiful contribution to the landscape. This is true, be it a Lowry urban situation, like Stockport redbrick viaduct, striding through the town and over the M60, or a Turner colour explosion, as seen in 'Rail, Steam and Speed'. Viaducts are now mainly accepted as features, except in the cases of Huddersfield, with its pigeonholes of workshops and small businesses, and Leeds, where they have become fashionable coffee houses, restaurants, and weird establishments for buying odd items of cloth to partially cover members of the in-crowd. There are also 'quaint little shops, manned by a funny little man or a wonderful little woman', for people from Harrogate to visit. Access is needed to be available for structural inspections, and these can be fun, grovelling through all the junk piled up under them. Out in the open, things became very different during my years.

Viaduct inspections in the late twentieth century became a thing of great excitement with the introduction of the Guzzunda. This was a rail-mounted wagon with hydraulic arms taking an inspection basket out and under the viaduct, or high bridge. Before this, inspection could only be carried out by scaffolding (expensive) or binoculars (shaky). The Guzzunda was an experience that outreached the Simon platform I had used to condemn Bradford Exchange roof. There you simply left the ground to seemingly climb up to the roof, a sort of automatic ladder. But the Guzzunda gave you a feeling of leaving the planet as you swept out over the land before coming back to the reality of the structure and up into its belly. Whatever, you had no apparent signs of support from below, and some sort of codicil needed to be added to the contract of needing a 'head for heights'.

As with all modern aids to more accurate observation, the Guzzunda revealed, at a close-up position, all sorts of worrying cracks and gaps. It was similar to the electric lighting in tunnels creating bulges. Ignorance is a great comfort, especially if, as so often happens, the bulges and cracks turn out to be benign.

My very first Sunday out from the York Office was to study the movement of viaduct arches under traffic. A small target plate about two inches square with a series of concentric rings was attached (via ladders) to the underside of the arch, and a tame locomotive used to run gently over it, while we watched the target by way of a theodolite. Invariably the viaduct was seen to move in a rotational manner, first pushing forward, then down, round and back up. Once again, this gained knowledge brought natural movements to light that immediately caused unnecessary worry.

Bridges over the railway are a very different matter to under-bridges, having a multitude of designs and directions, and character again. Roads might cross at an angle, making for some marvellously intricate skewed brickwork. By far my favourite overbridges are some of the first to be built – those along the Leeds to Selby line. With amazing foresight and optimism, these prototype bridges were constructed to accommodate four tracks beneath, even though at the time two tracks were thought to be evermore sufficient. They are in gloriously shaped flattened arches, sort of parabolic comes to mind as a description, but I bet I get letters about that. The only drawback of these matching sets is that the forethought as regards the railways of the future was not reflected in any expectations for the road traffic above, so they are generally narrow, in packhorse style, and in some places necessarily spoilt by crude but efficient widening extensions.

★

'Oop theer, just past t'quackyduck.'

Yes, it was said to me just as suddenly as that. I asked for a repeat and received a sad thicko condescendingly louder and slower rendition from the signalman.

'Along theer, sithee, Tommy and t'gang are just a bit p-a-s-t t-h-e quack-y-duck!'

As was usually the case, I never had the courage to go for a second repeat, so I wandered off in the direction indicated. I saw Tommy Sykes and his lads in the distance, so my objective had been achieved. It was as I passed under a narrow iron trough carrying a stream of water over the railway that the penny dropped. Ever since such have been known to me as quacky-ducks.

There is another quite spectacular aqueduct just over a mile away at the mouth of Standedge Tunnel, where water is carried river-wide over the slow double tunnel lines, and down under the old fast singles. It is an overflow from a small reservoir ('rezer-voyer') above the tunnel, which had at times broken through its walls to violently flood the tracks. Such a failure is offset now by way of some massive buttresses.

This leads us inevitably back to the tunnels and their various characteristics. All the tunnels I have worked in or walked through have been basically honest. What you see as you approach them is carried into the tunnel beyond. Bramhope is pretentious at the one end, but as that faces the gentility of North Yorkshire, this is only to be expected. But the tunnel that breaks all the rules of behaviour and presentation is the deceitful Stanningley Tunnel, between Leeds and New Pudsey. (In passing, I can boast that the whole of New Pudsey station is half an inch higher than designed, thanks entirely to me. I subtly altered track levels through the station as building work was starting, and the platforms, etc. levels used the tracks as a datum.)

Stanningley Tunnel is an outrageous 500-yarder, presenting two reliable-looking portals, with the one at the Leeds end perhaps betraying a little of what lies within. The Bradford end is a broad, high personification of sincerity. It virtually poses in the manner of those muscle-bound quarter-wits in the Mr Universe strain, and manages to hold the position for quite a few yards in, while the other end has a Uriah Heep presentation of contrived humility. Passengers get no real perception of all this, but if you're the poor unfortunate on the roof of the tunnel inspection wagon, it almost literally strikes you if you're not quick enough. For within a few paces of entering via an adequate-looking portal, the tunnel roof suddenly comes down upon you so that you have to flatten yourself on the wagon to avoid trouble. Here is the tightest bit of tunnel, or bridge for that matter, that I have ever come across. My measuring rods arranged at the rear of the wagon could not be drawn in sufficiently or quickly enough, and were unceremoniously snapped off, all three. Stanningley is a clear case of never judging a book by its covers, or a tunnel by the daylit bits at the ends. Now for me, the deception which Stanningley Tunnel puts out, and the hidden crush conditions just inside, makes for the character of the hole. You can sense it giggling as you fall flat on your belly when the roof jumps down with a 'Boo! Gotcha!'

This tightness eases a little as you get into the tunnel, to broaden out to very comfortable by the time the posing Bradford end is reached. What's more, the whole thing moves!

Not much, but enough for us to take regular readings of the roof profile twice a year. Having said that, I must stress that I have no fear for the stability and safety of Stanningley Tunnel. All movements seem to be seasonal, no doubt as ground water levels change, but I wouldn't like to have a property on the surface too close to the tunnel line.

So, from the utter deceit of Stanningley we move at last to the stability and nobility of Standedge. The name 'Standedge' is a group title for a family of tunnels, all over three miles long. Referring to the youngest, the Slow double line, it is regarded as the king of tunnels in my experience. Admittedly the counterpart to Standedge, Woodhead Tunnel is a shade longer, and much newer than Standedge, but it was only longer because the sad losers who designed it extended it at one end with two yards of superfluous concrete just to make it longer!

One thing now missing from the double line tunnel is the funereal gong a quarter of a mile in from the Marsden end, on the Down line running out of the tunnel, warning anyone at the tunnel end on the dangerous blind curve of an approaching train. This was activated on a treadle system as the train ran over its lever end. From inside the tunnel it was the sound of doom, with the effect of the sunken cathedral. This was perhaps the only sinister aspect of an otherwise heart-warming tunnel.

Is there a perception of global warming in that Standedge has not, to my knowledge, been closed in recent winters due to icicles at the Yorkshire end? These used to form like massive iron bars at the tunnel mouth and for many yards into the tunnel. They had to be big because the tunnel is big, probably the highest and widest in my collection. For drivers of steam locos there was a danger of the icicles falling into the cab, and for the later diesel operators the potential that they could smash windscreens. Traffic rarely stopped, since the Huddersfield PWay and Works departments anticipated the problem and the tunnel inspection wagon was brought in at night for the back-breaking purpose of smashing the growths before they could become dangerous. They certainly added to the impressive entrance at the Marsden end.

I have experienced feelings towards claustrophobia only in extreme situations (I have never tried potholing, but I fear that that would be such a situation). In younger days I did once crawl through the firebox of our church's coke boiler to look up the chimney. There was an element of panic trying to back out as my clothes rucked up and hampered my reverse gear. I mention claustrophobia with Standedge Canal Tunnel in mind. This is the basis for the Standedge family, for it was used in the construction of first one of the single line tunnels and again for the other, for access and the removal of spoil. It also provided a number of extremely generous air shafts, which are thankfully over the canal and consequently stood back clear of the railway tunnels. These are immense structures, some of which I have stood within, but never to look up, as the sheer volume and strength in the falling waters tumbling down the holes does not allow for looking up. Finally, after the twin single line Fast Tunnels came the very generous double line tunnel, the only one remaining active nowadays, although there is talk – just talk, you understand – as regards one of the singles. Very much like Morley, except Standedge is exactly level throughout, but for the long dip at the

Diggle end where the water troughs used to be. I can vouch for it being level as I had once to perform a survey using a level, with readings taken every four sleepers, for three miles and a bit – 4,276 separate readings. This was for one of Don's more whimsical projects.

But what a fine roomy tunnel it is, with the tunnel inspection lads holding their tapping rods at full stretch! Both single lines were fairly generous with regard to clearances, but not on the scale of the big sister. In my early days of Standedge experience there was a permanent tunnel gang repairing sections of the brick roof. Work was carried out with no effect on traffic, again the overhead clearance being good enough to allow for scaffolding across the roof. This was moved to new locations on Sundays, usually just carrying on from where they'd left off.

At Diggle there is small ghetto in the form of a group of sheds where the gang's cabin would be, with roaring fires in two large rooms. Here the aging PWay Supervisor, Dick Simms (Mr Simms to all but Don), would pass away his Sunday shifts in the comfort of the cabin with its chaise longue sofa, while the gang worked probably a mile and a half away in the depths of the tunnel.

One thing missing from the Diggle Hilton was a lavatory of any description. One dark single line tunnel with three miles of warning was used instead, so that the first two hundred yards of the Down Fast were particularly hazardous. The railway never bothered about anyone simply needing a pee, as all were lads together, and pausing 'to run a drop off' was part of any survey or gang's day. The use of the tunnel merely concentrated what was common for most of my time over a short area, whereas the whole length of the railway was a virtual sewage farm. Even the Royal Train had no more than a hole in the floor of the lavatory, hence the pole and long bucket duty wherever it stabled. This was the reason for the 'Do not flush while standing in a station' notice. Complementary was the inhospitable nature of surveying just outside stations, especially Leeds with its mass of point work.

'Oh, sod it! I'm going to be lucky this week!' was the occasionally heard remark at night from some unfortunate wiping down a badly placed hand on the rail in some available grass.

'Being lucky' after misfortune of this kind was the folklore compensation for landing in such a situation.

Tunnels should be put on an equal status as station platforms in making the plea not to flush. The results are not as easy to see in the light of a torch beam.

With the fallout from the 'great and good' Dr Beeching, the Fast lines were closed up the Colne Valley, and with that the single line tunnels fell into disuse. One huge benefit, once we had levelled the floor a little, was that cars and gang buses could be run into them, even allowing for a three-point turn in the middle at 'the Cathedral' where both single lines are exposed to each other. Towards the end of my time, myself and one other organised trips for office staff through the tunnel in their cars, something of an experience for them.

Sadly, all is not perfect at Standedge, in terms of the tracks, for sharp curves are encountered at both ends, with accompanying speed restrictions: 40 mph at Marsden and 55 at Diggle. I was commissioned to provide a scheme involving new tunnel bores at the ends to achieve something like 65 mph, but these involved a quarter of a mile of entirely new tunnel. On the plus side, photographers love the sight of a train emerging from the tunnel, on maximum cant and apparently rolling over on its side.

Going back to my thoughts on claustrophobia. This has never been a problem in a tunnel, except perhaps Bramhope, because you could not see either end until close to them, but the canal tunnel at Standedge can be seen at odd spots where cross adits give you a view of a few yards of the canal. It is hewn out of the solid rock, with no lining, and has all the appearance of a flooded dungeon. At the moment progress is being made towards running small launches through, but I'm not at all sure that I want to take part.

So, because of the canal and its enormous air shafts up to 500 feet deep, the Standedge railway tunnels do not suffer the downpours they would experience were they directly under the shafts; yet the movement of air keeps the tunnels reasonably clear, and the offset shafts keep them fairly dry. This makes the double track tunnel at Standedge the king of all tunnels that I have come across, with the regal characteristics that this epithet carries.

Now that is the point where this chapter ended. I have now realised, during a few days in North Wales, that I have not chosen a tunnel or bridge with what I see as having the greatest character. For bridges, some of Brunel's efforts cannot be beaten for sheer beauty, but not necessarily character. For me this shines out in two bridges by Robert Stephenson, one crossing the River Conwy, and the other, an ex-Stephenson, crossing the Menai Straits a mile or two further on. They are, or rather now only one is, box girders. The Menai one was burnt out, somewhat fortunately for the local roads authority, who had it reconstructed as dual rail and road bridge, accommodating the excellent A55 running through to Holyhead.

To view the Conwy pigmy version, you have to nip round the back, as the usual view is obstructed by a very ordinary road bridge. It looks like a glorified square drainpipe with suitable adornments to blend in with Telford's famous road bridge and the looming castle bursting out above it. Now, putting this bridge down as being full of character may be because not only is it a bridge, but it must also qualify as a tunnel, being 137 yards long! There is simply something odd watching a High Speed Train of several coaches in length, half disappearing in at one end, and the rest bursting out at the other. I think that it is the drainpipe analogy that does it; it's so children's toy train set, or Blue Peter amalgamated bog roll construction. Whatever, in all my searching for character, this is an eccentric-looking bridge, and surely not pretty.

I could have left it at that, nominating the Conwy bridge as my most characterful bridge and tunnel alike, except my sure choice in the tunnel department lies not many miles from Conwy, on the line to Blaenau Ffestiniog.

It's not so much the tunnel structure and entrances, but the amazing effect that it has on the first-time passenger. Starting from the busy town of Llandudno Junction, the single line travels alongside the tidal section of the River Conwy as far as Llanrwst. From here to Betws-y-Coed, the river hides behind trees and cuttings, before arriving at the full-blown tourist centre, with all that such carries with it. Things, on this single line from here on, start happening. The countryside becomes much more remote and lonesome. There is a feeling of travelling back in time as you progress, seeing a Roman bridge and a stranded castle. Even the sheep seem to be petering out as the way is made through very narrow rock cuttings on quite tortuous curves. Hills and mountains form an everlasting backcloth. You are travelling deeper and deeper into isolation; what the townie views as absolute desolation. There is nothing but limitless rough grassland with the occasional lonely tree and rocky outcrop. All this is glimpsed through gaps in the thickening lineside scrub, all of which seems to be closing in on you. You are climbing ever upwards into a cultivated desert. Loneliness and separation from the world you knew begins to overwhelm you; then the edges of the railway close in, as what starts as another claustrophobic vertical rock cutting grows towards engulfing you and the train. You are now heading for the forbidding face of one of the mountains, and as it becomes certain that you are to be exterminated, a small black hole appears and you plunge from bleak wilderness into the close fitting confines of the single line tunnel. Two miles away is a spot of light, seemingly marking your entry into the afterlife.

Four minutes later the most amazing sight greets you, as you sweep out of the tunnel into another world. You find yourself running along the floor of an enormous quarry, with three sides of this new world covered with broken slates stretching up to the sky. Blaenau Ffestiniog tunnel has taken you from an absolute desert of desolation into the antipodean valley of bygone industrialisation. I can only see it working in this direction, but our long confined tunnel has connected two completely opposite worlds. Its character lies in the yards before each end rather than within.

Treasure Hunts – a Digression

If you are looking for some way to completely waste an evening, destroying good drinking time, a way to infuriate, irritate and see little else but red, then sign up for an office treasure hunt.

I used to hate these. They cropped up every summer. Having the clever article who'd organised it following us around, as our team was always in last place (no, that should be both times – once not believing it could be so bad, and once again because you didn't think that you could not be so numb as the first time). He'd be smirking as we fell into all the laid traps and distractions, jumping about round the answer if we were showing no interest, or finally taking pity, and showing us. John Marshall was the worst/best at setting the course and questions; it seemed to fall to him evermore, once the rule stating that last year's winner sets this year's horror fell through. His clues were always perfectly obvious, when you knew the answers, but impossible when you only had half your mind on the job, with the rest of it on the culminating pie and pint, when this farrago was all over. In this state you were tuned fully into gullibility, and because of boredom, fell for every red herring presented.

Just the once did John come unstuck, when, following his third careful check with a dummy team, a week before the event, the council came and tarmacked over some vital signs on the road. This sealed it for John, since he was strange enough to really want to take part in one in future, and he resigned.

Dave Holmes thought it would be a good idea if the Project Section (then just three of us) took over the designing of the course. Summer was always a slack time for us, and we both felt totally confident in Dave Thornton running the section for a day, while we toured West Yorkshire looking for clues. I was more than happy with this, determined to get my own back on J Marshall and wife, Sheila, who was just as bad.

The routine was exactly that each year: routine. All meet in cars at a suitable car park; collect sheets of clues; set off round the undisclosed route; finish up around nine at a forewarned pub. Devising it involved one morning nipping round a possible course, noting odd things down, writing up a set of clues, if possible with a railway bias; then there's one check later – preferably with a semi-intelligent being to test the clues on, and unable to attend on the evening. It's between that last check and the actual day that several things are bound to happen.

John's piece of road will still have been tarmacked, of course. A strangely shaped tree, that has withstood a century of gales, storms, tempests and pestilence, falls over. Then it happens to be fallow time on the farm; things have been planted and the farmer is sat about with nothing to do until they grow, besides milking the hens and collecting the cow's eggs, and he goes and mends that particularly distinctive gate that's been off its hinges since a year last Michaelmas. They paint the vital telephone box with a clue written inside the directory, and everyone returns with streaks of red paint and tempers to match. Some poor GPO lad cops it for making a poor job of the painting because our lot have fingered it and smudged the glass. The grave you picked out has been opened up for another inmate, with soil piled up against the particularly interesting headstone. On the door of No. 19, in the village, the nine has been refixed the right way up. The occupants of what is now No. 16, which is at the end of the lane, are pestered all evening by strangers looking for the non-existent No. 19. A new bus timetable has been introduced. A bull has been put into the field with the tree in the middle, and is idly reading and nibbling at a plastic noticed clue nailed to the tree.

Dave insisted that 'nothing could go wrong' between the final check and the hunt evening, two weeks later; yet he had to pay four dinner-time visits to our finishing hostelry, to check that arrangements there were OK.

We had some unpleasantness at the very first search spot, near a pub. The clue was simply something like 'Look out for the duck's toilet'. Down the lane was a small stream running through a pond. It was obvious from the ground where the ducks liked to stand and cogitate, and we left a further clue fastened to a shrub there. However, Dave and I hadn't taken any notice of the pub, it being the first to be encountered, and with it being at the beginning of the lane. There was increasing hostility from the barman in 'The Mallard and Swan', as people trooped in to examine the toilets. They told him, refusing to buy a drink so early in the evening, that they were just checking up.

We followed the stragglers round so that nobody should get lost. This was a mistake. On reaching clue number five or six, which had simply said 'It's in the pipe', we found the whole company gathered together, and looking ugly. Starts had been staggered, which helps in that followers don't simply watch where the leaders find something. Both Dave and I had thought this particular clue a good idea, there being the gift of a road drainage job in the vicinity, and the pipes were something like ten inches in diameter and ten feet long. They were arranged along the roadside in an adjacent field. What seemed to upset the punters was that there must have been a thousand of them spread out for a quarter of a mile. A sense of humour was an essential quality to go on a Holmes/Collins hunt, and we thought they knew that.

One hunt finished in Arthington village, and was won by the Engineer, Geoff Holmes, and his team of semi-professional treasure hunters. Between them they knew the history of every church on the trail, the name and licensee of every pub, the date and times of every minor social event, the names of every flower in the garden, and what the village postman's dog was called. Dave and I decided that he had just got together a team of ringers, and the boss's winning envelope with the first prize in it was disdainfully chucked across the lounge floor towards him. Geoff picked it up, and reduced us to dust by ignoring the insult and inviting the organisers, Dave and me, and partners, round to his house (which was only a couple of miles away) for a coffee.

This was the first time for any of us to be inside a boss's house, and nervousness took over. Our first mistake was in assuming that one of us knew where *chez Holmes* was, and it was easy to mistake Geoff's instruction of 'left out of the car park' to mean 'right out of the car park'. Here were the organisers of the office treasure hunt, failing to get from the pub to the house, which apparently involved just two directional instructions. Should we pretend that we had misheard the invitation, and just go home? We couldn't. Dave's initiative brought him to a phone box, and using the emergency call-out list in his pocket, he rung the Holmes villa.

He then realised that he could not ask for directions to it since he had no idea where he was to start with. However, it turned out that this phone box was unique, in that it was apparently the only one in North Leeds. Dave took down directions, and five minutes later we were back in the pub car park. There we found the Assistant Engineer, Nigel Trotter, who had been at another function, now being ferried by his wife, Liz, who had taken part in what Nigel had described as a 'crippling waste of time', but had not avoided the get-together afterwards. We arrived as the Holmes were obviously thinking in terms of cocoa and bed. Nervousness was now peaking.

I picked one of those biscuits that are thoroughly dehydrated, and when introduced to the mouth tend to swell larger than the space would allow. I also found myself fingering a very bare patch on the arm of the easy chair that I was engulfed in. This was spotted by Mary, the hostess, who explained that the first-class three-piece suite was being re-covered, and the present one had been brought in from storage in the garage. The bald spot seemed to mesmerise me the more, and I could not take my hand away from it. I also badly wanted somewhere to hide the rest of my biscuit.

Dave now bravely announced that he wished to use the toilet. We noticed when we entered the house that we were in a lobby with several doors leading off it. Dave was told the third door from the right. Somewhat confused by the alcohol, Dave opened what he thought was the right door. From outside, in the poshest estate in Leeds, came the overloud cry, 'I'm in the garden, now, Mr Holmes, I take it that this is where you meant me to have a pee?'

Liz, meanwhile, was watching her husband like a hawk, obviously wondering if his natural talent of doing something embarrassingly bad was about to surface. We left just as I swallowed down the first bite of the erupting biscuit, itself having been wondering in whatever direction it was to make its escape. The rest of it went to blowing up some of the Holmes's feathered fauna, come the dawn.

It was shortly after this that Dave began to fall ill, and he was increasingly not around in a social sense anymore. Yet the world cried out for more treasure hunts; this meant doing them on my own.

Now they had to be organised on foot, and with a talent for spotting the opportunity, I arranged for the first to start at the office door in Aire Street, and lead up to our church's Social Club. The canal was the obvious route. I often walked it to work, and it was about a mile and a half from door to door.

Competitors had to pick out the usual clues, with a few novelties, like placing in correct order photos of various locations, which were presented to them later, back in the club room: large mooring rings, signs on bridges, lock numbers, all that sort of thing. Again the crowd turned ugly when shown two different pictures of canal water.

Along the route, the river running below the canal opened out to form a wide still lake, with the associated waterfowl. Pictures of a choice of birds were pinned up in the club, extracted from a compendium of the world's rich stock of such things. The question was, which five birds, from the twelve illustrated, had they seen on the river? It was sad to see the results of intelligent beings acting as momentary twitchers. In Armley, a mile from Leeds centre, there were spottings of six South Atlantic wandering albatrosses, two golden eagles and a penguin. There had to be an extra mark awarded to the competitor looking beyond the river into the trade park on the other side, adding a Kentucky fried chicken to his list of birds. This hunt finished with a walk through the two parks in Armley, Gott's and Armley itself.

I felt that these two recreation areas held a lot of potential, along with being handy for the club, so the following year I set up another within the parks. There were two pieces of misfortune, one only of possible disaster. A large heap of road chippings was a magnet for the clue setter, and as I was well up in collecting little plastic medicine bottles, I hid twenty in the granite bits, all with an item of treasure inside. What I wasn't aware of was that the pile was load one of two, the second arriving after I had just lightly covered over the bottles.

Another clue on this hunt was 'Challenge the dirty old man for a bonus clue'. Here I dressed myself in a scruffy old mac, with the collar turned up, and added an obviously false red beard, flat cap and thick glasses. In this get-up I wandered round the park, getting pretty close to some entrants, but was only challenged once – by Denise, who claimed that she'd been looking for a DOM all her life. Where this presented a problem was when I was standing on the mansion steps, and the PWay Assistant Engineer, David Kealey, and his wife, Beryl, came to within a couple of yards of me. I was ignored because they were arguing rather bitterly between themselves, mainly about the 'idiot who had set these stupid questions'. Beryl then walked swiftly away with the comment, 'I never wanted to come on your blessed treasure hunt, anyway. I've had enough, I'm going back to the car!' I stood firmly fixed to the spot as the boss's deputy turned and spat out in my direction, 'Women!' He then stalked after her, without giving me a second look.

Life was now becoming particularly busy for me, with the first suggestions of a remodelling of the whole of Leeds station and approaches, and I was called upon by headquarters to carry out staging assessments of their rough plans. My next treasure hunt would have to be my last; so, still working alone, I decided on something easy for me and spectacularly different for the hunters. It was to be a treasure hunt *by train*!

Now before you say anything, I'm fully aware of the possible pitfalls within. When you find that the whole evening depended on three separate trains running faithfully to the pocket timetable that I'd presented everyone with, you might shut the book right now, wanting to have no further part in the ramblings of one who is naively gullible. Oh you of little faith! We who were paid by the organisation had that faith in abundance. It is the faith and optimism of a modern vicar laying out 200 hymn books for morning service. I was absolutely sure that nothing could go wrong.

Which is why I had contingency plans, just in case.

Perhaps the beauty of this hunt was that, apart from free-range liberty in crossing a city between two stations, the participants were battery hunters, all encaged and all experiencing the same situations as they happened on the night.

It was a simple plan. All would buy a West Yorkshire Day Rover ticket for about 50p. They would all catch the same train out of Leeds station, following me as a tourist group to the right platform. They would travel to Bradford (the train stopping at Bramley and New Pudsey), with self ensuring that none of our expeditionary force got off, mistaking Bramley for Bradford. Then came the walk across Bradford from the Interchange station to Bradford Forster Square. For this 10-minute stroll they were allowed three quarters of an hour. They all had a little map, and Bradford itself did them proud with an abundance of signs. Here there was a slight worry for the organiser in getting them all onto the Ilkley train, disembarking at Guiseley. But when there it was a straightforward cross-over to the other platform, and twenty minutes or so later catch the Leeds train. Simple, and I'm not going to embellish the tale by saying that any of the trains failed. They didn't, and were spot on time throughout. I did find this slightly boring, and the carefully contrived contingency plans were left unused.

In fact the whole event might have proved boring if it had not been for the interest latterly shown in the event by the British Transport Police.

Leaving Leeds at a steady pre-remodelling speed of 15 mph, there were many lineside offices and works premises with useful names and other signs. Clues came fast and furious here; furious because they were at both sides of the line, and there was much dashing about to and fro, along with jubilant shouting. Before matters got out of hand, I had a quick word with the guard, who couldn't understand why the 17.30 from Leeds to Bradford, on a summer Thursday evening, had taken on all the social rapport of a football special.

I discovered en route that, as he went down the train checking tickets, he was telling the civvy travellers that we were a party from a local institution, and that the carers had dispensed with their white coats for the informality of the evening. Passengers were assured that the gathering was composed of the more docile inmates.

My church stood on the route, with its world-famous organ, which inspired some obscure clues, like having a stab at the number of pipes in it. At least one member of each team had been inside the church, as this had been the Holy Grail at the end of the previous year's park hunt. Answers varied from the thirty visible in the front of the casing, to half a million. Here a bit of poor photocopying led to some confusion, a few of the crew denying any knowledge of an organ having pips in it, let alone pies…

Bramley station was reached with no great mishap, but it was interesting that the few people getting off were obviously advising the waiting dozen on the platform to hang on for the next train, a quarter of an hour later. I have no idea what dreadful reasons they were handing out, but only one got on. He turned out to be the genuine nutter you often find sitting next to you on a bus or train, and the regular travellers could be seen to be turning into a crowd as they overflowed into the empty seats next to those who looked like their own.

A mile further on was the site of the former Stanningley station, the location of Leeds District's workshops and stores. Johnny Bass, for a quid, had been persuaded to come back after his tea, and dress in his famous Hitler coat, cap and boots. Added to this, Johnny was grasping, in his non-saluting hand, a surveyor's marked staff. With him being around five feet tall, wearing a six-footer inspector's black coat, the question on the sheet was 'How tall was Hitler?'

The coat comfortably covered the beer crate that Johnny was standing on, so a great deal of confusion was started among those who knew him well, and his impersonation, and others who only saw what they saw. By now half the train was joining in, having tumbled to the game, and John was somewhat disconcerted to receive a barrage of returned Nazi salutes from all three coaches. (Oh, those happy non-PC days of yore!)

We next came to our second station stop, New Pudsey. Now here was an enormous disappointment for me. Within the previous week, New Pudsey Station had appeared as a location shot on Monty Python's Flying Circus (you can check that, if you have the complete works). All the treasure hunt sheets had been compiled and printed when a dozen 'flying circus' clues shot through my mind, all wasted. Instead there was some mind-boggling question like, 'How many steps up to the car park?' This is mundane barrel-scraping treasure hunt stuff. Sorting out the technical staff from the clerks, the length of Stanningley Tunnel was next required. Duckett's crossing had the warning bell ringing, followed by a short hole (No. 9) alongside the track of a cross between a golf course and putting green. A few minutes later, and we were plunging into the bowels of the earth known as Bradford.

Up to now, most of the Great General Public had enjoyed the fun, occasionally joining in. There were just the embarrassed few slunk down into their *Evening Posts*, but not taking a single word in. After I had ensured that nobody from the group had either decided to go on to Manchester, or simply fallen asleep, I had them momentarily under control. It was at this point that the deviousness of the Finance Department team beat any expectations of mine, and in the course of that, began to cause mayhem on Bradford Interchange Station. All that the hunt required was a passport shot, with all the team members on it, from one of those little curtained portaloos you found on stations at that time.

Head of Finance, Alan Burgess, short in inches but high in financial acumen, saw an opportunity. He gathered as many of the teams together as he could, mostly in twos or threes, and explained how considerable money could be saved by using all four pictures the machine allowed on four different teams. This meant his team of four crammed in first, 50p was inserted, and following the first flash they all tumbled out, to be replaced by Team Two. This went on, or was planned to go on, through Teams Three and Four. By the time that Team Two and a Half were in position, there was a heap of One and some of Two on the floor, Team Three clambering over the top of them, and what remained, namely Four, trying to heave them back out. Furthermore the photographic studio had moved several inches. This was seen as a fracas, a brawl, and most definitely a disturbance of the peace by the station staff.

It took ten minutes in the Station Manager's office to sort this out, with me showing him the hunt questionnaire and him demanding the name and address of our superior. This we could help him with, as the very same was awaiting his turn in the photo booth.

Sadly, the resulting pictures did not justify the attempted financial prudence. The first picture was fine, but from thereon in, all we had was an assortment of arms, legs and bums in what looked like stills from a Kama Sutra rally. Added to the various teams' disappointment, I had to disqualify all but the first, that of the enterprising Finance Section, since one of the Finance team had got wedged down the side of the spinning round seat, and so contributed, in some part or other, on all other three pictures, being unable to get out of the way. There was also the side question as to why he had seen it to be necessary to take his umbrella in with him, as this exploded between Two and Three.

What had been planned as a 30-minute meander across Bradford, now became a 15-minute yomp. Fortunately, the main inter-station requirement could be solved later. This was an interesting exercise. It had become the norm for a single cinema to show no less than three films at the same time. I have no direct experience of this, but assume that they were shown on different screens in different theatres. Anyway, the challenge was to imagine that if all three were shown on the one screen, what then would be the title of the resulting film be, using the actual ones that were advertised on the day. These were *Camelot*, *Friday the Thirteenth* and *Clash of the Titans*.

I'd had Dave Holmes, now pretty ill, check through the script before the day, just for old times' sake, and so that I could compassionately put Dave's name on this one last treasure hunt. Despite being in great pain, Dave could not stop being Dave. His inspired suggestion for the resulting film was *The Day King Arthur Put His Sword Away Carelessly*.

So, more by luck than judgement, I had the same number of competitors that I'd started with piling on to the 18.35 two cars to Ilkley, at Bradford Forster Square, for chucking off at Guiseley. They only had to avoid disembarking at Shipley and Baildon on the way, neither place being easily confusable with Guiseley. I suppose that you're still wondering about the British Transport

Police's involvement, aren't you? But hang on a bit longer, we'll come to that later.

Let's just take a look at the 18.35 Bradford to Ilkley. By this time the last of the rush-hour commuters were at home on the right side of their glasses of sherry, and were preparing to shunt themselves up to the dinner table, ready for whatever well-earned titbit the little lady had concocted to gently close down their brains before venturing into the soaps. If, however, they had left the train at Baildon, then they would more than likely be awaiting what cook had devised, while the aforementioned 'little l' had spent a hard day under the hairdryer at that marvellous new salon in Ilkley, followed by a spell in the queue to be seen in, viz., taking one's turn for a coffee and cake at Betty's Café. (For the benefit of the reader in the South of England, there is a small oasis up here called Baildon, where almost everyone lives like you do.)

In short, the only passengers to be seen on the 18.35 would be a couple of briefcased brown-nosers staying on after the boss had left at half five, three dizzy shop girls swapping their days, and a bloke attempting a return to Ilkley, having dropped off to sleep the first time. Five, six if you're lucky, seven if you include the guard. It was the same day after day, plus or minus two or three. Today was different, the passenger total being augmented by twenty-five unexpected excited extras, many by now looking the worse for wear. I had a word with the guard, telling him that they were all on Day Rovers, and he settled back almost into his usual 18.35 comfort.

The triangle at Shipley gave plenty of scope for minor clues, and we began the long climb up to Guiseley. Cruelly, for the driver, this involved having a stop at Baildon, halfway up the hill. The briefcases alighted here, to immediately drop into the wife's little runabout, she having left the arduousness of the kitchen to Cook, who was a veritable treasure. About five joined the train, which then continued the climb up to Guiseley. Here the coaches were seen to heave towards the platform as our lot offloaded. There was a slight panic here, as the more legitimate passengers noticed the speedy evacuation, and assumed a crisis, and so tumbled off themselves, only to be comforted by the relieved guard and persuaded back on board.

Guiseley platforms were littered with clues, some in the form of cartoons of notable members of staff pinned to the joists of the wooden waiting shelters, and virtually out of sight. It was with some interest that ten years later I was again at Guiseley in connection with the electrification of the line, and I noticed the pictures, slightly yellowed, but still well in place, thanks to a powerful stapling gun.

The sun was still well up in the sky when we all piled onto the 19.20 back to Leeds. A fairly brisk downhill sprint allowed for only a few questions, but one that sticks in mind was an optician's chart that we had blown up on a plywood sheet and nailed it to a dead tree in an anonymous field. Obviously the question was as to how far down the chart you could read, thus:

T

REA

SURE

HUNTS ARE

A LOAD OF BOLLUX

Most teams guessed the answer and were right.

So, spot on time, we arrived at Leeds ready for the trip up to the club for marking and drinks. It was at this point that the wheels came off.

It was all down to the question at the top of page 1: 'How many times did you see the phantom flasher?' This all started after my first, depressing, run round the circuit when I felt that potential for peculiar clues was pretty low. I had to invent more happenings of the Johnny Bass type. The idea of a repetitive flasher was the first and most obvious idea. Dave Thornton was still young and amenable, and shared my take-it-or-leave-it attitude to treasure hunts, from the point of view of taking part. I had my flasher, he had transport; only the details of when and where he could appear remained to be sorted.

The fairly relaxed timetabling of the evening trip allowed plenty of time for Dave to manage to appear at least once on each leg, and we felt that three flashes should be enough. Locations chose themselves; Duckett's crossing, with its warning bell whenever a train was approaching, was where a narrow lane crosses the railway, about half a mile beyond Stanningley Tunnel. Another easy spot was in the old Kirkstall goods yard, with access straight off a main road. That dealt with the first and third legs, but somewhere on the Bradford to Guiseley stretch was hard to come by. Shipley was an obvious location, were it not for the fact that there were more signal boxes, and hence nosy signalmen, per yard than anywhere else on the District. We settled for a small field above what used to be Emmerdale Farm country before it got silly. A trial run round all three proved that Dave would need a newspaper to kill time, he had so much to spare.

The actual flash was to be no more than Dave opening a dirty old ankle-length mac in true flasher style, possibly a couple of times, as the train passed by. Beneath he was to wear normal clothing. All those on the right side of the train spotted Dave at Duckett's, and yelled approval. Unnoticed among the noise was a sharp scream. With everyone settled again, it became obvious where the scream had come from. It was a lady in a hat; now think about it, you don't get many ladies in hats on 17.30 commuter trains. She was all talcum, Dame Edna glasses and with traces of blue rinse poking out from under the hat. The poor guard got it full belt.

'Did you see him? Absolutely disgusting!'

The guard had not been paying attention, more occupied with when he could lever this crazy bunch off at Bradford.

'You must have done! Long macintosh. Completely... he was... he hadn't... well, he only had the coat on. I want to see someone about it. See to it at the next station!'

'Bradford. Love... er, madam, I'll raise the Station Manager. There's nothing I can do from here.'

'That's not good enough, he'll have disappeared long before!'

'Are you sure he was, ah, er...?'

'Of course I am! I know what I saw.'

Perhaps Dave's choice of clothing beneath the mac could have been better, especially as far as a myopic old bat with unsuitable glasses was concerned. He had on casual light fawn trousers with an off-white t-shirt, along with my red beard from the park, dark shades and a battered trilby. In the space of a moment, blurred around the edges, he might have appeared 'oh natural', as the French put it. Anyway, we'd hit a spot of bother, but I knew that Dave was already safely on his way across the valley to Esholt for Flash 2, so he could hardly be traced.

When we offloaded at Exchange Station, the old former reality virgin was still berating the guard, who was first intent on his duties of changing ends with the driver. Eventually, on a tight schedule, he found someone to take care of her, the Station Manager apparently being out of his office, trying to sort out a brawl around the photo booth.

Now here's what I was to find out later. Lady Bracknell had kicked up such a stink that the British Transport Police were called. There! I told you that if you had enough patience the cabaret would be on! Sergeant and constable arrived in time to see a rugby scrum disassembling itself on the concourse, releasing the Station Manager back into circulation. They were about to take some interest in this, until a bundle of feathered hat, twinset and flyaway spectacles gained their attention by smacking the sergeant on the shoulder. From this point they all went into conference, the upshot of which was that all Bradford guards were told to keep a lookout for a crazy nudist.

Dave's appearance at Esholt was brief, curtailed to one flash only, due to him slipping on the steep grass banking while flinging his coat open. It was convincing enough for the three dotty shop girls who mentioned it excitedly to the guard as he came looking at tickets. The guard asked the driver, who had had the best view, and the story was confirmed. They together thought on to report it when they got to Ilkley. The guard also mentioned that if anyone else encountered a demented crowd of excitable individuals, they were harmless and best left alone.

The driver and guard (our third of the trip) of the Guiseley to Leeds train were not phased by the loading of our uncoordinated party, as it was now the time for clubbing groups to be doing the evening trip into Leeds, and the train was now three parts full. Dave, in Kirkstall old goods yard, produced his finest performance of the day, managing three quick flashes in total. Again the driver spotted our lad, and mentioned it to the guard when we arrived at Leeds, and the latter tapped up a couple of the constabulary meandering about the concourse, also mentioning that there was an invigorated party with problem potential for their presumed trip back to Guiseley later that night.

'Hello, hello, hello,' said the two uniformed bastions of the law (or rather perhaps just 'Hello, hello', seeing as there were only two of them. These sharp-witted pair were now associating reports of a travelling circus together with appearances of this flasher, and with CID potential, were putting one and three dozen together. The sergeant picked me out from the throng, most of who had dissipated into the main concourse. He was a large man in all respects, and looked as if he could fell you with a flick of his eyelash. I'm not short, but he looked directly down his nose, and over his chinstrap at me. He beckoned me ominously to one side.

'Ayoop, Mike. Are you with this lot?' Sergeant Jack Booth was a regular customer of mine, in the buying of safety footwear, for which I was an agent.

'Hi, Jack!' Then inspiration. 'Do me a favour. Could you make it look as if you're asking me to accompany you to your office, please?'

Instantly Jack turned from friendly copper to Kneecap Booth of the Transport force. From friendly whisper he changed to menacing boom.

'If you've got a moment, I'll ask you to accompany me, *sir*. There are a few points that need clearing up. Now come along easily and there's no need for any trouble.' 'Sir' was said in the most disrespectful and sarcastic manner imaginable, as if he had just scraped me off his boot (Size 10, black, wide fitting, steel sole and toecap, item H241).

I had just a moment to turn to one of the few remaining punters and say, 'Just hang on a minute, this can't take all that long to sort out.'

'I'm in no great hurry, *sir*,' (there it was again) 'and my colleague can take down the names and addresses of what's left of your party. They are with you, I take it?' And off we toddled, with his hand most un-affectionately placed under my elbow, to the police office on the concourse.

I rejoined the main party ten minutes later, and we all made our confused way up to the Church Social Club. I didn't see it as necessary to point out that Jack and I were old pals, and his unexpected intervention made the final question that bit easier to answer:

'What was the most unusual thing that you saw on the trip?'

There was a current advertising hoarding showing a cat with two heads, each examining two varieties of a feline tinned delicacy. This was what I had had in mind, but was completely missed. Instead the universal answer was: 'Mike getting arrested.'

Coming of Age

'It has been decreed,' announced Cranium Colossus, head of Britannia Rut based in Eboracum, 'by Emperor Caesar Kickbum, that the East Coast Main Rut, at present dedicated to wheelbarrows, is to be Equestrified. Equestrification is to spread throughout the glorious Roman Empire, starting with the ECM Rut.'

'What,' said Twoplank Thickus, 'is Equestrification?'

'Horse power, of course. Didn't they teach you anything up the Collegium?'

'What,' pressed on Twoplank Thickus, 'have horses to do with the Great Rut?'

'The Rut is to be converted into a Double Rut to take passengers by horse and carriage from Londinium through to Auld Reekium by way of Eboracum in three classes of travel. First class will be by covered chariot, Second open chariot, and Third strapped to a plank fastened to the back of a chariot. The route will be known as the 'Equestrian Caravan Main Link', or ECML.'

'How can it get to Auld Reekium? There's a damn great wall that Hadrian slapped up bang in the way!'

'The wall at that point will be replaced by a guarded fortress, a new castle upon the Tyne, where only the rut will pass through.'

'What's it going to be called?'

'Newcastle upon Tyne.'

'Hades Goryous! What genius thought that up?'

'There is only one man who can see such a scheme through the tricky environs of Eboracum,' said Cranium Colossus, ' and that is Sinus Projectimus, assisted by Oral Loquacious, and they are duly appointed Project Managers for the complete re-rutting of the station area of Eboracum.'

'It is only VI years before the date for equestrifying,' announced Sinus Projectimus, 'so we must start meetings every month from now on. There will be Projector Meetings,

Progression Meetings, and during the work, meetings every Monday morning.' Vellum despatches went out to all departments, and the first Projector Meeting was arranged.

The Chief Rut Engineer was represented by Trigono Metrus and Straytan Curvus, and they were responsible for all the rutwork designs and estimates on the ground between Londinium Caesar's Cross to Berwick. The CRE would issue detailed plans of the rut and the rut crossings. For the actual construction of the ruttage around Eboracum, this work was assigned to the Divisional Rut Engineer at Cambodunum. (Which, because it is a difficult name to scratch onto a piece of granite or tap out on a computer keyboard, becomes known more simply as Leeds.)

The DRE at Leeds set up a special Project Team led by Baldas Cootus and Givtheman Upinus, assisted by Barnum and Lodgus, an Eboracum double act.

Around the table were representatives of every interested party, including such notaries as Semaphor Boardus, Telecom Beaconium, Porterus Major, Charioteer Steerum, each with IV assistants to hand. Financial advisors were headed by Titus Duksars and Stitchedup Pockets, and numbers were made up by such peripheral, but noisy individuals as Humerus Sillybugga and Pessimista Glumpuss. Regular refreshment breaks of crushed olives, wine and grapes were served by members of the Tealadii tribe.

Meanwhile the Bureaucratii were meeting in the Senate Chamber of the Kremlinorum in Eboracum, discussing the finances of the project, and most importantly which Sectorum should underwrite particular ruts.

'These absolutely top-hole plans show dual ruttageway going right through the city walls,' remarked Plumbus Gobbus from the chair.

'Well, I'm not picking up the tablets for that,' retorted Sectorum Magister Chariots, 'No rut! That's definitely Sectorum Magister Carts.'

'Mercantile Carts or Populus Carts, Carts Localum or CXXV Inter-City Carts?'

'I would suggest, chaps,' remarked the chair, 'that as it is within the city walls, it must be Sectorum Magister Poles Dragged Along the Ground.'

'Leave off,' said Sectorum Magister Poles Dragged Along the Ground, 'Inner-city has got to be Sectorum Magister Boots.'

'Double ruts,' argued Boots, 'whether through towns, cities or holes in chuffin' walls, ain't for boots, else why is there two of them? And I want that minuting.'

'Hold up,' pleaded the Secretariat, 'me chisel's buggered.'

'And where's the bloody Plonk Maiden from the Tealadii?' went on SM Boots. 'It's gone ½ past X and I'm gaggin' here.'

Baldas Cootus and Givtheman Uppin burnt the evening oils studying the plans of the complexities of the rutwork through Eboracum, Sinus Projectimus placing all sorts of obstacles in their paths from the other departments. A centurion's worth of foot soldiers slaved throughout the site, many dying on the job, and being buried beneath the line of the interconnected ruts, pushing aside the many archeologically significant remains of Ancient Britons. Man was replaced by man as the immense pressure that they were under saw them off. All this so that Emperor Caesar Kickbum could ride in triumph into Eboracum station, where he dined lavishly on curly sandwiches and evacuated sausage rolls. Leaving his horse and concubines in left luggage, he looked over the site and pronounced it good.

And so it was to be again, one thousand, nine hundred and fifty years later.

★

John Midgley and I had been kept together for what was to prove, in my case at least, the greatest challenge. John already had the Selby Diversion under his belt; indeed, it was in its final stages when Leeds and York Divisions joined up, and hence John and I as two project leaders amalgamated. Bowing to greatness, I took no part in these closing stages, and didn't even offer to, as I well knew what Midge's attitude would have been. This being the case he could claim Selby as wholly his. I had many smaller, but more complex permanent way projects to put my name to, probably in all adding up to an equivalent of Selby, without the main problem of that being a linked unit, one part affecting another throughout.

The Selby Diversion came about when the Coal Board decided to work a rich seam of coal in that area, with the East Coast Main Line running slap bang through the middle. This, and the consequent subsidence, would have led to numerous movable and crippling speed restrictions, with the associated compensation. On Leeds Division we were well up on the subsidence phenomena, it being a distinct roller-coaster-style feature of all lines south of Leeds, with areas around Barnsley moving several feet nearer to hell. (Nothing of significance should be read into that.) Thus there came about a 13-mile-long brand new railway route avoiding the new Selby coalfield, with the opportunity of faster point and crossing work at either end – pioneering stuff, which Midge and his team were responsible for installing. BR were none too bothered about the disruption to traffic as the connections at either end were installed, they were getting rid of a dodgy bit of railway over a swing bridge at Selby, with a whopping speed limit on it.

While this was going on I was working, with the odd assistant, on the relaying and restoration of track through tunnels at Woolley and Huddersfield. As I have noted in earlier writing, they [the authorities] had been pushing me on to projects from an early age, each one being more complex and problematic than its predecessor.

I was good at relatively small concentrated chunks, as John was at long-term stretches, an ideal combination for York remodelling. Added to this, I was forced into a 6-month absence due to the onset of pulmonary fibrosis, and John took the reins, with one small exception, managing as well as I might have. And so it came to pass that Baldas Cootus (known as Mike) and Givtheman Uppin (Midge) were summoned by Emperor Caesar Kickbum and Cranium Collosus to attend initial project meetings at HQ Eboracum (York).

After a morale-boosting opening, Caesar and Collosus withdrew to their two penthouse suites in the York Kremlin, and sat waiting the five years when they could re-emerge and take the national plaudits and any CBEs going. All future meetings were chaired by members of a breed known as project managers. This animal had many varying features and dimensions, but all had the same characteristics, and soon became in my book the contemporary versions of my favourite genus – the character. Some were upbeat and optimistic to a point where they instructed the rest of us to be the same; others saw problems, and lived in a state of nervous pessimism. The odd one or two were actually engineers of a sort, but tended to be more supportive of disciplines they knew less about. Then there was the deep sigh merchant, who made it our jobs to cheer him up with positive news. I was ensconced with one of these, in a meeting room on the sixth floor of Aire Street offices in Leeds, overlooking the station. There were about fifteen of us, mostly from York, a low turnout; the project manager sat at the head, with me at the foot of the long table. Half of the rest sat with their backs to the windows, and the others opposite, with only an outlook on the darkening sky. Snow was starting to fall, and I could feel the atmosphere becoming edgy as the majority contemplated a disruption to their journey home. This was early on in the Leeds remodelling discussions, so I more or less had the floor, with my initial sketches.

Operations saw the necessary track blockages as impossible to cope with. Telecoms could see no way that they could keep communications going. Inter-City saw vast diversions for their trains, and a shuttle service for London from Wakefield – a crippling prospect for business. The snow was now falling heavily, and settling. Regional Railways said that at best the commuter traffic would have to be cut to half in this, the busiest station outside London. Freight saw that they were being sidelined, and that they would have no access to their compound for weeks. Snow had now crept three inches up the window pane. Parcels saw their offloading area as completely blocked off, which would mean moving all their operations to Bradford. Signals could see no significant points where they could commission new chunks of railway. There was a virtual white-out beyond the window, that was fascinating me; only one of two who had a view of the disappearing tracks. Headquarters hierarchy were beginning to argue with their local representatives. Muttered squabbling went right around the table. The gloom-ridden chairman tried calmly to ask for order, but the arguing became louder. Yorkies were resigned to their fate of being stranded in Leeds, and hotels were being compared. Bickering became louder until the Project Manager screamed out with anger, demanding some sort of control. All fell deadly quiet. After what must have been only ten seconds, but seemed like an hour, I broke the silence.

'Do you want some good news?' I asked quietly.

'Oh, please,' said the chair with his head in his hands, 'something positive, please!' Obviously wanting some optimistic point about the doom-laden scenario of the depressing prospects of the project, he added, 'We need to go away with something promising to report back to HQ!'

'Well,' I said, 'I've just seen a train moving.'

There was a round of applause.

The track layouts of York station and its approaches were outrageously complex, much of the conglomeration having historic rather than operating reasoning. The whole was an accumulation of minor changes throughout the years within the greater disorder, and was a potential nightmare for the advancing aspirations of the electrification engineers. A scheme to electrify the whole area necessarily brought with it the semi-permanence of any layout, so the opportunity was there to rationalise and improve the two miles of railways approaching York, with the station standing at the hub. Speeds in, out and through York were crippling, and for the flash-trip visiting American tourists adequately represented a complete and detailed visit to the city. Now, a minute saved on the prestigious London to Edinburgh route was worth mega money. All in all it would be a revolution akin to the ancient Equestrification.

Midge and I were suddenly landed with two major projects: electrification from Doncaster through Leeds and York, to close on Darlington, and the complete track remodelling of York. For support we had the reliability, plus sideline activities, of Pete Wilder, along with his senior, a sadly inadequate one who just could not keep up. This poor lad was from a different century, and had been badly placed in a progressive unit like Projects. Perhaps that is a little unfair, as he was a wizard at track realign-

Arthur Barnard and Pete Lodge (Barney and Lodgey) on site at York. Photo: Phil Jagger.

Wendy Gaunt posing for an official photo.

Half a second later.

John Freeman doing something. Best not to ask what.

Two typical project managers, in this case Nigel Rutter and Ken Mackay.

George Woodcock, the steadying influence over John Freeman.

Nigel Trotter, sometime Assistant Area Engineer.

A most formidable, but jovial, Lily Tuke, a favourite clerk.

The gallant Norman Hebron, champion of the Dark Arches.

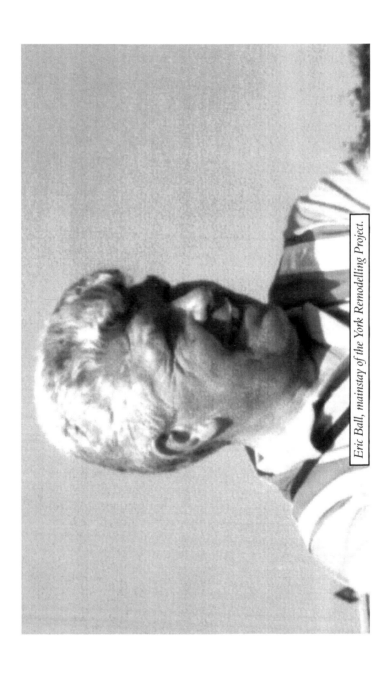

Eric Ball, mainstay of the York Remodelling Project.

Moira and John Midgley with Morris Smith presenting John's long service award.

Standedge Tunnels, Marsden End. From the left, Up Fast, Down Fast and the live double line Up and Down Slow. Note the 'Quacky Duck!'

Viaduct Inspection Unit on a trial run. 'Guzzunder' Tests. Photo: British Rail.

Dramatic defining picture of the York Project, with PUMs (see Glossary), running to site. Note the Minster in the background. Photo: British Rail.

A second defining York Project picture. Phil Summers at home during a week of thirteen-hour nights. Photo: Jacky Summers.

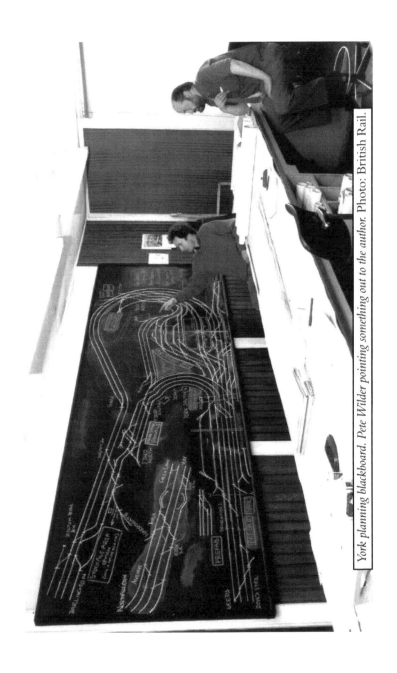

York planning blackboard. Pete Wilder pointing something out to the author. Photo: British Rail.

Much-replicated design of one of the first flat-arch railway bridges on the Leeds–Selby line.

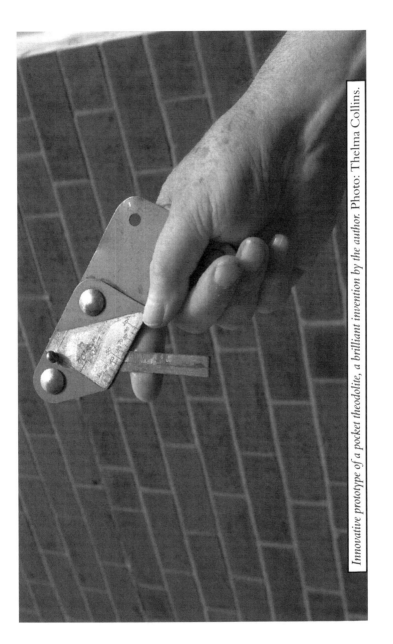

Innovative prototype of a pocket theodolite, a brilliant invention by the author. Photo: Thelma Collins.

ment schemes, essential where the aforementioned permanence of overhead electrification is to come, but a sad misfit in the drive and speed of the day's requirements. Looking at 100-year-old railway plans, we find everything precisely drawn and coloured up in watercolour, indicating many hands and plenty of time. This was where our colleague would have fitted like a glove; but adornment was inessential and drawing office work had to be stripped to the muscle and bone.

Many track renewal plans for the whole job gradually oozed out of the Chief Civil Engineer's Office at York, and careful studying of them led both Midge and me to the conclusion that the job would be impossible, mainly because we would be expected to remodel the whole of the two miles or so without stopping normal traffic.

'It's impossible!' said Midge after a day spent poring over the various drawings. 'We'll need a good team to do it.' 'It' being the aforementioned impossible. He elaborated, 'Yorkies could do it, or at least t'reet ones. You'll have to tell Morris [our Engineer] that it can't be done wiout picked aht Yorkies.'

'Pete Wilder's a Yorkie,' I pointed out.

'Oh aye, burram wantin' workers, three teams of two goin' ower ten hours a day – that's not Pete Wilder. He's too busy laackin' wi kids.'

This would be open to misunderstandings nowadays, but all it then meant was that Peter involved himself with many outside activities, including the Scouts. I had to agree that he would not fit in to the aggressive scenario that John was foreseeing. I also pointed out that the other member of our team was also a Yorkie, and quite unable to cope with the Midge onslaught of a pro-gramme. As it turned out, our present resources had to cover loads of investigation and preparation work before the job could start properly, and Pete Wilder was well made for such 'pokin' abaht and muckin' arahnd' as my colleague would have Peter's job description.

Peter fully accepted the way we saw things going. He was by no means a constant 6½-day-week man, and would not consider the intense work, but he was in his element, in the same way that I used to be, in seeking out drains and outlets, and arranging plant and cameras to assist. Then a necessary minor remodelling came up which needed doing in order to give us a bit more planning leeway. This we put to our senior assistant. He did nothing, went sick, and lacking doctor's notes, took holiday – and at the end of February at that! Reluctantly we had to put the junior, Peter, onto the planning, resourcing and execution, leading to a successful 5-week job.

In the course of this work, something interesting occurred. The new through station at York had been built on Roman burial grounds. This we knew, but not precisely where the bodies were interred. It was also not of any particular interest to us, either, but when we had got the initial team together, including Wendy, I gave her a mission that suited her (down to the ground, I might say): to trawl through York Library and find out what were the chances of our work digging up Sinus Projectimus, or any of his mates. She came back with a map of the burial grounds that to our dismay almost fitted perfectly the area of our worksite. We were going to operate with a Roman burial ground directly below us almost throughout.

By rights we were supposed to report this to the York archaeological people. From Midge's past experience, these 'interfering pillocks' were empowered to stop the job should so much as a Roman toenail appear, in order to record and investigate more substantial human bits. Electrification engineers were destined to dig 2-metre-deep holes for their masts, so they were bound to notify the authorities. Our 2-foot-deep excavations (you will notice that the Leeds Division Project Team dug in imperial, while the nationwide electricians dug in metric) would be unlucky if it struck any remains, but we were aware of the instructions. This is why I feel obliged to announce, for the first time, that, as far as we are concerned, the Romans invented the black plastic bin liner, and used it to bury their dead in.

I refuse to admit that Peter found any bones while digging; I might even discover that he was on leave if any had been dug up, as were, by coincidence, Midge and myself. However, I do know that the Ancient Romans interred a few of their dead in said plastic bags, and dropped them into a disused drainage pit a short distance from where we were working. We called it resourcefulness. We also called Pete Wilder, who, as I said, might well have been on leave, resourceful. So there!

Peter was left very much to himself over the next eighteen months of intensive investigations. This was a period where Midge and I spent all our time together, arguing, discussing, rejecting and cautiously plotting. Whenever a new bit of 'could we?' work arose, Peter was despatched to investigate on site, in among his drainage discoveries. We also had fortnightly Project Meetings to attend, and later fortnightly Progress Meetings, becoming weekly, and then daily every morning in the thick of the operations. Midge dealt with these daily ones, he having the ability to walk into any group of managers, and despite being the junior on paper, declaring that the meeting would last twenty minutes, tops, or they went on without him. This was also the time when we were getting monotonous and unwanted engineering visits and press interviewing from all sorts. Midge declared 'You're better at bullshittin' than me, so you can see to all that!' – him being my supposed underling! With that statement, our two roles were defined; I just felt that I should have decided it, not Midge!

I realised now that both Midge and I were well known among the project manager fraternity, and would be renowned for rather different approaches. Any PM coming fresh to us both, as happened at York, would most likely go through his colleagues until he could work out by a process of elimination what methods, requests or reactions he would be able to assume or adopt in getting some issue past both of us. He would also have divined which of us to address in order to obtain an offer to do something or other. He could get me to summarise in easy-on-the-eye sketches of a simple approach to the whole job, and he could get John to accept or eliminate any detailed design matters, and he would also know on what issues we would stand tight together. I understood the project manager's position as a devil's advocate for other departments, which John interpreted as taking sides. I wanted to work with, while John felt he had to work despite, project managers.

This would have been best understood by being at the south

end of the site amidst the Third Stage one morning, where John and I were examining a piece of installation of the night before which had required considerable negotiation and cooperation with and of other departments, through the PM. I had needed to slightly change tack in negotiation, John had had to fight. Across the tracks, two of the project managers were examining the same piece of delicate trackwork.

> MAIN PM (Brian Frodsham) calling across to us: Nice piece of work, well done!
>
> ASSISTANT PM (Nigel Rutter): You'd had to take on a lot with this one!
>
> JOHN, addressing someone five streets away from where we stood: No f—ing thanks to f—ing project managers, f—ing the job up all way along, and making it almost f—ing impossible to f—ing do owt! They want to try f—ing doing it their f—ing selves, with all the f—ing help they give us!

Condescending smiles from both PMs. But John said in a subdued way to me, 'Ah shouldn't orter have said that abaht them, should I? D'yer think ah might have made things worse? You don't think they'll drag Morris in, do you?'

Position achieved: the PMs have got a very tricky section of the work done, with all departments having had to cooperate to extremes. John, having done the job despite PMs apparently supporting every other department at our expense, has had his chance to vent his feelings on those who built brick walls across his worksite; but now, characteristically, was wondering if he might have gone a bit too far.

One attribute that both Midge and I had attained in the project managers' black book was stubbornness. We had both displayed this separately before we joined up, John making it quite clear to those many grades higher that his approach was the only one, and others could work round it, or get stuffed. His approach would have been devised only after close discussions with the Signals department, for whom he had a mighty respect. When we became a unit along with them, and ever had differing views, these would be fought out in private, and whatever the outcome, we would all stick to it come what may. I had once distinguished myself by being locked in a room with an electrification engineer, both having separate viewpoints, until we came to some agreement. We didn't, and forced the project manager to make an informed decision. The fact that it had gone against me did not alter Midge's opinion of me; it was the fact that I had refused to buckle that went home with him.

Project meetings and progress meetings both demanded a vast number of departments attending. On average this involved fifteen other bodies, most represented both at headquarters and local level, each requiring either two or three persons to be in attendance. Should there be something particularly contentious coming up, then the divisions would bring out their most senior men for the day. Some representations varied slightly between project and progress meetings, so that I had to find an easy way of remembering who was who and worked for which and were called what.

Early in my meetings experience, at such that were meetings as opposed to rallies, I hit upon a foolproof identification process. I produced pages of caricatures to refer to, this being an amusement of mine. While, John, at my side, was producing vicious doodles that would have sent a psychiatrist demented, I was sketching or improving on my collection of faces, with names and departments. This was all done during immense periods when the two of us were totally uninvolved, which was often. John felt, and sometimes said, that seeing as we were the ones doing the work, along with the Signal Engineer, meetings should be about our work, not 'frigging abaht wi t'others'. John could accept the Signals as having almost as difficult a job as we had. But getting back to my sketches: these would become most difficult at times when John might put down his pen and pointedly look over my shoulder, suddenly exclaiming, 'Nowt like him!' or 'That's a goodun,' or, 'Oozthat s'posed t'be?'… or finally, 'Bloody Hell! He'd best not see that!' – nicely blowing my cover.

These interminable breaks in concentration on our part were due to the most outrageous wasting of time by others. John and I, returning to our project office at the back of the old York Division offices one dinner time, had to explain to the staff present that we two, their illustrious leaders, had been at a meeting where the proposed colour of the signalman's chair in the new control centre was discussed for an hour and a half! I know that I am sometimes guilty in these annals of slight exaggeration, but in this I kid you not!

From a very early stage, each department established its own part of the table at which to sit for every meeting. Being old hands, Midge and I were always halfway down the long row, slightly out of the line of sight of the chairing PM, and close to the door. This was also where the side table for refreshments was kept.

Spanning many years, we experienced serious changes in the catering approach. My earliest memories are of two ladies entering pushing a trolley of cups and saucers, coffee pot or tea urn (respectively a.m. or p.m., half past ten or three), milk and sugar, and a plate of assorted biscuits. Individual requests were sought and delivered, one by one. This was always a most welcome break. Then the biscuits disappeared under financial tightening, unless the PM felt that some achievement had been made, or tricky situation was to be faced, and he bought a packet, using his expenses claim.

Following this, the womanpower was halved and the drinks became self-service, with her just providing pot and crockery. Such was progress that at my latter meetings, a year or two later, the PM was provided with tokens for us all to troop out to the vending machine in the corridor.

During the middle period of self-service, something occurred which forever after had Midge chuckling away.

I dislike too much milk in my tea. I had been watching one member of another department, oddly enough the Quantity Surveyors, kindly acting as 'mother' on one occasion during the period where we were trusted to pour our own. Midge had drawn his tea and had stepped aside; I was next. I had noticed rather generous amounts of milk being dispensed, so was anxious that mine was not over-supplied. I was invited to say 'When', and the acting butler made as if to pour in the milk. As he tipped the jug, I called out 'When!' before any measurable milk had left the jug. So unexpected was this, seeing as he had not, in his terms, actually poured any, that the 'maid' jumped back, startled, and trod on two sets of toes, only to be pushed forward, so dispensing most of the remaining milk in a random manner. Much apologising ensued, together with mopping down, and we returned to our seats. Midge had disappeared, and I could hear, down the outer corridor, a sound I had not heard before other than in a donkey enclosure. It was Midge laughing. He returned with a damp face and hiccups. It was only during his many times of recounting the story that I realised just how much commotion and comedy my urgent cry had caused. I suppose you had to be there!

After countless almost fruitless hours, the PM managed to compile all the requirements of the various departments. Operators demanded no interruption to the normal service outside Sundays; Signals needed to be able to commission new sections of layout, only when they could be identified with some old routes. Until then the new tracks could not be used; station managers needed nearly all platforms available to them; electrification engineers needed assurance of final alignments and levels, and a requirement for us to work ahead of their strict programme. That was just four of the fifteen! Midge and I joined in heartily, John frequently informing the company and most of the surrounding offices that 'if they wanted this frigging job doing at all, they'll have to fit in with what we could do'. 'Bollux' was often used in response to the impossible, followed by 'Because I bloody well say so!'

Occasionally mayhem erupted. This usually emanated from something that Midge or I had said would have to be the case. Once we'd got all the other departments shouting their corner, Midge would sit back with a defiant look of immobility, while I resorted to shouting 'Rhubarb' into my hands. It was at times like this that the pair of us had made a final statement of fact, adamant that there was no way of altering it.

We did on occasions have a situation where another department was being particularly obstructive, or was purposely not understanding the immovability of a position that Midge and I had had to take up, purely because, within the restrictions placed upon us, there was no other way to achieve something. I have known John get frustrated by ignorance or sheer stupidity in others to the point of a stiffly vibrating finger waving across the table along with verbal abuse. This was rarely the case with confrontations with the Signals, as we both accepted the complexity of each other's problems. John and I took to having 'secret' meetings with our Signals counterparts, even involving them in our staging planning. It was usually the operating departments that got the full frontal of John, on two memorable occasions arriving at a point where he had gone through his usual routine, and had developed it to placing one knee on the table. This really frightened the PM. On the other hand there were times when John would keep unusually quiet out of a sort of shyness and embarrassment.

Example: we'd had the Signals people, along with their Siamese twin, Telecoms, over to discuss and agree between us some common points to our mutual advantage, thus forming an impenetrable joint front at the next meeting. Something that had appeared on the plans and in Signals & Telecommunications notes was the TAN building. In our conversations John had discovered what this meant. When we were all gathering for another session in the arena of argument, the S & T were a bit late, and the PM, Brian Frodsham, was musing through the vast minutes, coming up against the TAN building. Admitting ignorance, he asked those gathered if anyone knew what it stood for, before the S & T got there.

John muttered to me, 'We know. It just shows you, them as shout a lot really know nowt.'

Brian and some of the others began going through signalling possibilities, and as they guessed and guessed wrong, I could feel Midge coming up to simmering point at the side of me. In one of those sudden silences that uncannily occur, John burst into a spluttering mutter.

'Terminal Access Node!'

There was almost a round of applause, and plenty of verbal admiration. John went straight back into his shell, chuntering as he went, 'I wish ah'd said nowt. They'll have me down as a clever bugger now. Why didn't you mek sure a stayed shut up? Tha's allus mekin' me look bloody daft!' He was frantically doodling his way through the minutes. He just could not do with any form of limelight.

It would take both of us the rest of the day to restore our sanity after many of these meetings, later working out what we had achieved and what we had been asked to prove conclusively to the chairman's satisfaction and understanding; this along with any consequences there would be, should our statement be questioned by the PM. So it was that for every single stance or demand we made about some small point within the whole, we had to spend valuable time working out laymen's explanations of 'why', 'when' and the penalties, both practical and financial.

There were three main phases of the York job: the Yards, York North, and York South. The Yards phase was fairly straightforward in relaying terms, as we were allowed long possessions through the Easter period, and there was little effect on passenger traffic. A wagonload of steel or a few tankers of oil don't generally mind standing for fifty hours, whereas passengers tend to get a bit snarly.

South and North posed completely different problems to each other in our staging, arranging the order of work. Common to both was the accepted need to keep a full passenger service going throughout. The civil engineer was responsible for surveying and producing the plans (Headquarters), with each sector (Inter-City, Regional, Freight and Parcels) putting their individual oars in and trying their best to pay for as little of it as possible, with Leeds Civil Engineer's Division staging the work within the restraints given, planning the operation in detail, and finally executing the installation.

These plans were drawn up for the best final results, not at all for our convenience. The assumption by the design people had to be that we came along with a helicopter, lifted out a mile of complex trackwork, and bunged in the new by the same method, all in eight hours.

John and I had to study them for each phase and together come up with a method of working within the restrictions of the plans, traffic, and close colleagues in the Signals and Telecommunications, who among all the others, were our best friends. When we had them finely honed and reluctantly agreed by all, we produced dozens of pages forming a complete book of intermediate sketches (my speciality). They would then be passed to our two resident project engineers, Arthur Barnard and Peter Lodge.

Here we had a selection from the organisational cream of our department, with Arthur taking the lead. Between them they produced hour-by-hour plans and charts of the complete works from our sketches and notes, including resources in materials and manpower spread over many weeks. Come the start of the job, and we had another two teams of technical lads, mostly of proven quality and ability. We had wanted three teams, but were pared to two, which meant each couple working up to 13-hour shifts, all week, alternating days with nights each week, with Arthur and Pete Lodge giving some site relief at weekends. A team of supervisors was dedicated to the job, managing all the gang work. By negotiating with the Divisional Civil Engineer and assistant, we had got ourselves a project team together – smaller than we felt comfortable with, but one that was without a single weak link.

Our planning ideal would have been a complete possession of the York area, and start at one end and go through to the other, probably over some twelve weeks or so. If we could have done that, then there would have been virtually no need for John and me. We were faced with many practical barriers and departmental restraints. Argument, discussion and quiet thinking were needed, with occasional visits to site, supposedly to tie up some minor points, but in reality just to get away from the office for a bit. We would do this either together, or with Midge (investigating details) or me (jus' paddling abaht), alone. These technical terms for site visiting were provided by Midge.

So both areas, North and South, posed their own particular difficulties. At the North end of the York complex, the East Coast Main Line was the principal user, with branches coming in from Harrogate and Scarborough, representing the full social spectrum of customers. Whenever we were on the station, and a train came in, we would investigate it for booty.

Harrogate trains terminated at York, and we occasionally leapt on board as passengers thankfully alighted, rubbing vibrating bottoms after a few miles of two-axle tram-like trains on old jointed track. We managed to salvage discarded newspapers such as the *Telegraph* business supplements, and *Guardian* reports on the future of integrated transport, and the *Times* comparisons of railways abroad. All these bore no relevance to the baby bouncer that they had just escaped from. Scarborough travellers, mostly boarding at Malton, left their copies of the *Express* and *Mail*, which both led with major exposés of the disaster of nationalisation under Labour and the disaster of privatisation under Labour, and the ways that the Tories were coping with nationalisation and their ideals of privatisation, until it happened. East Coast Main Liners between London and Edinburgh stood for no more than fifty seconds – barely enough time to pick up in-house Inter-City magazines which explained to the public how many improvements were in the pipeline, and how those improvements were essential to be made on what was, as announced on another page, already a perfect system. Clearly discarded papers ran through the full spectrum from the *Sun* to the *Telegraph*, the former with completed crosswords and the latter with two anagrams worked out and no more. All these provided some basis for discussion during rare slack times in the office. Leeds traffic left very little for us, as the journey time was so short, and Selby trains provided nothing, as they were virtually empty.

Most of the day away from meetings was spent studying the many plans, and ideas about our staging diagrams. We had a few copies of each plan involved, a large blackboard, and a rainforest of paper. There was an awkward agglomeration of lines throughout, and we had to find useful space within to lay as large lumps of track as we could, all the time keeping traffic moving. We struggled late into the evenings on long tables, frustrated by only being able to see ourselves laying in small lumps at a time. Then one day, suddenly, in the evening darkness, alone but for the cleaners, together we arrived at what has always been our 'eureka' moment. We saw a way, which when explained to others, looked obvious, and allowed for a large chunk of the layout to be completed, to be joined in and commissioned later over a long weekend. We sat back and grinned at each other like idiots. That was a moment that I have savoured ever since.

There were four main lines at the South end, and we early on realised that we had to split the whole job into five stages concentrating on the two halves, dealing with one pair while the other remained operational. All very well except for all the interlinking crossings. Lots of little eurekas here, but nothing dramatic. The whole job was condensed into two books of staging sketches, which we defended to the end at all subsequent meetings, but were open to minor improvement suggestions from Barney and Lodgey. All this happened a year before the first sod was lifted in the Yards at Easter in 1988. Autumn of that year was filled by the North end, and late winter and spring of 1989 with the South. It was a happy, fairly relaxed, Christmas that year.

I would like, at this point, to run through a list of the main players on the civils side. You won't miss anything by leaping on a few pages, but I owe it to my past comrades to acknowledge their outstanding work.

On paper, I was in charge of the DCE's work. In practice, sharing the planning and heartaches on an equal footing with John Midgley. Then as we approached the sitework and through-out it, I took on the public relations side, meeting visitors and press, and generally defending our line up to the hilt. Again I bow to my number one's summary of my duties as 'bullshitting and keeping the buggers off my frigging back'. John, once more in his terms, 'did all the wark'.

With John, I very soon realised that I was in the presence of greatness in the world of railway permanent way engineering. There follows shortly a whole chapter devoted to the lighter side of this great character, but it must not be allowed to deflect from the unmatched genius which that character enclosed. Intense teamwork together resulted in a plan of attack of which we were both proud, and in the course of it were some splendid ideas. Who had them we neither of us remembered. John's philosophy tended towards tried and tested methods, whereas I, when faced with major obstructions, was open to some revolutionary means. This came about from our two rather different experiences in major project work. John had attacked long traffic-free sites, whereas mine were often compressed and open to interference. In the end we had a mix of our two standpoints. John's obvious technical superiority over me meant that he quite naturally took on the role of day-to-day site engineer in charge. It would have been counterproductive should the both of us be issuing instructions, so it had to all come from one source – John. He never ever in my knowledge suggested that I had got it easy; he revelled in hands-on control. We conferred, but the word went out from John.

Almost in the Midgley league was Arthur Barnard, inevitably 'Barney' to all. He was worthy of a much higher station in life, but had mastered the skill of staying where he was (which I had ultimately failed at). In support of this attitude is the crude fact that promotion from the ranks, with their associated overtime, means a considerable drop in take-home when you dipped your toe into the management scales. Barney was perfect to work alongside, though in theory, under Midge. They had very similar approaches and the results were, without exception, good. Although I had tremendous respect for all members of the team, Arthur had me in awe. His knowledge and attack on the job, along with his overall attitude, was exceptional. There were two aspects to his work. First there was the prior planning from the staging which John and I had produced (which he accepted as 'not bad'), with detailing down to every single man and minute of continuous action. This was followed by on-site setting out, and amendments to his plans as these became necessary (weather inevitably led to varying daily successes).

Here, I thought in amazement, was someone who was actually the equal in grade of the sad case that I had had to dump at the very beginning. Whereas I could describe differences in approach between individuals, I could not grasp that Arthur and my lost soul were paid at the same rate. There was not an element of similarity, or comparison in ability. Barney had, I hope, the personal satisfaction of beating me at my own game once, but never knew that I had accepted defeat long before any confrontation between us emerged. Although I took something of a back seat on the site work (with the advice that position engenders), I still felt that my respect for such as Barney was reciprocated. Apart from anything else, Arthur looked fearsome, and his understated opinions of the work of others was equally formidable.

Making up our initial team was Peter Lodge. Peter built on his existing great strengths working with John and Arthur, and was a perfect companion to the latter in the planning, setting out and personal execution of weekend site work. He was another of the York Mafia, and part of the social whirl which that demanded. These people either worked absolutely in harmony with each other, or were eagerly dismissive of anyone not up to their standards. I put a lot of this down to their off-piste activities, where bonding was more than just apparent. Peter was, if anything, a little more urgent than his mate, but I very soon learned to listen hard to anything either had to say, and act upon it. Peter's main purpose in the site office appeared to be in answering to the calls of 'Oi, Pete'. You hardly ever heard 'Oi, Barney', for instance.

There were now five lads who took the brunt of the 13-hour continuous shifts. Two would come on around 7.30 in the morning, overlapping with the night shift pair, who would return that evening. The two pairs alternated nights and days, swapping over every weekend. We should by health rights have had more of these site lads, but it would have virtually meant closing down the rest of the District work. At the end of York North, one lad dropped out and another joined the team for the final part. Stretching the lads to limits must have been difficult decisions for our top management to make, but far be it from me not to carry on heaping criticism on them. After all, compared to us, they did nothing all day!

If you can regard a naturally gifted and determined member of your team, coming initially as a fairly green recruit, as partly a success for yourself, then I had two in my working life. Dave Thornton was the first, living in my initial musings under the alias of Eddy Stapleton. Phil Summers was the other. To prove himself in professional circles he did far more than me, lacking the launching site of a university career. It was such as Phil that proved official advanced education was of little value compared to a natural approach to work. Both Dave and Phil have since gone on to great things, coming from being tongue-tied reclusive young lads to having great individual strengths. Not just a good engineer, the developed man, Phil, in my presence, performed an act of personal control and heroism in giving the eulogy at a well-loved colleague's funeral. Phil was a determined worker and a very good friend. He was so good that Midge willingly accepted him into the York team despite the fact that he was Leeds. If the present railway industry can still recognise and keep hold of rare people like Phil Summers, then I still have hope for the future.

Rick Thompson was not an obvious choice on superficial showing. He liked his beer, and talked of it in terms of slabs, rather than tubes. In this he might have been a risk. He was a bit of a maverick – no, quite a lot of a maverick – but he amazed us all by seizing on the office tie, when it was first introduced, and putting it round the usually open neck of his shirt. He turned out to be possibly the hottest team player we had, with vigorous loyalty. This probably came as part of the package with him being very involved with the Territorial Army. Here, though, was to us the biggest drawback to having Rick on the team. Had World War Three been declared during the course of the job, we could well have been in trouble!

Next there was, to me, a virtual unknown, and someone untried as far as I was concerned – Peter Cushing. He had the support of the rest of the Yorkies, but seemed to me to be less assertive than the others. I was to find that this was a front for quiet confidence. His worth boasted by his colleagues proved to be fully justified, though he did have a very annoying side to him, both at work and in his private life. He appeared to be perfect. Composing one *Annual Newsletter* I realised that over the years he had never had a mention, and sent out minions to discover the inevitable darker side. This proved to be a failure. Peter was most importantly a brilliant team man, and technically very efficient... but I refuse to believe that he's faultless. One day, when he becomes, as he most certainly must, the chief civil engineer of a re-nationalised combined railway, the tabloids will reveal what has eluded me all these years.

Almost in the Rick Thompson club was Scott Brogden, that is in knowing which end of a bottle to open. No problems, but these two knew how to relax after the job! Scott was efficient, without trying to make a name for himself. Quieter than most of the others to the point of him being short of words, Scott is best summed up with the following short story: Almost midnight and his tank full, Scott searches for some privacy to have a leak and picks the house garden near where he is standing. This happens to be the only house in the street where the occupant is still up, and looking out of the window into the dark. Scott is virtually facing him, and easing off his wants successfully. The owner bursts out into the garden with, 'What the hell do you think you're doing?' Word minimalist, Brogden, replied, 'Not a medical man, then?'

Now here was a surprise for all. John Barnard (no relation to Arthur) was 'forced upon us' from Headquarters, mainly for experience. We reckoned that at best he could only be a useful passenger. He was quickly accepted by all due to his ability to muck in, and very soon came to be considered an equal member of the team. Coming from the seclusion of Head Office work to the District is a big enough culture shock, but to be plunged into work that would make many of his new colleagues quake, John amazed us all, particularly Midge and me. Arthur referred to him with only a week behind him as 'Ar kid'. This meant full acceptance. However, he almost fell at the last fence, struggling manfully with a T-bone steak at the York Remodelling Team Steak Dinner. How easy is it to get the last bits of chewy steak down with a dozen others cheering you on?

In the office we had Wendy as the single all-round clerk, where the Selby job ran to two clerks. She had to be good at every clerical task, even though her skills lay mainly in pay and wagons. Wendy has cropped up quite a bit in patches throughout these ramblings, and although a character in her own right, she is my first great working personality. It overflowed from her, leading to highs and giggles, and to the inevitable tumbles and doubts. I have said elsewhere that many times she managed to infuriate Midge, by being an assertive female, being an assertive female from Leeds, and being a competent assertive female from Leeds who did a brilliant job, even though she sometimes appeared to be too relaxed to be performing that well.

In the latter stages we were joined by Gary Phillips, a technical officer of late suddenly forbidden, for medical reasons, from going on the track. Gary was naturally distressed about this, but did well to cover it up. When I felt that there was no danger to him I had him accompany me onto site, where he at once became alive and exuberant. Garry acted as a kind of linkman, taking some of the heat off Wendy, and was by no means a waste of space!

This leaves one of the most important elements – the supervisors, and here we are back to my favourite topic. Eric Ball unquestionably led the team, and was included in any practical discussions. Eric had a most expressive face that could be illuminated and coloured any time he met a situation that went against his straightforward logic. I suppose Eric was fiery to many, but anyone not going along with him was seen to be purposely getting in his way, as did other people's trains, such as the operators. Eric had a remarkable similarity in attitude to his team leader, Midge, who he referred to as 'John, lad'. He was a man who perhaps did not fully appreciate his vast practical abilities, and would see himself as simply doing his job. But how well he did it, and how reliable he was! Eric was built along the lines of a rugby fullback, and was as agile as one too. But above all, Eric, well known to the York lads, was a discovery for me, and, as I say, took me back to my now decelerating character collection. Only true characters cannot detect it within themselves. This is well illustrated by a quote from the *Annual Newsletter* of the time:

> ERIC BALL to John Midgley: The trouble now, John lad, is that there're no characters around.
> JOHN: Ay, you're right there, Eric!

How these two could look at each other, and not see what was before their two pairs of eyes, was amazing. Eric ranked very highly in my collection, only failing to reach the purity of a top rank character in that he was eminently sensible. In the white heat of relaying action he would speak to any person of any rank or department in exactly the same way. The following illustrates it:

Eric, needing to take a short train of wagons from one side of the main line to the other, a task taking no more than a minute, rings the signal box to get permission. The signal person tells him that he'll have to wait a while, which Eric might expect if a train was approaching. He was told that one such was just leaving

Darlington, heading in his direction. Darlington is thirty minutes away, a fact which the signalman is left in no doubt about after Eric has turned crimson, and then filled the air with lots of effing and blinding.

To confuse matters, Leeds had provided one of its finer relaying supervisors in the form of Eric French. Frenchy, to keep things clear, had had an uphill struggle to establish himself in this foreign territory, but once he passed the Midge test, and had familiarised himself with the area and inmates, he shone out because of his approach to the job. Balley would bellow out his instructions, and chase about the site making sure; Frenchy spoke his requirements, and never broke into a trot. Time for a little story.

All railway engineering wagon types are distinguished by a code. I have yet to find out the source of this code, but always accepted that a particular type of wagon was referred to by the name of a fish or sea mammal. There are even side-tipping vehicles called mermaids. Common wagons were mackerel, catfish, herrings and dogfish. There were also trout and sharks. (Exceptions were the Engineering Department's EDs.) Running about the York site were stone hopper wagons, walrus, sea cows and sea lions. We now had a hot addition to our standard equipment in the site radios, essential for such an intricate job, but still fairly new. The problem with them was that all supervisors had them, and the same system was being used by all site departments, the range even reaching into the nearby headquarters buildings, so there was no such thing as a private conversation – something Eric Ball discovered on a few occasions, leading to some acrimony.

The scene is set here in a fish and chip shop, just off the site, but well within radio contact. Frenchy, complete with striking high-visibility vest, is in the queue with a short list in his hand. His radio crackles into life, all eyes and ears turn to him:

> 'Eric Ball to Eric French. Where are you, Eric? Over.'
> 'I'm in the chip shop, Eric. What do you want? Over.'
> 'Get me a couple of fish, please, Eric, and a breadcake. Oh, and I'm sending six empty sea lions down to you.'

So provoking a myriad of expressions and questions from the rest of the queue.

We played about with this fish for wagons idea in the *Newsletter*, coming up with kippers, as herrings with hot smoking axle boxes, piranhas, EDs with lethal drop doors, and a penguin that we saw as being the Engineer's saloon around dinner time.

It would be easy to leave the accolades there, but mention must be made of the other supervisors and the lads in the gangs. There were too many to be named, but all, being known by Midge, and well up to the job before them. More than I can detail – yes, but far less than we would have wished for. Herein lies the proof that they all did the work of more than one man.

Although the total worksite was long, there would inevitably be times when the lads were concentrated in a relatively small area. Yet in the entire fourteen months or so, we only had two complaints from the public about noise. We had taken disturbance to neighbours on board at the outset, and John and I apparently made an outrageously controversial suggestion that, instead of noisy generators going all night, we should take our lighting power directly from the mains. It becomes a long story, and not relevant here, but instead of the usual flood of complaints about the constant noise at night, we had one complaining about the lack of it! Without the steady clatter of pounding lineside generators, the pleasantries passing between the lads could be heard in the stillness of the night. Trackmen, whether maintenance or relayers, do tend to be oversensitive about the behaviour of their comrades, such that they will throughout the night shift call to notice any shortcomings they see in those around them, especially when it comes to one man digging and his comrade standing watching.

'I say, old friend, you appear to be doing nothing while I am steadfastly continuing in muscular effort. Do you not feel a need to pull your weight a little more?'

'It is true what you say, but at the moment I would appreciate it if you would keep your opinions to yourself while I regain some strength in my back.'

There is a danger that this is paraphrasing the actual wording of the conversations, the precise details not being relayed by the complainant over the phone, but I think the picture may be drawn from the above.

The second complaint came from houses opposite the private girls' school alongside the South stage. It was said that our lads were to be found playing football on the girls' hockey pitch at 5.30 in the morning. The game was said to be strenuous and verbally volatile. We answered the press to the effect that it was a little beyond comprehension that the lads we knew would be exercising with such gusto on a voluntary basis.

(This is an example of where John would sit back and allow me to deal with things. His response to our complaining neighbours would be to the effect that 'the frigging railway was here before you, so you can go stuff'. This frankness does not go down well with the neighbours or the press, so it was my job to once more paraphrase Midge's sentiments in a more acceptable manner.)

Some of the gangs even managed to make a name for themselves on the national media. By horrible chance, with an element of good fortune for us, BBC TV had been planning a fortnight's live documentary on railway engineering. This was a bit of a nuisance, but quite by accident they had arranged it for the two weeks immediately preceding the start of the York South end phase – thankfully, rather than during it. A Portakabin studio had been set up just off site, on scaffolding. It turned out to be a handy place for the lads to stand under when it rained. A lot of preamble stuff and interviews were being recorded within and the sound engineers had to battle with a sheltering Dave 'Phucket' Oldham rallying his lads, or explaining to one of them, in his own inimitable manner, how he feared that the lad had acted a little rashly in some way or other, or had incurred his displeasure by some misdemeanour.

Dave had been brought in with his scrapping gang to deal with all the old track that was generated during the remodelling. This involved stripping it down, stacking sleepers and cutting up rails into lengths that could be manhandled. Prior to the job going ahead, masses of estimates had been done, including any assets we might realise from this scrap. I'll mention here that the multi-million pound job came in at 2% under estimate on our side. Most of this was due to the Barney/Lodgey planning combo, slightly refining a particular approach, but much was due to Dave's enthusiasm, and carefree attitude as to what was legitimate scrap. If it went 'ping' when hit with a hammer, Dave scrapped it. Redundant railings disappeared, an abandoned loco shed had all its rails and chairs stripped out, and the odd condemned wagon stuck in remote sidings was tastefully put out of its misery.

Dave was one of Leeds' more able relaying supervisors, and had landed this weekday job of handling scrap in a very profitable way. I have to be careful what I say about Dave as his son, Stephen, lives just across the road from me, and looks a good foot taller than anyone he stands next to. In fact Dave's idiosyncrasies have been discussed elsewhere under an alias. At this moment of writing, Dave is pretty fireproof in these annals as he still has a job to go to.

York station trackwork came under the day-to-day care of Taffy Venables, a most affable and very experienced permanent way supervisor on the maintenance side, as opposed to relaying. Taffy was well involved with the project, as his ground knowledge was invaluable. Furthermore, seeing as the most intense area of his empire was undergoing this complete renewal, it could have been argued that he had a great proportion of his railway temporarily under the care of others. Be that as it may, Taffy was drawn into the work during the week. For a period he was occupied preparing the new units of switch and crossing work before they were run to site and installed. This was involving the pioneering experimental use of a special glue. I only mention this because as he ran short of this component, he reported it to Pete Lodge, adding that he could not progress much further without a fresh supply. Pete reported back to the nerve centre, which was Wendy, in an urgent manner that was so typical of him. Also typical was his lack of comprehension when Wendy went into one of her violent fits of giggling. 'All I said was that Taffy was stuck without this glue!'

★

Midge's traditional methods stood us in good stead at the North end, but revolutionaries saw the South as an excellent test bed for some new relaying equipment emanating from France, of all places. John was very doubtful of using PUMs, particularly as the acronym was in French, and he could not remember what it stood for in that language (as I can't either – I could look it up, but it wouldn't enhance the story). We settled for PUM's meaning *Machines pour le Picking Up*.

What they did was lift from the construction site complete crossovers up to 150 yards long, walk them across onto the main lines and run them down to site before lowering them precisely into their final position. We're talking here of a massive unit of switch and crossing work with concrete instead of timber. If we hadn't had this equipment the same work would have been done over several weekends, but our unit was fully welded up and virtually ready for traffic in hours rather than weeks. This is the only really technical piece of information within. I have to mention it because of the sheer excitement it engendered in us. John was virtually singing as we walked alongside the first unit to go in using this method, and many other departments had come out to watch. All this novelty added to the sheer scale of the operation, attracted the press, both railway and local, along with visiting bodies from various spots around the world. It was here that John insisted on the clear demarcation between his work of doing the job, and mine of seeing to the Public Rabbiting.

Apart from Europe, we had small parties of engineers from Thailand and Japan, with individuals from other faraway countries. We also entertained a very pleasant Frenchman from the PUM company, who drank beer. John immediately classed him as not bad, 'considering he's a foreigner'. (It was one of John's foibles that 'goin' abroad is OK, except there's a load of foreigners all over t'place'.) Our greatest challenge was the Poles. Despite protest, Morris Smith, the Engineer, insisted that John was included on this one. 'What's t'bloody point? Ah can't gabble in Pole!' Of the visitors, many had basic English, but none had basic Selby.

'Call 'emselves engineers? Aif on 'em can't cotton on to a single friggin' word ah'm sayin'!'

Morris had received strict instructions as to how to entertain this particular group. They were to get an illustrated talk from me in the Leeds office, then travel out to site, lunching on the way. This was where the special instructions came in. On no account were these Polish gentlemen to be entertained on licensed premises.

Once more I am in danger of appearing racist, but these were our instructions. We had to keep the Poles and alcohol as far apart as possible. This apparently arose from an unfortunate set of incidents down south somewhere, and their fame spread before them. As a quick point of information, can you guess how many licensed and unlicensed premises there were between Leeds and York in 1989. Answer: twenty-four and one respectively – research carried out by Roger Bean, Chief Administration Assistant. The one acceptable eating house was a Little Chef. This is why a party of fifteen prominent Polish railway engineers descended on it one early spring day in 1989.

As the meal wore on, we both became aware of an increase in the noise level as our visitors got high on chicken, chips and peas. Plus, as it turned out, a multitude of hip flasks. Our Poles had been treated in a similar way for most of their trip to England, and had grown wise. Morris was at a loss what to do, just watching the situation slip away from his well-planned grasp. Much of the afternoon was cancelled, as it had involved small parties examining the railway at close quarters, and our guests were acting far too cheerfully to be trusted.

Midge would often arrive at points of apparent despair, particularly over things like manpower, small failures of his staff and the impossibility of keeping up to schedule. Only once did this become deep gloom and worry me, so much so that I got Nigel Trotter, Morris's PWay Assistant, to come over for a council of war. Midge was unusually sat with his head in his hands, muttering violently and occasionally beating the desk with a desperate fist as our visitor arrived. Nigel purposely took one of the less imposing chairs, put his feet up on the table, swung back and said, 'Right then, John, what problems have we really got?'

John burst; out it came, point after point, Nigel acting as if to make notes. When John finally dried up, Nigel looked at his doodlings, and went through everything, a piece at a time. John slowly deflated and slowed down, as every problem that had become inextricably mixed with another was sorted and answered. It took Nigel half an hour, before upping and announcing a site visit, followed by some grub at the Railway Institute. He had not sorted out any of John's problems at all, but he had disentangled them and put them in proportion. John followed quietly, already wondering why things had seemed so complicated. Occasionally an 'Ah, but,' would emerge before he'd sort it out himself. John got on with, and approved of Nigel, but was also infuriated by him. When he left us, John warmed up again a little with, 'All right for Trot, he doesn't have to deal with the pillocks that we do. It's OK for him just swannin' in and sorting stuff. He doesn't have to talk to them. He's not too bad though, Trot, ferra gaffer, is he?'

There were a few of the minor mishaps during the intense work, all of which either I or John dealt with. I would issue a large figure-one-shaped piece of paper (aping the official disciplinary Form 1), with an accusation and warning chosen from the many options written thereon (one of which was of not being Pete Cushing). This could defuse a situation. John would explode with a short-lived 'upping', immediately getting down to putting the matter right.

We had only one major mistake on the job, when an entire night's work had been installed at too high a level, putting the track too close to the heavy lattice bridge spanning the south end. John took confession from a tired team and erupted more than I'd ever seen outside a project meeting. Drastic measures were called for, and quietly. After many discreet phone calls he managed to get hold of a new machine which was on test not far away, and work it secretly down to site for the next night. This hammered and consolidated the track, in effect lowering anything new – which was not its purpose in life, but produced the right result.

My personal moment of conflict came with the great Arthur. This was a contest that I knew I would lose, but had a principle of seniority at stake. We had a drain to dig, using my old pal the rail-mounted trencher. It would run alongside the South stage and finish, a little deeper than I would have liked, in a culvert under the main lines. Arthur wanted to extend it further back to start opposite an unwanted pond in the grounds of a private school, so helping them with a problem. This would have meant digging further and deeper, way beyond the design. We discussed this from all points of view, until I had to lay it down that we would not extend at extra cost, just to do a school a favour. The deeper a drain goes, the less effective it is, and it would be at its deepest alongside the main new junctions. Arthur was defiant, but shut up. He had far more experience than me of draining flat areas like the Vale of York, most Leeds District tracks, and therefore drains, being on good gradients. It was like high noon again.

After the night of the drainage work, I found, as I had expected, that Arthur had sacrificed some of the effectiveness of the drain by extending it as he had wished. It was a defiant Arthur who faced up to me on the Monday morning. He was perhaps a bit deflated when I made little comment, but issued him with one of my fake Form Ones for going against instructions.

What Arthur knew well, as I did, from experience, was that the very act of digging a trench alongside the railway and filling it with clean stone is for many years as good as laying the pipe at the bottom of it. Lots of drainage jobs I have done never had any water in the pipes for years after, but the drainage of the track worked.

Arthur's pond disappeared, and we continued together with only minor mutterings from both sides. On occasions like this there are either many correct ways to do a job or none perfect. Arthur's just had the advantage of combining two jobs with minor detriment and with undetectable costs.

There were plenty of celebrations when the York job finished. Marquees, public presentations and an award from the Institution of Civil Engineers for the year's finest piece of work, which went to Morris Smith as our leader. Public talks or lectures followed, with me travelling to all sorts of exotic places, at least for a nailed-down Yorkshire lad, from Exeter to Edinburgh. I took these on myself, it not being Midge's world at all (as if it was mine!). For local Leeds and York venues, he would come along too, just to help with the questions, which he would do well. Then it all died down, and we filtered back into the Leeds office, Peter and Phil staying with a much simplified Projects Section, and Arthur going back into PWay Maintenance, next door. These two more or less ran the section while I became swamped with plans for Leeds remodelling, the main job on being the electrification of lines from Leeds and Bradford to Skipton and Ilkley.

If you are ever on York station, go over the footbridge across the East Coast Main Lines and you will see on the wall to the left a sign commemorating the work which John, I, and the small team completed successfully, on time and within budget. The sign covers another in dried goatskin commemorating the completion almost two thousand years earlier of the Roman Rut between Londinium and Auld Reekium, and the introduction of Equestrification.

One day soon after the official closure of the job, I found a small envelope on my desk with a hand written note inside on standard Railway paper. It was from the undemonstrative Arthur Barnard. In neat straightforward terms it said that he felt it had been a privilege to have worked with two such professional engineers as Midge and me. He cannot know what that gesture meant to me. It was one that surpassed anything that the Chief or our Engineer or the Institution of Civil Engineers had said or done. It became one of the most treasured moments of my railway career.

Midge

'I've got far too much work on to start having to delegate as well.'

British Rail was not a company to work for if you sought great acclaim or accolades. Very rarely were you called up to the boss's office to receive a bouquet of flowers and a box of gift-wrapped cigars. Only once did I share a glass of £2.50 champagne with the boss, Morris Smith, at nine in the morning (the launch of the Area Civil Engineer's staff colour magazine). Surprise bookings at the City Varieties with dinner afterwards were in short supply. Days at the casino fell into the category of hen's teeth and rocking horse manure. 'Well done!' was an expensive expression from higher management. So it was a great honour when an unconscious compliment came my way.

Moira Midgley, John's wife, boosted my ego more than anything ever did at work when, with John out in the kitchen making coffee, she said, 'John's ever so pleased. He came home after your first day out together and said that he thought he'd at last found an MS 2 that he could work with.'

MS 2 was Management Scale 2; John at the time was MS 1, one disgruntled step down. To be accepted by Midge was the greatest accolade a fellow railway engineer could receive. It went deep with me!

That first day out together was John driving me around various sites on the Selby Diversion – thirteen miles of brand new railway that he had constructed; an immense achievement of which he was enthusiastically proud, and which should have been better reflected in his grading. As we were about to drive off to another location he was struggling to find reverse. John gave me the first taste of Midgespeak: 'We'll get going in a sec, when ah can finnagear!' This, along with many contributions from our mutual clerk, Wendy, formed the basis of a collection of stories and quotes from a man who I regard as the choicest character in my entire collection.

Midge, one day finding a solar powered calculator in a puddle in the gutter outside his house, took it in, gave it five minutes' rinse in the dishwasher, sneaked it into the spin dryer along with a light wash, and brought it proudly to work. By that time pocket calculators were about 50p apiece, or free if you bought twenty gallons within two months at the right garage, and everybody had one, but the gutter model had come to John out of the blue. What's more, it just about still sort of worked, even after lying in mud and water, and being lovingly restored in a way that only John would find quite unremarkable. He also happily accepted that it only worked with provisos – just so long as he held it up within a foot of a fluorescent tube. He was often to be caught standing on his desk holding the thing up to the ceiling in a state of contortion, stabbing long numbers in from lists at his feet, and returning to the light before the display forgot where it had got to. Full summer sun was also effective, except for the display tending to become invisible, so calculations were done more or less blind out in the yard, after which he rushed back inside to copy down the answers before they faded. On the many occasions it failed him, he would considerably improve its potential by slinging it across the room, together with his famous remark, 'These things are friggin' useless when they don't wark!'

When I went out with him, on that first trip together, he was just winding up the great Selby job. He had a shed-cum-office to himself and his small section, attached to the timber buildings that had been York District's home. His work there, which had achieved rare recognition from on high, could not have been easy, as I realised when I met his team. This included a flash, vapid, confident bloke, a stupefying nymphomaniac and an incontinent smackhead. I viewed them with interest, and took note of John's experience of dealing with such, reckoning immediately that this bloke's man/woman management must be really something. However, when we got down to forming our team for the York Remodelling Project, we had a great diversity in manpower to start with. In fact we'd only two.

Pete Wilder was one, a happy, unambitious achiever, more a

pal than a colleague, and too much so for Midge to quite approve of. 'Ah don't have mates at work, just folk what ah've to gerron wi.' Peter showed no aptitude for disagreement, but steadily tackled whatever task was put before him. This, in the early days of York, meant stepping in to cover his immediate senior's inabilities. It transpired that this bloke was just not up to modern life, its pressures and its pace. He beat Midge completely, especially during a time when they had to work closely together while I was off ill for six months. John happily took over the Leeds Projects Section, and just about managed with half of the material he had inherited in any kind of working order.

He came to visit me at home one day, obviously distressed, and it took no prompting to get it out of him. John became very broad and urgent when upset and in new territory, in terms of experience and emotions. Happily, though weighed down with insurmountable problems on the York job at times, actual depression was alien to John, but sadly he was to have his share later in life.

'Ah can't do wiit! In all my time ah've nivver come up agin a fellow crying at work. It's bloody creepy. Ah just giv 'im a simple bitta drainage t'find and foller and put reet. Fust he goes off sick, then he's back and blubbin' that he can't cope wiit. Bloody hell, Wilder'd have etten t'job, for all he's not much use! He's had to bail aht that booger time and agen. He's doin' all t'tricky work and t'other booger's doin' nowt. Ah've had to rethink Pete Wilder a bit, 'cos ah'd've got nowt done wiout him. Mind, he's still laackin' abaht in't bloody Boy Scouts, so he can't be all that good! But wat d'yer do when a bloke gets dahn on t'floor cryin'? You'll have t'come in fer a day, ah'll send Pete up forthee wi't'car. He's OK, is Wilder, when tha gets used to him, tha knaws! We'll have to go inter t'cellar for you to deal wi t'useless booger, ah can't do wi havin' him cryin' up in t'office agin. Thur were bloody girls abaht! You'll have t'come in and givvus a hand. Yer not deein'!'

I was off work, as intensive treatment was in process after my lung problem had been diagnosed. Even with five months gone I was not fit for doing all that should have been required of me, but I found Midge an uncharacteristically sympathetic being. Even so, he had relished being back in charge, and was obviously distraught at this, his one and only admitted failure. I went in for the half day and interviewed the collapsing heap that was our senior technical man, as well as I could. For John's sake, we met in the depths of the office cellar, and discovered that the lad could not face the oncoming work associated with the York Remodelling Project. It is to the Railway's credit at the time that it took many months to have the sad article removed to the lightest of work. He had no chance when York got going fully, so he had to be removed from the team.

Midge was the most down-to-earth brilliant achiever when at his work, but in private in the office he was something of a loner, for all his 'one of t'lads' blustering. I may be wrong, but in our position I might have been one of the very few that John would take into his confidence when sober. This was underlined towards the end of our time together in the most devastating way possible, which I'll come to later.

I only knew John in the role of a manager. It was obvious from his achievement on the Selby Diversion that he could manage what we now have to call human resources. Indeed, John might have been one of a few that could relate to that title, for, up to the situation above, he had been given a widely differing bunch of human resources as assistants, and yet had always brought the job to a very satisfactory conclusion. I suspect that John had ever been the achiever, and had treated his colleagues as just less able than himself. It would be interesting to know when he first started issuing 'uppings'.

If you received a Midgley upping you were in no doubt about it. Minor failures he could cope with, producing a mere snapping, but serious misjudgements or miscalculations would be discovered by John, and send his upping meter nudging full. When he next met the miscreant he would be brief, precise, linguistically clear and very noisy, finishing up with, 'So thee see to it!' The result was always effective, and a more cautious and careful technical officer would be the outcome. Uppings lasted minutes rather than lingering on, and would be set aside immediately, but they would not be forgotten. I cannot recall him ever reporting anyone, except to me, even after repeated failures, with the one exception of the weeping misfit. In that case he happily left it to me to follow things through on an official basis.

Where John was an almighty failure was in tact, respect, toler-ance, public relations, diplomacy, delicacy, and in understanding and accepting ignorance in others, particularly neutral project managers. These he could not understand; they both wanted the job doing well, while at the same time putting as many obstacles in his path as was possible. He had no time for any of the other departments, with the exception of Signals, and could not understand why the project managers even listened to them. The PM's explanation that he had to 'act as devil's advocate' for all these minor impedimenta meant nothing to Midge other than treachery, betrayal and obstructionism on the team leader's part.

Wendy was our clerk for the York Remodelling Project, dealing with all aspects of clerical work involved, and a lot of the reported detail as to what went on in the Midge presence is down to her, and her book of quotations. She was a major problem for Midge. Before Wendy, females had adored him and fawned on him, or were angered by him and went into sulks; they either did everything for him they decently could or tried to ignore him; they worshipped his authority or left the room crying when he shouted at them. One of them even cut his hair for him in the office, and went out to buy him new shirts! At all these things Wendy was a complete and utter failure. John tried to put her down and find faults and flaws, but was always presented by her with perfect details of progress in terms of materials and finances. She did not conform to his view of women as being reluctantly necessary clerks or heaving sex objects. Where Wendy failed so dismally was in her tendency to crack up and start giggling the more John ranted. The wilder he got then there was a greater chance of some lovely quotes, and there could be nothing as annoying as being in a rage against incompetence and having the clerk sniggering away and writing things down in her book. Midge would sometimes collapse, deflated while in full flow, and look puzzled. He would then quietly ask what he'd said that was so bloody funny. He found Wendy, except for any absence in her of noisy application of counter-correction, far too much like being at home for him. He never managed to listen to himself before he said something that forced her to write it down, with her shoulders heaving. Here are a few of many to be going on with.

Quote Break No. 1 (more of an introduction):

From the latest addition to the Lingaphone Language Courses – Midgespeak – some useful phrases:

TYPIKALLEEDS – Not the manner in which things were achieved on the York Division.

EEORTA-GERRAN-UPPIN – That man has left himself open to chastisement and disciplinary action of some kind.

WYZEE-WANTIN-THAT? – I have my suspicions as to the man's motives in requiring this information.

WEERZMIMUG? – I have put my cup down somewhere. Why were you not watching where?

EEZGORRA-GERRA-GRIPONIT – I feel that our colleague has not yet assimilated the basics of the matter in hand, and needs to investigate more deeply the requirements to achieve success in this particular department of his work.

BOLLUX – There is an element of doubt in what's just been said.

There was at the time an opinion that John was somewhat held back in position by his forthright approach and local East Riding accent. It has to be regarded as an early manifestation of racialism.

★

John Midgley was a presence you did not forget. He stood over six feet tall and had an impressively menacing face, which defaulted to a deep look of suspicion at times of uncertainty. This was set under a mop of black hair, brushed down in all four directions. My first sights of John were on his visits to Leeds on Monday mornings after Leeds and York Districts had merged, to be housed in 'Cramptup' House in Leeds. He was very obviously disgruntled at having now to waste time travelling from York to make his weekly demanding requests for materials, generally stone ballast, for the terminating Selby Diversion work. He should really have gone into the Monday Morning Engineers' Meeting to put his requirements forward along with the rest, but he would have found this beneath his dignity, and it would mean mixing with a bunch of highfalutin halfwits, as he saw most of his surrounding superiors.

He would stand uncomfortably in the strange surroundings (to him) of the Leeds Drawing Office, handling a slightly aggressive cigarette and not giving his former York colleagues more than a glance. His expression was glowering at the Materials Clerk and the Wagon Clerk, the latter then being Wendy, she who was destined to become alternately 'No bloody use' and 'Couldn't do wiout her' depending on whether Wendy's determination over the phone from York had achieved all that he had demanded.

John wore a loose corduroy jacket with a dangling belt, over very thin trouser legs. He was ever so slightly bow-legged, but had never ever been told so! On their annual appearance on the holiday snap, his exposed legs proved that he was doing a service to mankind by normally keeping them covered up, unless you saw the thick coating of hair achieving that object. He had large farmer's hands, an inheritance from his family background. He wore his clothes severely, but correctly – never, except for that holiday snap, without a tie. From all aspects John had to be admitted to having a 100% masculinity, together with a rugged handsomeness. Any newcomer was treated with deep suspicion until he had proved himself acceptable. Younger lads were things he trod in.

On one occasion in the early days of working together the two of us nipped over to the Chief Civil Engineer's PWay Drawing Office in the headquarters building, to discuss some aspect of the ongoing York project. In our wooden hut over in the goods yard, the section never stopped for meals, only relaxing at appropriate moments in the course of the day. We were therefore flummoxed by the almost total absence of any staff. (York HQ still worked the 1½-hour dinner break, when most of them went home – this never happened in our office.) There were two youths reading their papers towards the end of the office, so we decided to quiz them about when people were expected back. I did the talking while John held his head down – these particular offices being among his chief hates. He lit up his usual 'slightly ill at ease' cigarette.

'Excuse me,' said one of the lanky white-shirted youngsters, 'but who gave you permission to pollute my air space?' To John.

'Tha wat!'

'This is my area, and I don't want you coming in here and contaminating it.'

'You talking t'me?'

I was quaking on the perimeter, not knowing how to divert this.

'You're the one who's infringing my liberties!'

To me. 'What the frigging hell's he on about?'

'Let's leave it for now, John. We can come back later.'

I turned to go, putting a guiding hand on John's arm to follow. This he did, out of confusion. All the way back down the office John was walking semi-sideways, nearside leg facing forwards and offside turned facing me. He was continually demanding to know if I'd any idea what the lad had been talking about, and trying to come to grips with it. We were almost at the doors when he fully cottoned on.

'*Tha wat*? The bleedin' jumped-up prick! Ay, thee – yes, thee, tha streak of piss! Dusta know who tha's talking to? Tha'd best not come anyweer near a proper office weer thur's work done, or ah'll have thi bollux toasted and strung up as door chimes!'

John started back down the office. At last the youth seemed to grasp that he was in a presence and made a move for the opposite stairs. John just stopped and watched him go. He was totally perplexed how anyone, let alone a strip of a child, had deigned to talk to him like that.

We made several quick visits to this office later, always to see this youngster beating a retreat.

By then I was almost fireproof as far as the Midge wrath went.

I could pull his leg as much as I pleased without danger of being annihilated. Off guard, John was a happily naïve character, and as soon as he relaxed he was off guard, In the 1984 *Christmas Newsletter*, I even went so far as to name him 'Wally of the Year' – a very brave move. The award went to him following his recounting tales of his visits as a private patient to a physiotherapist in York (he was comfortable doing this, because of suffering a perpetual bad back, since it was a middle-class thing to do). She was a large German lady with two consulting rooms labelled 'House of Commons' and 'House of Lords', which John found particularly amusing. Come to think of it, I cannot remember John being over-amused, openly, about anything much. Anyway, the award was presented thus:

Wally Prize No. 1 went to John Midgley for his sense of timing and positioning in choosing to discus the ethics of World War II with his masseuse while lying on a slab in only his underpants. She was a 17-stone German lady, and was in the process of walking up and down his defective spine at the time.

Wally Prize No. 3 again went to John for continuing the above conversation even after the Wagnerian lady had told him that she had been a proud member of the Hitler Youth, and still took a dim view of dissidents.

(Out of interest, the second prize went to Pete Lodge, who thought that a good place to leave his expensive leather jacket was in the four foot space between the rails on the East Coast Main Line. He had to walk a mile up the track to pick up his watch, glasses, keys and odd amounts of loose change.)

John only revealed parts of his early life while we were out on car journeys or wasting time on a train. In the working environment very little other than a quick aside interrupted shop talk. He was brought up on a farm, and was therefore middle class. This was something that John was adamant about, and would fly into one of his declamations whenever I asked how he made that out, as I felt that I was firmly working class.

'Because mi' dad were a farmer! Stands to reason. He could tell folk what to do, so he must have been middle class!'

Middle class or not, John's father was not over-hot ('nobbut oweryat' as our hero would have it) at counting. Otherwise he would have noticed that his hens, rather than increasing in number, were in decline greater than Sunday meals explained. Investigation would have led to the discovery of a mad son laying waste to the farmyard on his motorbike. Chickens, as is often reported, cross roads, and should feel even more sure of themselves when crossing a farmyard, but not when there is an uncoordinated son of the land screaming round on a bike.

'Ah allus used to mow down one or two, so ah shoved them under t'hedges. They weren't all wasted, 'cos if t'old lad said we'd have chicken for Sunday, ah'd nip out and whip a couple on t'latest inter t'kitchen afore he could!'

It was from the farmhouse that John would be collected for a Sunday's work on the railway, and he was quite unconcerned, though his townie mates were a bit shaken, when they called early one morning to find that the outside door had blown open during the night of a blizzard, and snow had drifted way up the staircase. This story came from them, and not our middle-class son of earthly majesty.

Before the railway, John left school to stay in the agriculture business, working at York's busy sugar beet factory. This was boring, shovelling lorry-loads of beet into a hopper, and somehow John found his way into the York District PWay Drawing Office. How good the drawing ability of this large-handed lad was I don't know, but during interminable project meetings sat at his side I watched some fantastic artistry emerge on the pages of minutes. Looking at these, I felt the urge to let John loose with a large glass tank, a mature tuna and a gallon or two of formaldehyde. I reckon that he could have made his fortune!

He became famous, as did many of his colleagues, for his reported sexual exploits. How true these were, and how much they were about keeping up fantasies, I never worked out; but John was determined that any bloke seen talking to a woman must be having it off. He it was, under an alias during my previous venture into these tales, who entertained a whole non-smoking compartment on a DMU from Hebden Bridge to Leeds with his fantastic appetite for the fairer sex; since we were facing forwards behind the driver, and were in high back seats, and he was oblivious to the compartment being fairly full. All women were declared lovely by John, until he moved to Leeds and encountered a former lady clerk visiting her old office. 'Friggin' hell, but she's ugly!' he said to me in one of his famous roaring stage whispers. 'Ah'd have to have t'leet off for her!' When I pointed out that she was happily married with three kids, he could not believe it.

John's more famous appetite, and better suited to an open communal life, was eating.

'Ofter mi'mother's, Sunday. Allus a great heap of beeast, tatties – two kinds, sprouts and tunnups! She knows ah need mi'grub!'

Moira, John's beloved and feared wife, was more into haute cuisine, but John would rant about her famous 'Spaghetti Bollucnaked'. Moira was a gorgeous and strong woman, who thought nothing of marching into a lads-together do one Christmas and yanking John out by his collar because she suspected something improper had been going on. He had to walk the full length of the room, bent over in her grasp, and protesting his innocence in front of all his colleagues.

When I first met Moira, she was a genteel and tidy hostess, definitely middle class; but the surprise was Midge. Full of bluster in the car and garden moments before, he suddenly went all damp lettuce in her company, and spoke only when he was spoken to. I never had any fears or doubts about those two!

John's eating was a legend, yet he kept a moderately slim body. During the York project, on one of many dinners out, with a visiting bunch of foreigners – in this case the Poles – John swept through his 'Little Chef' gammon and chips. His last shovelful stopped on its way to the barn door where he kept his eating machinery, and dropped off his fork. He was staring across the room.

'What's up?' I asked, as I bunged a modestly laden fork into my mouth.

'It's Morris [Morris Smith, Engineer at the time]. You'd nivver guess what he's just done! He's only cut a bloody chip in two!'

With John dumfounded, let's relax with another quote break, leading on from his mother's famous dinners:

'I'm like a pig when I'm eating pork!'

After a conversation with a project manager on the phone:

'These people don't talk like I think!'

Explaining a change of duties:

'Eric's not Andy any more. Andy's Eric now, if tha sees what ah mean. That were a loada gibberish worra ah just said then, weren't it?'

'...Aneesez, Mike Collins, oozee? And ah sezeeze that baldeddebugger ooze inchargevme.'

And on the radio intercom during York:

'It's all quiet aht theer, Gordon. Is Eric's gob on strike?'

'I've had a bellyful of babies.'

And:
'I ain't been out since ah cumin.'

A rare appearance in the newsletter of Mrs Midgley:

'You'd been banging away a bit before I twigged!'

And returning to the enigmatic master:

'I'm no good at getting big things into little holes!'

And finally an example of the bleeding obvious:

MIDGE: Ay, Pete, we've a loada Pakis to show round York in January!
PETER: Where are they from?
MIDGE: Pakistan!

★

My relationship with John was fiery at times, as we argued over the best ways of tackling the many aspects of York remodelling. John was a firm believer in the tried and tested, whereas I had always been a fan of innovation. While Pete Wilder did most of the current work of the section, John and I were poring over the mass of track plans. It was during necessary breaks from deep concentration that he opened up a bit about life in general. He was well aware of his weaknesses, particularly in terms of how he spoke and who he spoke at, involving some discretion on my part, but in eruptions at times on his. One of his frequent moans was that because of who he was and how he presented himself, added to his personal pessimism (we were well matched there) he could never see himself as getting further promotion. 'They'll nivver make me an MS 2, you'll see!' In this, he turned out to be right, but not in the way he expected.

By now, I was responsible for a regular divisional staff full-colour magazine, free to all. As the main writer, with Wendy's assistance, and the only photographer, I was called on to snap important presentation ceremonies, of all kinds of staff. This provided me with an example of Moira's amazing control over John. When being presented with the annual golfing trophy, by the Permanent Way Engineer, a speech was demanded from John. All that I managed to record, and not report later was his, 'Well, bugger me, I'll go to t'foot of our stairs!' I didn't even get that much out of him at his long service award, when Moira was invited in to meet Morris Smith, the Engineer, and receive an extravagant bunch of flowers. Moira did all the talking, touching on all the valuable work that John had done without any material recognition; John (and Morris, more or less) just kept quiet.

The various Engineers rather enjoyed these presentation mornings, when couples were conveyored in at 20-minute intervals, for the wife to be kissed, and the boss to be looked up to. I avoid comparing Engineers as much as possible, especially when they're still around, but I think that on the whole Geoff Holmes was the better operator at this. I only really have Morris to compare with as an onlooker, but Geoff certainly had the edge, as an engineer, when it came to the kiss and embrace.

After York, and the climb-down from intensive work, the project team broke up and the lads went back to their regular posts, leaving Midge and me together with two assistants. Because of his experience, John was getting more and more new work, but it was boring stuff – he was no longer 'getting his hands dirty'. A new job, scaled MS 3, came up, of co-ordinating all weekend work and materials, and heading a team of clerks and technical staff. John reluctantly put in for it, dreading another brick wall and knowing that a jump of two grades was impossible. To his amazement he leapt the two rungs and got the job.

'There you are,' I told him. 'You said you'd never be an MS 2, and you were right!'

It was in this new post that Midge had to try out the new concept of mobile phones. Up to then, on big jobs like York, a radio walkie-talkie system was in use. This was all right for a moderately spanned site, but too often we were out of range of each other. Also, no messages could be private, as every other person switched on could hear it all, including other departments. This, in the hands of such as Midge and Eric Ball, led to mis-understandings and possible legal action. Mobile phones were unbelievable, and a first few were put into John's hands. This was new technology, always something which took him time to accept, appreciate and absorb. Within the Leeds office he tried it out, with me scribbling furiously over at the other side of the office, as he launched into one of his hilarious soliloquies.

'Oi, Pete! D'yer know how to work this thing? Young Lindsay' (a high flyer landing briefly in charge of us) 'young Lindsay wunt let on, sez everyone knows how – I don't – and he goes off forra fortnight, and I'm left in charge! I'm trying to ring this phone here… No, not this one in mi hand, yer silly booger, that one theer on t'desk, t'ordinary phone. Look, 0532 – that's Leeds intit? – why d'they mek these numbers so bloody small? I keep stabbing two at a time – can't get mi finger in… – Izzitbooggery! They're the same size as anyone else's!… Have I put 0532 in? Well, you should have been looking… Didda slot a nine in for outside first? It is outside intit, even though it's inere? Right, 033, no hold on, it's 411 now, intit, 411591? How do I start agin? Bloodyell, Lodgey, you're no bloody use at all! Don't you know owt? No, givvitere, let's avanuther crack at it… Reet, oh – five – three – Where's bloody three – didda hit six instead? There – three – two… wotsnext… Hurry up, it goes off if you don't look sharp. Four – won – won – five – Why aren't these numbers in order – no they're not! Weerwozza – won! How many wons did ah stab in? Duzzit matter? Nothing's happening! It's not working! Wotsupweeit? D'yerpress this – or this – worrabout this – Send – no, yer've med mi press it twice now! Orr, bloodyell, t'phone's ringing, answer it, Pete… ay! *No! Giuzzitere…* it's me! Ay, ahm talking tomissen… Ah've cracked it. Dunnitbimissen – owabout that, then?'

'What did you press in the end, John?'

'Buggered if I know – have to do it again. *Now watch worram doing, this time!*'

Which leads us naturally into some more Midge quotes:

JOHN at dinnertime, balanced on a high drawing office chair: I can't go to sleep 'cos I tumble ower every time I drop off!

In the York Project Office: It's all very well making decisions, but we're here to work!

At a Team Briefing on alcohol: Drunk and drigs rebillihabitation…

MIDGE at the section's annual dinner in an Italian Ristorante: 'Fancy this Spaggetty aller Putenesser, and this Pisser Caprickiarsole looks OK; wash it down wi this red, Verdickio Classy; dunno boot starters though… Reckon I'll have a dolloperthis.'
'That's the owner, John!'

About his immediate boss, one winter's day: Cold weather got Dick hot and bothered last week.

'I've booked the Meeting Room every Monday afternoon this week.'

'Caravan Park were all right, except it were owerful of caravans.'

…And finally this, outside the office by Mrs Moira Midgley, at a time when the pair were taking up serious caravanning. They were walking round a specialist store. From opposite sides, through the assembled crowd of shoppers:

MOIRA: Hey, John, come and look at this. It's a better tool than yours!

JOHN: How's that?

MOIRA: Well, you don't have to suck it to get it going!

★

We're going to have a holiday break here, as Midge returns to the office after a week abroad, with clerk Graham Whiteley. Now the best offer for a flight to Spain was to be had from a company called Winglessjet, operating from an old airfield outside London. To make things easier (and more complicated) for themselves they hijacked Paul Major to drive them down from Selby (Midge) first and Bradford (Graham) because there was a threat of a railway strike.

'Gotmi photos back today, wanter see em? Thissuns packing luggage; there's mine, sitha, two paira shorts, two tee shirts, toothbrush and two bitsa chicken for t'journey. That's Whiteley's – eighteen changes of clothes, fancy booits, galloner suntan, and that parcel, am not tellin' yer what's in theer, but thur mustabin' a gross – brought back nobbut only four wiim. Notice… thur's no tickets!

'Thissuns as we set off from Selby; well it were dark and Paul Major's head gotint road – he were drivin cosser t'train strike. This is pickin' up Whiteley in Bradford – ah know yer can't, it's still dark, aifpassfour in t'mornin', tha knaws. This is dawn in Barnsley on emwon motorway – ah know yer can't! – am still sat behind Major's head. Thissuns Whiteley's house in Bradford agin. No, it's not outer order, weer back theer to pick up iz tickets worreeforgot, daft booger. 'Undred miles on t'clock, and we've got noweer!

'Thissiz mi bag agin, juss afore they were about to blow it up wi a controlled explosion. Theer bloody daft down London; put yer bag down to go gerra paper, and before yer knowit, thur's some mad sod wirin' it up to crack it open!

'Yer not seein that woner that woner that woner, this... now this is a snapper Whiteley's breakfast. Allus gorrup and ordered *'Dos breakfasts, parbervor'*, but Whiteley were slow offertmark mornings... aifpasseven, and no sign of him. Ah allus giim another ten minutes after ah'd finished mine, then ah'd see his off anall.

'Anthisis in t'old streets; they were reet narrer and ancient, real cultural. There's Graham theer, no theer, theer, sitha! Tekit ower to t'light. Now canyer seeim? Ah know it's mostly ovva dog's bum, but that weren't theer when ah were pressin' t'shutter. Ah can see it's squattin', burra were tekin' Whiteley, ah tell yer! Amahbooggery perverted! Ahm tellin' yer, thurwur no dog when ah were tekin' it. Oh, t'hell wiit... ahm not showin' yer no more!'

I must put a note in here to remind you that we are still talking about a master at strategy and planning, who would have been furious at his companion's lack of it in leaving his tickets at home. In fact, after jotting all that down (and playing havoc with 'spellcheck'), I am still referring to this same brilliant engineer when working. You might easily forget that!

★

When Morris Smith replaced Geoff Holmes as Engineer, we, as was customary, treated him with deep suspicion. We soon learnt that he often finished a sentence with a kind of laugh, which we discovered did not necessarily mean that he'd said something funny, and that a like response was not to be expected. I first encountered him on a visit into the office during my long illness break coping with my lung problem, and was made to talk to him, humped over a chair back, apparently gasping my last. He knew me, or rather of me...

'I believe you produce an annual newsletter for the office. I shall, of course, want to vet it before it is issued.'

Bad start, Morris! At first I thought I'm not in the best position regarding work, yet stories about folk in the office have been getting through. I thought that the wisest thing would be to forget the newsletter that year. Others thought differently, accusing me of cowardice, and crumbling to a new boss, where it was my clear duty to expose him as well as everyone else. I took the point, and six months later produced a newsletter, but despite his heavy hint, printed it without approval. It was the most innocuous issue yet, and caused Morris no problems. What he didn't know, and still doesn't, was that I produced an underground supplement that was only available by application. That really had the goods in it! (That bit about Morris still not knowing assumes that you are reading this before he does. As I am sure, from a legal point of view, that Morris will cough up for an early copy; there're probably only one or two of you to whom the statement will apply, so the rest must assume that the sentence no longer stands. I wish I'd never started that bit now.)

Apart from his ominous little laugh, heads of sections found another problem with Morris – his writing. This appeared at the top of letters sent down for us to deal with, apparently indicating his directions or suggestions as to the stance we should take. None of us had a clue what they said, and to the most part, dealt with them in ignorance. Despite ten years of training, reading Don Newell's delightfully distinctive, but illegible writing, I was beaten by Morris's. It made Don's look like copperplate.

Its main feature was that, unlike most people, Morris wrote horizontally, rather than vertically, or if not quite horizontal, then at a very acute angle to it. From a distance his writing looked like several broken lines, a bit like a drunken bar code. You had a bit of a chance with it if you viewed it slightly tilted and edge-on. Better still, though, we had a nark up our sleeves. If any part of his instruction was underlined, then it was deemed important, and we would take it up to Morris's secretary, Stephanie (late of the glamour on the table tennis). She was not too good at the early stages, but became amazingly reliable after a few months' experience, only because she was in a position to go in and question the scribe on anything beyond even her. To his credit, Morris also had difficulty reading it, so even he was sometimes impotent.

When his photocopied invitation to all MS staff came to us

each personally, we were forced to recruit Steph. It turned out to be a sort of Christmas reception at his house on an evening in early December.

'Wotzit say?' asked Midge, who also had one. 'Dun't look too good t'me.'

'Well, it can't be all bad, since he's drawn a sprig of holly in the corner,' I observed.

'Thought that were a word! Holly, you reckon; it'll be summat abaht not drinking then, or enjoying yourself at all… Ah bet he's arranged a special carol service for management at his chapel – well, ah'm out ferwon!'

Having no sense of disgracing myself by not understanding the letter, unlike a couple of young PWay managers huddled in the glass office in the corner, I was first up to see Stephanie for a rough translation.

'That's "Christmas", there,' she said, with great confidence. 'Now then, how about the rest?'

I propped up the cupboard in her office while she studied the note, putting some words down on her typewriter, sometimes swivelling round to the diminishing light from the window. Eventually we had the bones of the thing, which she typed out. Essential words (apart from Christmas, which wasn't exactly a wild guess at the beginning of December) we had 'party', 'social', 'our house' (address given – you could easily have ended up in Scunthorpe – but Steph knew what it was anyway), 'Valerie and I', 'parking', the date, and most importantly, 'casual dress'.

I brought the bits down to Midge. He brightened up a bit at the words 'party' and 'casual', but he might have been thinking of the wild orgies he was known to take a part in as an occasional feature of the village rituals of Thorpe Willoughby, his base near Selby.

'You going, then?' he asked me.

'Not right keen on works parties, but I'll give it a try. I know Thelma'll think it's a good idea, just to have a gander round the house.'

'Moira will too. She's dying to meet Morris to give him another earful abaht my grade after Selby and York. P'raps it's not a good idea to tell her. Mind, ah s'pose she's bound to find out, anyway! There's a wives' mafia in York.'

We let some of the others, like George Woodcock, John Marshall and Jack Todd, see our translation of the hieroglyphics, but left the whiz-kids to find out for themselves. We needed those three to be there for balance, all being more or less of our generation and attitude. Besides which, George tended to laugh a lot when he'd had a drink, and Jack's dry chat, leading to the forthright, could prove refreshing. John Marshall would be driving, so he'd be concentrating too much on remaining capable to prove to be anything of an ice-breaker. But the smarmy rockets of young management would be difficult to stomach as they smooth-talked Morris and Valerie. We'd forgotten about Nigel Trotter, the PWay Assistant. Light-hearted enough at work, but tending towards the pure daft away from it.

I always found that Nigel was to be relied upon to do more or less the right thing, though some might disagree with that when it came to a work situation. By the time our little party (Marshall's and us) got there, he'd found the most comfortable chair, without it being one of those that you sink to the floor in, and the sides and back come in to trap you. He was resplendent in a wildly Christmassy pullover – red, green and white with a robin, holly and berries – along with a large 'Merry Christmas' emblazoned across his chest. That should have been the standard for 'casual dress'.

Others had simply chickened out. All the rest, except the host, were wearing suits of varying severity, along with unspectacular shirts and low-key ties. One let the side down so badly as to resort to Morris's official office tie! Morris himself looked unusually comfortable in light trousers and an open-necked shirt. I was just taking my coat off when Midge arrived with Moira. With a 'How do' he examined the surroundings – he looked distinctly uncomfortable. We were in a large reception area, with unsignposted routes off in all directions. John then caught a glance of the assembled company through the part-opened door. 'Aww, bugger!' he said to Moira, 'Cummon, weer off home.'

'Don't be stupid, John,' she said. 'We've only just got here. What's the matter? Take your coat off.'

'Ah'm leaving it on. This is all your fault.' This remark was apparently split between Moira and me. What I'd done or said, I did not know, and certainly couldn't think of anything I might have done in collusion with Moira. She had removed her coat and was resplendent in a very attractive dress, edging on party style.

'You,' he said, rounding on me, 'said you'd come casual. And you', (to Moira) 'told me I was OK! Look at them in theer!' said John. 'D'they think that's supposed to be casual! Look at 'em!'

'Take your coat off, and stop making a fuss,' hissed Moira, before exchanging a few pleasantries with Morris and Valerie. Moira was the sort who could have cheered up a Christmas party on Death Row.

Slowly, very slowly, Midge's coat came off. I was not ready for it.

'Bloody hell, Midge, that's a bit sharp!' I said to the muttering bundle.

John was straight out of a magazine, in deliberately slightly torn, but clean jeans, a light brown 'Crocodile Dundee' sleeveless shirt, cut at the shoulders, and with a variety of dangling trimmings, bronze metal-edged pockets, the whole bottomed off with embroidered cowboy boots (borrowed, I suspected, from Graham Whiteley). The plunging neckline of the shirt, with medallion, revealed a sight akin to a dustbin lid on a barber's floor.

The reaction of the assembled company was worth seeing. The ladies were split at the sight between complete disdain, from the porcelain fragile princess squatting at her husband's feet, to many restrained welcoming remarks from those who had met John before. Altogether there was a noticeable drop in temperature, and a frost was forming. I was still in shock, so it was left to Nigel to grumble that someone had to top his festive jumper, then turning to his Liz, complaining that she always held him back, and another time *he'd* decide what was casual.

Then followed a long and splintered stage-whispered bollocking of me, from the antipodean dress-down artist sat at my side.

'What the buggery d'yer mean turning up in that?' I was wearing slacks and a bright, open-necked checked shirt, sleeves rolled up above the elbow. 'Tha's med me look a right pillock; ah thought tha said tha were coming casual! Look at me in this! Moira said it'd be just the thing, and look at these others. Bloody syuits and ties. Nige is OK, ah s'pose, considering his age, but what sort of party's this goin' t'be? Ay, whose is that skinny tart, theer?' (He meant the porcelain figurine.) 'Ah'm not goin' t'end up withat, ah'm telling thee! Thur's no bloody handles on it, for a start!'

This was when a cold flush hit me. Never in my wildest had I imagined that Midge was expecting the kind of party common in Thorpe Willoughby at Morris's, the sort where you lose sight of your wife or whatever half an hour after you'd arrived, only to fish her out from some entanglement around one o'clock in the morning. I looked around the stable possibilities for the Midge stakes. We were two distinct camps, with as usual Nigel Trotter in the middle. Steady middle-aged engineering assistants had brought along matching wives in twinsets, or discreet blouses and skirts, whereas the young whiz-kids, like the one belonging to the painted ornament, had brightly dressed young maidens in tow. Nigel, himself a whiz kid in his time, but with a slow burning fuse, had the delectably comfortable Liz with him, bridging the void.

Morris came round with the first order for drinks.

'Pint, please, Morris,' said Waltzing Matilda at my side.

'We've only got cans, I'm afraid, John.'

'Fine, I'll have a couple to be going onwi, ta.'

Morris wisely brought in a four-pack and set it down beside John, very deliberately placing the compulsory glass in his hand. Other drinks followed on trays, handed round by a diminutive, polished young boy. These were mostly small cut glass jobs, with the occasional umbrella stuck out of them. I decided to keep John company by settling for a can of Guinness for myself. He had managed to empty a couple of tubes before everybody else had been served, and at last sat back in his chair. He was now in that brief transitional period between uncomfortable muttering and over-relaxed chatter.

We all sat around the perimeter of the room, sipping and mumbling, and moving very little in embarrassed paralysis, looking for all the world like lumpy wallpaper. George had been forced into one of the Venus mantraps which masquerade as comfort, and apart from two knees, a couple of hands and part of his head, he had virtually disappeared. There was a forced daft grin on what face we could see, along with a marked determination not to fall asleep. Mrs George's elbow was active in assisting him in that.

From time to time the youngster would wander in with a tray, and take orders for more drinks.

'D'yer reckon that theer's Morris's kid?'

'Dunno; suppose so. Ask him.'

'Ayoop, young'un, ista Morris's sprog?'

The lad looked blank and went pink; he turned and wandered back to the drink store. He was obviously telling his mother that one of the men, the one dressed in a tea towel, was asking for a drink that he'd never heard of before.

We had no idea as to the size or design of the house, as we had arrived in the dark, and had not been invited to accompany our coats upstairs. From what we were able to see we were in a splendid large building, in its time furnished with servants. Evidence of this was there in the form of push buttons set in the moulded border running all round the room. Bored with the women, John's eye was drawn to these.

'Wotsthese for here, d'yer reckon?' John was an unlikely candidate for period drama on TV where such furnishings would be normal.

'They're for getting the servants in to poke the fire, or serve the drinks.'

'Morris doesn't have servants, does he? Nah,' he said, answering his own question. 'D'yer reckon they'll still work?' His fingers were already caressing the nearest.

'One way to find out!'

Midge toyed with it, took another draw at his glass, looked at me in his quizzical way, and back at the button. He pressed it.

'Hello, everyone!' said Valerie, walking into the room for the first time.

'Bloody hell!' said Midge. 'Did I do that?'

Now, needing to add another aspect to the gathering, and ready for anything, John called out to his host, 'All right if we smoke, Morris?'

'Fine,' replied the boss, 'so long as you fancy a walk round the garden at the same time!'

'Ah tek it ah can't smoke, then,' John muttered to me. 'I need some grub if ah can't!'

This might have been a little loud, for Valerie immediately announced that supper was served in another room. We were led into a second very large space at the opposite side of the entrance hall. John's eyes lit up. There before him was a gargantuan spread. Four cans down, and another pack supplied, John was now firmly in party mood. Out of general nervousness, both of the occasion and with watching what I unreasonably took as being my responsibility, I wasn't far behind him. Thelma was keeping up pretty well, with Moira taking it steady, as she was the driver. John had now left his worries about his shirt way behind him, and was mixing well with the crowd. It was at this point I wished that I'd had a camera, for here were all these suits holding modestly filled plates, alongside something from a tent near a billabong going walkabout among them, having liberated one of the serving plates, now piled high. His free arm was wandering round a few female shoulders, even attempting the figurine but getting a frosty 'Excuse me!' in return.

Across the table he called, 'Ayoop, Mike, wotseez?'

'They're vol-au-vents, John.'

'Vol-au-vents! Vol-au-vents! What's a bleedin' vol-au-vent?'

This had to happen in one of those silences when, quite by accident, everyone stops speaking at the same time. Moira was round the table in one, dragging her errant husband over to a corner, and into a long, discreet and finger-wagging conversation with him, he being now well into his second pack. Jack Todd, finding this most amusing, began to laugh. I mentioned Jack's laugh in the early pages. On this occasion it rose way above the nervous chatter that followed John's intervention, with Jack trying to control a plate, a glass and uncontrollable tears. When Jack laughed like that, you knew that he was now delightfully comfortable, the laugh being either highly infectious or slightly embarrassing.

Morris cleared the air, coughed and clapped his hands. It was time for the speech. Unfortunately he'd been told a joke the day before, and in the course of talking rambled into the joke without warning. Nobody realised we were experiencing the cabaret, and the joke settled dead level with the carpet. Morris tried to give it the kiss of life with one of his light chuckles, but the moment had passed. Then we had the Morris we knew – the light-hearted speech of thanks for all that we'd done over the year, drifting into his usual address as to the state of the railway industry. The Channel tunnel was in progress at the time, and was foremost in all railway conversation. Morris, well away by now, provided me with material, just in time, for the newsletter.

'The tunnel,' he said, winding up, 'will make a great difference to the railway as a whole!'

I grabbed a table napkin and scribbled it down. Quote of the year, I thought!

★

Finally, a report, as it appeared in the 1992 *Newsletter*, of a typical John Midgley response to a difficult domestic situation.

FIRST AID FOR THE NON FIRST AIDER
No. 34. DEALING WITH A SUICIDE ATTEMPT

Scene: In the Midgley garage, bottling his home-made wine.

Enter distraught neighbour (DN) in tears:

DN   John! John! Come quick, Cyril's acting peculiar. [Some names have been altered to protect the individual.]

JOHN MEDIC (JM):   Wassermatter wiim?

His legs start moving out of curiosity towards the neighbour's house; head – full of reason and trepidation – tries to go in directly the opposite direction.

Both enter house. Cyril is slumped in a chair, white as a sheet, tongue lolling out of the side of his mouth, mumbling.

JM: Seems all right t'me. Wotsup?

Midge

DN: He's taken twenty paracetemols! He's going to die!

[First Aid Rule No. 1: Establish the facts quickly, and inform the emergency services on their arrival.]

JM: Howderyerknow he's teken twenty?

DN: For crying out loud – does it matter? Look, he's pressed out twenty from this pack.

JM: Ay, but thurmayabin some gone already.

DN: I know he's taken twenty! Just look at the state of him!

JM: He allus looks like that.

[First Aid Rule No. 2: Always try to calm, comfort and reassure the patient and family.]

DN: Look! I am absolutely sure he's taken twenty paracetemols!

JM: Well, bloodyell! Twelve's normally enough to do you in!

DN, plus three children, now break into uncontrollable sobbing.

JM: Haveyer called nambulance?

DN: He won't let us! Keeps slamming the phone down. Please do something.

[First Aid Rule No. 3: Alert the Emergency Services as quickly as possible.]

JM: Look, Cyril, yerknow wotsupwithee dunntyer? Yer bloody crackers man. Yer don't tek twenty a them things and live! I'm offterget help, Moira'll know what to do.'

He returns home.

JM: Gerroff that phone, summthin important's cummup!

Mrs JM:	This is important, shut up and go away!
JM:	Yer don't understand, this is vital! Cumwime!
Mrs JM:	Will you go away, John, and stop interrupting.
JM:	Cyril's topped hissen! He's teken twenty tablets!

Mrs JM twirls round, and reappears in a very fetching nurse's uniform, slams down the phone and turns into Wonder Woman (WW).

| WW: | Why didn't you say so?! Come on then, there's no time to lose! |

[First Aid Rule No. 4: Do not panic. At all times keep the situation in perspective.]

| JM: | Ayoop! Don't go offerin a lift ter t'hospital, aver golf match in arfanour! |

★

About four weeks after this episode, I was set to leave home for work at 7.30 one morning when the phone rang. It was Midge.

'I won't be in today, Moira was killed last night.'

I was struck dumb; his usual accent had gone, and there was no mistake as to what he'd said. For seconds I couldn't answer; all that eventually came out was, 'Ring you later.' I turned to Thelma, for what I didn't know. We just stood there stunned, holding each other. Eventually I left, and arrived in the office a bit before eight.

The news had gone before me. Phil Summers, a mainstay on the York job, and a neighbour of John's, looked up from the table where two or three had congregated. His face was white and devoid of all expression. He said, 'You've heard, haven't you?'

I nodded. Wendy was quietly sobbing into a hankie. It was at that moment that I realised that our mutual feelings for John went far beyond friendship. I find myself wet-eyed writing this.

Later that morning, after so many people had come up to me to find out what I knew, the 'committee' decided that someone should ring John, and arrange to go and see him. They very soon concluded that it should be me. I was the only person he had rung, all the rest finding out from Phil.

I went into the boss's glass box, willing myself to ring; the then boss himself stayed outside with the others. Thankfully they all turned their backs on me. I rung. It was John himself.

Moira had been leading the family pony, with their youngest, Paula, mounted, along a lane leading back to their home. It was a very bright evening, with a dazzling sun in their eyes. It was also in the eyes of the lunatic driving at some speed, never seeing them, and hitting Moira full force. The pony panicked, and took Paula back home at a gallop. John rushed out to the spot to find the police already there. He could see that Moira was dead.

Going with my instinct, but against my honest inclinations, I fixed up to go over to Selby two days later, and for John to pick me up in his car at the station. I was whisked to his house where all three children were in a whirl of unnatural activity. They had a picture of Moira, and wanted a mount – I promised to get one to them as soon as I could. It was a horrendous but beautiful visit.

A Nostalgic Interlude – Rain

Leeds remodelling initial project meetings almost tumbled over themselves to interfere with our celebrations on completing York. They were, as before, long meandering arguments between the various operating departments of the now identifiable components of the railway transport system, Inter-City, Regional Railways, Freight Services and Parcels. Each one would state their track requirements, usually hanging on in pecking order to the company ahead of them in 'importance'.

Lush sweeping lines, with trackside adornments on a rolled-out sheet would be produced by Inter-City. A copy would be made for Provincial Railways, who added ruled lines running off from I-C drawings. Additional lines at the insistence of the Operators were sketched in, merely to make the two minimalist requirements operable. Freight were prepared to be identified with the odd passing line sketched on ruled pages torn off a pad, while Parcels handed in a brown paper envelope with a platformed siding, and what appeared to be two turntables on the back of it. (These later turned out to be the result of putting two damp coffee mugs on the envelope.)

It was then the turn of the Civils headquarters to collate all these impossible entities, and, along with the S & T, produce initial discussion drawings. So while I was required to attend all the meetings, the first six months' worth would scarcely involve me to no greater extent than pouring the tea out.

We were on the top floor of the Aire Street Offices, overlooking the west end of the Leeds station complex. I always chose a seat where I could at least watch the trains passing in and out of what is this very busy station. You could see all the complicated web of cross-overs, slips and diamonds and approach lines for a mile distant in some cases; in fact the need for modernisation was blatantly obvious, for once involving additional lines for a change, rather than the traditional 'rationalising'. Floor six was the ideal vantage point to study the major part of the job; that is, unless it was raining, as it was on this particular day. It was streaming down the south wall of windows, occasionally being caught in the wind and driven hard against the glass in a rapid-fire attack of shrapnel. The railway was invisible, and my thoughts and pencil doodled away in monotony.

My very first project meeting in York had scared me rigid. It was straight after my appointment as the Leeds Project Assistant, and I remember coming home in a haze and telling Thelma that I was seriously thinking of packing this in. I deplore boredom. It really frightens me. For smaller projects on the Huddersfield Area, meetings would be on stools in my office around a table of plans, with mugs of tea, everyone involved, and over and done with in the space of an hour. This one at York had managed three hours in the morning and two more after the dinner break, which in York was an interval of 1½ hours. Gradually I became immune to them, aware that my turn would come all too soon, where I would be the one holding forth for the full length of the meeting, protecting my ideas, re-sketching and insistent about my non-negotiable staging sheets. Until then I had to work out my own diversions, once I'd caricatured everyone round the table.

I fixated on the drenched windows, watched the endless repetitive patterns of the rivulets and mused on earlier, happier encounters with the elements, while at Huddersfield, with Bill Boyes, Wilf Warburton and Percy Kellet…

Cue wobbling screen and drifting back in time music.

'In rain or fog or falling snow,
Into the cabin you must go…'

This was probably the first rule of permanent way work that I was taught, and certainly the first that I conscientiously obeyed.

'It's lookin' black ower t'wife's mother's!' A pessimistic prognosis from Percy.

'Dusta reckon it's headin' ower this way?' A hopeful question from Wilf.

'Can we get this bit done, please? I will at least have something down on paper if we finish this bit off today, before it starts.'

'Ay, but just bear in mind that Bill ain't ower handy wi t'car. He's quite a few fields off. Look sharp, and we might beat it!'

Ten minutes later we three had hurried along to join Bill back in the car, the last hundred yards being taken at speed as large chunky raindrops struck and penetrated our minimal summer clothing. We clambered back inside, me in front alongside Bill, and the other two climbing into the back after flipping the front seat up. This was not due to any respect for the senior man on paper – giving him the front seat. It was more knowing that he'd be stood out in the rain while the underlings eased themselves over the back of the folded front seat. The more we struggled to get out of the rain, the more we got entangled with each other and the seat belts, and the wetter I became. We were in no way assisted by Bill continuing to read his broadsheet in the driver's position. By now the windscreen was completely obscured with streams of rain pouring down it.

'Tha's nivver given up for a few drops of rain, hasta?'

We jointly gave Bill some advice as to his immediate future.

'Thur's folk as would give their reet arms to be stood out in a heavy downpour. Ah were watchin' this thing t'other week abaht rain in America, and how thur were folk as chased arahnd t'country tryin' t'get caught in thunderstorms. Daft abaht leetnin' and such. Took photos of it. Tried t'get near them theer whirlwinds wot they 'ave ower theer, hurricanes or such. Balmy! Mind, all Americans are balmy – and so's thur TV. Hasta seen that theer Lucy woman, and her wot waggles her nose and meks things disappear. Then they've a programme boot a talkin' 'orse. Crazy! Burra reckon chasin' rain's as daft as they come.'

We three were busy adjusting ourselves and shuffling about trying to find a bit of dry seat. There was little interest in Bill's TV critique.

'Ah'd say we're gettin' enough rain t'look at reet 'ere, wiout chasin' t'bloody stuff. Sithee, it's bloody bouncin'. Does this car leak at all, 'cos ah c'n feel a draught from someweer…'

'Me and Don chased rain once,' I volunteered. I was trying to conceal the slightly open window I'd organised next to myself in the front. Three damp blokes plus one dry, squashed in a small car, with rain streaming down every side, lends itself to a certain heavy atmospheric ambience. 'At least hail, rather than rain. Same thing, though. D'yer remember, Bill, that hailstorm last March?

'Ay, it come down wi'a reet wallop.'

'First we heard was from Marsden, up the valley; signal bobby reporting that his box windows had been smashed by hail, and he'd need them replacing urgent.'

'True, burree were somethin' of a stranger to t'truth, were that lad. It were 'is cold frame glass wot'd copped it, burree weren't bahn t'admit that, weree? Nice crop of lettuce he'd got theer, and he weren't prepared t'lose it, so he reports that t'signal box windows had got busted. We thought it were nobbut ower odd that hail could brek side windows.'

'I'm not sure what Don was worried about to have us chase this storm right the way up to Low Moor through Heckmond-wike and Cleckheaton. I think he were just fascinated with it. When it got to us in t'office it laid a good six inches on t'ground. Like golf balls, weren't they, Bill?'

'I were abaht t'say tennis balls, but tha's not as good a liar nor what I am. I think from what he said, Don was nattered abaht it startin' off some bank slips, burra reckon tha were nearer t'truth abaht him wantin' t'go rubberneckin'.'

'There were doorways and ginnels well made up. Around six foot deep in t'wind. Folk were shovelling it up like buggery to stop it melting into t'houses.'

'Nivver found no real damage though, didsta? Not while you got back. Them two silly sods traipsin' up and dahn t'railway looking for disasters didn't notice till they got back to t'office that wi chasin' abaht in't hailstorm, instead of just standin' still, all t'roof of t'car what they were in got a reet hammerin'. All little dimples, it were.'

'Why d'yer reckon rain sometimes comes down as hail or snow? Rain's allus cold, so ah reckon it could come down as what it chooses, so why hail?'

'Has tha not heard of hard watter, Bill? It's all t'rage dahn south. Ah think hail's just heavy watter, 'cos it feels it when it cops thee.'

'How abaht snow then?'

'Well that's just really soft watter, surely. Ah heard tell that t'rain in t'Arctic is always made wi very soft watter, so it comes dahn as snow.'

'So how coom we get all three 'ere, then?'

'It depends weer t'winds blowin' from. If it's a northerly it's bringin' Arctic rain wiit, and tha'll have noticed that hail often happens wia hot south wind.'

'That,' I said full of educated wrath, 'is a load of bollocks!'

'He'll shut up if we get off, Mike. May as well pack it in here. This lot ain't goin' t'give up ower easy.'

'No, let's hang on a bit longer, it's not dinner time yet.'

Wilf and Percy could never be criticised for their lack of willingness to work at all sorts of times, but Rule No. 1, above, always had a strong influence on their thinking. We were down at Cooper Bridge, a bit outside Huddersfield, facing the River Calder at a point just up from where it joins the Colne. We had been overlooking the river before any visual clarity disappeared due to the downpour; rather mysteriously drawn up alongside us was a smart convertible with its roof down and nobody in sight.

Bill cleared a patch of windscreen and set the wipers going.

'Ayoop, thereer, two on 'em, sithee, just comin' out from under t'bridge. T'blokes just zippin' hisself up sithee! What's afoot, dusta think?

'Bugger! They've seen us. They're off back under t'bridge.'

'Good luck to them, that there leaks like a sieve. They'll be as wet under there as out here in no time.'

'They'll be a bloody sight damper when they get back inter t'car! Ah'll bet it's ankle deep in theer bi now.'

'They'll not come out afore we've shoved off, I'll bet!'

'Mebbee we should hang on a bit, like Mike says. It could get interesting.'

'If this lot was snow instead of rain I bet it'd be three foot deep by now, 'cept it's rain and not snow, and it's t'middle on July.'

'Do you really mean three foot of snow?' At times I could be rather pedantic when a point of scientific accuracy was involved. 'You know that it takes all of six inches of snow to make an inch of rain. You're suggesting that we've had six inches of rain now if you say three feet of snow.' Figures were becoming a little tangled up now.

'Tha can't have six inches o'rain. It doesn't stand up, dun't rain.'

'S'pose tha had one inch of rain covering a back yard, say. That'd be about six inches all told, ah reckon.'

'Ay, but if tha had six inches falling in one spot and spreadin' out t'mek one inch, tha's forgettin' that t'rest on t'yard's gettin' same six inches, so it'd be all mekin' up.'

'That's all very well burrit's rainin' t'same outside t'yard as well. Rain dunt suddenly stop, tha knaws!'

'Rain's got to end somewhere, all ah'm sayin' is at t'edge it can't be standin' at an inch just goin' straight to nuthin', cannit?'

'It's looking a bit brighter over there, don't you think?'

'That'll be the edge weer he says that watter'll be stood one inch and suddenly nuthin'. Just dun't mek sense! Ah reckon tha has t'be a professor or summat to understand edges. Like t'edge of everything. Like at infinity.'

'Bill's well up with academics and doctors of engineering like that, aren't you, Bill?'

'Nah then, that were only a bit of fun, tha knaws.'

Bill had the previous week been responsible for at least a couple of near coronaries during the visit to the area of a leading American railway corporation engineer who was looking round, in the company of Don and Steve Bell, our District Engineer at the time, along with a dignitary from Headquarters at York. Our visitor was a Dr Cochrane, whose field was in all sorts of engineering.

'We'd that Dr Cochrane bloke that's been sniffing around over the last couple of weeks, and him there went and disgraced himself as usual.'

'We've had him round t'Leeds office an' all. We was introduced by Kye – called us the new cleus of t'organisation, or summat! Ah weren't sure whether he was pullin' us plonkers.'

'Well, Don knew that he couldn't trust him there to keep his trap shut, so he tried to get him out of the office for the visit. But he stayed long enough to be in the line-up for introductions. "How do, Dr Cochrane," says he, "pleased to meet thee. Would you mind if I asked thee a question?" "No time for questions just now, I'm afraid, Bill," says Don and Steve together almost.

"Dr Cochrane's got a very tight schedule." "Hold on, there," says the American, "I'd like to hear what Bill's got to say."

'Both Don and the boss are looking a bit more than apprehensive, and the white shirt from HQ is looking at his watch. "It's nowt much, Dr Cochrane," says Bill, "I just wanted bit of advice, like." "Fire away, my friend," says the Yank. "Well," says this daft bugger, "I've been having a bit of trouble wi mi shoulder when ah gets me arm up so far, and ah thought p'raps tha might have an idea what's wrong wiit, like!" "Dangit, Bill, I'm not that sort of bloody doctor!" says him, laughing his head off. "Tell you what, pardner, how about you showing me round this set-up – I've heard plenty from this lot already!" '

'He were a proper gent!' said Bill. 'Ah took him all round t'offices, and t'shops, and he were reet interested. Med mi go wiem to t'George for a drink and a bit of snap after!'

'And Don and Steve Bell were both in a sweat all the time you was talking to your "doctor".'

'Sod this rain! It's worse than ever now!'

'Stair rods,' remarked one of the amateur meteorologists present.

'Cats an' dogs,' added another.

'What's tha think that means – "rainin' cats an' dogs"?'

'Ay, and what sorts of dogs? I mean cats are just cats – theer eether black, white, orange or brahn, but a cat's still a cat, intit? But dogs are all sorts. Fancy callin' an Alsatian and a poodle and a cheerywawa thing all t'same – dogs, like. Thur nowt like each other. And how come all them diff'rent sorts breed t'mek mungrils when they're like chalk an' cheese. It'd be more likely t'have a cow mating wi'an 'orse, than a bulldog getting' stuck inter a Pekingese, wun't it?'

'That dun't answer t'question, do it? Abaht rainin' cats an' dogs.'

'No, but mi point is that if it were them theer toy dogs, they wouldn't wallop thi like what a Gurt Dane would, would they? So it matters what sort of dogs they're talkin' abaht. As ah sez, rainin' little poodles'd bi t'same as cats, like, but think abaht gettin' clobbered wi a load on Alsatians!'

Someone made some sort of remark about poodles on the

ground after it had stopped raining, but it was met with a silence and pitying stare.

'What's tha reckon, Bill? What's it mean, rainin' cats an' dogs?'

I butted in here, having seen it only a week or so ago in a Sunday paper 'Strange phrases in common usage' sort of article.

'Actually, it's an old Norse saying, because cats are associated with storms and dogs with the wind. You're not meant to take it literally; it's never rained cats and dogs, but it has rained frogs and fish sometimes. It's a phenomenon that can occur in a waterspout, lifting them out of the lakes and sea and depositing them on grounds. There's a number of authenticated accounts to substantiate the theory.'

There followed a long pause as this piece of wisdom sank in, each examining their various expressions and after that looking blank at me. Then…

'So, what's tha reckon, Bill? What's it mean, rainin' cats an' dogs?'

'Ah'm not bahn t'foller Confushus 'ere. Worraloada cobblers!'

'Looks like a fair dosing of fish still coming down out theer, and ah think ah spotted a coupla frogs and a tin on sardines drop past on thi side, Percy.'

'Nobody wants to be told anything, nowadays. There's loads of good info you can pick up from books and papers. Anyroad, have you noticed where this lot's coming from?'

'From up theer, Mike!'

'No, I mean which direction do you think it's moving.'

'Downards!'

'There's no hope for you two! Can you see any brightness around?'

'Theer's a patch of blue yonder.'

'My father always said that if there was enough blue sky to make an elephant a pair of trousers, then it'd come out fine.'

'By gum! Thi dad were a bit of a deep thinker, weren't he, Mike? Wonder he didn't get to do t'weather guessin' on telly.'

'They're not guessing; it's a piece of science is meteorology. Did you know that for any one place they're always 80% accurate?'

'Well, ah knaws weer t'other 20% were – allus ower me!'

'Tha knaws theer's some truth in that. Ah reckon some places are dead unlucky for weather.'

'Meaning…?'

'Well, tek reservoyers. They must put them someweer wot has more rain nor other places, otherwise all ower'd be a reservoyer, wun't it? Stands t'reason they builds 'em weer thur's most rain; nah, them places ah'd say were proper unlucky!'

This, I could see, was taking us down one of those byways where it is most unwise to follow. An abrupt change was needed.

'That blue you saw – is it getting any bigger?'

'It's moving abaht a lot. Hold on, it's reflection of tha shirt in't windscreen. Didsta dad say owt abaht blue shirt reflections and elephant dress-makin'?'

'My dad was, I've got to admit, a bit daft at times. He was a source of great embarrassment to my mother, and us kids sometimes.'

'Like…?'

'Well he was useless at DIT and…'

'DIT? Wassat?'

'Do It Thissen. Anyroad, he'd these couple of pictures to hang. They were stood in the back bedroom for months 'cos he'd got no nails. Eventually our mum got so annoyed she went and bought four ounces of four-inch nails from up Town Street. My dad marks where t'pictures needed to be and dipped into the bag of nails. Daft-like, he starts giggling, and tells my mum that these nails are no good because t'points are at the wrong end. When he gets like that, he doesn't know when to give up. He gets no reaction from mi mum, so, still sniggering away like a loony, he puts his coat on and takes them all the way back to Bretherick's, ironmongers, and tells t'man behind t'counter that he wanted to swap them for a packet with the points at the right end. Bretherick's man takes the bag off him, turns it round, and gives it him back. My dad gives up then. We don't go to Bretherick's much any more now.'

'Ah woodn't have got one step away from t'wall, if I'd tried that trick on our lass at 'ome.'

'That wasn't the worst of him, though. He once got these blokes in to lay roof insulation – y'know, that prickly stuff in rolls what we're all being told to fit. Anyway these two lads finish t'job and my dad's paying them. It was obvious that these two weren't much more use to society for anything but unrolling packs of insulation, which doesn't require much thinking power – ninepence to t'shilling, both of them – so my dad asks them if they're sure that they've laid it the right road up. He says he doesn't want it upside down so that it gets colder in winter and hotter in summer! The lads looked at him, and then at each other. Our dad was obviously some kind of thing they'd never come across before. But they says that they've always put it that way up because it unrolls along the roof, but they go off promising to have a word with their boss about it. Meanwhile my dad's chuckling away again and my mother's giving him what for.'

'Tha can get away withat by reckonin' t'be a carricter, and not just plain barmy.'

'Why,' said Bill, who'd been a bit quiet through the last couple of tales, mainly because they were just the sort of thing he'd do and say, and didn't regard it as 'barmy' at all, 'why, goin' back to cats and dogs sayin's and such, why dusta reckon we say "right as rain"? Wot's reet abaht rain, other than we might get back for an early snap when this bugger knaws when it's time to giup?'

In actual fact I'd nearly had enough, but I wasn't going to admit it. 'I'm going to check this rain, I'm getting out to see if it's really as bad as it looks.'

I got out. I got back in. 'It is as bad as it looks!' I said.

In that brief moment I found that my window had been wound up.

'Y'know,' said Wilf, 'us simple buggers wi no university eddication just tek it for granted that if it looks like it's pissin' down outside, from inere, then it must be really pissin' dahn. An eddication like wot tha's got, Mike, learns thi to query these things by means of gettin' aht, gettin' wet and gettin' back innagen, so havin' it sprayin' ower us three 'cos tha's experimented and experienced it, like.'

'Do I detect a hint of sarcasm in that, Wilfred?'

'Please thissen, think wot tha wants,' he replied, winking at the other two.

'Straight up, Mike, no messin',' came in Bill, 'wiout bein

funny or owt, didsta learn owt at all at college that tha uses now on t'railway? Ahm not muckin' abaht, Mike' – detecting a lowered eyebrow on my part – 'us lot didn't have t'chance, I just wonder wot we missed aht on.'

'In three years at uni, I reckon I learnt a bit more number work which comes in handy, but loads and loads of geology, hydraulics and strength of materials, that's been no use at all. What I didn't learn was how to set up museum pieces of survey- ing tackle like what we have on t'railway. D'you know, we were handling theodolites and levels that you just screwed onto the legs and they were level automatically. No, I reckon I might know a bit more about general all-round civil engineering than you three, but compared to you lot, I know very little at all about railway work.' I added, in case I'd complimented them too much, 'And they never taught us how to cope with daft buggers working as chainmen either. We chained for each other.'

They obviously appreciated most of this, but most important, it was true. Experience is the only way to learn. It's just that they were overfull with experience.

'Oh, come to think about it, there are two things where I bet I could beat you three at, hands down…'

A noticeable slight bristling within the car.

'I was taught for a full term about surveying by way of using the stars, and all six of us on our course spent a whole day on t'uni sports field taking measurements and doing calculations to work out the radius of the earth.'

'And how much use has that been on t'railway, then?'

'Buggerall! What's more with six of us working it out independently we came up with six different answers. I can say with confidence, from that afternoon, that the radius of the earth lies somewhere between one and half a million miles, and fifteen foot six, which you can't honestly fault!'

'By gum, lad, that's bloody useful t'knaw. Ah'm impressed!'

By which I took it that Bill was not impressed.

'It nivver rains but it pours!' said Percy suddenly.

'So?'

'No, ah mean that's another daft sayin', i'ntit? What abaht fine drizzle and a leet shower? Why d'they mek out it nivver rains but what it's pourin' dahn?'

This was another phrase that my article in the paper had covered, but past experience suggested to me that I should keep quiet about it.

'It'll be them friggin' Norse mates of his agen. "Rains" don't mean rains, and "pour" don't mean pour. Tha can bet on it!'

'Them Norse were... ayoop, movement under t'bridge. Dusta reckon theer bahn t'mek a dash ferrit? What didsta have to set wipers goin' for just then, Bill? They 'appen din't knaw we was still in t'car.'

'Wot's it like now, out theer?'

'Back to stair rods!'

'Oh well, that's an improvement on cats and dogs, ah'd say.'

'Cats and dogs again, I knew it reminded me of something. Have you told these two about Autumn Mists yet, Bill?'

'Oh, that stuffed racin' 'oss up on t'estate? Bloody fine piece of work that, for a taxi driver!'

'*Taxidermist*, you twerp! Anyway, Bill was up there again this week, being as usual the mischievous little prat. Right got old Henry Russell-Abbotson going, didn't you, Bill?'

'Autumn Mists were a lovely 'oss, but on t'racetrack it were bloody hopeless. It'd get better odds now it's stuffed than it ever got alive. But it were summat of a pet t'them, and worth preservin' as a good-lookin' animal.'

Bill used to drive up to the 'Big House' a couple of times a year with a load of clapped-out sleepers in his relaying days. They were used to build bins for manure and stuff. He was on first-name terms with the squire, Henry. Bill was just the sort of bloke anyone in their right mind could take to. As you've gathered, Autumn Mists was a magnificent beast to look at, but liable to stop and graze between fences. He meant a lot to the Russell-Abbotsons so they'd had him stuffed and placed in their very roomy hallway. Henry regularly groomed and polished him, or rather dusted him down and buffed up the bits he could. We were passing a day or two back, and Bill decided to pop in for old time's sake while I had my sandwich in the car. He wandered into the barn where he could hear the Hon. Henry working. I'll let Bill take over from there – he tells it better than me.

'Ah'll tell thee wot, though, yon Jack Coggan's allus been a bit jealous o'me mixing wi the likes of old Henry. Right closet Tory, Jack is.'

'That's true,' I agreed. 'Went to a meeting in York with Jack, and we both bought papers for the journey. He got t'*Express* and I bought t'*Mirror*. Called me a bloody Commie for ever afterwards.'

'Which goes to explain the red and yeller flags wot tha purloined off Jack Senior and cut out a yeller hammer and sickle to stick on t'red. Puts it up whenever Coggan's comin' across. Anyroad, ah were up at t'Big 'ouse last Thursday. Could hear t'old lad in't barn, so ah went inter say " 'Ow do", like. I looked carefully at him and then at t'vice on t'bench, and realised he'd one of Autumn's hooves innit and were polishin' it up, burra weren't bahn t'let on ah knew. "What's that?" says I, "that what you're buffing up?" "It's a hoof," says he.

'Ah says to him, like, "Well bugga me!" "Wot's up, Bill, lad?" says he. "Well," says me, "ah knaws ah'm a bit on a townie, an' that, iggerent of country things, like, burra nivver thought as 'ow they come off!" "What's tha onabaht?" says he, only a bit posher, like, 'cos he's Eton and Oxferd, is ol' Henry. "Ah'm on abaht 'osses 'ooves," says me. Ah says, "Ah nivver knew that!" "What?" says he. "Abaht them comin' off," ah says, "tha seez 'em walkin' in t'fields an' dahn t'road, an' jumpin' fences, an' such, burra nivver knew that their 'ooves come off!' Henry starts splutterin' a bit, not quite up wi me. "D'they just unscrew, or has tha t'prise 'em off, or are they on press studs?" ah says. "You don't mean…" he says, tryin' to jump in, burra just goes on. "Nay," ah says, "ah've worked it out!" Thay have t'screw off, else they'd come off while they were runnin'." Henry's gone a sort've pink colour bi now. "Well!" says I, "tha learns summat new ivvery day, dunt'tha? Ah suppose t'blacksmith just teks 'em off an' 'ammers on a new shoe, like. Bloody 'andy, ah reckon. Jus' wait while ah tell t'lads toneet dahn t'club! An' ah bet t'wife won't believe it. Burra've seen it for missen. Bloody amazin'!"

'An' then ah just walks off wi a "s'long, Henry", and mutterin' an' shekin mi 'ed, like. Henry dun't knaw weer t'put hissen. He's stutterin' away, like, wi, "N-n-nay, Bill, that's not reet, tha's got wrong idea," an'stuff. Burram away back to t'car, an' ah can see 'im in t'mirror pacin' oop an' dahn, shekin' his 'ed an' lookin' sort of bewildered, like, an' tryin' t'wave me back.'

'You're bloody evil, you are! Poor bloke wouldn't be able t'sleep after thee. An' wot's tha bahn t'say t'him next time tha sees 'im, eh?'

'Ah'll worry abaht that when t'time comes, burra bet he's a bit befuddled, like.'

'He's in a different world, is old Henry; apart from t'way he let's you talk to him, he's a good hundred years behind the times.'

Here at last some silence broke out, except for the gentle beating of rain on the car roof. Struggling surreptitiously, I managed to lower the window a fraction of an inch again. Four blokes constrained in a car surrounded by water can become claustrophobic. All round, the windows were heavily misted up.

'Tell thi what, Percy,' said Wilf, 'we could do with thy magic cloth just now.'

'Thee shurrup!'

'What magic cloth?' I asked, sensing some unrest in the camp.

'Percy, theer. Small advert in t'paper 'boot a magic cloth. It could mek winders sparkle 'cos it had special chemicals in it. All you needed to mek the dirtiest outside winders fresh and stoopendusly clean.'

'Well,' Percy joining in, 'ah weighed it up, like. This cloth cost one pound ten, and it said it'd do an average house ten times afore t'chemicals wore out. Now t'winder cleaner sets thi back twelve and six every visit, so I reckoned it were reet on t'advert weer it said that t'cloth'd pay for itself in no time.'

'True,' added Wilf, 'burree found out theer were a snag when 'e gorrit, didn't thee? Advert said buggerall abaht thi needin' to buy a set of ladders as well!'

Bill chuckled away, and Percy went his vivid red. Wilf hadn't finished.

'Allus bin a mug for t'small ads, hasn't tha, Percy? Thur were one 'e sent off fer a vacuum cleaner at thirty bob only. Jumped at it, 'e did. When it cem it turned aht to be t'same magic cloth as before. Note wot cumwiit said it were ideal for cleaning vacuums!'

'Alreet, then,' Percy responded. 'But tha couldn't wait for

them fizzy tablets that med thi teeth whiter than white, cud thi?'

'Well, ah'd allus bin proud of mi teeth. All mi own still. Just goin a shade yeller wi age, like.'

'Ah, so when they cem he were all for chewing a couple when he fahnd on t'label that tha'd to put t'teeth in a glass of watter fust!'

It went quiet, as there were no more comebacks for either of them. A sullen, sulky silence fell on the car. The rain was still there, but not as heavy.

Time for a bit of thinking usually sprang a tangent off the circle of conversation.

'I wonder what t'railway'll be like in an 'undred years' time. Ah reckon that tha wain't haveter sit in a bloody car wi t'rain thumpin' dahn waitin' t'do a job. Ah mean, when tha thinks how far we've come, and of what's happened in t'last 150 year.'

'Ay, there were a time when tha nivver gorron a train wi out gettin' off mucky. When they smelt bloody awful, you couldn't get nowt t'eat, and tha could get no peace what wiall t'others arahnd thi. Tha'd be bunged t'gether like animals, and t'ride were as rough as an Excuse Me in a disco. Tha'd go at thirty all t'way, and t'station's were nobbut a few planks on stilts.'

'Tha means arahnd t'1860s, when tha were crammed in t'open wagons, tight up agen t'person sittin' next but one!'

'Nay, ah'd two week ago in mind, between Wakefield and Barnsley. Nowt'll change! It nivver has, and it nivver will!'

'I think you're wrong, Wilf. There's a mass of new technology coming out.'

'What is this 'ere technology stuff, anyroad? We nivver had technology in our day. Weer's it sprung up from?'

'It's using science in a practical way, that's all.'

'Tha what? Gi'us a f'rinstance.'

'Well, it's like using water or steam to drive turbines and things; or making electricity. It's building bridges using mathematical and physical sciences, it's...'

'We'd have used bricks and stone.'

'Yes, but you'd maybe have overused the materials, made them over-strong, like.'

'So what? They stays up; that's what matters. This here technology of thine – it's just engineerin', i'nt it? So why invent a new name?'

'*Il pleut beaucoup*,' I said, just for something to divert the conversation.

'Tha wot?'

'Just giving a new name to pissing down!'

Wilf rubbed the window to look at some more rain.

'They could've parked yon car wi no roof in an 'andier spot than that, tha knaws. It'll be nobbut ower damp inside it bi now!'

'Jack Pinder's our parkin' expert nah. Went into Dewsbury station car park last Sunday morning. Zips arahnd lookin' for t'andiest spot. Only one other car in t'whole field. Jack 'its it! All t'space in t'world, but Jack manages t'clobber only car arahnd.'

'What about women parking?' I put in. 'Give our lass an half-full car park and she's all at sea, Up and down looking for t'prettiest spot or something. Put her in one with only one or two spaces and she's happy!'

'Ah still wonder why rain's allus cold.' Wilf was still peering out at the most miserable of scenes. 'T'ottest day on t'year – sudden storm – and t'rain's ice cold. Ah mean it were fair warm enough afore this lot started, but open t'car door an' tha's cold. Can't be much fun for them two under t'bridge, cannit?'

'Stompy in t'Messengers wor on abaht t'cold and these 'ere superconductors – he were looking through t'boss's *Railway World* for nude pictures. Poor lad sees a magazine and straight off reckons it must have mucky pictures innit! Failin' them he were bungin' his mind up wi superconductors. All he'd picked up were that they worked better cold than 'ot. Ah says to 'im, why did he think that t'Railway had winter and summer timetables? Told him that t'electric trains ran faster in winter than summer 'cos t'wires come closer to bein' superconductors 'cos of t'cold. Believes every word, the soft sod!'

This inspired another pause in the conversation. I was beginning to go with the crowd, but thought that we should give it a bit longer as there was some brightness outside. From way back in the conversation Bill suddenly comes out with, 'So what abaht infinity, then? What's that all abaht? Ah mean, when tha's got to infinity, what's outside it? And why does t'world turn reet rahnd in exactly twenty-four hours and not twenty-four and a quarter? And another thing, are them cow's yonder black wi white markin' or white wi black?'

'Infinity,' I said 'Is—'

'Ayoop, 'ere comes another load of eddicashun. Pin thy ears back, lads!… Well, go on, then, don't keep us in suspenders!'

'Infinity,' I repeated, 'goes on for ever, and when you get to the edge of infinity, there's still more further on. It's rather like him there. When he starts talking bollocks he can go on for ever, until he takes breath, and after that there's still more bollocks to come. Right,' I concluded, determined that this was one road too far, 'let's get off back home!'

'No, hang on a bit,' said Wilf. 'Yon couple looks like mekin' a dash ferrit. We're not to five minnits, are we?'

The Leeds Area Annual Newsletter

'Armpit!' It was thus that a new young clerk from Hemsworth introduced himself. Hemsworth is at the heart of the former mining community of Yorkshire, having a language all its own. It's where they got 'coil from t'oil'. Same county, but quite different from the popular conception of the Dales farmer's way of speaking, being much more lazy.

Hemsworth was notable as being the constituency that were a donkey with a red rosette to put up for Parliament, it would win with a landslide of votes. Should the Conservative candidate achieve more than two votes (him/her and his/her wife/husband), then there would be a witch-hunt to seek out those perverted individuals with no sense of tradition who voted blue.

Our new lad, Pete ('I am Peter' – in case you're still wondering about the opening quote), was no different in making himself known.

Peter was for a while the stationery clerk; should you be enquiring about some reinforcement rings for filing holes in paper, he'd tell you, as if you'd no idea, that what you were looking for were 'weshas'.

Other items in the Hemsworth/English Dictionary were:

Waste bin	Where have you been?
Tint	You are incorrect.
Gearsit	Would you please give me it.
Want gotnon	We do not stock that article.
Eesezitziz	He claims to own that item.

Peter Lowe was food and wine for the annual newsletter.

★

Before 1976, around Christmas time, annoying little 'jokey' scraps of paper would appear, copied by means of typed stencils. They were much on the lines of the childish gags which keep cropping up in your e-mail inbox nowadays. Nobody would claim responsibility for them, and they were usually lifted from somewhere else and were often offensive and filthy. For this reason I put it about that we would collect these into one sheet and grade them for humour content, discarding the trash. From that moment they stopped. So was born the *Divisional/District/Area Civil Engineer's, Leeds Annual Newsletter*. It wasn't difficult to produce; you only had to keep your ears open. Once it became established as a way of reporting and making public odd misfortunes that happened to those among us, there were many eager contributions.

These contributions were made in the hope that they could become bargaining points to allay some of the contributor's own false moves and mishaps. There was no chance of that at all! What follows now cannot include some of the best material because you had to know the foibles and habits of particular individuals. However, dotted around within were bits of satire against the establishment and management figures, along with those great one-liners that occur in any conversation. I have collected these together, and here included them as a final chapter, as I consider them as having less of the nature of in-jokes than most.

This is how most of the newsletters started; after a list of congratulations to all those who had been promoted in the last twelve months (for example, Don Newell from Area Assistant District Engineer, Huddersfield to Area Assistant Divisional Civil Engineer, Huddersfield, which merely means that after another reorganisation the jobs have been given new names, more work, more responsibility, less manpower but not more cash) there followed, in the first edition, a detailed description of how to gain entry to our new office called Compton House, or Cramptup House, as the *Newsletter* would have it. I kick off with the very first words of introduction to our first edition, comprising a tour of these new characterless offices:

> One enters the new accommodation by way of an Entrance Hall
> after tripping up three darkly carpeted steps. I say that one enters,
> because everyone else slips in via the fire door at the back. This
> magnificent hallway, illuminated by four AA batteries set in star-
> light effect in the black ceiling, leads straight through to the open
> back door, and the unwary can easily make their visit exception-
> ally short.

There then follows a blow-by-blow guide of the offices either
side of the corridor, and their contents, down the centre of the
ground floor. You could almost trickle a line of salt down here,
dividing the 'tops' from the 'bottoms', if it wasn't for the
'Enquiries and Reception' manned by two approximately
uniformed messengers. This tour then went on throughout the
whole office and the people within; but here let's just be satisfied
with a look around this welcoming lobby.

The main feature of the entrance was a small paying out window. This would be occupied on pay days by one of the clerks. In
the early days of Cramptup House this could be 'little' Wendy.
She was always known as 'little'. True, there were certain things
that were 'little' about Wendy – the little grin which was there
nearly all the time; the little voice which hinted at mischief – and
'little' because she never seemed to grow any older. As to height
and sense of respect, I have no visions or allusions of Wendy ever
looking up to me.

The little voice came in when she talked to her window sill
full of concrete gnomes, rejects from Johnny Bass's home
industry at Stanningley Shops using only genuine BR materials.
Should you try to humour her by attempting small talk with one
of the models, she would look at you pitifully with that little sad
smile and say in that little voice, 'They can't hear you, Mike.
They're made of concrete, you know.'

Wendy was on duty at the payout window one day when a
dishevelled member of the workforce turned up to be paid. From
the point where Wendy said, 'Hello, name please,' there followed
a lengthy descent into farce. She was trying to establish who he
was and his work number, while he was trying to book a bed for
the night, having mistaken Wendy for the supervisor of the
Salvation Army hostel next door. Wendy's response to any

situation that becomes silly was to collapse into an uncontrollable fit of giggles, which only went to confuse the situation further. Wendy was destined to play a much larger part in my life when, as a superbly experienced clerk, she joined our York Project Team.

So we meet Wendy again, someone who crops up in most of the Leeds years, and who contributed more than most to the Newsletter, either due to her hobby of collecting accidental quotations, dropped out unthinkingly, or by producing plenty herself. Her throws of mischief would often come when she was receiving sympathy for one reason or another – she had a skin no thicker than most when it came to mistreatment. She might have attracted it through familiar comment, but never ever by flirtation.

★

Unfortunately, by far the larger part of the Newsletter does not translate into general reading, as there would have to be a lot of background explanations of the characters being pulled apart. I will satisfy myself by bringing you a few that can more or less stand alone.

The first edition introduces a few of the main characters around in the Drawing Office and beyond of the mid-'70s to '80s. These people are characters in a way different from those I have introduced elsewhere, taken more from the educated ranks. As I have pointed out in the past, it was only the advances in the educational system when folk were not rejected on the examinational evidence of one day at the age of eleven. So here goes with some potted extracts.

Racing News – a rundown of this year's Grand National runners:

Jockey	Horse	Pedigree	
R Bean	Bad Loser	Out of Practise	by Never Winning
L Tuke	Jaws	Out of Breath	by End of Day
J R Newell	No Betting	Out of Conscience	by Stitched Up Pockets
M Collins	Acting Management	Out of Depth	by Miles
N Edwards	Skint	Out of Gambling	by Picking Losers
J Marshall	Collecting Expenses	Out of Sight	by Half Past Ten

Otherwise:

Roger Bean: From Chief Clerk to Administration Assistant, stern and unwielding, short fuse when losing at table football, notability – only person to manage to bend the bars holding the small players. Superficially highly respected, but underneath game for a laugh.

Lily Tuke: Frightening but soft lady with a three-floor voice (you could hear her coming from two floors down when she had one of her frequent differences with a member of the technical staff to sort out.) Was welcomed by a chorus of chicken noises. Big-hearted daughter of the pits.

Bob Newell: In his early days a furiously staunch Evangelical, with a mission to save the world. Grew into a genial but equally furious table football enthusiast, a game which necessitated him stripping down to a string vest during cup matches on hot days. Would realise about the vest around mid-afternoon, and replace his shirt.

Mike Collins: Unsure of his ability to do the job in hand until he surveyed his alternative colleagues on offer. Always mid-table at sports. Tended to write himself out of tight corners.

Neville Edwards: Packaged enthusiasm. Literally threw himself into all social activities with tremendous optimism and with an ability level slightly lower than his apparent potential. Fought desperately against promotion, but ultimately failed.

John Marshall: Solid reliable character. Former joiner who was quite happy to be left alone to do his job his way. Sturdy office cricketer in all departments. Had a greater knowledge of shops and where to get things than anyone else in the office. For example, he was the first to discover the enormous bath towels and everlasting soap for sale in pit canteens.

★

This first *Newsletter* was innovative in that the first tentative steps were taken to make fun of the top management on the District, namely the Engineer himself, Geoff Holmes – one to be wary of, as his former life out on an Area had taught him all the tricks. He had a refreshing attitude to local departmental councils (LDCs) and what should have been confrontational meetings. Beforehand he would informally invite the opposing chairman to his office, ask what was being demanded, state where he would be starting from, and reveal how far he was prepared to compromise. He was a 'Good Thing' in *1066 and All That* terms.

His PWay Assistant for most of the early days was David N Kealey, acknowledged as being an outstanding engineer. Also, with him being of less than average height, this formed the basis for his treatment in the newsletter. His nickname of Little Donkey was obvious, especially when it came to allocate roles for the imaginary Office Nativity Play. The post of Works Assistant was ever changing, but there were two golden periods, the days of the full fathom of Ray Collingwood, especially when standing next to DNK, and the time of Nigel Trotter, who had done so much in public in his days as a lad that his reputation went before him and was not allowed to lie down. Nigel was both a remarkably able boss to confer with, having a management approach that I found to be brilliant and natural, and being at lighter times a genial crackpot.

As an aid to the above members of management, a questionnaire was devised to find suitable candidates for senior technical officer posts:

1.   Can you sleep

(a) With your eyes open? *10 points*

(b) Only with them shut? *2 points*

(c) Only with them shut and you lying down? *0 points*

2.   Think of a song you sing regularly in the office, Do you

(a) Know a full verse? *0 points*

(b) Know only a couple of lines? *5 points*

(c) Know only the title? *10 points*

(d) Not even know the title? *15 points*

3.   Do you regard Sundays as a day for

(a) Rest at home? *2 points*

(b) Work at home? *0 points*

(c) Paid work? *10 points*

(d) Paid rest? *15 points*

4.   What is a theodolite?

(a) Someone from Theod *5 points*

(b) A surveying instrument *0 points*

(c) An Irishman's spare lamp *10 points*

5.   Put your hand in front of your face. How many fingers have you up?

(a) Five *0 points*

(b) Two *10 points*

(c) None *5 points*

(d) Don't know *15 points.*

★

In 1978 Inter-City was the Word:

INTER-CITY 125 MAKES THE GOING EASY.

It was something they put in the coffee.

As Geoff Holmes had, in his history, only briefly left the District, for him to be remodelled as a proper manager in York, and sent back as The Engineer, he was well-known to many of us as 'Geoff'. However, he did throw out a rather new aura, and it took time to weld him back into the genial person he was before becoming The Engineer. He had an alarming knowledge of photography, and we were now and again treated to audio-visual shows of the highest poetic quality.

In 1979 we had a scoop; we managed to get hold of the diaries of two ladies, one being Betty, Geoff Holmes's secretary, and the other, Mary, Mrs Geoff Holmes. One week makes for interesting comparison:

	Betty's Diary	Mary's Diary
Monday	Must use one of fifty-two excuses for him to have to get out at 9.50 (Monday morning meeting 10.00).	Old snap tin and trousers day as on all Mondays. Apparently he goes out and sits on a spoil heap throughout the day at Normanton contemplating his lot.
Tuesday	LDC meetings at 10 and 2. Remind him that it is the staff Treasure hunt this evening. Write down names of organisers and any other members of the staff he is likely to meet, as a reminder as to who they are.	Have to burst hot water bottle as this is one of those days when it's the only way to get him up. Annual drag. Get old sofa out of garage as he always seems to bring riff-raff back to house after this do.
Wednesday	PBD (Chief Civil Engineer) is coming today.	Put out his knee pads and hide the cat for when he comes home.
Thursday	Saloon trip, Ilkley and Skipton branches.	Make sure we have no visitors and arrange for the children to be out all evening while he gets all those filthy stories he picks up out of his system.

| Friday | Day before he goes on holiday. Brief (sorry) Mr Kealey. Try to find Mr Trotter. Arrange for R Bean (Admin Assistant) to have audience since it's he who really runs the Division. | Get camera undersealed. Dissuade him from going to the office in his shorts and Bermuda shirt. |

★

Among this year's annual awards was one for Lily Tuke winning the 1979 West California Hog-calling championships. From here!

★

UNCLE BOB NEWELL'S CAMPAIGN GIFT SHOP – This year's specials:

Get your Stop-The-Nuclear-Ban-on-Gravity-Abortions-Not-Bombs-For-Women-Against-Men-Clean-Up-To-The-Bringing-Back-Of-The-Wearing-Of-Ties-To-Prevent-Cruelty-To-Gay-Freedom-for-The-Workers-Against-Drinkable-Coffee-And-Home-Rule-Prevention-Of-Want-Of-Bombs-Up-Maggie's-Vest Badges NOW. Made from Commonwealth Non-toxic fission-free recycled dustbin lids.

Third World Tea. Genuine tea from real tea bags unstitched by un-exploited native hands. Tastes like no other tea you've ever tried. Indistinguishable from shredded tarpaulin. Caffeine-free; coughing inevitable.

Campaign Coffee. Got gutsache, halitosis, cramps, spots before the eyes, or just spots generally? No? Then try Newell's knockout coffee. Five different beans, their supporting twigs and a sample of the earth they grow in go to make up every jar.

★

INVESTIGATIONS by top scientists from Derby Research in Bramhope Tunnel have resulted in the famous bulge in the wall having a large kaolin poultice slapped on it. Latest information, following a visit from the Mothercare SAS, is that the tunnel is in fact pregnant and is expecting a culvert in the New Year. Solicitors acting on behalf of the nearby Arthington Viaduct are suing for divorce. The 11.15 Leeds – Harrogate Inter-City 125 has been cited as co-respondent.

★

DESPERATE for news this year, we welcome information from Mr John Freeman that he entered the Dewsbury Budgerigar Show and won first prize. Apparently a budgie came second.

★

HINTS ON THE MAINTENANCE OF OFFICE CARS

[It is apparent from the text that clerks Andy Burton and Darren Buttle had some minor mishaps with the office transport in 1981 by way of the unsubtle hints they have initiated below.]

1.   Frozen windscreens can be prevented by putting quality newspapers over them the night before. If you forget, don't worry. You can adequately clear the screen by pouring boiling water over it, which may give a crazed appearance. This can be rectified using a small hammer.

2.   If you have locked the keys inside the car, all can be put right with a fire extinguisher – by heaving it through the rear window. Not yet tested is the putting out of a fire using a bit of bent wire through the crack in the door.

3.   No petrol? Move the theodolite in the boot and refix the gauge wires.

4.   To indicate left turns to cyclists on your nearside, use a badly adjusted windscreen washer.

5.   Worn tyres? Drive down an old track formation at 50 mph to produce a new tread pattern.

6.   Rear tyres flat? Carefully release boot catch and stand well back. When everything has settled down re-fasten boot and move debris to side of the road.

7.   Front tyres flat? Empty ashtray.

★

Departmental reorganisations happened on a regular four yearly basis. They usually involved changing the name of the District to Division to Area etc., giving the organisers the chance to redesign posts without going through complex negotiating machinery. They were all designed to improve efficiency, attitude and morale. With minor exceptions they achieved nothing at all. One such was OP, Organisational Planning, around 1982. The *Newsletter* did not comment on this directly, but rather concentrated on the inevitable amalgamations to be made under Son of OP, whenever that might appear. Thus:

Parts of Liverpool, Darlington and Paddington Divisions will combine to become the Paddlingpool Division.

Basingstoke, Bath, Waterloo and St Pancras Divisions will become the B & Q Division.

Nottingham and York combine to become the Not the York Division.

And finally,

Sections of York, Cannon Street, Sheffield, Darlington and Bristol will combine to become the new Can I Feel Your Bristols, Darling Division.

★

Within a section of headlines and brief reports, all expanded elsewhere in the *Newsletter* in 1983 were:

MORE BLOOMERS DROPPED BY BEAN. 'HE'S GONE TOO FAR THIS TIME' SAYS DCE, 'I'VE HAD AS MUCH AS I CAN TAKE!'

In an unfortunate incident today, superclerk Roger Bean tripped and fell in GC Holmes's office while carrying a tray of plants from Poppleton Nurseries. Said Mr Holmes 'It's all a mistake, he should have taken them into David Kealey's office next door, back down the corridor; mine is full of flowers.'

CHAINMAN FOILS ESCAPE ATTEMPT: YORK MEN UNDER HEAVY GUARD

During a demonstration of escapology on Leeds City Concourse, a would-be Houdini from York failed to free himself from a sack in which he was chained, despite desperate contortions, due to his assistant having left him no room to manoeuvre. While he thrashed about, a passing 18-stone railway guard was tripped and fell on top of both men.

TRAINS HIT BUFFERS – CHIEF CIVIL ENGINEER SAYS 'IT'S A GOOD JOB THEY DID: I'M GLAD.'

In a freak accident at the Registry Office wedding of twins a gust of wind caught their headdresses which then struck two men buffing up the brasses on the door of the adjoining British Rail Headquarters. Commenting on the incident the Chief Civil Engineer said he would like to congratulate the men on the brilliant shine they achieved. He added that he would like to take this opportunity to announce his forthcoming sex change operation, and said that in future he wanted to be known as Gladys.

★

In 1984, a natural successor hobby was introduced to all train-spotters who had crossed off every number in their Ian Allan books.

EXCITING HOBBIES No. 42: COLLECTING BRIDGE NUMBERS

Have you tried the new and enthralling hobby of Bridge Spotting yet? The Editor of the twice-fortnightly *Practical Bridge Spotting*, Reg Isterdmoron, tells us of their useful starter's kit of a three-hour video showing rivets and flanges in their original livery and a fascinating CD of bridge sounds, including the creaking of Footbridge Number 38 based at Copley Hill, Leeds, and the famous Marble Arch 'Yahoo-hoo-hoo' echo in Leeman Road, York.

So here, exclusive to the *ACE's Newsletter* is our own Spotter's Starter Pack of six popular bridge numbers. We are offering Number One, Number Two, Number Three, Number Four, Number Five and Number Six, with two culverts thrown in free. All these were recently spotted between Dryclough Junction and Greetland.

Number One is a high-powered version of the standard stone arch, with the famous Gresley abutments, while Number Two is actually two side-by-side tunnels, and it quite takes the breath away as it appears coming out of the mist – a dramatic sight with its twin bores, and, typical of its class, a dark interior. Number Three is what the ardent spotter will know as a 'namer', the ever-popular 'Bankhouse'. Next seen were Numbers Four and Five, a matching pair from the same foundry of 1869 Wrought Iron Staniers. Number Four was spotted spanning the Sowerby Bridge road and features on the CD (the unforgettable sound of a re-routed double-decker bus being sliced in two). The keen spotter will note the 1897 amendment of a fourteen-inch lift to Number Five. The utilitarian 0–5–0 Number Six is probably the gem of this collection, spotted recently spanning the River Calder, the banks of which were littered with a hoard of those sad cranks, river spotters.

If you take up the sport, please send any interesting numbers you may spot to be included in our future editions.

★

Note: Clerical officers were graded CO 1 to CO 5

THOUGHT FOR THE DAY:
A CO 2 IS A CYLINDER OF GAS FOUND IN PUBS

★

Safety was on its way into overkill, as we delicately put it, leading to the creation of Safety Engineers.

SAFETY MAN '84

Further adventures of our careful hero.

Safety Man 84 smiled as he sat in his kitchen surveying the carefully laid out meal before him. Everything was perfect. Safety Woman 84 called out a cheery 'Bufulgmomdrling' which lost a lot during its journey through her protective fume-absorbent mask, BS 2091. This was to ward off the possible potentially toxic mixture of waste gas and hot pig as she fried the bacon.

Safety Man 84 donned his protective goggles, BS 2092, and carefully dug into his grapefruit. Safety Child 84 fitted his ear protectors, BS 2145, before adding milk to his Rice Krispies, just in case there should be a particularly loud snap, a rather heavy crackle or an overenthusiastic pop. Although he was not in great danger, Safety Man 84 pulled on his combined goggles and earmuffs. He found these did tend to protect his hands when he failed to hear Safety Woman 84 calling for him to do the washing-up.

The bacon cooked, Safety Woman blew a loud blast on her warning horn and called out 'Toast Alert!' Swiftly, Safety Man 84 and Safety Child 84 put on their Safety Helmets, BS 5240, to protect them from the chance eruption of toast from the pop-up. This was also the signal for Safety Man 84 to pull on his protective gloves BS 1651, to avoid the chance of marmalade rash caused by the concentration of citric acid in the fruit.

All done, Safety Man 84, smiling his contented smile, BS 4093, rose from the table, stubbed his toe on the leg, fell over the cat and impaled himself on the hallstand.

★

I feel we can include this in-joke, as Nigel Trotter is known in these pages. Nigel is a keen photographer.

PHOTOGRAPHIC TIPS by PN TROTTER

1. Do not sit on a fence to photograph bridges being blown up if you are likely to be thrown off the fence by the blast.

2. If you have to sit on such fences, make sure that there is something soft to fall into.

3. Pig muck is soft.

★

1985 was dominated by the appearance of the York Remodelling Project – see 'Coming of Age' chapter. Among the rest are some quotations, the first of which is so wrong, it's unbelievable. You don't have to know Jaquie to appreciate the significance of her comment during a discussion on her workload: 'Well, I've nothing outstanding!'

> PHIL HARGREAVES, deep-thinking clerk, talking about Leeds Rugby League Club: What with the ground, the buildings and the stands, they've got loads of cholesterol.

★

Every Christmas there would be an 'explanation' of what days we would not be expected to come in to work over the holiday period. Every year we were no clearer:

> 'The mandatory holiday will this year be the Wednesday and Thursday of Christmas week, and Tuesday as well, or the 26th, the 24th, and 25th taken in any order. New Year's Eve this year falls on the 31st, while New Year's Day occurs in the following year, and we have already used this year's allocation for that day early on in the current year.
>
> If anyone did not save a day of annual leave from their personal allocation, then they must take one day out of the following year, preferably the first, or even earlier if this does not apply.
>
> The office will be closed on Friday. One day's annual leave will be taken in between the period between Christmas and the New Year on Tuesday of the following week, but as this falls on

the 30th it is covered by the extra day granted in the previous year's pay agreement.

Anticipating this, staff should have saved one day of the present year's allocation to be taken as they wish between 28–30 December, not inclusive. The other extra day should be taken as agreed when there will be the least loss of effective work. On past records this should be the day when the Administration Assistant removes the fuses. Essential staff will be required in the office on the other days.

★

Throughout the 1985 *Newsletter* there appeared at intervals all original apologies from various staff for their inability to attend the annual retired codger's reunion:

From Mrs Meritorscrew, for her former joiner husband, William.

On behalf of our old digger friend who specialised on trax-cavators, Mrs Tupanbustit excuses her husband, Duggie.

From Mrs Dedonmied, from her former roofer husband, Alan.

Mrs Ussatackinthe-Restroom, for the illness of her former clerk husband, Billy.

And Mrs Tlypickled writes of her former York Drawing Office technical officer husband Percy Stan.

From ex-drainage ganger, Mr Bootswiwater, on behalf of himself and his wife, Phyllis.

And of her labourer husband, who spent his life at the bottom of holes, Mrs Kerserred excuses her husband, Ernie.

From the regions horticultural nursery Mrs Loadamanure writes of her husband, Laurie.

From the wife of the former stationery clerk, Mrs Armipencils, for her husband, Howard.

And finally from Mrs Lowsatall for her ex-estimator husband, Warwick.

★

By 1986, rumours of the coming of privatisation were rife, hence this:

British Rail plc. announce their first issue of shares. The question is asked what this offer provides for the man in the street. Answers are listed:

Bigger dividends than the TSB or Gas.

Unit trust reliability.

Greater flexibility for your money.

Golden Rail Away-in-a-Manger trips to the Holy Land.

Extra bonuses the longer you hold stock.

Rail vouchers to use against travel.

A variety of surprise coupons for fringe services.

Less expenditure on 'Have you seen Syd?'-type advertising.

Lower overall risk than any other share offers.

Initially, looking down the list, an outstanding offer – don't miss it!

AIDS

It is BR policy to inform and protect their staff from AIDS. To this end the Administration Assistant instructed the Supplies Clerk, Neville, to order a supply of condoms. This is the reason for the arrival of 200 cruets of salt and pepper.

Jaquie comes out again with two quotes:

Looking through her drawer of Christmas decorations – 'I've got balls and bells.'

Also:
'You didn't have that this morning when you showed me all you'd got!'

Then:
'You should see the fingerprints on me!'

And finally:
'Has Nigel said anything to you about my hanging baskets?'

To give you some idea about Jaquie, the office t-shirt was issued this year. It came in three sizes:

1. The 'Neville', inscribed 'Leeds ACE'.

2. The 'Denise', inscribed 'Leeds Area Civil Engineer'.

3. The 'Jaquie', inscribed 'Leeds Area Civil Engineer, a Division of the Chief Civil Engineer's Department, York. For enquiries see round the back.'

Jaquie also announced that she was into biorhythms, studying her personal curves. She was welcomed to the club. We'd been watching them for years.

Oh, yes, the newsletter was sexist, but to both sexes, and it had very little to do with PC, as yet unknown, and all the better for that!

By 1987 a much loved and eager relaying supervisor had emerged in Donald Coates. Donald spoke quickly, and in his race through life, his brain was ever a yard behind his mouth, therefore he was always good for quotes. Also, to somewhat pacify his clamouring workforce, he would automatically demand more men for a job, regardless of how many had been actually allocated, hence:

> If Grand Old Donald Coates
> Had 10,000 men,
> He wouldn't start on any job
> Without another ten.

DONALD: York Relayers are at Benidorm this weekend! (Beningborough).

'Logic should have prevailed.'

'We should have shingles for relaying.'

★

Boredom at multifunction meetings prevailed, hence from personal experience:

THINGS TO DO IF BORED IN THE MEETING ROOM

1. Imagine what the meeting would look like if the ceiling was a mirror.
2. Try taking your chair to its lean-back limit. If there is a spare one at your side, do the same with that, trying to balance it at its limit point. This can become compulsive – it is possible that you will become noticed if you attempt to balance all the empty chairs.
3. Gently blow towards each light switch pull string until it moves.
4. Do not look at the clock.
5. Do not try unzipping the chair covers behind your back in case it isn't a chair cover.
6. If bearded, scratch beard, blow, and watch the scurf dancing in the sunbeams.
7. Make a list of things to do if bored in the Meeting Room.
8. Watch the crack in the adjacent lift shaft opening as the lift falls away.
9. Work out who else is using this list.

★

On 11 March 1987, No Smoking Day, Morris Smith issued a recommendation that the office comply with this.
In 1988 he proposes to extend this edict to Mother's Day, Father's Day and St Valentine's Day.

★

Reliable JAQUIE (in a roomful of men): There's only me hasn't got one, it would appear.

From this point on the *Newsletter* has a large input from Wendy's little book of quotations – ones that make her double up and start crying. It doesn't matter who the authors are, it's what they come out with that counts.

BRENDA, on having gone into the Gents by mistake, is asked:
'Who was in there?'
'I don't know, I didn't look at his face.'

TICKETS are now available for the ACE's Ball.
Please note: this is a dance not a raffle.

★

1987 had marked the arrival of Morris Smith, to replace Geoff Holmes, who, along with David Kealey, was taking an early retirement. As that year's Christmas party bingo had it: 'Rats leaving sinking ship, on its own, number two.' This year's was a muted edition, mainly because the incoming Engineer had announced that he would need to vet it. Hence an underground sheet only available to applicants. On this, now revealed under the government's 20-year Freedom of Information Act, appeared the following (team briefing had just been introduced, a sort of Chinese whispers of information being passed down):

TEAM BRIEFING:

A Director of Unsolicited Gifts has been appointed to receive all future bribes.

Corrections: Due to the principle of passing the message down step by step, one or two items can get subtly changed, arriving at the bottom level somewhat misleading.

When the gangs were told 'Morris Smith has an appointment for a sex change, Monday at noon', it should have been heard that 'Morris Smith was appointing six chainmen one day soon'.

Another item suffered variously, but should have been 'Mr Smith is booking four in each month'.

In the innocent general edition there was the usual crop of quotes:

PAUL: I've nothing against homosexuals, so long as they don't ram it down your throat.

ROGER DUDLEY (of Nigel Trotter): He's trying to get me to think!

DENISE, local political activist: Those were his exact words – virtually.

And then one we never really understood from,

WENDY: If you squeeze your knees together, glue comes out.

We were here in the middle of the York Remodelling Project. The first night was spectacular, and heavily populated with watchers, including me. A later arrival was Morris Smith. One thing to know is that there is a similarity between Morris and myself regarding hair; we are both topless. Hence:

JOHN VEYSEY to Morris Smith, the Engineer, in the dark and from behind: What the hell are you doing here, you f—ing bald-headed old c—?
MORRIS (turning round): Hello John!

★

We must stop for a while and take a short explanation for what turned out to be a quite fascinating story. Leeds City Station is built in the daftest place, over the River Aire. This involves a substructure of dozens of archways. Down there is now one of the places to be seen in Leeds, with its way-out shops and cafés. Many railway engineering sections used to be housed here, including works staff and relaying gangs. Master of the Dark Arches was Norman Hebron, an undoubted gentleman, and about the most pleasant chap you could wish to meet. Norman had a small office and pay window off the main road, Neville Street, under the station, which led through to the male toilets and hence the gang quarters, wagons and buses. An annual audit was required, and a clerk from the Area Civil Engineer's Office had to do it. This year, Neville Edwards chose Lily Tuke to take on the task. Lily was one of those perpetually busy people, both at work and within church circles in Knottingley. She could be demure, but in the offices rarely got the chance, having to save herself for home. She could not be ignored, and made sure of this with a voice that travelled before her in the office, and no doubt ruled many a jumble sale at home. Lily could have walked into *Last of the Summer Wine*, and immediately taken a leading role. Now the story, remembering that the ACE's Pooh-Bah was the Admin Assistant, Roger Bean:

Let it be said at the outset that Dark Arches Norman runs a tidy dungeon, though the décor of the bog can, at times, struggle to achieve an '18' certificate. So when a figure of protected purity like Lily Thunderthroat Tuke is despatched to stock take in Norman's Grotto, there are certain areas that may not pass her particular whiteness test. Wrong-footed from the first by hearing 'It's Neville's treat for you, Lily' instead of 'It's Neville Street for you', her expectations were dangerously high. Add to this that Norman is the epitome of chivalry, and has doused Lily with four or five mugs of tea by 11, with the consequence that, by 11.15, she is standing like a pair of closed scissors, needing relief. Once more the gallant Norman comes to her rescue, by taking a T2 possession (given up to pass things) of the Gents' toilet, while Lily powders her nose and recovers her power of speech.

Lily now emerges like an enraged Attenborough, having discovered the ancient cave paintings of the tribes of *humanus sewermindus*. [The story goes a little foggy here regarding Lily's aforementioned purity of mind, in that she apparently understood most words she had seen.] 'Tut-tut,' she exclaims to Norman, 'you really must tell your lads that they must not write such things.' Norman tries to explain that his cherubs are unlikely to take a great deal of notice of him. A mixture of evangelism and optimism persuades Lily to take it on herself to address the men while they are assembled in the mess room. This goes down like a Durex on a hedgehog. Not one to give up, Lily now informs the lads, all eager to return to their work, it now being the end of their allotted break, that she will report the matter to Roger Bean. [Here again the story wears a bit thin, apparently, as this does not reduce the lads to jelly – rather the opposite in fact.] Norman, again coming to the rescue, pacifies Lily by promising to have the offending material removed by the following day.

So Lily returns on the morrow, having had an embarrassing evening at the Mothers' Union meeting, where she had asked around about the odd words that she had seen, but had not understood, and finding that only the Vicar's wife could explain. Once more Norman hammers the PG Tips, and come 11.15 the Tuke tea-meter is blowing a fuse. Norman slaps another injunction on the bog so that Lily can relax uninterrupted. 7½ seconds later there is a scorched-edge Lily-sized hole in the door as she emerges somewhat overwrought, voicing discontent to the extent that starlings fail to roost within 400 yards for the next three weeks. Norman goes in to see what has produced an explosion in Lily of an enormity sufficient to recreate the Universe. Covering an entire wall Norman sees a graphic illustration, carefully labelled to allay any doubts, of our Lily and the Venerable Bean in intimate conjunction.

Little remains to tell, except that Lily, starting with the Lord God Almighty and working her way up to R Bean himself, lists people who must see this gross offence. The LGA, not having a Leeds extension, cannot be reached, and the clerical seniority settles on Neville to view the outrage. Lily mounts a strict guard on the door, while the unlucky Neville is summoned from Aire Street. However, Lily, unlike the rest of the world, is unaware of a back entrance to the Gents. The time taken for Nev to descend from Floor Six to the Dark Arches is just half a minute longer than that taken for a small party with sponges and buckets to nip in the back door and bring a purity to the cavern never seen before.

★

Time for a few more quotes:

> MAN ON PHONE: Hello, have you any vacancies for guards?
>
> WENDY: Sorry, you've got the wrong number.
>
> MAN: Oh! This was the number I was given.
>
> WENDY: (hoping to be able to transfer him) Are you ringing from outside?
>
> MAN: No, I'm ringing from the next-door neighbour's hallway.

From WENDY, who has a little experience with livestock: Goats are pigs to move.

Unusually from MIKE COLLINS: It isn't the same; it never was the same.

In the York Project Office, phone rings.
GARY: Hello.
GEORGE MCHOOLIGAN: Hello, is Mike there?
GARY: No.
GEORGE: I had it mind that I had a meeting with him at ten.
GARY: I'll check in his diary… No, he's written nothing in his diary.
GEORGE: That's funny, neither have I.

The following little tale is typical of the mini-blunders that occur to staff, only to end up in the *Christmas Newsletter.*

One of the many troubles that beset Nigel Trotter, Assistant Engineer.
Sends wife and daughters away to Manchester for a week in the car.
Daughters decide they want to come home early, so they need their travel cards.
Nigel posts the travel cards, first class, to them from York.
Wonders in passing why lots of men are stood around at the York main sorting office.
Wonders why man puts a large sack over the postbox as he is leaving.
Wonders why local papers are full of stories about an extended postal strike.
Wonders why daughters don't turn up.

★

The sad thing, in what follows, is that the document up for treatment is a genuine guideline that was sent to all departments.

MANAGEMENTSPEAK TRANSLATED TO MIDGESPEAK

A fine piece of Managementspeak has come to hand, and is used below to form a basis for translation. In this I asked a colleague to provide a comprehensible alternative. It may be that my choice of assistance (John Midgley) was a little misguided.

Statement: General management skills. Overview – Business declines result from one thing: poor management. Conscientious leadership leads to greater productivity, heightened profits and morale.

Approach to effective organisation: the dynamics and mechanics of motivation. The keystone of effective management within the ever-widening radius of modern competition may be readily identified as personnel management / human relations. The collective employment ego is of paramount significance. Ergo, people must be viewed as assets in which the company wishes to invest. Investing in manpower is an important strategic task, with full cost justification.

Translation: You've gorra keep in touch wi t'lads, see that they're framing reet, meckshurr they've gorragrip on things.

Those in whom the success of a company depends are more effective when they, the staff, are fully cognisant of the direction the company is heading (viz. corporate strategy) and can relate their own personal contribution to it. A well-led management must possess a cohesive and distinctive vision of success. It is increasingly clear that in order to sustain high performance levels, employee care / job enrichment must be assigned top priority and is deserving of assiduous consideration by mid to senior management.

Translation: You scrat they're backs and they'll scrat yours.

An in-depth re-examination of management planning methodology as regards raw materials motivation is overdue. Esprit is the sole index of/off-shoot of/by-product of successful corporate working activity. A basic consideration must be that responsible and competent management must be seen trans-parently to wash their faces on the bottom line.

Translation: Keep tabs on t'lads or you'll gerrammered for costs.

Regarding positive material elements, they must be distinctly identified and accounted for to the end that they are correctly situated and orientated at the dis-inertial stage of any operation. Anti-correctivication at the genesis leads to an antithesis of a successful end.

Translation: On t'day of t'race, tackles gorrabe in t'reet 'ole, and reet road round, norarseabahtit.

To summarise: Motivation is an exacting task. The motivational make-up of individuals varies. The issue of remunerational packages is only half the equation. Managerial responsibility towards staff emotions must be focussed if real gain and optimum performance levels are to be achieved. THE MIND OF THE EMPLOYEE IS LIKE A PARACHUTE – it only functions when open.

The greatest sense of achievement is found in tackling familiar workaday situations as regards financial theory and practice, and discovering solutions that may otherwise have remained dormant.

Translation: You've gorragivem anuppin now and then, to keep them on their toes, and sometimes a carrot. Reminds me, wunnerwots for tea. Up mi mother's Sunday, three times back fermore, gurt slabs abeeast, tatties, tunnups, piled upitwor. Wannee borin'? Wot were allthatabaht? Buggerme, if ah come out withat tripe they'd laugh at me. It's these fancy courses ah blame. Yercant teach 'andlin' blokes on a bloody blackboard. Ah learnt backerra tractor, not playin' Lego an' doin' jigsaws…

Perhaps all that should have gone in the Midge chapter, except both he and I were disgusted at managementspeak at project meetings, 'sending an idea up the flagpole and seeing if it flutters' and 'all singing from the same hymn book' sort of stuff.

★

In 1989 we had to comment on the new faulty coaching stock that had just been introduced:

HAVE YOU TRIED THE REVENGE TOILETS on the new coaching stock? When they go through tunnels, you get your own back.

★

DRAMA ON THE 16.45 TO YORK, 5/10/89.

It has to be remembered that this train is stuffed with the cream of the Area Civil Engineer's highly trained and totally responsible staff, also that it is ordinary loco-hauled coaching stock.

Going through Micklefield Junction at 70 mph, a door flies open. Extensive active discussion as to what to do next takes place. Mr Tumman decides to dash the full length of the train to fetch the guard. Fears of being sucked out, an inability to counter the force of the speeding train, of fouling the kinetic envelope or of just getting home late abound.

Eventually Mr Tanner wakes up, asks what the fuss is about, and pulls the communication cord. Result: train slows down, stops with a jerk, open door swings back and slams shut, just at the moment that Mr Tumman reappears with the guard to show him a closed door and a swinging communication cord.

★

Numerous quotes from that year:

UNA: John Wilson didn't have me for five years without something sinking in.

DENISE: Do you realise, if you get the job, I'll have to come underneath you.

JOHN: Do you fancy one, Lily?
Lily: Aye, give me one, John, it'll help clear this pain in my head.

DAVE: The marks on the rail looked pretty fresh. I reckon they were done last week, or the week after.

STEPHANIE: I've had the man on my hardware. It had dust in its cracks so it wouldn't play with me properly.

PAUL: If I don't give her one today, I'll not get it in before Christmas.

GARY, of Wendy and her extravagant earrings: Sometimes you can hear her tinkling down the corridor.

DONALD: Recoveries have been going full stop at York.

UNA: She's getting a divorce – from her husband.

JOHN: I can understand padded bras – I can see the point in that.

BOB: Have you heard about the tunnel? They've decided to put it underground.

And a selection of Wendy's own inimitable quotes:

'When I was born my mother apologised.'

'My hands and knees are older than the rest of me.'

'This isn't funny; hee, hee, hee, hee.'

'I'm my Grandma's daughter.'

★

A short story about one of the technical lads, Ian Dickson. You have to wonder at the need, after cock-ups, for the victim to have to come in and tell everyone all about it.

Ian Dickson, a clear-headed lad, was wishing to protect his valuable photographic equipment (camera, telephoto, camera-can't-lie-adjustment kit), and he purchased an expensive special bag, designed to guard against knocks, bangs, dropping it, fire, earthquake, flood, etc., and duly packed it to go on holiday.

Luggage was then taken out to the car and stashed away in the boot, in a very careful manner so that nothing could fall over, or be crushed. It is at this point that the miracle bag failed miserably, possibly because he forgot to place it in the boot, left it in the drive and reversed the car over it.

★

Quote of the year came from Jean, examining John Marshall's photographs of a young lady, when she said, 'Mine don't come out like that!'

Though WENDY finished the year's entries with: I can't keep these legs together.

★

1990 was an odd year for me. York was out of the way and I had been given the job of producing a full colour glossy house magazine, along with carrying on with projects. These were mainly the electrification of the Ilkley and Skipton lines, and the embryonic planning for Leeds remodelling, a much more complicated job than York.

I was somewhat snowed-under now, and I relaxed by writing letters to people concerned about the imminent electrification of the line at the bottom of their garden.

There is, though I say it myself, some skill in answering complaints like:

'My brother-in-law lives with us ever since his wife was killed by a train. If you cut down the bushes for this electrification, he will be able to see the wheels of the passing trains going round, and this drives him to the brink.'

Another lady complained that the electricity would make the railway too dangerous for her children to play on.

A local sculptor asked if we could spare him some wood from the tree trunks that we were clearing for him to carve. We dropped the main portions of five large trees in his garden, obscuring everything else. He tried to look pleased.

So I was getting plenty of quotes from the general public, thus not needing any internal ones, but still they came.

'I know what I'm thinking of, but I can't think it.'

SCOTT BROGDEN was asked about his visit to Disneyland: It was all right, except it was full of kids.

Reliable DONALD (on Tuesday): Can we have the site meeting on Wednesday, I can't make it tomorrow?

Morley Town Centre. BR property affected is Tunnel Shaft No. 4 at the junction of Queen Street and Middleton Road. According to a letter sent to everyone this has been declared a conversation area.

★

Now introducing a new friend, picked up during the York Project.

ALL CREATURES GREAT AND SMALL

Featuring York chainman, John Barker.

No. 1 The Dog

John acquires a stray dog from York Dogs' Home

Dog loves John, and barks a lot to say so.

John gets engaged (to a lady – not the dog).

Dog still loves him, but now tends to look over shoulder and bark more.

John gets married.

Dog is now really unsettled and barks a lot more.

Mrs John finds the dog a problem since it is always barking.

Dog starts packing its suitcase and barks a lot more.

John takes dog back to Dogs' Home, complaining that it's always barking.

Dogs' Home reluctantly take dog back, but ask for John's name for their records.

'Mr Barker,' says John.

No. 2 The Horse

John arrives home to find four horses in garden.

John puts in a complaint to nearby York Racecourse.

John notices horses have big hairy ankles.

John then identifies nearby farmer as owner.

John's garden now looks like a farm.

John asks landscape gardener for estimate to restore garden.

Farmer refuses to pay full amount, claiming that four nervous horses have improved garden in one important way.

From JOHN FREEMAN: The ultimate statistic – one in one of us die.

UNA quotes:

I pull them down at dinner time and Les pulls them back up in the afternoon.

Every time I pull them up, it comes out.

And:
WENDY: It could be twins, you know.
UNA: Well, these things come in threes.

WENDY: He likes to keep his image, and every now and then I blow it for him.

'Ooo, look, the sungulls are sea bathing.'

PETE LODGE on phone: Hello, is that Pete Lodge?

Also PETE: Tuesday dinner times, starting Thursday the 24th.

★

1991 saw things taking off as we left them the year before.

DONALD: He's misinterpretated me. This raises implicamentations.

'That's a Catch 29 situation!' (RICK: 'As bad as that, Donald?')

'Up at Newcastle we'll be working over the underhead cables.'

'Going back to that question; it depends what I asked.'

'Well d'you know? Yesterday was the hottest day under the sun.'

And from the genteel STEPHANIE: I've changed my position a little bit so you can fit in.

And a great favourite in those days, from JOHN FREEMAN: In a word... I don't know – or should I say in two words... I don't know.

Finance Section. Phone rings, NEIL WOOD answers it:

'Hello!'

'Is there an Enwood there?'

'No, nobody called Edward here.'

'No – not Edward, Enwood.'

'No – there's not even anyone called Enwood... oh, hang on. Not Enwood – N Wood!... Speaking!'

PHIL SUMMERS, trying Nestlé's Cappuccino: Don't like it – it's not my cup of tea at all!

This year we included THE REGIONAL RAILWAYS YEAR SONG, with acknowledgements to Michael Flanders.

> JANUARY brings the snow,
> Ooops, wrong sort – all go slow.
> FEBRUARY's timetable fails,
> Ice and snow stuck to the rails.
> Depend on MARCH, and you'll risk all,
> (New Year wishes – if you're fiscal).
> In APRIL miss the sweet spring showers,
> In the cabin for hours and hours.
> MAY's frost by night and heat by day,
> Buckled rails bog up PWay.
> Torrential JUNE with lightning cracks,
> Slips in banks block miles of tracks.
> In JULY the hot strong gale
> Brings down wires – electrics fail.
> All AUGUST's holiday trains run true
> Unless the staff are on theirs too.
> SEPTEMBER's trees take on new hues
> And now we know that means bad news...
> ...For in OCTOBER Management grieves,
> Their 158s won't run on leaves.
> Pierce NOVEMBER's fog with signal's spot –

> Is it working? No it's not.
> Freezing, wet DECEMBER, then...
> Bloody JANUARY again!

★

By 1992 the *Newsletter* is clearly photocopied (early ones were on typewriter stencils, and only half the text was there) and runs to thirty-six pages.

And still the quotes come – what's more, you only get a selection in these pages.

PHIL KIRKLAND (who should have appeared more): These park rangers have mobile transport.

CALLER: Is Brian there?
BARRY: Yes, speaking.

JUNE: Nev's in a meeting with John, and he's having me next.

WENDY: If we had more women in charge there'd be fewer cock-ups.

MALCOLM: If we have to have double standards, then we must all work to the same double standards.

EDDIE: I'm sick and tired of moaning.

DONALD: I went to the dogs last night, backed a horse, and it came in second.

And one that hurts – DAVE DOUGLAS: Just ignore Mike, I generally do.

Young clerk, Simon Bedford, got a quick lesson in life when he accompanied Lily to Newcastle on some mission. Stood together on the station, expecting a lift, Lily approached a vague-looking bloke, apparently looking for someone:
LILY: Are you waiting to pick me up?
GEORDIE: Nay, canny lassie, I'm looking for the Gents.

★

INTERVIEWS – AN ABSOLUTELY FAIR SYSTEM DEVELOPED BY FINANCE

How often is the interviewer influenced by the appearance of the candidate? His or her physical features, or dress sense. No more. With the Finance section's move to progressive interviewing, the persuasion of a pretty face can no longer sway the jury. How? Simply change the venue for the interview from York to Leeds, and don't bother to tell the candidate.

MAJORGATE SCANDAL

The young lady reported to have spent a weekend of activity with Paul Major this year has denied a press interpretation of a statement she made earlier, that it had been 48 hours of intense passion. 'I was just miss-under-stood,' she claimed.

TERENCE WARD, picking up chairman Winston Spencer in the Chapeltown area of Leeds, late Saturday night, can't quite locate the correct place, so he drives slowly along the kerb, hoping to spot Winnie. Lights are low, and generally red in this area. A young lady approaches and asks Terry if he's looking for assistance. Terry asks her if she can handle a level staff...

★

THE SEARCH FOR CHRIS THISTLETHWAITE OF ELDRETH

This was reported to me by George Woodcock who sits opposite John Freeman. (John is nothing if not persistent. He once rang the Japanese Embassy in London to enquire about a new Japanese excavator that no local plant contractors had heard of.) John here is on the trail of Chris Thistlethwaite of Eldreth.

'I'm ringing that bloke Thistlethwaite with the culvert at the Old School House.' [Dials 822460 – no answer]

'Tell you what, George, I'll ring Clapham Post Office, they might have an idea where he'll be.' [Does so – they don't know him, but recommend the Flying Horse Inn, Clapham 9201]

They don't know him either, but do know Miss Julie Preston

who also lives in Eldreth. [Rings Miss Preston 51261]

Julie knows him, and that he has a shop next door to her friend's, Judith Milenthorpe. [Rings Judith, 57229]

Judith is very helpful, and has a number to contact Thistlethwaite in emergency – 822460.

John dials, Thistlethwaite answers, John looks again at the number he's just used, 822460.

'George, you're not going to believe this…' But George does.

★

THERE ARE A LOT of ardent royalists in the Relayers, as a body. They can be heard on Sunday mornings around 4.00 chanting 'I'm for King Cold, I'm for King Wettfrew, and I'm for King Fedup.'

A STAB AT SOME OF THE YEAR'S QUOTES:

Phone conversation:

PAUL in Leeds: Chris, your ballast request doesn't actually say what wagons you want.

CHRIS, in York: Well… I don't know one wagon from another. Hang on, I'll ask Eddie Piercy, it's him that wants them, and he's our expert on wagons. (Sound of quick retreating footsteps. Sound of slower ones returning.)

CHRIS: Errr… he says he wants bigguns.

PAUL: I'm going out for twenty minutes, if anyone wants me, Wendy.

WENDY: Why should anyone want you, Paul?

PAUL: Because I'm a large cog in a small wheel, or should I say a large tooth in a small cog.

WENDY: Eh?

PAUL: …I'll be back in twenty minutes.

Pete Lodge doesn't appear much in this section, but when he does it's worth it.

'Half of summat that's big is bigger than three-quarters of summat that's small, isn't it?' The point being that, when questioned, he goes on to justify it.

'This is Pete Lodge here, downstairs, upstairs.'

KEVIN: What's the procedure for us learning to drive?
PHIL: You go on a fortnight's crash course.

WENDY: You can't walk round Leeds in a straight line any more.

'I do eventually drop them.'

Not enough has been reported on KEITH THOMPSON: 'When you go to the dentist's today, it's an arm and a leg job.'

★

JOHN HODGSON, another York chainman, was in Peterborough for an interview in the Training School.

He walked into the office, and asked a man at the door, dressed in full safety gear, if this was the right place for the interviews, going on immediately to add that he was a bit nervous about the whole thing, and that nervousness tended to cause him to talk rather a lot, hoping that this would not go against him, as he can, under these circumstances, rather ramble on a lot, adding that time was passing and it would help to settle him down if the safety man could assure him that he was actually where he should be.

However, John had to remain in doubt, as the display dummy dressed in full safety gear was giving nothing away.

★

MARTIN THEOBOLD, a newcomer: There was a good video about leaves on the radio last night.

PETE LODGE: What we want at Bingley are some plumbers on tap.

And a last Wendy phone conversation for this year:
CALLER: Hello! It's me again.
WENDY: Oh, is it?

CALLER: Oh, it's not you!

WENDY: No, it's me.

It's Pete and Midge again:

LODGEY: Ayoop, John, are those new shoes?

MIDGE: Yup. But look at these old uns though. Ahvadem nigh on six or seven years. Gone right through York job withem. Done some miles, these; and look arrem. Nigh on perfect. Gorram off Mike Collins; sells safety shoes, tha knows. Look at them soles. Bit worn but solid. Great shoes they've bin. Look at these uppers; no splits or owt. Ahve hardly worn owt else, and they're still good ferra bit longer; and comfortable too; you'd nivver know you'd gorremon. Brilliant!

LODGEY: So you've got the same again?

MIDGE: No.

SUPER-PEDANTIC

Dave Douglas, for some time Assistant Engineer on:

1.   THE WEATHER. Why do they say 'changeable'? I mean, once it's changed from wet to dry it's changeable, isn't it? So why do they say it when they really mean variable between two or more modes of weather? I mean, it could mean sunny, cloudy, wet, frosty, windy, hot, cold, brass monkey: all they mean is it could rain and then not. So why…?

2.   AIRCRAFT. What do they mean by a 'Near Miss'? There's no such thing, is there? What they mean is a 'Near Hit', isn't it, so why don't they say it? A 'Near Miss' is actually a hit, isn't it? So why…?

From the same Dave, an item that I don't want to believe what I thought I'd heard at first:

'Denise can fax better than Jenny could. She can do five at a time, where Jenny could only get one in.'

BOB FALLAS, Training Section. Wandering slowly into the Print Room buried in a copy of the *Leeds A–Z* Road Map. Eventually he comes alive, exclaiming 'Ah! Found it!'

QUESTION: Do all the Trainers need a *Leeds A–Z* to find their way from the fourth to the fifth floor?

★

And so it all came down to the final edition, that of 1993. Final because life at work was no longer a joy for me. With the approach of privatisation there was no place for projects, as these speculated on a future, and the railways could see no future the way they were going. How right they were! With the gross mismanagement which was to follow, and temporary emergency close-downs that resulted from atrocious maintenance, the railways all but died. Certainly the reliable, safe, reasonably priced outfit that was British Rail was to disappear, as inexperience took over. We were getting managers of sections into the drawing offices who had gone through the minuscule training that I had seen in my time out at Huddersfield, as young hopefuls. They dismissed such as me, whom they had passed on the way up, and just clung onto the ladder, reaching for the next rung. Bitter? Yes. All that I had worked for was sinking under 'progress'. I have lived to see people that I admired, who had achieved great things in the past, lowered and moved either to retire early, or just leave.

More and more sarcasm and bitterness, masquerading as satire, had crept into the *Newsletter*, and I no longer liked what I read, most of which I had written. However, there were still daft moments to savour, and I have selected the happier items for this run into life's buffers.

GRAHAM BROWN: They look at you stupid when you ring them up.

Picture young Shelley struggling onto the bus with a load of shopping, having to stack it away in order to pay, fighting her way to a seat, packing all the bags around her, and then looking out of the window and noticing her car in the car park, exactly where she'd left it.

MIKE COLLINS, complaining about the fact that office problems aren't mentioned in Team Briefing: Things don't come up like the lift.

GARY FLETCHER: I'll stick my neck out and say "Yes, cut it off."

JAMES: Where's Keith?
SHELLEY: I don't know. He was in the toilet last time I saw him.

CHARLIE BATTY: I'm not having anyone working at night, unless it's daylight.

★

I used to have double spreads dedicated to John Freeman, the reasons being that he was fair game for the complications of life; he was incident prone, where others are accident prone. Also, as with most who appeared in the pages, he could take it with a grin and a sigh of resignation. The next bit illustrates the difference between incident and accident prone.

JOHN FREEMAN'S NEW COOKER.

Fatal combination No. 1: John Freeman, a length of electric cable, one end attached to a new cooker, the other, hanging loose, together with a plug and a screwdriver.
Analysis of the thought process that follows: Earth is generally a browny sort of colour, maybe black, or a dark red, but mainly brown. Green is a colour that signifies life. Blue is just a pretty colour, associated with the right, and goes well alongside the green.
Result: Liquidised fuses, kitchen wall gains a Bonfire Night mural, green van parked outside, minimum call-out charge £40. [Remember, this is the 1993 Newsletter.]

Fatal combination No. 2: John Freeman, a now correctly wired plug, a book of instructions and an 'On' switch. 'We'll test it out, Mary, by putting it into 'self-clean' mode.'
Result: Oven warms up gently to around 200 °F over next hour. Slight smell put down to newness. Later, stronger smell, black smoke and a horizontal canary in cage. Put down to leaving all polystyrene packing inside oven.

Here the worth of the man is shown, in that he comes to work, tells George his story, knowing full well where it will end up. While we're with the good and great man:

> JOHN FREEMAN on the phone: Can I smell cigarette smoke?

> On the phone again, JOHN: Is Neil Sutcliffe there, please?
> ANSWER: No, he's out with Pete Mills.
> JOHN: Oh, can I speak to Pete Mills, then?

For a time John Midgley became John Freeman's boss.

> MIDGE: This overtime sheet John does is a work of art; I've never understood one yet!

★

A Shelley break:

> 'I got home and I thought, Where's my trousers?'

> 'Tomorrow my car broke down yesterday, and me mum's getting that chef to have a look at it.'

> 'Is there anyone there who knows what I'm talking about?'

> 'I'm in a rush, so when I get home I'm going to jump in the shower and iron my jeans.'

A Pete Lodge break:

> 'We're doing a lot of investigations into flooding at Kirkstall, so you'll know what's happening if you see anyone floating about.'

> 'I've spoken to the Property Board verbally.'

> 'Did I hear my voice then?'

These are two sound-only ones:

SARAH: I'm a bear lover.

And WENDY: How many "I"s has Iain got?

For some reason Wendy insisted on these going in:

MIKE COLLINS: I want to see an invisible barrier here.

And: Have you got any of those sticky holes?

★

Now, over to Leeds Area Assistant's Office, like Huddersfield in the old days, but for Don Newell (the boss) read Bob Doyle, and for Mike Collins read Terry Ward.

Bob Doyle is closeted with Morris Smith in the Divisional Office. They decide to go out on a site visit. It is chilly, so Bob rings over to his office in Whitehall Yard, half a mile away, for someone to fetch his high visibility coat over.

Cath begins the search for Bob's coat, totally unaided by an unsympathetic audience. She finds it, in an act of bravery, hung up in the Gents. She confronts everybody, including Terry Ward, and they confirm that that is Bob's coat. She delivers it to Aire Street, and Bob.

(Later, Bob admits that on reaching site, and putting it on, he discovered that his arms seemed to have grown six inches, and his chest beyond the range of the zip.)

Meanwhile, back at Whitehall, the day draws to a close, and all leave, Terry being the last has to lock up. It is now that he discovers that his coat has been stolen during the day, from right under his nose.

He looks everywhere, even in Bob's car. It isn't there, but oddly enough, Bob's is. He next tries ringing Cath at home, but she has not got there yet. It is now that the contents of the pockets of his stolen coat dawn on him: keys (including the office), chequebook, credit cards, etc.

He takes immediate, if late, action, ringing round all the credit card companies and the bank, cancelling everything. Finally he rings BT Police and arranges an all-night patrol, as the Whitehall compound keys were in the coat.

He now goes home (with borrowed coat sleeves skimming the ground), rings Cath, who enlightens him as to a possible mix-up; rings Bob who agrees that his coat was over tight and full of keys, chequebooks, credit cards, etc., etc.

★

And now we can bring you a scoop as, along with the longest clerk in Leeds, Graham Whiteley, we trace the real Father Christmas!

THE REAL SANTA CLAUS

'I've met the *real* Santa Claus,' announced Mr Whiteley during a discussion following Wendy's visit to a declared substitute at Tong Garden Centre. According to the Shelley/Wendy faction of the Provisional Wing of the 'Track Down the Genuine Santa' Brigade, he is resident in British Home Stores. 'Not so,' says Graham, 'I've met him – in Harrods!'

A story of magical fantasy emerged, as Graham described the amazing Grotto, where, along with many other emissaries, he waited with his young daughter, Olivia, in excited anticipation of the approaching audience. When their turn came, they were ushered through large double doors into a darkened corridor with a golden light at the end. Making their way between glittering snow-laden branches and the twinkling gossamer of a thousand elves, they came upon the light that radiated from a golden sleigh, heavy with gaily wrapped presents of every shape and size. Attendant fairies and pixies shepherded them to a velvet bench, almost at the feet of the avuncular bundle seated astride the sleigh – the awesome figure of Santa Claus himself!

'Ho! Ho! Ho!' exclaimed the great man, 'and what's your name?'

'Graham,' said Graham.

'I think Santa was talking to the little girl,' whispered one of the fairies. But Olivia was too spellbound to answer.

'So!' boomed Santa, 'and where do you come from? I need to know where to deliver your presents, don't I?'

'We're from Bradford,' said Graham.

'Well, I'll go to t'foot of our stairs!' said Santa, 'Bradford! Well booger me! I've some reet champion memories of Bradford.

Dusta knaw t'Alhambra?'

'Course I do,' said Graham, 'everyone knows t'Alhambra in Bradford – best theatre in Yorkshire!'

'Ah played theer in '77,' went on Santa. 'Dusta remember Lonnie Donegan's Skiffle Band? I was on t'washboord. Bloody great panto run that was. And cansta still get a grate curry in Bradford? Dusta knaw t'Sikh's Shed in Gurt 'Orton Rowd?'

'Do you mean t'Maharajah's Palace?' says Graham.

'That'll be it nah. It wor nobbut a doorway and six tables then…'

During the next twenty minutes, a crescendo of muttering arises from the waiting throng without, along with the gentler sound of scales from a little girl's eyes falling to the ground.

★

Running out with a few final quotes:

British Home Stores, and Shelley notices an elderly lady staring fixedly at her.

'Eee, I'm sorry, love, but you're the very image of my granddaughter!'

'That's because I am, Grandma,' says Shelley.

Tales of clerks Simon and Sarah:

SIMON: Me and Sarah have had a trial erection, and we're happy about it.

SARAH: Do you want me to get on the desk, Simon?

And, SIMON: Sarah enlarged it for me.

SHELLEY: I had every intention of going to the toilet, but the bar was in the way.

GRAHAM, examining the TV listings: *Invisible Man* looks good tonight.

And finally, Christmas, MORRIS SMITH in his morale booster at the retired codgers do: Accidents are falling.

And so, on Page 283 of the omnibus edition of the *Leeds Civil Engineer's Newsletter*, after 'A stand still on stationery has just been announced,' appearing for the first time in seventeen years, came the words:

THE END

A Glossary of Railway Terms (glossed over within)

These do not appear in alphabetical order; rather they are here in a railway wife's natural questioning order.

permanent way   Usually shortened to PWay, which gives the immediate impression that it is the gutter in a urinal. It is actually the name for the track, and all that goes with it. Up to recent years the term 'permanent' could have been queried under trades description, in that the track did not remain fixed, but would bounce up and down at joints. In summer it could add a playful sideways movement that we knew as a track buckle, but this became none PC and was replaced by the more reassuring 'misalignment'. PWay consists of rails fastened down to cross members called sleepers, and could be either uninterrupted plain line or points / switches and crossings, where a second track leaves the main line or joins it. In the old days, the passing of a train over the joints between rails gave the passenger a reassuring 'clickety-click', rather than 'crunch-crunch', which tends to indicate that you've left the track. The sound was in a rhythm dependant on the lengths of the rails. These were usually sixty feet long, but could be forty-five or thirty, especially on single lines, that is railway where there was only one track rather than double. Railway fathers, if mine was typical, told their children that the rails are saying 'had-dock-and-chips' (60-foots) or 'rice pudding' (30-foots). I was never convinced.

works   Otherwise the engineer's Pooh Bah, referring to practically everything else in the railway civil engineer's kit. This included bridges, tunnels, viaducts, buildings, cabins, signal boxes and stations, along with the various trades associated with structures. Works artisans were plumbers, brickies, plasterers, woodworkers, gas and water inspectors, fire inspectors – in fact most of the Yellow Pages. If you want to be confused, the Works department also looks after toilets, which includes my initial urinal pee-ways.

rails   Come in two main types, bull head and flat bottom, which rather describes your worst nightmare on a blind date. Generally speaking, bull head is now only seen on minor routes or sidings, and looks as if it could be put in either way up, whereas today's railway runs on flat-bottom rails, which amazingly have a flat bottom with a central vertical web and are topped off by a running head.

rail chairs   The completion of the rail to sleeper unit. Bull head sits in comfortable looking chairs with side support arms, the whole screwed down to the sleeper with the rail held in place by a key. This is usually a wood block, but can be a sprung metal fitting. (Handy duffel-coat party opener for sad individuals who start every statement with, 'Do you know that...?': the wooden keys for bull head were normally of oak, but in tunnels they were of teak, since that wood contained oils, and was resistant to rot – now there's a bit of knowledge to change your day!)

chair screw   Holds rail chairs down to the sleepers. Also appears as a challenging position in the Kama Sutra.

baseplates   Flat-bottom rail lies on these, attached to the sleepers, and has in the past been clipped to the plate by a panoply of weird and wonderful means. Railway component manufacturers came up with one improved design after another – each one, like computers, being better than the last. That was true right from the moment when a modest chief engineer designed a fastening that he named after himself, in which there were about twelve components per fastening, each capable of disappearing. We seem to have settled for the most effective and rather beautiful Pandrol clip, now in a few different forms, but basically a round bar, curling seductively onto the rail and through the sleeper housing. Easily handled, a joy to insert and a boon to the railway industry. (Dear Pandrol, the name's Mike Collins, contactable through the publishers.)

sleepers The cross members of the track, holding the rails apart securely and at the right distance (see *gauge*). They can be of soft or hardwood, reinforced concrete or steel. Softwood sleepers are impregnated with creosote, except in hot weather, when it becomes your trouser knees that are impregnated. Jarrah was a favourite hardwood, coming cracked and split even when new, but staying the same after many years. In old 60-foot panels of track there would be twenty-four sleepers to the panel. I got this rhythm fixed in my mind to the extent that I could measure out a field to within 1% accuracy; one thing that I take away with me after thirty-three years on the railway. In unjointed track (wait for it – we'll get there later), wooden sleepers would be at twenty-eight if hard and thirty, soft, per 60-foot length. Reinforced concrete, in a wild variety of designs, came in at twenty-six. Old jointed was very comfortable to walk on (except when icy or covered in moss), whereas twenty-eights and thirties drove the walker into the rambler-strewn cess at the side. Continental travellers may find concrete blocks held to gauge by a connecting iron rod – sort of reinforced fresh air. There are also some steel sleepers, but they are better suited to hot and dry climates like Africa, Central America and the Thames Valley.

rail joints Between track panels there was always a gap so that the rails could expand and contract. I think that they were designed to be about a quarter of an inch in average conditions, that was one day in April and another in October. Hence the 'clickety-click' became 'clunkety-clunk' in the depths of winter and 'de-de-de-de' in heat (am I getting too technical for you, or are you still with me?)

fishplates Spanning the gap between rails, fishplates come in pairs bolted to the rail ends usually with four slotted holes to allow expansion to occur. Signs of spring used to be snowdrops, carpets hung out in the street and railway track gangs greasing the backs of fishplates. Despite this, in the first hot weather, a man was often despatched to clout rail ends with a hammer, receiving back a satisfying 'ping' when the rails jumped together.

points or switches and crossings Are means by which trains can change tracks from one to another. They are referred to as P & C or more usually S & C (the former sounding like a glass lavatory door). Switches are planed rails on sliders that direct traffic onto another line, and the crossing is the V-shaped rails where one rail crosses another. (Fathers of old had more interpretations of the sound of a train going through crossings, but I think we've taken that as far as we need.) The whole unit was called a 'lead' or a 'turnout'. One of these joining up with another on the opposite line became a crossover. This may be pushing comprehension to the limit, so we will not go into tandems, three-throws, slips and diamonds

check rails Ran alongside running rails where there was any danger of a wheel trying to escape, as in crossings and on tight curves. They acted as a guide for the flange of the wheel. Since they were not run on, there was a certain amount of supervisory perturbation when fogmen were found attaching their warning detonators to them.

running and outside edge	The edges of the rails where the wheel flange ran alongside or didn't, respectively. On severe curves the outer running edge could suffer side-wear as the wheel forced its flange up against the rail, catching it as it tries to slip over. An outside edge, on the other hand, leads to catching it in the slips.
gauge	Is the distance between the two running edges of the track. George Stephenson decided that this should be 4'8½". This was in answer to his suppliers when asked, and he stretched his arms out and said, 'This much.' (Try it.) Brunel adopted the same approach, but he always carried a walking stick, so naturally his gauge was nearer to seven feet. Stephenson's was eventually adopted throughout the system, which accounts for an unbeatable offer of heavy timber poufs made from the sawn-off ends of sleepers in the Bristol B & Q. The British Railways Board decided to make it 4'8 3/8" around 1970 in certain conditions, thus saving on the manufacturing cost of axles. (This is another smart-arse piece of information for gricer parties, except leave out the axle bit.) Incidentally, the Stephenson gauge is also the exact distance that an average technical officer's chin lands after tripping up over the first rail. (Just accept this as a fact – don't go trying it!)
gricer	A proclaimed lover of all things to do with railways, except for track, bridges, tunnels, viaducts, stations, signalling, railwaymen and women… and frigging diesels.
void	A gap between the bottom of a sleeper and the supposedly supporting ballast.
voidmeter	A device for measuring fresh air.
fourfoot	Describing the space between the rails, except it isn't.
sixfoot	Describing the space between tracks, which it is

cess   A designated strip alongside the formation where you can walk or stand clear. In reality, a nature reserve one foot wide and hundreds of miles long. Favourite haunt of flora dedicated to producing long creeping limbs with vicious spikes and stinging leaves attached. These either trip up the walker or disguise open drain manholes. All you can say in its favour is that you were free from any danger from trains when walking in it. On the other hand, you are not safe from spiky bushes, the constrictor ramblers, miscellaneous rubbish, ducts with lids missing or broken, S & T mystery cupboards, deconstructed animals, flushing train toilets, tree roots, treacherously slippery drain catchpit lids, and the world in general.

curves   Can be simple or compound, i.e. a single radius throughout or a successive number of different radii. An example of a compound curve is the Venus de Milo, a simple one is the Hunchback of Notre Dame.

chainage   The position of any location measured in miles and chains. If you consider this to be well out of date, then think on; if the railways were any older then this would be in leagues and paces. When the rest of Britain eventually goes metric, the railways will introduce yards and feet.

continuous welded rail (CWR)   This is rail without joints. Except for the intrusion of S & C, there is one continuous rail from London to Leeds, or, hopefully, two, side by side. Engineers dipped their collective toes in this particular pool by starting with 300-foot lengths, with long fishplates (called Long Welded Rail). They got bolder as the track became a structure able to withstand heat and cold. CWR is stretched so that it is without stress at a predetermined average temperature. Sort of stressed, but pulling itself together.

de-stressing   A daft term which is exactly opposite to what it means. It is in fact stretching rails so that in cold weather they are stressed, and comfortable in warmth.

adjustment switches	Rapidly becoming a thing of the past. These were overlapping tapering rails at the joining point between CWR and jointed track, which in theory could open and shut several inches. They were known affectionately as 'breathers', or in ignorance, many times, as broken rails.
wheel burns	Spots on the rail head where loco wheels have spun before moving off. In steam days they could be deep (10 mm the best I ever saw), but under lighter diesels they are more superficial. Both need removing before they become un-plated rail joints.
cant	A spell-check nightmare. It is the difference in height of the high (outer rail) of a curve over the low (inner rail). Poshly called 'superelevation'. In effect it makes the passenger's ride more comfortable instead of pushing him up against the coach side. Compare with dodgems. It also helps protect the track against side wear and damage to the outer rail on a curve. It leads naturally to the…
coffee-cup test	Where the coffee should stay fairly level in the cup even when going round a curve. It should be stressed that there is no particular quality in coffee that means it has to be the observed liquid; whisky will do equally as well, but leads to more heartache if the test fails.
platelayer	Literally a man who laid the blocks and plates that formed the first railways. With the completion of railway building, platelayers were absorbed into the rapidly developing railway restaurant business.
relayer	Really someone who many years later took over the platelayer's job, re-laying exhausted stretches of track. A retired relayer is said to have gone broody.
lengthmen	Were formed into small maintenance gangs overseeing

	stretches of railway. They were often consumed with pride and would boast about their length.
snap tin	A container for a chainman's sandwiches.
slips	Earth movements that endanger the railway. In cuttings these are usually of soaked surface material slipping onto the railway. On embankments of made ground they are often in the form of circular slips taking material away from the tracks and showing as a bulge at the bottom. Slips in cuttings are simply dug up and loaded; embankment slips generate a large amount of discussion, argument, expense and head scratching.
up and down	The identification of the two tracks. They might have Fast and Slow, Goods and Main, or even destinations attached. Do not be deceived by these titles. Trains both fast and slow cause similar damage if you decide to stand in front of them. An Up line usually runs towards a major town or city, Fasts being used to avoid minor stations as opposed to Slows. It is an affront to all Yorkshiremen that their Ups go to London and Manchester.
'Near enough for t'Railway'	A description of a result or a setting-out detail, or a measurement which is perhaps not quite correct but is considered adequate. Usually associated with the threat of approaching bad weather.
ballast and formation	The supporting material under and on the shoulders of the tracks. In remote areas and sidings this can still be ash, but is more usually stone. In the 1950s there was a love affair with power station slag, but this was found to fall apart under traffic. Penmaenmawr, in North Wales, a source of much stone ballast, is a pleasant little coastal holiday resort. It used to be bigger, but a great deal of it now lies underneath railways.
bussing passengers	Usually comes down to replacing the last train with a taxi carrying a single late reveller past an engineer's blockage of the track. Said passenger often in

	no state to notice that he is no longer on a train.
stone train	Train of ballast wagons used to distribute stone onto the track. On Leeds District it also applied to an inconvenient train transporting stone from a quarry and disrupting a track possession at Skipton. Suggestions by engineers to bus this traffic invariably turned down.
relaying and re-railing	The first referring to the complete renewal of track and ballast, the second purely changing the rails, probably from temporary jointed rails to continuously welded ones. All in all, it still means a Sunday, so detail is unimportant.
ballast cleaning	A means for removing the ballast, sieving it, and returning the cleaned stone to underneath the track. It sounds clever, and it is clever!
bang road	Travelling 'bang road' is moving a train in the wrong direction of the line, though at the time it is the right direction. Usually conducted under an engineer's possession of the line. Why 'bang road' though? Discuss and write your answers using both sides of the paper.
pulled off	An old semaphore signal in the clear position. Nowadays 'pulled off on the Up' is open to misinterpretation.
lookout men	Persons appointed to shout 'Look out, men!' when a train is approaching.
snowmen and fogmen	Both more or less redundant now, with global and point warming taking over. One was set to clear snow from points and the other to put detonators on the track to indicate signal positions.
put the wood in the hole	Usually translated to 'Put t'wood in t' bloody oil'. An invitation to shut the cabin door.
drains	One of carriers, pickups or blocked. Normally in the cess, but in the sixfoot through platforms. Carriers take water from a high point to a low one, pickups take up water along their length, and blocked ones do neither.
rag man's trumpet	This is an inexplicable term for the Rail Mounted Trencher, invented, for no particular reason, by

	Dave Holmes. It was similar to a ballast cleaner, except its purpose was to dig a drainage trench by means of a chain of buckets. It was very efficient in tipping water and spoil over the technical man walking in the trench behind the buckets, checking depths. This was not its main purpose in life, but was the aspect most satisfying to the operator and the attendant gang.
possession of a line	Total control of a line with normal traffic diverted. Today more often known as a drug user.
Thermos flask	Essential for night work, keeps hot things hot and cold things cold. One Colne Valley lad noted for putting hot tea and an ice lolly in one.
light engine	A locomotive running without a train. As heavy as any other should it hit you.
train	A locomotive with coaches or wagons.
wagon	A truck.
truck	A wagon.
running a drop-off	A means of personal relief. Paradoxically best done well away from the PWay.
overbridge	A bridge over the railway.
underbridge	A typical question on *Richard and Judy* after being told what an overbridge is.
mining subsidence	An exciting phenomena, transforming the railway and structures into the basics of a theme park.
tunnel	An overbridge longer than fifty yards. Forty-nine yards and no muck money, two more yards and qualifying to be paid muck money. Why is life so damned unfair?
viaduct	Series of more than five consecutive spans. Usually named after the place it is avoiding.
S & T	Signals and telecommunications engineers. Two interconnected departments, the signals part of which tends to talk sense at project meetings. (Almost as much sense as the Civils.) They are also

	known as the 'Sick and Tired' department, referring to their attitude to project managers.
chainman	For full details see the first book, chapter one. He was either the most important piece of equipment on a survey, or a source of disruption. He did all the measuring and setting out of survey lines, the surveyor was his clerk. A chainman's working day lasted from first thing to first race.
muck money	A bonus paid to chainmen for working in a tunnel. Obtusely, the surveyor who was guaranteed to come out dirtiest, courtesy of the chainmen, got nothing.
tapes, measuring, dumb end	This refers to the ring end of the tape as opposed to the reading end where a measurement is announced. Experience shows it to be anything but a dumb end when the holder has to negotiate all sorts of unsavoury material in order to reach the point in question.
theodolite and legs	The measuring device and its supporting adjustable tripod. Theodolites can measure angles in both horizontal and vertical planes to very high degrees of accuracy. They carry a multitude of confusing knurled screws in a surveying form of Russian roulette. Touch the wrong one and you're buggered.
level and legs	Sometimes confused with the above, but is actually quite different. A graded staff is placed on objects where relative levels are needed, and the level telescope moves round in a perfectly horizontal plane and takes the readings. Not as many knobs involved, but screwing the wrong one still leads to disaster. Cap nebs and long noses are a grave danger, as was the fact that the target appeared upside down, leading to some tragic positions in trying to rectify this.
survey book	When you have packed the car with a level, a theodolite, a set of legs for each, a measuring staff, a

string line, two tapes, your snap tin and drinks, high visibility reflective clothing, several wooden pegs, nails, and a sledge hammer, and set off to site, the survey book is the thing that you have forgotten and have left behind. If you turn the book over and examined the back pages, these would be marked in a surveyor's code, e.g. 'Four times, two fish and a b.c.'

district, division, area

All terms for a sub-section of a region. The three are used in rotation for the same thing as an excuse for removing posts and increasing work, and are changed at five- or six-yearly intervals. So a district engineer will get an increase in his administration area, a decrease in his manpower, an increase in his workload and a satisfying maintenance of his current pay rate.

rule book

When thoroughly read through, and stringently obeyed, you will find that you are permitted only to stand in the middle of a deserted field, and nothing more.

stationary and stationery

Papers in the pending basket.

newspaper and aluminium foil

The difference between chainmen's and management's sandwiches.

Portique Universale de Manutention

I said that I couldn't be bothered to look this up for you, but this is the PUM system we used on York remodelling. So there you have it. Work that into the conversation during cocktails if you can!

卞尺丹几乙し丹卞と

Translated Language Learning

Aladdin a'r Lamp Rhyfeddol

Aladdin and the Wonderful
Lamp

Antoine Galland

Cymraeg / English

Published by Tranzlaty

ISBN: 978-1-83566-068-3

Original text by Antoine Galland

From *''Les mille et une nuits''*

First published in French in 1704

Taken from The Blue Fairy Book

Collected and translated by Andrew Lang

www.tranzlaty.com

Un tro, roedd teiliwr gwael yn byw
Once upon a time there lived a poor tailor
roedd ganddo fab o'r enw Aladdin
he had a son called Aladdin
Roedd Aladdin yn fachgen diofal, segur a fyddai'n gwneud dim byd
Aladdin was a careless, idle boy who would do nothing
Fodd bynnag, roedd yn hoffi chwarae pêl drwy'r dydd
although, he did like to play ball all day long
hyn a wnaeth ar y strydoedd gyda bechgyn bach eraill segur
this he did in the streets with other little idle boys
Roedd hyn yn drist iawn i'r tad ei fod wedi marw
This so grieved the father that he died
Roedd ei fam yn crio ac yn gweddïo, ond doedd dim byd yn helpu
his mother cried and prayed but nothing helped
er gwaethaf ei phledio, ni throdd Aladdin ei ffyrdd
despite her pleading, Aladdin did not mend his ways
Un diwrnod roedd Aladdin yn chwarae yn y strydoedd fel arfer
One day Aladdin was playing in the streets as usual
Gofynnodd dieithryn iddo ei oedran
a stranger asked him his age
Gofynnodd iddo os nad oedd yn fab i Mustapha y teiliwr.
and he asked him if he was not the son of Mustapha the tailor
"Rwy'n fab i Mustapha, syr," atebodd Aladdin
"I am the son of Mustapha, sir" replied Aladdin
'Bu farw amser maith yn ôl'
"but he died a long time ago"
Roedd y dieithryn yn ddewin Affricanaidd enwog
the stranger was a famous African magician
a syrthiodd ar ei wddf a'i gusanu
and he fell on his neck and kissed him
'Myfi yw dy ewythr,' meddai'r dewin
"I am your uncle" said the magician
"Roeddwn i'n dy adnabod di o'th debygrwydd i'm brawd."

"I knew you from your likeness to my brother"

"Dos at dy fam a dywed wrthi fy mod yn dod"

"Go to your mother and tell her I am coming"

Rhedodd Aladdin adref a dweud wrth ei fam am ei ewythr newydd ei ddarganfod

Aladdin ran home and told his mother of his newly found uncle

"Plentyn," meddai, "roedd gan dy dad frawd."

"Indeed, child," she said, "your father had a brother"

"Roeddwn i bob amser yn meddwl ei fod wedi marw"

"but I always thought he was dead"

Fodd bynnag, paratôdd swper i'r ymwelydd

However, she prepared supper for the visitor

a hi a adarawodd Aladdin i geisio ei ewythr

and she bade Aladdin to seek his uncle

Daeth ewythr Aladdin yn llawn gwin a ffrwythau

Aladdin's uncle came laden with wine and fruit

Syrthiodd i lawr a chusanu'r man lle arferai Mustapha eistedd

He fell down and kissed the place where Mustapha used to sit

ac efe a wnaeth gais i fam Aladdin beidio â synnu

and he bid Aladdin's mother not to be surprised

Eglurodd ei fod wedi bod allan o'r wlad ddeugain mlynedd

he explained he had been out of the country forty years

Yna trodd at Aladdin a gofyn iddo ei grefft

He then turned to Aladdin and asked him his trade

ond crogodd y bachgen ei ben mewn cywilydd

but the boy hung his head in shame

a gwaeddodd ei fam yn ei dagrau

and his mother burst into tears

felly roedd ewythr Aladdin yn cynnig darparu bwyd

so Aladdin's uncle offered to provide food

Y diwrnod wedyn prynodd Aladdin siwt wych o ddillad

The next day he bought Aladdin a fine suit of clothes

Ac efe a'i dug ef dros y ddinas

and he took him all over the city

Dangosodd iddo olygon y ddinas

he showed him the sights of the city
Yn y nos daeth ag ef adref at ei fam.
at nightfall he brought him home to his mother
Roedd ei fam wrth ei bodd yn gweld ei mab mor brydferth
his mother was overjoyed to see her son so fine
Y diwrnod wedyn fe wnaeth y dewin arwain Aladdin i mewn i rai gerddi hardd
The next day the magician led Aladdin into some beautiful gardens
Roedd hyn yn bell y tu allan i gatiau'r ddinas
this was a long way outside the city gates
Eisteddasant wrth ffynnon
They sat down by a fountain
a thynnodd y dewin gacen o'i wregys
and the magician pulled a cake from his girdle
Rhannodd y cacen rhwng y ddau
he divided the cake between the two of them
Yna aethant ymlaen nes cyrraedd y mynyddoedd bron.
Then they journeyed onward till they almost reached the mountains
Roedd Aladdin mor flinedig nes iddo erfyn am fynd yn ôl
Aladdin was so tired that he begged to go back
Ond roedd y dewin yn ei dwyllo â straeon dymunol
but the magician beguiled him with pleasant stories
ac arweiniodd ef ymlaen er gwaethaf ei ddiogi
and he led him on in spite of his laziness
O'r diwedd daethant i ddau fynydd
At last they came to two mountains
Rhannwyd y ddau fynydd â dyffryn cul
the two mountains were divided by a narrow valley
"Fyddwn ni ddim yn mynd ymhellach," meddai'r ewythr ffug
"We will go no farther" said the false uncle
'Dangosaf i ti rywbeth rhyfeddol'
"I will show you something wonderful"
"Casglwch ffyn tra byddaf yn cynnau tân"
"gather up sticks while I kindle a fire"

Pan gynnau'r tân taflodd y dewin bowdwr arno

When the fire was lit the magician threw a powder on it

a dywedodd eiriau hudol

and he said some magical words

Roedd y ddaear yn crynu ychydig, ac yn agor o'u blaenau

The earth trembled a little and opened in front of them

Datgelodd carreg wastad sgwâr ei hun

a square flat stone revealed itself

ac yng nghanol y garreg yr oedd modrwy bres

and in the middle of the the stone was a brass ring

Ceisiodd Aladdin redeg i ffwrdd

Aladdin tried to run away

Ond daliodd y dewin ef

but the magician caught him

ac a roddodd iddo ergyd a'i trawodd i lawr

and gave him a blow that knocked him down

"Beth dw i wedi'i wneud, ewythr?" meddai'n druenus

"What have I done, uncle?" he said piteously

Dywedodd y dewin yn fwy caredig: "Peidiwch ag ofni dim, ond ufuddhewch i mi."

the magician said more kindly: "Fear nothing, but obey me"

"O dan y garreg hon y mae trysor sydd i fod yn eiddo i ti"

"Beneath this stone lies a treasure which is to be yours"

'Does neb arall yn gallu ei gyffwrdd'

"and no one else may touch it"

"Mae'n rhaid i chi wneud yn union fel dw i'n dweud wrthoch chi"

"so you must do exactly as I tell you"

Wrth sôn am drysor anghofiodd Aladdin ei ofnau

At the mention of treasure Aladdin forgot his fears

gafaelodd yn y cylch fel y dywedwyd wrtho

he grasped the ring as he was told

Ac efe a ddywedodd enwau ei dad a'i dad-cu

and he said the names of his father and grandfather

Daeth y garreg i fyny yn eithaf hawdd

The stone came up quite easily

ac ymddangosodd rhai camau o'u blaenau

and some steps appeared in front of them

'Ewch i lawr' meddai'r dewin

"Go down" said the magician

"Wrth droed y grisiau hynny fe welwch ddrws agored"

"at the foot of those steps you will find an open door"

"Mae'r drws yn arwain i mewn i dair neuadd fawr"

"the door leads into three large halls"

"Golchwch eich gwn a mynd drwy'r neuaddau"

"Tuck up your gown and go through the halls"

'Peidio â chyffwrdd unrhyw beth'

"make sure not to touching anything"

"Os byddwch yn cyffwrdd ag unrhyw beth, byddwch yn marw ar unwaith"

"if you touch anything, you will die instantly"

"Mae'r neuaddau hyn yn arwain i ardd o goed ffrwythau braf"

"These halls lead into a garden of fine fruit trees"

"Cerddwch ymlaen nes i chi ddod i gilfach mewn teras"

"Walk on until you come to a niche in a terrace"

"Yno fe welwch lamp wedi'i goleuo"

"there you will see a lighted lamp"

"Arllwyswch olew y lamp"

"Pour out the oil of the lamp"

"Ac yna dod â'r lamp i mi"

"and then bring me the lamp"

Tynnodd fodrwy o'i fys a'i rhoi i Aladdin

He drew a ring from his finger and gave it to Aladdin

ac fe wnaeth gais iddo ffynnu

and he bid him to prosper

Daeth Aladdin o hyd i bopeth fel yr oedd y dewin wedi dweud

Aladdin found everything as the magician had said

Casglodd ffrwyth o'r coed

he gathered some fruit off the trees

Ac, wedi iddo gael y lamp, efe a ddaeth i geg yr ogof

and, having got the lamp, he arrived at the mouth of the cave

Gwaeddodd y dewin ar frys mawr
The magician cried out in a great hurry
"Brysiwch a rhowch y lamp i mi"
"Make haste and give me the lamp"
Gwrthododd yr Aladdin hwn wneud nes ei fod allan o'r ogof
This Aladdin refused to do until he was out of the cave
Hedfanodd y dewin i angerdd ofnadwy
The magician flew into a terrible passion
Taflodd ychydig mwy o bowdwr ymlaen i'r tân
he threw some more powder on to the fire
ac yna fe fwriodd swyngyfaredd arall
and then he cast another magic spell
a'r garreg wedi ei rholio yn ôl i'w lle
and the stone rolled back into its place
Gadawodd y dewin Persia am byth
The magician left Persia for ever
Dangosodd hyn yn amlwg nad oedd yn ewythr i Aladdin
this plainly showed that he was no uncle of Aladdin's
Yr hyn yr oedd mewn gwirionedd oedd consuriwr cyfrwys
what he really was was a cunning magician
Magician a oedd wedi darllen o lamp hyfryd
a magician who had read of a wonderful lamp
lamp a fyddai'n ei wneud y dyn mwyaf pwerus yn y byd
a lamp which would make him the most powerful man in the world
Ond roedd yn gwybod yn unig lle i ddod o hyd iddo
but he alone knew where to find it
a dim ond o law un arall y gallai ei dderbyn
and he could only receive it from the hand of another
Roedd wedi dewis yr Aladdin ffôl at y diben hwn
He had picked out the foolish Aladdin for this purpose
roedd wedi bwriadu cael y lamp a'i ladd wedi hynny
he had intended to get the lamp and kill him afterwards

Am ddau ddiwrnod arhosodd Aladdin yn y tywyllwch
For two days Aladdin remained in the dark

Roedd yn crio ac yn galaru am ei sefyllfa
he cried and lamented his situation
O'r diwedd fe roddodd ei ddwylo mewn gweddi
At last he clasped his hands in prayer
ac wrth wneud hynny fe rwblodd y cylch
and in so doing he rubbed the ring
Roedd y dewin wedi anghofio tynnu'r fodrwy yn ôl oddi
wrtho
the magician had forgotten to take the ring back from him
Ar unwaith cododd athrylith enfawr a brawychus allan o'r
ddaear
Immediately an enormous and frightful genie rose out of the
earth
"Beth fyddech chi'n ei wneud i mi?"
"What would thou have me do?"
"Fi yw caethwas y cylch"
"I am the Slave of the Ring"
"Byddaf yn ufuddhau i chi ym mhob peth"
"and I will obey thee in all things"
Atebodd Aladdin yn ddi-ofn, "Gwared fi o'r lle hwn!"
Aladdin fearlessly replied: "Deliver me from this place!"
a'r ddaear yn agor uwch ei ben
and the earth opened above him
Cafodd ei hun y tu allan
and he found himself outside
Cyn gynted ag y gallai ei lygaid ddwyn y golau, aeth adref
As soon as his eyes could bear the light he went home
Ond roedd yn llewygu pan gyrhaeddodd yno
but he fainted when he got there
Pan ddaeth ato'i hun dywedodd wrth ei fam beth oedd wedi
digwydd
When he came to himself he told his mother what had
happened
Ac efe a ddangosodd iddi y lamp
and he showed her the lamp
Ac efe a gawod iddi y ffrwythau a gasglasai efe yn yr ardd.

and he shower her the the fruits he had gathered in the garden
Roedd y ffrwythau, mewn gwirionedd, yn gerrig gwerthfawr
the fruits were, in reality, precious stones
Yna gofynnodd am fwyd
He then asked for some food
"Alas! 'Plentyn' meddai
"Alas! child" she said
'Does gen i ddim byd yn y tŷ'
"I have nothing in the house"
"Ond dw i wedi sbio bach o got"
"but I have spun a little cotton"
"A byddaf yn mynd i werthu'r cotwm"
"and I will go and sell the cotton"
Aladdin yn ei bade yn cadw ei cotwm
Aladdin bade her keep her cotton
Dywedodd wrthi y byddai'n gwerthu'r lamp yn lle'r cotwm
he told her he would sell the lamp instead of the cotton
Gan ei bod yn fudr iawn dechreuodd rwbio'r lamp
As it was very dirty she began to rub the lamp
Gallai lamp glân nôl pris uwch
a clean lamp might fetch a higher price
Yn syth ymddangosodd athrylith gudd
Instantly a hideous genie appeared
Gofynnodd beth hoffai ei gael
he asked what she would like to have
yng ngolwg yr athrylith fe lewygodd
at the sight of the genie she fainted
ond dywedodd Aladdin, gan gipio'r lamp, yn eofn:
but Aladdin, snatching the lamp, said boldly:
"Rhowch rywbeth i'w fwyta i mi!"
"Fetch me something to eat!"
Dychwelodd yr athrylith gyda bowlen arian
The genie returned with a silver bowl
Roedd ganddo ddeuddeg plât arian yn cynnwys cigoedd cyfoethog
he had twelve silver plates containing rich meats

Ac roedd ganddo ddau gwpan arian a dwy botel o win

and he had two silver cups and two bottles of wine

Dywedodd mam Aladdin, pan ddaeth hi at ei hun:

Aladdin's mother, when she came to herself, said:

"O le daw'r wledd ysblennydd hon?"

"Whence comes this splendid feast?"

"Peidiwch â gofyn o ble y daeth, ond bwyta, fy mam," atebodd Aladdin

"Ask not where it came from, but eat, mother" replied Aladdin

Felly dyma nhw'n eistedd yn y brecwast nes roedd hi'n amser cinio.

So they sat at breakfast till it was dinner-time

Ac Aladdin a fynegodd i'w fam am y lamp.

and Aladdin told his mother about the lamp

Roedd hi'n erfyn arno i'w gwerthu

She begged him to sell it

"Gadewch i ni gael dim i'w wneud â gythreuliaid"

"let us have nothing to do with devils"

ond roedd Aladdin wedi meddwl y byddai'n ddoethach defnyddio'r lamp

but Aladdin had thought it would be wiser to use the lamp

"Mae cyfle wedi ein gwneud ni'n ymwybodol o'i rinweddau"

"chance hath made us aware of its virtues"

"Byddwn yn ei ddefnyddio, a'r cylch yr un modd"

"we will use it, and the ring likewise"

"Byddaf bob amser yn ei wisgo ar fy mys"

"I shall always wear it on my finger"

Ac wedi iddynt fwyta'r holl genhedlu a ddaeth, gwerthodd Aladdin un o'r platiau arian

When they had eaten all the genie had brought, Aladdin sold one of the silver plates

a phan oedd angen arian eto fe werthodd y plât nesaf

and when he needed money again he sold the next plate

Gwnaeth hyn nes na adawyd unrhyw blatiau

he did this until no plates were left

Yna gwnaeth ddymuniad arall i'r athrylith

He then he made another wish to the genie
a rhoddodd yr athrylith set arall o blatiau iddo
and the genie gave him another set of plates
ac felly y buont yn byw am flynyddoedd
and thus they lived for many years

Un diwrnod clywodd Aladdin orchymyn gan y Swltan
One day Aladdin heard an order from the Sultan
Roedd pawb i aros gartref a chau eu caeadau
everyone was to stay at home and close their shutters
Roedd y Dywysoges yn mynd i ac o'i bath
the Princess was going to and from her bath
Atafaelwyd Aladdin gan awydd i weld ei hwyneb
Aladdin was seized by a desire to see her face
Er ei bod yn anodd iawn gweld ei wyneb
although it was very difficult to see her face
oherwydd ym mhob man yr aeth hi'n gwisgo gorchudd
because everywhere she went she wore a veil
Cuddiodd ei hun y tu ôl i ddrws y bath
He hid himself behind the door of the bath
ac efe a ddisgleiriodd trwy gilfach yn y drws
and he peeped through a chink in the door
Cododd y Dywysoges ei gorchudd wrth iddi fynd i mewn i'r bath
The Princess lifted her veil as she went in to the bath
ac roedd hi'n edrych mor brydferth nes i Aladdin syrthio mewn cariad â hi ar yr olwg gyntaf
and she looked so beautiful that Aladdin fell in love with her at first sight
Aeth adref felly newidiodd fod ei fam wedi dychryn
He went home so changed that his mother was frightened
Dywedodd wrthi ei fod yn caru'r Dywysoges mor ddwfn fel na allai fyw hebddi hi.
He told her he loved the Princess so deeply that he could not live without her
Ac roedd eisiau gofyn iddi mewn priodas ei thad

and he wanted to ask her in marriage of her father

Wrth glywed hyn, byrstiodd ei fam yn chwerthin

His mother, on hearing this, burst out laughing

ond o'r diwedd byddai Aladdin yn drech na hi i fynd o flaen y Swltan

but Aladdin at last prevailed upon her to go before the Sultan

Ac roedd hi'n mynd i gario ei chais

and she was going to carry his request

Casglodd napcyn a gosod ynddo y ffrwythau hud

She fetched a napkin and laid in it the magic fruits

Y ffrwythau hud o'r ardd hudolus

the magic fruits from the enchanted garden

Mae'r ffrwythau yn disgleirio ac yn disgleirio fel y tlysau mwyaf prydferth

the fruits sparkled and shone like the most beautiful jewels

Aeth â'r ffrwythau hud gyda hi i blesio'r Swltan

She took the magic fruits with her to please the Sultan

A hi a aeth allan, gan ymddiried yn y lamp

and she set out, trusting in the lamp

Roedd y Grand Vizier ac arglwyddi'r cyngor newydd fynd i mewn i'r palas

The Grand Vizier and the lords of council had just gone into the palace

a hi a osododd ei hun o flaen y Sultan

and she placed herself in front of the Sultan

Fodd bynnag, ni chymerodd unrhyw sylw iddi

He, however, took no notice of her

Roedd hi'n mynd bob dydd am wythnos

She went every day for a week

A hi a safodd yn yr un lle

and she stood in the same place

Pan dorrodd y cyngor i fyny ar y chweched diwrnod dywedodd y Swltan wrth ei Vizier:

When the council broke up on the sixth day the Sultan said to his Vizier:

"Rwy'n gweld menyw benodol yn y gynulleidfa-siambr bob

dydd"

"I see a certain woman in the audience-chamber every day"

"Mae hi bob amser yn cario rhywbeth mewn napcyn"

"she is always carrying something in a napkin"

"Ffoniwch hi i ddod atom y tro nesaf"

"Call her to come to us, next time"

"er mwyn i mi gael gwybod beth mae hi eisiau"

"so that I may find out what she wants"

Y diwrnod wedyn rhoddodd y Vizier arwydd iddi

Next day the Vizier gave her a sign

Aeth hi i fyny at droed yr orsedd

she went up to the foot of the throne

ac arhosodd yn penlinio nes i'r Swltan siarad â hi

and she remained kneeling till the Sultan spoke to her

"Cyfod, gwraig dda, dywedwch wrthyf beth yr ydych ei eisiau"

"Rise, good woman, tell me what you want"

Roedd hi'n betruso, felly anfonodd y Swltan i ffwrdd pob un ond y Vizier

She hesitated, so the Sultan sent away all but the Vizier

ac fe'i hanogodd i siarad yn onest

and he bade her to speak frankly

Ac addawodd faddau iddi am unrhyw beth y gallai hi ei ddweud

and he promised to forgive her for anything she might say

Yna dywedodd wrtho am gariad treisgar ei mab at y Dywysoges

She then told him of her son's violent love for the Princess

"Dw i'n gweddïo'n daer arno i'w hanghofio hi," meddai

"I prayed him to forget her" she said

"Ond roedd y gweddïau'n ofer"

"but the prayers were in vain"

"Roedd e'n bygwth gwneud rhyw weithred anobeithiol os wnes i wrthod mynd"

"he threatened to do some desperate deed if I refused to go"

"Ac felly yr wyf yn gofyn i'ch Mawrhydi am law'r

dywysoges."

"and so I ask your Majesty for the hand of the Princess"

"Ond yn awr yr wyf yn gweddïo i chi faddau i mi"

"but now I pray you to forgive me"

"A dw i'n gweddïo dy fod ti'n maddau i Aladdin fy mab."

"and I pray that you forgive my son Aladdin"

Gofynnodd y Sultan iddi yn garedig beth oedd ganddi yn y napcyn

The Sultan asked her kindly what she had in the napkin

Felly mae hi'n datblygu'r napcyn

so she unfolded the napkin

a hi a gyflwynodd y tlysau i'r Swltan

and she presented the jewels to the Sultan

Cafodd ei daro gan harddwch y tlysau

He was thunderstruck by the beauty of the jewels

Trodd at y Vizier a gofyn iddo, "Beth wyt ti'n ei ddweud?"

and he turned to the Vizier and asked "What sayest thou?"

"Oni ddylwn i roi'r Dywysoges ar un sy'n ei gwerthfawrogi am bris o'r fath?"

"Ought I not to bestow the Princess on one who values her at such a price?"

Roedd y Vizier eisiau hi ar gyfer ei fab ei hun

The Vizier wanted her for his own son

felly ymbiliodd â'r Swltan i'w dal yn ôl am dri mis

so he begged the Sultan to withhold her for three months

efallai o fewn yr amser y byddai ei fab yn dadlau i wneud anrheg gyfoethocach

perhaps within the time his son would contrive to make a richer present

Rhoddodd y Swltan ddymuniad ei Vizier

The Sultan granted the wish of his Vizier

a dywedodd wrth fam Aladdin ei fod yn cydsynio i'r briodas

and he told Aladdin's mother that he consented to the marriage

ond ni chaiff hi ymddangos o'i flaen eto am dri mis

but she must not appear before him again for three months

Arhosodd Aladdin yn amyneddgar am bron i dri mis

Aladdin waited patiently for nearly three months

Ar ôl i ddau fis fynd heibio aeth ei fam i fynd i'r farchnad

after two months had elapsed his mother went to go to the market

Roedd hi'n mynd i'r dref i brynu olew

she was going into the city to buy oil

pan gyrhaeddodd y farchnad dod o hyd i bob un yn llawenhau

when she got to the market found every one rejoicing

Felly gofynnodd beth oedd yn digwydd

so she asked what was going on

"Ydych chi ddim yn gwybod?" oedd yr ateb

"Do you not know?" was the answer

"mab y Grand Vizier yw priodi merch y Swltan heno"

"the son of the Grand Vizier is to marry the Sultan's daughter tonight"

Heb anadl, rhedodd a dweud wrth Aladdin

Breathless, she ran and told Aladdin

ar y dechrau cafodd Aladdin ei lethu

at first Aladdin was overwhelmed

Ond yna meddyliodd am y lamp a'i rhwbio

but then he thought of the lamp and rubbed it

Unwaith eto ymddangosodd yr athrylith allan o'r lamp

once again the the genie appeared out of the lamp

"Beth yw dy ewyllys di?" gofynnodd yr ysbryd

"What is thy will?" asked the genie

"Mae'r Sultan, fel y gwyddoch, wedi torri ei addewid i mi"

"The Sultan, as thou knowest, has broken his promise to me"

"mab y Vizier yw cael y dywysoges"

"the Vizier's son is to have the Princess"

"Fy ngorchymyn i yw eich bod chi'n dod â'r briodferch a'r priodfab heno."

"My command is that tonight you bring the bride and bridegroom"

"Meistr, rwy'n ufuddhau," meddai'r genie

"Master, I obey" said the genie

Yna aeth Aladdin i'w siambr

Aladdin then went to his chamber

ddigon sicr, am hanner nos roedd yr genie yn cludo gwely

sure enough, at midnight the genie transported a bed

ac roedd y gwely yn cynnwys mab y Vizier a'r Dywysoges

and the bed contained the Vizier's son and the Princess

"Cymerwch y dyn newydd hwn, athrylith," meddai

"Take this new-married man, genie" he said

"Rhowch ef allan yn yr oerfel am y nos"

"put him outside in the cold for the night"

'Dychwelwch nhw eto ar doriad dydd'

"then return them again at daybreak"

Felly cymerodd yr genie fab y Vizier allan o'r gwely

So the genie took the Vizier's son out of bed

a gadawodd Aladdin gyda'r Dywysoges

and he left Aladdin with the Princess

Ac meddai Aladdin wrthi, "Fy ngwraig wyt ti."

"Fear nothing," Aladdin said to her, "you are my wife"

'Fe'ch addawyd i mi gan eich tad anghyfiawn'

"you were promised to me by your unjust father"

"Ni fydd unrhyw niwed yn dod i chi"

"and no harm shall come to you"

Roedd y Dywysoges yn rhy ofnus i siarad

The Princess was too frightened to speak

A hi a fu farw noson fwyaf diflas ei bywyd

and she passed the most miserable night of her life

er bod Aladdin yn gorwedd wrth ei hochr ac yn cysgu'n gadarn

although Aladdin lay down beside her and slept soundly

Ar yr awr benodedig y genie fetched yn y priodfab crynu

At the appointed hour the genie fetched in the shivering bridegroom

fe'i gosododd yn ei le

he laid him in his place

ac efe a gludodd y gwely yn ôl i'r palas

and he transported the bed back to the palace
Ar hyn o bryd daeth y Swltan i ddymuno'n dda i'w ferch bore
Presently the Sultan came to wish his daughter good-morning
Neidiodd mab y Vizier anhapus i fyny a chuddio ei hun
The unhappy Vizier's son jumped up and hid himself
ac ni fyddai'r Dywysoges yn dweud gair
and the Princess would not say a word
Ac roedd hi'n drist iawn
and she was very sorrowful
Anfonodd y Swltan ei mam ati hi
The Sultan sent her mother to her
Pam na allwch chi siarad â'ch tad, fy mhlentyn?"
"Why will you not speak to your father, child?"
"Beth sydd wedi digwydd?" gofynnodd
"What has happened?" she asked
Y Dywysoges ochneidiodd yn ddwfn
The Princess sighed deeply
Ac o'r diwedd dywedodd wrth ei mam beth oedd wedi digwydd
and at last she told her mother what had happened
Dywedodd wrthi sut roedd y gwely wedi ei gario i ryw dŷ rhyfedd
she told her how the bed had been carried into some strange house
a dywedodd hi am yr hyn a ddigwyddodd yn y tŷ
and she told of what had happened in the house
Nid oedd ei mam yn ei chredu yn y lleiaf.
Her mother did not believe her in the least
ac fe'i bathodd hi i'w hystyried yn freuddwyd segur
and she bade her to consider it an idle dream
Y noson ganlynol, digwyddodd yr un peth
The following night exactly the same thing happened
a'r bore wedyn ni fyddai'r dywysoges yn siarad chwaith
and the next morning the princess wouldn't speak either
ar wrthodiad y Dywysoges i siarad, bygythiodd y Swltan dorri ei phen

on the Princess's refusal to speak, the Sultan threatened to cut off her head

Yna cyfaddefodd bopeth oedd wedi digwydd
She then confessed all that had happened
ac fe wnaeth hi gais iddo ofyn i fab y Vizier
and she bid him to ask the Vizier's son
Dywedodd y Swltan wrth y Vizier am ofyn i'w fab
The Sultan told the Vizier to ask his son
A mab y Vizier a ddywedodd y gwir
and the Vizier's son told the truth
ychwanegodd ei fod yn hoff iawn o'r Dywysoges
he added that he dearly loved the Princess
"Ond byddai'n well gen i farw na mynd trwy noson arall mor ofnus."
"but I would rather die than go through another such fearful night"
ac efe a ddymunai gael ei wahanu oddi wrthi, yr hon a roddasid iddi
and he wished to be separated from her, which was granted
a bu diwedd ar wledda a gorfoleddu
and there was an end to feasting and rejoicing

Yna daeth y tri mis i ben
then the three months were over
Anfonodd Aladdin ei fam i atgoffa'r Swltan o'i addewid
Aladdin sent his mother to remind the Sultan of his promise
Roedd hi'n sefyll yn yr un lle ag o'r blaen
She stood in the same place as before
roedd y Swltan wedi anghofio Aladdin
the Sultan had forgotten Aladdin
Ond ar unwaith cofiodd ef eto
but at once he remembered him again
Gofynnodd iddi ddod ato
and he asked for her to come to him
Wrth weld ei thlodi roedd y Swltan yn teimlo'n llai tueddol nag erioed i gadw ei air

On seeing her poverty the Sultan felt less inclined than ever to keep his word

a gofynnodd gyngor ei Vizier

and he asked his Vizier's advice

fe'i cynghorodd i osod gwerth uchel ar y Dywysoges

he counselled him to set a high value on the Princess

pris mor uchel fel na allai unrhyw ddyn sy'n byw ddod i fyny iddo

a price so high that no man living could come up to it

Yna trodd y Swltan at fam Aladdin, gan ddweud:

The Sultan then turned to Aladdin's mother, saying:

"Mae'n rhaid i fenyw dda, Sultan gofio ei addewidion"

"Good woman, a Sultan must remember his promises"

"Byddaf yn cofio fy addewid"

"and I will remember my promise"

Ond rhaid i'ch mab anfon deugain o fasnau aur ataf yn gyntaf.

"but your son must first send me forty basins of gold"

"A rhaid i'r basnau aur fod yn frau o emau"

"and the gold basins must be brimful of jewels"

"Rhaid iddyn nhw gael eu cario gan bedwar deg o gamelod duon"

"and they must be carried by forty black camels"

"Ac o flaen pob camel du mae yna un gwyn"

"and in front of each black camel there is to be a white one"

"Ac maen nhw i gyd i'w gwisgo'n ysblennydd"

"and they are all to be splendidly dressed"

"Dywedwch wrtho fy mod yn aros am ei ateb"

"Tell him that I await his answer"

Mam Aladdin yn isel

The mother of Aladdin bowed low

Yna aeth hi adref

and then she went home

Er ei bod hi'n meddwl bod y cyfan wedi'i golli

although she thought all was lost

Hi roddodd y neges i Aladdin

She gave Aladdin the message

Ac ychwanegodd, "Efallai y bydd yn aros yn ddigon hir am eich ateb!"

and she added, "He may wait long enough for your answer!"

'Ddim mor hir ag yr ydych chi'n meddwl, Mam,' atebodd ei mab.

"Not so long as you think, mother" her son replied

"Byddwn i'n gwneud llawer mwy na hynny i'r Dywysoges."

"I would do a great deal more than that for the Princess"

ac efe a alwodd yr athrylith eto

and he summoned the genie again

ac ymhen ychydig funudau cyrhaeddodd yr wythdeg camelod

and in a few moments the eighty camels arrived

ac fe wnaethon nhw gymryd pob lle yn y tŷ bach a'r ardd

and they took up all space in the small house and garden

Gwnaeth Aladdin iddynt fynd allan i'r palas

Aladdin made them set out to the palace

ac fe'u dilynwyd gan ei fam

and they were followed by his mother

Roedden nhw'n gwisgo'n gyfoethog iawn

They were very richly dressed

a thlysau ysblennydd oedd ar eu gwregysau

and splendid jewels were on their girdles

a phawb yn tyrru o gwmpas i'w gweld

and everyone crowded around to see them

a'r basnau aur a ddygent ar eu cefnau

and the basins of gold they carried on their backs

Aethant i mewn i balas y Sultan

They entered the palace of the Sultan

ac fe wnaethant benlinio o'i flaen mewn cylch lled

and they kneeled before him in a semi circle

a mam Aladdin yn eu cyflwyno i'r Swltan

and Aladdin's mother presented them to the Sultan

Nid oedd yn oedi mwyach, ond dywedodd:

He hesitated no longer, but said:

"Gwraig dda, dychwel at dy fab"

"Good woman, return to your son"

"Dywedwch wrtho fy mod yn aros amdano gyda breichiau agored"

"tell him that I wait for him with open arms"

Collodd hi ddim amser wrth ddweud wrth Aladdin

She lost no time in telling Aladdin

a hi a barodd iddo frysio

and she bid him make haste

Ond galwodd Aladdin am yr athrylith yn gyntaf

But Aladdin first called for the genie

'Dw i eisiau bath persawrus' meddai

"I want a scented bath" he said

"a dwi eisiau ceffyl yn harddach na'r Sultan's"

"and I want a horse more beautiful than the Sultan's"

"Ac yr wyf am i ugain o weision fod yn bresennol i mi"

"and I want twenty servants to attend me"

"A dwi hefyd eisiau i chwech o weision wedi gwisgo hardd aros ar fy mam

"and I also want six beautifully dressed servants to wait on my mother

"Ac yn olaf, rydw i eisiau deng mil o ddarnau aur mewn deg punt."

"and lastly, I want ten thousand pieces of gold in ten purses"

Dim cynt oedd wedi dweud beth roedd eisiau ac fe gafodd ei wneud

No sooner had he said what he wanted and it was done

Marchogodd Aladdin ei geffyl hardd

Aladdin mounted his beautiful horse

Ac efe a dramwyodd trwy'r heolydd

and he passed through the streets

Taflodd y gweision aur i'r dorf wrth iddynt fynd

the servants cast gold into the crowd as they went

Roedd y rhai a oedd wedi chwarae gydag ef yn ei blentyndod yn gwybod nad oedd

Those who had played with him in his childhood knew him not

Roedd wedi tyfu'n hardd iawn

he had grown very handsome

Pan welodd y Swltan ef daeth i lawr o'i orsedd

When the Sultan saw him he came down from his throne

cofleidiodd ei fab-yng-nghyfraith gyda breichiau agored

he embraced his new son in law with open arms

Ac efe a'i dug ef i mewn i neuadd lle yr oedd gwledd wedi ymdaenu

and he led him into a hall where a feast was spread

ei fod yn bwriadu ei briodi i'r Dywysoges y diwrnod hwnnw

he intended to marry him to the Princess that very day

Ond gwrthododd Aladdin briodi yn syth

But Aladdin refused to marry straight away

"Yn gyntaf mae'n rhaid i mi adeiladu palas sy'n addas ar gyfer y dywysoges."

"first I must build a palace fit for the princess"

Yna cymerodd ei absenoldeb

and then he took his leave

Unwaith adref dywedodd wrth yr athrylith:

Once home, he said to the genie:

"Adeiladu i mi palas o'r marmor gorau"

"Build me a palace of the finest marble"

"Gosodwch y palas â iasbis, agate, a cherrig gwerthfawr eraill."

"set the palace with jasper, agate, and other precious stones"

"Yn y canol byddi'n adeiladu neuadd fawr i mi gyda gromen"

"In the middle you shall build me a large hall with a dome"

"Bydd ei phedair wal o aur ac arian"

"its four walls will be of masses of gold and silver"

"A bydd gan bob wal chwech o ffenestri"

"and each wall will have six windows"

"A bydd y toiledau y ffenestri yn cael eu gosod gyda thlysau gwerthfawr"

"and the lattices of the windows will be set with precious jewels"

"Ond mae'n rhaid bod un ffenestr sydd ddim wedi ei haddurno"

"but there must be one window that is not decorated"

"Ewch i weld ei fod yn cael ei wneud!"

"go see that it gets done!"

Daeth y palas i ben y diwrnod canlynol

The palace was finished by the next day

Aeth yr athrylith ag ef i'r palas newydd

the genie carried him to the new palace

Ac efe a ddangosodd iddo sut yr oedd ei holl orchmynion wedi cael eu cynnal yn ffyddlon

and he showed him how all his orders had been faithfully carried out

roedd hyd yn oed carped melfed wedi ei osod o balas Aladdin i balas y Sultan

even a velvet carpet had been laid from Aladdin's palace to the Sultan's

Yna gwisgodd mam Aladdin ei hun yn ofalus

Aladdin's mother then dressed herself carefully

a hi a rodiodd i'r palas gyda'i gweision

and she walked to the palace with her servants

ac Aladdin yn ei dilyn ar gefn ceffyl

and Aladdin followed her on horseback

Anfonodd y Swltan gerddorion gyda thrwmpedau a symbalau i'w cyfarfod.

The Sultan sent musicians with trumpets and cymbals to meet them

felly mae'r aer yn atseinio gyda cherddoriaeth a cheers

so the air resounded with music and cheers

Aethpwyd â hi at y Dywysoges, a gyfarchodd ei

She was taken to the Princess, who saluted her

ac roedd hi'n ei thrin yn anrhydedd mawr

and she treated her with great honour

Yn y nos dywedodd y Dywysoges yn dda wrth ei thad

At night the Princess said good-by to her father

a hi a aeth allan ar y carped ar gyfer palas Aladdin

and she set out on the carpet for Aladdin's palace

Roedd ei fam wrth ei ochr

his mother was at her side
ac fe'u dilynwyd gan eu gwŷr o weision
and they were followed by their entourage of servants
Cafodd ei swyno yng ngolwg Aladdin
She was charmed at the sight of Aladdin
Ac Aladdin a redodd i'w derbyn hi i'r palas
and Aladdin ran to receive her into the palace
"Tywysoges," meddai "beio eich harddwch am fy hyfder
"Princess," he said "blame your beauty for my boldness
'Rwy'n gobeithio nad wyf wedi eich siomi'
"I hope I have not displeased you"
Dywedodd ei bod yn barod i ufuddhau i'w thad yn y mater hwn.
she said she willingly obeyed her father in this matter
am ei bod wedi gweld ei fod yn olygus
because she had seen that he is handsome
Ar ôl i'r briodas ddigwydd aeth Aladdin â hi i'r neuadd
After the wedding had taken place Aladdin led her into the hall
Yma ymledodd gwledd yn y neuadd
here a feast was spread out in the hall
Ac mae hi'n swp gydag ef
and she supped with him
Ar ôl bwyta buont yn dawnsio tan hanner nos
after eating they danced till midnight

Y diwrnod wedyn gwahoddodd Aladdin y Swltan i weld y palas
The next day Aladdin invited the Sultan to see the palace
Daethant i'r neuadd gyda'r ffenestri pedwar ac ugain
they entered the hall with the four-and-twenty windows
Roedd y ffenestri wedi'u haddurno â rhuddemau, diemwntau, ac emralltau
the windows were decorated with rubies, diamonds, and emeralds
gwaeddodd, "Mae'n rhyfeddod byd!"
he cried "It is a world's wonder!"

'Dim ond un peth sy'n fy synnu'

"There is only one thing that surprises me"

"Ai trwy ddamwain y gadawyd un ffenestr heb ei gorffen?"

"Was it by accident that one window was left unfinished?"

"Na, syr, fe'i gwnaed hynny trwy ddyluniad," atebodd Aladdin

"No, sir, it was done so by design" replied Aladdin

"Hoffwn i'ch Mawrhydi gael y gogoniant o orffen y palas hwn."

"I wished your Majesty to have the glory of finishing this palace"

Roedd y Swltan yn falch o dderbyn yr anrhydedd hon

The Sultan was pleased to be given this honour

Ac efe a anfonodd am y gemyddion gorau yn y ddinas

and he sent for the best jewellers in the city

Dangosodd iddynt y ffenestr anorffenedig

He showed them the unfinished window

ac efe a'u gosododd hwynt i'w haddurno fel y lleill

and he bade them to decorate it like the others

"Syr" atebodd eu llefarydd

"Sir" replied their spokesman

'Allwn ni ddim dod o hyd i ddigon o emau'

"we cannot find enough jewels"

felly roedd gan y Swltan ei emau ei hun nôl

so the Sultan had his own jewels fetched

Ond buan iawn y defnyddiwyd y tlysau hynny hefyd

but those jewels were soon soon used up too

Hyd yn oed ar ôl cyfnod o fis nid oedd y gwaith yn hanner

even after a month's time the work was not half done

Roedd Aladdin yn gwybod bod eu tasg yn amhosib

Aladdin knew that their task was impossible

a'u perswadiodd i ddadwneud eu gwaith

he bade them to undo their work

Ac efe a'u bathodd hwynt yn dwyn y tlysau yn ôl

and he bade them carry the jewels back

Gorffennodd y genie y ffenestr wrth ei orchymyn

the genie finished the window at his command

Synnodd y Sultan dderbyn ei emau eto

The Sultan was surprised to receive his jewels again

ymwelodd ag Aladdin, a ddangosodd iddo y ffenestr wedi gorffen

he visited Aladdin, who showed him the window finished

a chofleidiodd y Swltan ei fab yng nghyfraith

and the Sultan embraced his son in law

yn y cyfamser, roedd y Vizier genfigennus yn amau gwaith cyfareddol

meanwhile, the envious Vizier suspected the work of enchantment

Roedd Aladdin wedi ennill calonnau'r bobl trwy ei dwyn tyner

Aladdin had won the hearts of the people by his gentle bearing

Fe'i gwnaed yn gapten byddinoedd y Swltan

He was made captain of the Sultan's armies

ac enillodd sawl brwydr dros ei fyddin

and he won several battles for his army

ond arhosodd mor wylaidd a chwrtais ag o'r blaen

but he remained as modest and courteous as before

Yn y modd hwn bu'n byw mewn heddwch a bodlonrwydd am sawl blwyddyn

in this way he lived in peace and content for several years

Ond ymhell i ffwrdd yn Affrica cofiai'r dewin am Aladdin

But far away in Africa the magician remembered Aladdin

a chan ei gelfyddydau hud fe ddarganfu nad oedd Aladdin wedi marw yn yr ogof

and by his magic arts he discovered Aladdin hadn't perished in the cave

Ond yn hytrach na darfod ei fod wedi dianc a phriodi'r dywysoges

but instead of perishing he had escaped and married the princess

Ac yn awr yr oedd efe yn byw mewn anrhydedd a chyfoeth mawr,

and now he was living in great honour and wealth

Roedd yn gwybod mai dim ond trwy lamp y gallai mab y teiliwr tlawd fod wedi cyflawni hyn.

He knew that the poor tailor's son could only have accomplished this by means of the lamp

Ac efe a gerddodd nos a dydd, hyd oni ddaeth efe i'r ddinas.

and he travelled night and day until he reached the city

yr oedd yn plygu ar sicrhau adfail Aladdin

he was bent on making sure of Aladdin's ruin

Wrth iddo fynd trwy'r dref clywodd bobl yn siarad

As he passed through the town he heard people talking

Y cyfan y gallent siarad amdano oedd palas rhyfeddol

all they could talk about was a marvellous palace

"Maddeuwch fy anwybodaeth," gofynnodd

"Forgive my ignorance," he asked

"Beth yw'r tŷ hwn yr ydych yn sôn amdano?"

"what is this palace you speak of?"

"Onid ydych wedi clywed am lys y Tywysog Aladdin?"

"Have you not heard of Prince Aladdin's palace?" was the reply

'Hwn yw rhyfeddod mwyaf y byd'

"it is the greatest wonder of the world"

"Byddaf yn eich cyfeirio i'r palas, os hoffech ei weld"

"I will direct you to the palace, if you would like to see it"

Diolchodd y dewin iddo am ddod ag ef i'r palas

The magician thanked him for bringing him to the palace

ac wedi gweld y palas, gwyddai ei fod wedi ei godi gan Genie y Lamp

and having seen the palace, he knew that it had been raised by the Genie of the Lamp

gwnaeth hyn ef yn hanner gwallgof gyda chynddaredd

this made him half mad with rage

Penderfynodd gael gafael ar y lamp

He determined to get hold of the lamp

ac fe fyddai'n plymio Aladdin eto i'r tlodi dyfnaf

and he would again plunge Aladdin into the deepest poverty

Yn anffodus, roedd Aladdin wedi mynd i hela am wyth diwrnod

Unluckily, Aladdin had gone a-hunting for eight days

Mae hyn yn rhoi digon o amser i'r dewin

this gave the magician plenty of time

Prynodd ddwsin o lampau copr

He bought a dozen copper lamps

a'u rhoi mewn basged

and he put them into a basket

ac efe a aeth i'r palas

and he went to the palace

'Lampau newydd ar gyfer hen!' gwaeddodd

"New lamps for old!" he exclaimed

ac fe'i dilynwyd gan dorf Jeering

and he was followed by a jeering crowd

Roedd y Dywysoges yn eistedd yn y neuadd o ffenestri pedair ac ugain

The Princess was sitting in the hall of four-and-twenty windows

anfonodd was i gael gwybod beth oedd y sŵn am

she sent a servant to find out what the noise was about

daeth y gwas yn ôl yn chwerthin cymaint nes i'r Dywysoges ei scolded

the servant came back laughing so much that the Princess scolded her

"Madam," atebodd y gwas

"Madam," replied the servant

Pwy sy'n gallu helpu ond chwerthin pan welwch chi'r fath beth?

"who can help but laughing when you see such a thing?"

"Mae hen ffŵl yn cynnig cyfnewid lampau newydd gwych ar gyfer hen rai"

"an old fool is offering to exchange fine new lamps for old ones"

Siaradodd gwas arall, wrth glywed hyn,

Another servant, hearing this, spoke up

"Mae yna hen lamp ar y cornice yno y gall ei gael"
"There is an old lamp on the cornice there which he can have"
Wrth gwrs, hwn oedd y lamp hud
this, of course, was the magic lamp
Roedd Aladdin wedi gadael yno am nad oedd yn gallu mynd â hi allan i hela gydag e.
Aladdin had left it there, as he could not take it out hunting with him
Doedd y Dywysoges ddim yn gwybod gwerth y lamp
The Princess didn't know know the lamp's value
chwerthin ei bod hi'n bade y gwas i'w gyfnewid
laughingly she bade the servant to exchange it
Cymerodd y gwas y lamp at y dewin
the servant took the lamp to the magician
"Rhowch lamp newydd i mi ar gyfer hyn," meddai
"Give me a new lamp for this" she said
Cipiodd ef a bade'r gwas i gymryd ei dewis
He snatched it and bade the servant to take her choice
a'r holl dyrfa yn gwawdio ar y golwg
and all the crowd jeered at the sight
Ond nid oedd y dewin yn gofalu fawr am y dorf
but the magician cared little for the crowd
gadawodd y dorf gyda'r lamp yr oedd wedi mynd allan i'w gael
he left the crowd with the lamp he had set out to get
Ac efe a aeth allan o byrth y ddinas i le unig.
and he went out of the city gates to a lonely place
Yno y bu hyd y nos
there he remained till nightfall
Ac yn y nos tynnodd allan y lamp a'i rhwbio
and it nightfall he pulled out the lamp and rubbed it
Ymddangosodd yr athrylith i'r dewin
The genie appeared to the magician
A gwnaeth y dewin ei orchymyn i'r genie
and the magician made his command to the genie
"Cariwch fi, y dywysoges a'r palas i le unig yn Affrica"

"carry me, the princess, and the palace to a lonely place in Africa"

Bore trannoeth edrychodd y Swltan allan o'r ffenestr tuag at balas Aladdin
Next morning the Sultan looked out of the window toward Aladdin's palace
a rhwbio ei lygaid pan welodd y palas wedi mynd
and he rubbed his eyes when he saw the palace was gone
Anfonodd am y Vizier a gofynnodd beth oedd wedi dod o'r palas
He sent for the Vizier and asked what had become of the palace
Edrychodd y Vizier allan hefyd, a chafodd ei golli mewn syndod
The Vizier looked out too, and was lost in astonishment
Unwaith eto, rhoddodd ef i lawr i swyno
He again put it down to enchantment
a'r tro hwn y credai'r Swltan ef
and this time the Sultan believed him
anfonodd ddeg ar hugain o wŷr meirch i nôl Aladdin mewn cadwynau
he sent thirty men on horseback to fetch Aladdin in chains
Cyfarfu ag ef yn marchogaeth adref
They met him riding home
rhwymasant ef, a'i orfodi i fyned gyda hwynt ar draed
they bound him and forced him to go with them on foot
Ond roedd y bobl oedd yn ei garu yn eu dilyn i'r palas
The people, however, who loved him, followed them to the palace
byddent yn sicrhau na fyddai'n dod i unrhyw niwed
they would make sure that he came to no harm
Cafodd ei gario o flaen y Sultan
He was carried before the Sultan
a gorchmynnodd y Swltan i'r dienyddiwr dorri ei ben
and the Sultan ordered the executioner to cut off his head
Gwnaeth y dienyddiwr wneud Aladdin penlinio i lawr cyn

bloc o bren

The executioner made Aladdin kneel down before a block of wood

Caeodd ei lygaid fel na allai weld

he bandaged his eyes so that he could not see

a chododd ei gwyddoniadur i daro

and he raised his scimitar to strike

Ar y pryd hwnnw gwelodd y Vizier fod y dorf wedi gorfodi eu ffordd i'r cwrt

At that instant the Vizier saw the crowd had forced their way into the courtyard

roedden nhw'n graddio'r waliau i achub Aladdin

they were scaling the walls to rescue Aladdin

Felly galwodd ar y dienyddiwr i atal

so he called to the executioner to halt

Roedd y bobl, yn wir, yn edrych mor fygythiol nes i'r Swltan ildio

The people, indeed, looked so threatening that the Sultan gave way

a gorchmynnodd i Aladdin gael ei ddatrwymo

and he ordered Aladdin to be unbound

efe a barodd iddo yng ngolwg y dyrfa

he pardoned him in the sight of the crowd

Aladdin yn awr yn erfyn i gael gwybod beth oedd wedi ei wneud

Aladdin now begged to know what he had done

"Ffug wretch!" meddai'r Swltan "dewch yma"

"False wretch!" said the Sultan "come thither"

Dangosodd iddo o'r ffenestr y man lle'r oedd ei balas wedi sefyll

he showed him from the window the place where his palace had stood

Roedd Aladdin mor rhyfeddu fel na allai ddweud gair

Aladdin was so amazed that he could not say a word

"Ble mae fy mhalas i a'm merch?" gofynnodd y Swltan

"Where is my palace and my daughter?" demanded the Sultan

"Am y tro cyntaf, dydw i ddim mor bryderus"
"For the first I am not so deeply concerned"

'Ond mae'n rhaid i mi gael fy merch'
"but my daughter I must have"

"Mae'n rhaid i chi ddod o hyd iddi neu golli eich pen"
"and you must find her or lose your head"

Ymbiliodd Aladdin i gael ei rhoi deugain diwrnod i ddod o hyd iddi
Aladdin begged to be granted forty days in which to find her

Addawodd pe bai'n methu y byddai'n dychwelyd
he promised that if he failed he would return

ac wedi iddo ddychwelyd byddai'n dioddef marwolaeth wrth bleser y Sultan
and on his return he would suffer death at the Sultan's pleasure

Rhoddwyd ei weddi gan y Swltan
His prayer was granted by the Sultan

ac aeth allan yn drist o bresenoldeb y Sultan
and he went forth sadly from the Sultan's presence

Am dri diwrnod bu'n crwydro o gwmpas fel madman
For three days he wandered about like a madman

Gofynnodd i bawb beth oedd wedi dod o'i balas
he asked everyone what had become of his palace

ond dim ond chwerthin a thrugarha
but they only laughed and pitied him

Daeth i lan afon
He came to the banks of a river

ymgrymodd i ddweud ei weddïau cyn taflu ei hun i mewn
he knelt down to say his prayers before throwing himself in

Wrth wneud hynny fe rwblodd y modrwy hud roedd yn dal i wisgo
In so doing he rubbed the magic ring he still wore

Ymddangosodd yr athrylith a welodd yn yr ogof
The genie he had seen in the cave appeared

Gofynnodd iddo beth oedd ei ewyllys
and he asked him what his will was

"Achub fy mywyd, genie" meddai Aladdin

"Save my life, genie" said Aladdin

'Dod â fy mhudys yn ôl'

"bring my palace back"

"Dyw hynny ddim yn fy ngallu," meddai'r genie

"That is not in my power" said the genie

"Dim ond caethwas y cylch ydw i"

"I am only the Slave of the Ring"

"Mae'n rhaid i chi ofyn iddo am y lamp"

"you must ask him for the lamp"

'Gallai hynny fod yn wir' meddai Aladdin

"that might be true" said Aladdin

"Ond gelli di fynd â fi i'r palas"

"but thou canst take me to the palace"

'Gosodwch fi i lawr o dan ffenestr fy ngwraig annwyl'

"set me down under my dear wife's window"

Cafodd ei hun yn Affrica ar unwaith

He at once found himself in Africa

Roedd o dan ffenestr y Dywysoges

he was under the window of the Princess

a syrthiodd i gysgu allan o flinder llwyr

and he fell asleep out of sheer weariness

Cafodd ei ddeffro gan ganu'r adar

He was awakened by the singing of the birds

a'i galon yn oleuach nag yr oedd o'r blaen

and his heart was lighter than it was before

Gwelodd yn amlwg fod ei holl anffawd oherwydd colli'r lamp

He saw plainly that all his misfortunes were owing to the loss of the lamp

ac efe a ryfeddodd yn ofer pwy oedd wedi dwyn ef o hynny

and he vainly wondered who had robbed him of it

Y bore hwnnw cododd y Dywysoges yn gynharach nag yr oedd hi fel arfer

That morning the Princess rose earlier than she normally

Unwaith y dydd fe'i gorfodwyd i ddioddef y Magicians Company

once a day she was forced to endure the magicians company

Fodd bynnag, roedd hi'n ei drin yn greulon iawn

She, however, treated him very harshly

Felly ni feiddiodd fyw gyda hi yn y palas

so he dared not live with her in the palace

Wrth iddi wisgo, edrychodd un o'i menywod allan a gweld Aladdin

As she was dressing, one of her women looked out and saw Aladdin

Rhedodd y Dywysoges ac agor y ffenestr

The Princess ran and opened the window

wrth y sŵn wnaeth hi i Aladdin edrych i fyny

at the noise she made Aladdin looked up

Galwodd arno i ddod i'w

She called to him to come to her

Roedd yn bleser mawr i'r cariadon weld ei gilydd eto

it was a great joy for the lovers to see each other again

Ar ôl iddo cusanu ei dywedodd Aladdin:

After he had kissed her Aladdin said:

"Rwy'n erfyn arnoch chi, Dywysoges, yn enw Duw"

"I beg of you, Princess, in God's name"

'Cyn i ni siarad am unrhyw beth arall'

"before we speak of anything else"

"Er eich mwyn chi a'm lles fy hun"

"for your own sake and mine"

"Dywedwch wrthyf beth sydd wedi dod o'r hen lamp"

"tell me what has become of the old lamp"

"Fe wnes i ei adael ar y cornice yn neuadd pedair ac ugain o ffenestri"

"I left it on the cornice in the hall of four-and-twenty windows"

"Och!" meddai, "Fi yw achos gwirion ein gofidiau."

"Alas!" she said, "I am the innocent cause of our sorrows"

a hi a ddywedodd wrtho am gyfnewid y lamp

and she told him of the exchange of the lamp

"Nawr rwy'n gwybod" gwaeddodd Aladdin

"Now I know" cried Aladdin

"Mae'n rhaid i ni ddiolch i'r dewin am hyn!"

"we have to thank the magician for this!"

"Ble mae'r lamp?"

"Where is the lamp?"

"Mae'n ei gario o gwmpas gydag ef" meddai'r Dywysoges

"He carries it about with him" said the Princess

"Rwy'n gwybod ei fod yn dod â'r lamp gydag ef"

"I know he carries the lamp with him"

"Oherwydd tynnodd hi allan o'i fron i ddangos i mi"

"because he pulled it out of his breast to show me"

Ac mae'n dymuno imi dorri fy ffydd gyda chi a'i briodi. "

"and he wishes me to break my faith with you and marry him"

Dywedodd, "Fe'ch torrwyd gan orchymyn fy Nhad."

"and he said you were beheaded by my father's command"

"Mae e'n siarad yn sâl amdanat ti am byth"

"He is for ever speaking ill of you"

"Ond dim ond trwy fy dagrau yr wyf yn ymateb"

"but I only reply by my tears"

"Os byddaf yn parhau, nid wyf yn amau"

"If I persist, I doubt not"

"Ond bydd yn defnyddio trais"

"but he will use violence"

Cysurodd Aladdin ei wraig

Aladdin comforted his wife

gadawodd hi am gyfnod

and he left her for a while

Newidiodd ddillad gyda'r person cyntaf iddo gyfarfod yn y dref

He changed clothes with the first person he met in the town

ac wedi prynu powdwr penodol, dychwelodd i'r Dywysoges

and having bought a certain powder, he returned to the Princess

Y Dywysoges yn gadael iddo fynd i mewn wrth ddrws ochr fach

the Princess let him in by a little side door

"Gwisgwch eich gwisg harddaf" meddai wrthi.

"Put on your most beautiful dress" he said to her

"Derbyn y dewin gyda gwên heddiw"

"receive the magician with smiles today"

'Peri iddo gredu dy fod wedi fy anghofio'

"lead him to believe that you have forgotten me"

"Gwahoddwch ef i fyny gyda chwi"

"Invite him to sup with you"

"a dweud wrtho eich bod yn dymuno blasu gwin ei wlad"

"and tell him you wish to taste the wine of his country"

"Bydd yn mynd am beth amser"

"He will be gone for some time"

"Tra bydd wedi mynd, byddaf yn dweud wrthych beth i'w wneud"

"while he is gone I will tell you what to do"

Roedd hi'n gwrando'n astud ar Aladdin

She listened carefully to Aladdin

A phan adawodd hi ei hun yn hyfryd

and when he left she arrayed herself beautifully

Doedd hi ddim wedi gwisgo fel hyn ers iddi adael ei dinas

she hadn't dressed like this since she had left her city

Gwisgodd wregys a gwisg pen o ddiemyntau

She put on a girdle and head-dress of diamonds

Roedd hi'n fwy prydferth nag erioed

she was more beautiful than ever

a hi a dderbyniodd y dewin gyda gwên

and she received the magician with a smile

"Yr wyf wedi penderfynu bod Aladdin wedi marw"

"I have made up my mind that Aladdin is dead"

"Ni fydd fy dagrau yn dod ag ef yn ôl ataf"

"my tears will not bring him back to me"

"Felly dw i'n benderfynol o beidio galaru ddim mwy"

"so I am resolved to mourn no more"

"Am hynny, yr wyf yn eich gwahodd i sefyll i fyny gyda mi"

"therefore I invite you to sup with me"

"Ond dw i wedi blino ar y gwinoedd sydd gyda ni"

"but I am tired of the wines we have"

"Hoffwn i flasu gwinoedd Affrica"

"I would like to taste the wines of Africa"

Rhedodd y dewin i'w seler

The magician ran to his cellar

a'r Dywysoges yn rhoi'r powdwr roedd Aladdin wedi ei rhoi hi yn ei chwpan

and the Princess put the powder Aladdin had given her in her cup

Pan ddychwelodd gofynnodd iddo yfed ei hiechyd

When he returned she asked him to drink her health

A hi a roddes iddo ei chwpan yn gyfnewid am ei

and she handed him her cup in exchange for his

gwnaethpwyd hyn fel arwydd i ddangos ei bod wedi'i chymodi ag ef

this was done as a sign to show she was reconciled to him

Cyn yfed roedd y dewin yn gwneud araith iddi

Before drinking the magician made her a speech

Roedd eisiau canmol ei harddwch

he wanted to praise her beauty

ond torrodd y Dywysoges ef yn fyr

but the Princess cut him short

'Yfed yn gyntaf'

"Let us drink first"

"A byddwch chi'n dweud beth fyddwch chi'n ei ddweud ar ôl hynny."

"and you shall say what you will afterwards"

Gosododd ei chwpan ar ei gwefusau a'i gadw yno

She set her cup to her lips and kept it there

Draeniodd y dewin ei gwpan i'r dregs

the magician drained his cup to the dregs

ac wedi iddo orffen ei ddiod fe syrthiodd yn ôl yn ddifywyd

and upon finishing his drink he fell back lifeless

Yna agorodd y Dywysoges y drws i Aladdin

The Princess then opened the door to Aladdin

a hi yn ysgwyd ei breichiau rownd ei wddf

and she flung her arms round his neck

ond gofynnodd Aladdin iddi ei adael
but Aladdin asked her to leave him
Roedd mwy i'w wneud o hyd
there was still more to be done
Yna aeth at y dewin marw
He then went to the dead magician
Ac efe a gymerth y lamp allan o'i fest
and he took the lamp out of his vest
Bathodd yr athrylith i gario'r palas yn ôl
he bade the genie to carry the palace back
y Dywysoges yn ei siambr yn unig yn teimlo dau sioc fach
the Princess in her chamber only felt two little shocks
Cyn bo hir roedd hi adref eto
in little time she was at home again
Roedd y Swltan yn eistedd ar ei balconi
The Sultan was sitting on his balcony
Roedd yn galaru am ei ferch a gollwyd
he was mourning for his lost daughter
Edrychodd i fyny a bu'n rhaid iddo rwbio ei lygaid eto
he looked up and had to rub his eyes again
safodd y palas yno fel yr oedd o'r blaen
the palace stood there as it had before
Brysiodd i'r palas i weld ei ferch
He hastened over to the palace to see his daughter
Derbyniodd Aladdin ef yn neuadd y palas
Aladdin received him in the hall of the palace
a'r dywysoges oedd wrth ei ochr
and the princess was at his side
Dywedodd Aladdin wrtho beth oedd wedi digwydd
Aladdin told him what had happened
Ac efe a ddangosodd iddo gorff meirw'r dewin
and he showed him the dead body of the magician
fel y byddai'r Swltan yn ei gredu
so that the Sultan would believe him
Cyhoeddwyd gwledd deg diwrnod
A ten days' feast was proclaimed

ac roedd yn ymddangos fel pe bai Aladdin bellach yn byw gweddill ei oes mewn heddwch

and it seemed as if Aladdin might now live the rest of his life in peace

ond nid oedd i fod mor heddychlon ag yr oedd wedi gobeithio

but it was not to be as peaceful as he had hoped

Roedd gan y dewin Affricanaidd frawd iau

The African magician had a younger brother

Efallai ei fod hyd yn oed yn fwy drygionus a chyfrwys na'i frawd

he was maybe even more wicked and cunning than his brother

Teithiodd i Aladdin i ddial ar farwolaeth ei frawd

He travelled to Aladdin to avenge his brother's death

aeth i ymweld â menyw dduwiol o'r enw Fatima

he went to visit a pious woman called Fatima

Roedd yn meddwl y gallai fod o ddefnydd iddo

he thought she might be of use to him

Aeth i mewn i'w chell a chrogi dagger i'w bron.

He entered her cell and clapped a dagger to her breast

Yna dywedodd wrthi am godi a gwneud ei gais

then he told her to rise and do his bidding

Oni bai ei fod yn dweud y byddai'n ei lladd

and if she didn't he said he would kill her

Newidiodd ei ddillad gyda hi

He changed his clothes with her

ac efe a lliwiodd ei wyneb fel hi

and he coloured his face like hers

rhoddodd ar ei gorchudd fel ei fod yn edrych yn union fel hi

he put on her veil so that he looked just like her

ac yn olaf llofruddiodd hi er gwaethaf ei chydymffurfiad

and finally he murdered her despite her compliance

fel na allai hi ddweud unrhyw straeon

so that she could tell no tales

Yna aeth i gyfeiriad Palas Aladdin

Then he went towards the palace of Aladdin

Yr oedd yr holl bobl yn meddwl mai ef oedd y wraig sanctaidd.

all the people thought he was the holy woman

Casglasant o'i gwmpas i gusanu ei ddwylo

they gathered round him to kiss his hands

ac maent yn erfyn am ei fendith

and they begged for his blessing

Pan gyrhaeddodd y palas mae cynnwrf mawr o'i gwmpas

When he got to the palace there a great commotion around him

Roedd y dywysoges eisiau gwybod beth oedd yr holl sŵn am

the princess wanted to know what all the noise was about

Felly dyma hi'n plygu ei gwas i edrych allan o'r ffenest iddi hi.

so she bade her servant to look out of the window for her

a gofynnodd ei gwas beth oedd pwrpas y sŵn

and her servant asked what the noise was all about

darganfu mai hi oedd y wraig sanctaidd a achosodd y cynnwrf

she found out it was the holy woman causing the commotion

roedd hi'n gwella pobl o'u anhwylderau trwy gyffwrdd â nhw

she was curing people of their ailments by touching them

roedd y Dywysoges wedi dyheu ers tro i weld Fatima

the Princess had long desired to see Fatima

felly y mae hi'n cael ei gwas i ofyn iddi hi i'r palas

so she get her servant to ask her into the palace

a derbyniodd y Fatima ffug y cynnig i'r palas

and the false Fatima accepted the offer into the palace

cynigiodd y dewin weddi am ei hiechyd a'i ffyniant

the magician offered up a prayer for her health and prosperity

Gwnaeth y Dywysoges iddo eistedd wrth ei hochr

the Princess made him sit by her

Ac roedd hi'n erfyn arno i aros gyda hi

and she begged him to stay with her

Roedd y Fatima ffug yn dymuno am ddim byd gwell

The false Fatima wished for nothing better

ac mae hi'n cydsynio i ddymuniad y dywysoges

and she consented to the princess' wish

ond cadwodd ei orchudd i lawr

but he kept his veil down

oherwydd gwyddai y byddai'n cael ei ddarganfod fel arall

because he knew that he would be discovered otherwise

Dangosodd y Dywysoges iddo'r neuadd

The Princess showed him the hall

A gofynnodd iddo beth oedd ei feddwl ohono

and she asked him what he thought of it

"Mae'n wirioneddol brydferth" meddai'r Fatima ffug

"It is truly beautiful" said the false Fatima

"Ond yn fy marn i mae dy balas dal eisiau un peth."

"but in my mind your palace still wants one thing"

"A beth yw hynny?" gofynnodd y Dywysoges

"And what is that?" asked the Princess

"Os mai dim ond ŵy roc oedd yn cael ei hongian o ganol y gromen yma"

"If only a Roc's egg were hung up from the middle of this dome"

"Yna byddai'n rhyfeddod y byd" meddai

"then it would be the wonder of the world" he said

Ar ôl hyn gallai'r Dywysoges feddwl am ddim byd ond wy y Roc

After this the Princess could think of nothing but the Roc's egg

pan ddychwelodd Aladdin o hela daeth o hyd iddi mewn hiwmor sâl iawn

when Aladdin returned from hunting he found her in a very ill humour

Plediodd arno i wybod beth oedd ar goll

He begged to know what was amiss

A hi a ddywedodd wrtho beth oedd wedi difetha ei phleser

and she told him what had spoiled her pleasure

"Rydw i wedi fy ngwneud yn ddiflas am fod eisiau ŵy Roc"

"I'm made miserable for the want of a Roc's egg"

"Os mai dyna'r cyfan rydych chi ei eisiau, byddwch chi'n

hapus yn fuan," atebodd Aladdin

"If that is all you want you shall soon be happy" replied Aladdin

gadawodd hi a rhwbio'r lamp

he left her and rubbed the lamp

pan ymddangosodd yr athrylith fe orchmynnodd iddo ddod ag wy Roc

when the genie appeared he commanded him to bring a Roc's egg

Rhoddodd yr athrylith shriek mor uchel ac ofnadwy nes i'r neuadd ysgwyd

The genie gave such a loud and terrible shriek that the hall shook

"Wretch!" gwaeddodd, "onid yw'n ddigon fy mod i wedi gwneud popeth i ti?"

"Wretch!" he cried, "is it not enough that I have done everything for you?"

Ond yn awr yr ydych chwi yn gorchymyn i mi ddod â'm meistr."

"but now you command me to bring my master"

"A dych chi am i mi ei hongian yng nghanol y gromen yma."

"and you want me to hang him up in the midst of this dome"

"Rydych chi a'ch gwraig a'ch tŷ yn haeddu cael eich llosgi i lludw."

"You and your wife and your palace deserve to be burnt to ashes"

"Ond nid yw'r cais hwn yn dod oddi wrthych"

"but this request does not come from you"

"Mae'r galw yn dod gan frawd y dewin"

"the demand comes from the brother of the magician"

'Y dewin yr ydych wedi ei ddinistrio'

"the magician whom you have destroyed"

"Y mae yn awr yn dy balas wedi ei guddio fel y wraig sanctaidd."

"He is now in your palace disguised as the holy woman"

"Y ddynes sanctaidd y mae eisoes wedi ei llofruddio"

"the real holy woman he has already murdered"

"Efe a roddes y dymuniad hwnnw yn ben eich gwraig"

"it was him who put that wish into your wife's head"

"Gofalwch amdanoch chi'ch hun, oherwydd mae'n golygu eich lladd."

"Take care of yourself, for he means to kill you"

Ar ôl dweud hyn diflannodd yr athrylith

upon saying this the genie disappeared

Aeth Aladdin yn ôl i'r Dywysoges

Aladdin went back to the Princess

Dywedodd wrthi fod ei ben yn ysgwyd

he told her that his head ached

felly gofynnodd i'r Fatima sanctaidd gael ei nôl

so she requested the holy Fatima to be fetched

Gallai roi ei ddwylo ar ei ben

she could lay her hands on his head

a byddai ei gur pen yn cael ei wella gan ei phwerau

and his headache would be cured by her powers

pan ddaeth y dewin yn agos at Aladdin yn cipio ei ddagr

when the magician came near Aladdin seized his dagger

a'i dryllio yn ei galon

and he pierced him in the heart

"Beth wyt ti wedi ei wneud?" gwaeddodd y Dywysoges

"What have you done?" cried the Princess

Rwyt ti wedi lladd y ddynes sanctaidd!"

"You have killed the holy woman!"

'Nid felly y mae hi' atebodd Aladdin

"It is not so" replied Aladdin

"Rydw i wedi lladd consuriwr drwg"

"I have killed a wicked magician"

Ac efe a fynegodd iddi pa fodd y twyllwyd hi.

and he told her of how she had been deceived

Ar ôl hyn roedd Aladdin a'i wraig yn byw mewn heddwch

After this Aladdin and his wife lived in peace

Olynodd y Swltan pan fu farw

He succeeded the Sultan when he died

Bu'n teyrnasu ar y deyrnas am flynyddoedd
he reigned over the kingdom for many years
Ac efe a adawodd ar ei ôl linach hir o frenhinoedd
and he left behind him a long lineage of kings

Y diwedd
The End

Printed in Great Britain
by Amazon